The Mystery of
The Wooden Leg

Steven Leonard Stearns

TXu 2-234-143 2021/15.01

ISBN 978-1945907753

The Mystery of the Wooden Leg

Written by Steven Leonard Stearns

Edited by Amy Oaks

Associate Editor: Griffin Mill

Proofreader: RaeAnne Marie Scargall

Layout by Michael Nicloy

Illustrations by Philip A. D'Amore

D'Amore Artistry | www.damoreartistry.com

PUBLISHED BY NICO 11 PUBLISHING & DESIGN

MUKWONAGO, WISCONSIN

www.nico11publishing.com

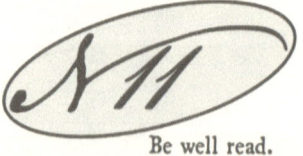

Be well read.

Quantity orders may be made by contacting the publisher via email:

mike@nico11publishing.com

Printed in the United States of America

Acknowledgments

As a public historian for the bulk of my life, I have always wanted to write a book of fiction. Little did I realize how much work it would take, particularly as young adults were my intended audience. This book has been a work in progress, sometimes put aside for months at a time, and the result of several re-writes. Its fruition is as much due to the support and guidance of others as it has been to my own industry.

A few good friends read my drafts and made excellent suggestions. Kay Steward and John Colton were particularly helpful. It seems to be a failing of many would-be authors (and I include myself in that assessment) to have an exaggerated opinion of their writing. Both Kay and John kept me grounded and helped me realize that not only writing my mystery would be hard work—but that it would require constant refinement.

Thanks also to my grandchildren who volunteered to read my "final" draft, leading to yet further improvement. As they are the book's target demographic, I gave strict attention to their comments and suggestions. In particular, I am grateful to Sean and Kevin Haynie.

No book goes anywhere without a good editor and publisher. Credit goes to Amy Oaks and Mike Nicloy for getting this book to the finish line. Also, readers will notice some most excellent line art throughout the book. My illustrator was Philip D'Amore, who caught my vision for the characters.

Finally, the book was driven by the characters themselves. They drove the plot and took me down alleys I had not intended to walk. In many respects, I felt a bystander to their story. We developed a connection that bordered on admiration (at least on my end). They are whispering to me, "Get going on the next installment." I suspect, dear reader, you will have something to do with that.

Steven Leonard Stearns

Prologue

Spring had come to Webster, Indiana, and it was time to clean up the attic. We had just moved into my parents' old home. My wife had done her job and purged the house of many marginal possessions. Those having some value were designated for the attic or garage. Since the attic looked the same as when my parents lived in the house, the challenge before me was obvious. The fact it had begun to rain eliminated the last excuse I had to postpone the exercise.

It was not long before I found myself bogged down by what I found. There was my old ball and glove I had been saving for my own son, but Alicia and I had a daughter. Then there were the Christmas tree ornaments, each nicely wrapped in tissue paper. How I loved that rocking horse ornament. About an hour into the process, and with little progress being made, I came across a medium-sized box that was bound with an unusual amount of tape. In large letters on the side, a magic marker had been used to write one word: "MYSTERIES."

I returned to the garage to get a cutting knife. My leaping up the attic stairs brought the comment from Alicia, "Having fun, are we?" Since I had never heard anything mentioned by Mom or Dad regarding a mystery, never mind mysteries, I was nervous to know the box's contents. It did not take me long to cut through the tape—even the spider crawling along the floor was not a distraction. The inside of the box exposed a musty smell, so I cracked open the circular window to my left. Inside were several folders. Each folder contained a bunch of written notes and a typed manuscript underneath. There were labels on each folder; the top folder read, "1: The Mystery of the Wooden Leg." The next folder read, "2: Mystery of the Montgomery Mansion." There were twelve in all.

I sat cross-legged to delve into these mysteries further. Opening Folder 1, I read the following cover sheet:

"The mysteries in this box represent the adventures of Johnny Turnbow, Jeremy Murkowski, and Heather Stippich—all residents of Webster, Indiana. They are cases the three of us became involved in during our school years. Someday, I am hopeful they will be of some interest to my children, their children, and many children to come. I swear to the truthfulness of the mysteries as I have described them. As I ready myself to attend law school, I thought it only proper, out of respect for my friends, that I preserve our exploits. I am giving a box to Jeremy and one to Heather's parents (as she is employed by the C.I.A., and I have lost track of her)."

Sincerely,
Johnny Turnbow
August 1992

My father had never, ever spoken of any mysteries to me. Perhaps he did not want me to follow in his footsteps. Perhaps he thought I would not believe him. It made me wonder if my mother ever knew. As my parents had died in an auto accident two years earlier on the way home from Chicago, I knew my questions would go unanswered.

Alicia found me two hours later reading Mystery 3. Before she could protest, I handed her Mystery 1. That led to both of us sitting on the attic floor in rapt attention reading my father's mysteries. Our daughter had SpaghettiOs for supper that night.

In the succeeding weeks, I decided to bring these mysteries to light and rework them some. Being trained as an editor, I was confident I would be up to the task. I decided to present them as works of fiction as opposed to local history. So, to the reader, I now present *The Mystery of the Wooden Leg*. You can enjoy it simply as another detective story, but if every so often you remember that Johnny, Jeremy, and Heather were real people, that's okay, too.

With love and respect for my father,

Rodney Turnbow
November 2018

The Mystery of
The Wooden Leg

The Plan

Harvey "Mad Dog" Scrima was not very tall. In fact, from the rear, he resembled an orangutan. His hair was matted to his skin and grew in every possible direction. His arms were too long for his body, and he walked rather stooped over. Mad Dog had never been on a horse his entire life but walked like he had. And you didn't mess with Mad Dog. His temper was known over at least four counties. One summer evening, it was said he threw a man twice his size off the Cumberland Bridge. He also took offense when called Harvey.

Harvey Scrima had acquired his nickname from a bar fight. Seems he'd taken a chunk from his victim's forearm. When he stood victorious, there was blood and flesh hanging from his mouth, causing him to look rabid.

"Skippy, hand me those plans again," barked Mad Dog. Harvey Scrima trusted no one but Skippy Forester. The two partners in crime had known each other a long time. Skippy was as tall as Mad Dog was short. That, combined with a beanpole frame, contributed to Skippy resembling Shaggy from *Scooby-Doo* fame. Skippy always wore a beat-up fisherman's hat over his balding head.

The state penitentiary, in all its wisdom, allowed inmates in their last year of serving time to share a cell. It was no surprise that Mad Dog requested Skippy as a roommate.

"Hey, Harvey, you sure you don't want to rob another bank?" asked Skippy. (Only Skippy could call Mad Dog by his first name.)

"Use your brain, mate," replied Mad Dog. "You want to do another three years or more in this poor substitute for a Motel 6? Besides, this job is a pushover. All we have to worry about is that old geezer, Tompkins. I figure we can haul away enough artifacts to bring us a tidy sum. The professor won't mind if we nick a few things, as long as he gets his wooden leg."

To assist them in their escapade, Mad Dog had gotten word to the other members of their gang. Two of them, Boris and Iggy Smothers, had received a lesser sentence—three years of probation. There had not been enough evidence to pin them at the scene of the crime. Professor McDougal, Professor of Anthropology at Bradford State University, had been most cooperative in ensuring messages were delivered. The remaining two, Jarvis and Tommy Bolton, were in cellblock six in another part of the penitentiary. Fortunately for them, Tommy and Mad Dog both worked in the prison's laundry and had ample time to go over the basic details of the plan.

Skippy was still not all that excited about the caper. "Harvey, why would someone want to pay so much to lift this wooden leg? Doesn't make any sense. And why did the professor pick us for the job? I mean, we just botched a bank heist."

Mad Dog lifted his head slowly, pushing the hair out of his eyes. "Listen, Skippy. You always ask too many questions. You know what it is? You lack faith. Yeah, you lack faith. Here this guy seeks us out, offers us a bundle to break into a museum—with no armed guards, by the way—to poach an old pirate's leg. What do we care why he wants the leg? He can use it to beat stray cats, for all I care. We do the job, take the dough, pawn the stuff we steal, and beat it out of town. Then we lay low while we plan our next bigger burglary."

Skippy opened his mouth as if to respond, but Mad Dog gave him "the look." Skippy knew better than to say any more. About the same time, a guard came walking down the cellblock corridor. Mad Dog quickly put the plan under his mattress bed.

*   *   *   *   *   *   *

Dr. Winston McDougal sat in his comfortable office on the third floor of Bluffton Hall. Bookshelves lined all the walls except for the one behind the professor's desk, where through the window he could look out onto the university commons. Books and papers were strewn everywhere. Only one small chair managed to rise from the piles. Any students showing up during his office hours were relegated to that chair or sitting on the corner of his desk.

The professor had tenure. He'd taught long enough to earn several perks, one of which being that the dark brown leather reclining chair served as a second home. Dr. McDougal wondered why he owned a house at all; he rarely occupied it. He so looked forward to his afternoon naps that occurred promptly at 3:30 p.m. every day.

It was a Wednesday afternoon, which meant he begrudgingly carved out an hour for students seeking his counsel. Well, it was 3:25 p.m., so his rather rotund, hefty body began slouching into the recesses of his chair. Soon his eyes could close, and any mortal concerns could be temporarily excused. So, you can imagine his agitation when there was a knock on his door.

His eyes fluttering for a moment, the professor reluctantly muttered, "Come in, if you must." When the knock was repeated, he shouted out, "COME IN!" Opening the door cautiously and peering around it was Emily Quig, perhaps the worst Principles of Archaeology student he had ever taught.

"Pro-pro-fessor," Emily stammered, "do you have a moment to answer some questions about this quiz?"

His eyebrows pinched, Dr. McDougal restrained himself and only uttered, "And where would we begin, Miss Quig? In the two weeks we have had class, you have already given evidence that you might be more comfortable in a Music Appreciation class."

Emily fought off her tears and tugged on her dark-brown ponytail as she sat down in the one chair. "Professor, this is the one class I really wanted to get into this semester. Without passing it, I am not going to be able to major in Anthropology. You just have to help me get through this course with a good grade."

Dr. McDougal remembered from signing her enrollment waiver she indeed had an interest in Anthropology as a major. In his opinion, she would be better off teaching third graders.

Then into his conniving mind came a brilliant idea.

He slyly smiled and asked, "How much do you like museums, Miss Quig?" He then looked her up and down and added, "By the way, how tall are you?"

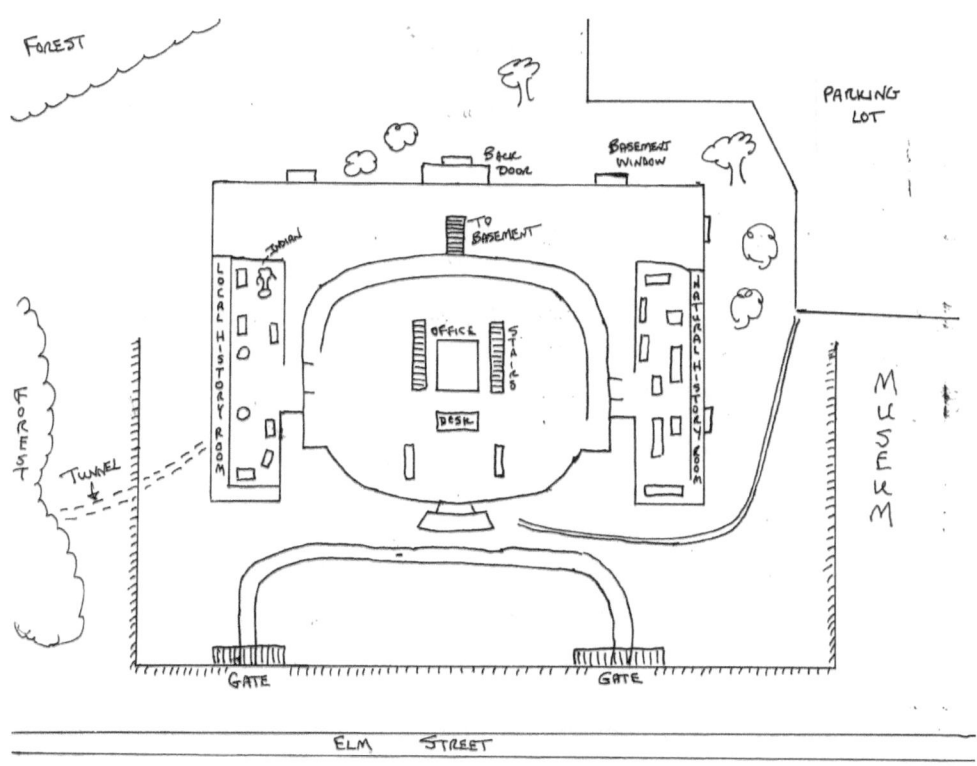

The Museum

Johnny Turnbow knew all about the county museum. He had passed it every day for three years—ever since enrolling in Mark Twain Elementary School in the third grade. This was his last year at Mark Twain. As a sixth grader, it was supposed to be the best. He could not wait to be a recess monitor. Not only would he be able to go to the front of the line any time he wanted a drink, but monitors were the last to return to class (they were supposed to survey the grounds for any lost items, trash, and anything unusual). That meant at least an extra ten minutes of recess.

He would miss the walk to and from the elementary school. While most kids had to take a bus, he lived close enough that he did not have to. That meant in the fall, he and his best friend Jeremy could plow through the piles of leaves (particularly if Mr. Crowley's car was not in the driveway). In the distance between Johnny's house to the school, he passed several houses and a vacant lot. Every house had heaps of leaves on the curbs, thanks to the numerous oak trees lining the streets. Jeremy usually managed to leap into every pile, scattering brown and copper projectiles into the air.

On rainy days, Johnny and Jeremy would race home while trying to avoid any puddles along the sidewalk. It was considered bad form to splash each other, not to mention having to catch it from their respective moms. Living in Indiana meant a fair amount of snow in the winter. Because he lived close, Johnny was expected to make it on time for school, even if the buses were late. They *never* closed school in Webster. Johnny used to lie in bed, listening to the howling winds outside, taking some comfort in the fact it meant a blizzard had snuck into town. Of course, no matter how much snow fell, it was never enough to close school; particularly with his dad manning the snow removal equipment at the maintenance lot. No, it would take quite a storm to shut down Webster. Johnny's Grandpa Matt told him that there was only one year (1951, he thought) when the snow had piled so high that it buried the telephone lines, and everything stopped. But Johnny realized he would be graduated from high school before Webster would ever see another storm such as that.

On nice days, though his mom did not want him to dawdle on the way home, there was always time to sneak into Riegleman's Pharmacy and beg Jeremy's brother, Buddy, for a scoop of ice cream at the soda fountain. Buddy would usually let them help finish off any container that was about empty, so they could not be picky. That being said, there was little in the way of ice cream that Johnny did not find acceptable. Well, watermelon did sometimes leave a nasty aftertaste.

Yeah, Johnny would miss those walks home. Sometimes the lights would still be on in the museum, which meant Mrs. Smothers, the cleaning lady, had not left yet. Johnny and Jeremy would stand near the gate, looking to see if the knight in armor was still standing in the hallway. (You could just see his arms through the tall right side window). Of course, there was no hope of going in. The museum closed at 4:00 sharp on weekdays. Mom would let him stop by once in a while on Saturday mornings if his chores were done or he did not have anything scheduled. With ball practice, piano lessons, and having to walk his sister Katie to her friend's house, it did not happen that often.

Johnny really liked the museum. It had a special smell when you walked in the door…something between musty and "new car." When you entered, you were greeted by this large circular information desk. "That's real oak, son," Mr. Turnbow would remind Johnny on nearly every visit. The desk had to be about four feet high, because Johnny had only recently measured at 4'8" and he was barely tall enough to sign the register. The curator, Mr. Thaddeus Tompkins, was funny about things like that. Everyone had to sign in. There was no admission, but you had to mark your attendance. However, you did not have to sign out. So, Johnny would always write his name in his best cursive. He thought it important—if anyone really did look at the ledger—for them to know he had visited.

To the right and left of the desk were archways to two rooms. On the left was the Amandus C. Hale Local History Room. It had all kinds of oddities. He liked the Delaware Indian statue the best; it was painted in bright colors, and the chief had a long war bonnet that draped to the floor. Jeremy said the bonnet contained real eagle feathers, but Johnny was not so sure. He had never seen an eagle up close, and there sure were a lot of feathers. Better yet, the chief had one arm extended with his palm up. If you put a quarter in the hand, the arm withdrew and came back out with a folded piece of paper containing your fortune for the day. Johnny did not have a lot of quarters to waste, but his dad did let him have two on his birthday, so he got a fortune for himself and for Jeremy. Jeremy's read, "A friend will give you an unexpected gift." That made sense, because he'd just received a quarter from Johnny. But Johnny's read, "If you watch for a miracle, it won't happen." That made no sense at all.

There were other interesting items in the room off the left archway, including the first phone used in town (donated by the Sullivan twins before they entered the nursing home), a huge bird's-eye picture of Webster in 1910 when there were only two main cross streets, and this wooden marble set that you could look at but not touch. There were a lot of books, and sometimes an adult would be sitting at one of the round tables reading. Johnny had never taken any off the shelf because, to be honest, he thought they might fall apart in his hands; plus, he had never read a book thicker than one inch before.

The room to the right was the natural history room full of stuffed animals and with several exhibit cases. The cases held everything from butterflies to rocks and minerals. On school field trips, there never was enough time to see everything. It was not surprising when he visited at other times that he could spend an entire morning just moving from case to case. He never even realized when he got hungry or thirsty. There was one tall case that contained a scene from a tropical forest. At different levels, there were different kinds of birds, reptiles, and even insects. The roach at the very bottom usually freaked out the girls—all except Annie Cummings, who just stared at it like she had never seen one before.

If you left either the local history room or the natural history room from the rear, connecting the two was a curved hallway lined on each side by a variety of portraits. They supposedly represented national and state leaders worth remembering. Johnny recognized two: General Ulysses Grant in full dress uniform with an impressive sword, and President Abraham Lincoln giving the "Gettysburg Address." Somehow a painting of a former mayor had worked its way into the gallery—no one could tell Johnny why. The lights were dimmed in the hallway to protect the paintings, which meant it always resembled sunset. Jeremy thought it would be a great place for a secret passage. Had quite an imagination, that Jeremy.

If you looked down at the museum from a helicopter, it appeared as a rectangle with an attached semicircle topped by a dome. It was built in 1897 and, despite a small fire in 1922, looked the same as it did originally. The years had taken its toll, and every time there was a heavy rain, Mrs. Smothers had to attend to the leak in the men's bathroom. For as long as Johnny could recall, Mrs. Smothers had been the one fixing the leaks, dusting and protecting the collections, and repairing what had to be repaired. She was actually more of a handyman than an overseer. She spoke with an accent, and Mrs. Turnbow explained to Johnny that he needed to treat her with respect. He got the impression life had not been kind to her.

∗   ∗   ∗   ∗   ∗   ∗   ∗

In a year it would be on to Central Middle School, which meant a bus ride downtown for Johnny. But Central would have to be patient. Johnny was going to make sure this was the best school year ever. The good news was that the Turnbow family was not moving to Huntington. Mr. Turnbow had walked into the house after work one evening and announced, "I spoke with Jones today, and he promised me a raise in January—the one I've been asking for if I stayed on. Call the realtor, Jenny, and tell him to take the sign off our lawn." And that was all there was to it. He winked at Johnny's mom as he said it, so they must have had an understanding about it or something. All Johnny knew was that now he and Jeremy could still be best friends— probably all the way through high school.

Johnny could not be sure, but sometimes he felt their friendship meant more to him than it did to Jeremy, as Jeremy had two brothers and Johnny had none. As Jeremy referred to it, he was the filling in the Hostess cupcake. Buddy, the oldest, just turned fifteen, and Hans, at nine, was the youngest. They also had a younger sister named Melinda. Johnny just had his sister Katie who was six, five years his junior. The Turnbows and the Murkowskis were only two houses apart on Elm Street. Ben Turnbow and Frank Murkowski both worked for the County Department of Transportation. They took fishing trips together, and on Friday nights, they bowled together in the city league. So, it seemed natural that Johnny and the Murkowski boys would become good friends.

Had Johnny not possessed thick red hair, freckles, and a pointy nose, he could have been mistaken for Jeremy's brother. Both were about the same height and build. When you walked behind them, each moved forward with short, quick steps…not to mention they had the habit of wearing similar plaid shirts. True, Jeremy did wear braces. But what truly set them apart was Jeremy's fine, light blonde hair that chose to lie neatly on the top of his head. His mother had it trimmed regularly, no matter the season.

The boys' birthdays were only a month apart; Johnny's was February 16th, and Jeremy's was March 16th. Their mothers, more often than not, held one huge birthday party around March 1st. This did not always sit well with the boys' brothers and sisters who felt shortchanged when it came to birthday treats, games, and overall excitement. Still, it was hard to stay angry at Johnny or Jeremy for very long. Neither had a mean bone in him. Jeremy had this infectious laugh that seemed to fill a room. When Jeremy started laughing, it made Johnny laugh.

They both loved baseball, spaghetti, pumpkin pie, maps, collecting rocks, fireworks, marbles, and playing Monopoly. They found computers fascinating, but since their families did not own any, unless the boys went to the library, they had no access. More than anything, though, they loved a good mystery. They had this understanding that whenever either of them heard any interesting news, they told the other first. And that is how Johnny learned of the surprising news concerning the museum.

Johnny had just walked in the door on Thursday afternoon after running an errand (they had run out of bread again—they may as well have had their own bakery with as much the Turnbows ate bread).

His mother called from the kitchen, "Phone for you, Johnny! And make it short; I have to call Mrs. Wiggins back." Johnny quickly threw his jacket on the couch and scampered into the kitchen.

"Yeah, this is Johnny," he said.

"Johnny, have you heard the news about the museum?" It was Jeremy, and he sounded beyond excited.

"No, I just got home from the store. Did it burn down? Did it get robbed?" Johnny was hoping this was going to be a really good story… something that would make the headlines of *The Webster Reporter*.

"Nothing as big as that," replied Jeremy, sounding a little deflated.

"Well, did that totem pole finally fall over? You always said it would."

The totem pole controversy had been going on since the third grade when Jeremy swore he saw it tilt a bit during a spring field trip.

"No, no," said Jeremy, now getting a tad irritated. "Just hold on a second and I'll tell you. Hans and I were riding our bikes past the museum an hour ago, and the gates were locked tight. We went back to check it out and noticed a big sign on the front door that said 'Closed.'"

"You're crackers, Jeremy. Of course it was closed. You know the museum closes early on Thursday in the summer," chided Johnny.

"No, no, not *that* kind of closed," replied Jeremy. "There was this huge sign that you could see from the road, and when we peered closer, we saw smaller lettering which read, 'until further notice.'"

"Must be some kind of renovation," Johnny suggested.

"Well," noted Jeremy, "I kind of thought that, too, but when I asked my dad if he had heard anything, he looked kind of puzzled, like this was news to him, too. I'm telling you, Johnny, there is something fishy going on at the museum."

They both agreed that if it were anything newsworthy, it would be in the evening paper. Later, they sat on Johnny's porch steps while waiting for Marvin Pollock to come whizzing by on his bike as he made his deliveries. Whatever faults Marvin had, and all agreed there were many, he did always get his papers delivered like clockwork. So, sure enough, at 4:08 p.m., there came Marvin around the corner.

"Hey, guys, catch this," yelled Marvin as the paper zipped toward Jeremy's forehead. Fortunately, Jeremy ducked. Unfortunately, Whiskers, the Turnbow's overweight, half-blind house cat, did not. It hit Whiskers with a dull thud. He made his best attempt at staying on all fours, but eventually he skidded to one side of the porch and fell over on his side. There he lay mewing in protest, waiting for Katie to come save him—which she did, but only after glaring at Johnny and Jeremy for their falling over, doubled up with laughter.

"Hey, quick! Get the paper," instructed Johnny.

Jeremy managed to get up enough strength to retrieve *The Reporter* and unfolded it to the front page. There was mention of a truck dumping its load of lumber in front of the 7-11 on Johnson Drive. There was also a feature on the foreign exchange student arriving from Italy for the coming school year, plus a news article on the latest space station repair...but nothing on the museum. They even reviewed all of the stories on pages two, three, and four, looking for the slightest hint of scandal. Nothing to be found.

Jeremy got up to go home when Mr. Turnbow pulled into the driveway. He barely acknowledged Johnny or Jeremy before running into the house, shouting, "Hey, Jenny, you won't guess what happened at the museum!"

The Wooden Leg

Mr. Thaddeus Tompkins had been curator of the county museum for as long as anyone could remember. Before him, his father Edgar had served faithfully, and before that, Dr. Reuben Tompkins had worn the hats of both director and curator for twenty-two years.

Johnny had heard his father say one evening after dinner, "You know, Jenny, they should just call it the 'Tompkins Museum.'" He had a smile on his face as he said it, but Mrs. Turnbow was not pleased.

"Shhh, the children will hear you," she chastised, turning away for a moment from loading the dishes in the sink. Johnny looked at his father, trying to show no emotion, but Mr. Turnbow just smiled at him and winked.

Ben Turnbow was only saying what everyone in town thought. He wasn't implying any unhappiness with the Tompkins' service over the years. Quite the contrary; the Tompkins had always been much respected. They did well enough, but they were not the social type, and the only time you ever saw a Tompkins was at church—the First Presbyterian Church at the corner of Elm and Pickett, to be exact. So, it was not surprising to find Thaddeus Tompkins sitting behind his desk that August evening, fingers drumming quietly. He was contemplating. The moon was full, and the only light in the curator's office was a small round lamp.

Mr. Tompkins appeared to stare into space, almost as if he were trying to become an exhibit himself. Finally, after several minutes, his bent frame rose slowly, and his withered right hand reached out and closed the cover of the 1875 rolltop desk. Thaddeus dreaded the last weekend of the summer. The town fathers, in all their wisdom, had decreed that on the Saturday and Sunday of Labor Day weekend, the museum would stay open until 6:00 p.m. If the extra hours were not bad enough, it meant he would have to put up with the riffraff from Shiloh

County. Shiloh County residents had voted down a museum several times, so they'd adopted the Benson County Museum as their own. Mr. Tompkins couldn't understand how anyone could have that attitude when they only visited once a year. But the fact they came at all caused him great concern.

The only time an artifact had been stolen from the museum was during such a weekend in 1947. It took two months to track down the stuffed owl. When it was found at a flea market in Indiana, it was in no condition to go back on display. Mr. Tompkins had to appear before three town council meetings to gain approval for a replacement. He was a young man at the time and took it personally. He swore never again would anything be stolen from the museum.

And so, on this Wednesday evening, his mind was once again on the wooden leg. For 363 days of the year, he managed to convince the museum board that the wooden leg needed to stay in a glass case in the second-floor hallway. Visitors infrequently walked up the squeaky, rattling stairway to catch a glimpse of this gem of the collection. It was the board's concession to security. When his great grandfather, Captain Robert Tompkins, returned from a trip to the Orient (after a stopover in England) bearing several wonderful specimens, no one noticed it. Well, what would *you* rather look at: snakes, precious jewels of all colors, colorful silks, chattering monkeys, or a weathered wooden stump? It was only years later when Thaddeus was straightening up the attic that he took a closer look. It surprised him that he had never noticed the markings earlier.

Turning the wooden leg to the side, at its very bottom where it met the floor, Mr. Tompkins noticed there was etched a miniature skull and crossbones. On the very opposite side, carved vertically, was one word: 'Death.' For Thaddeus, it was an eyebrow-raising experience. That very week, he traveled down to Bradford State University, eight miles south of Webster, and consulted with an old friend of the family, Dr. Winston McDougal. Normally, Thaddeus did not drive his 1965 Ford station wagon any farther than necessary. However, this was worth the risk of any mechanical malfunction. He made sure he wrapped the wooden leg in clean linen to protect it during transport.

"You have a fine specimen here, Thaddeus," noted Dr. McDougal. "I've only seen one other like it. It came from a shipwreck off the coast of Borneo." When Mr. Tompkins questioned him further, Dr. McDougal reluctantly admitted the leg could have come from a ship captained by none other than Blackbeard the pirate. Thaddeus' eyes grew as big as saucers. He was sure it would put his curatorial career on the map (it didn't), and would cause attendance at the museum to almost double (not even close). To state it accurately, after a few weeks on prominent display, most of Webster went back to admiring the Delaware Indian statue. Had Mr. Tompkins any marketing skills at all, he would have networked with other museums, along with the Indiana Museum Association, to spread the word about his valuable wooden leg. Because he had never fostered such associations, however, his idea of trumpeting the valuable artifact was to arrange for an article in the Sunday edition of *The Webster Reporter*. Tucked away on page seven of the arts section, it received scant attention.

The result was, if Thaddeus Tompkins had been a man of few words before he knew of the wooden leg's value to the collection, he became almost mute thereafter. This was primarily due to the combination of dashed hopes and dreams and an increased paranoia over the safety of the leg. He seemed to treat visitors with only the barest respect. The one time of the day he showed any life at all was when he got to lock the museum doors. It was only after the wooden leg was moved to the second floor, accompanied by some stern admonishment from Supervisor Higgins, that Mr. Tompkins became more civil.

Supervisor Reginald Higgins, a portly, middle-aged man, took his job very seriously, particularly around election time (every four years). 1982 being an election year, when schoolteachers began to complain about Thaddeus' rudeness, he decided to pay the curator a visit. Supervisor Higgins generally avoided the museum. If it disappeared into thin air, he couldn't have cared less. The supervisor longed for the day he could replace the aging structure with something more useful—like another convenience store, for example.

He also had no use for Mr. Tompkins. In the supervisor's words, he was a "prune-faced, gnarled hunk of a man" whose best days were behind him. "If Thaddeus had any decency," he shared with his wife, "he would crawl under a log and expire!"

It was no surprise, then, that his visit with Mr. Tompkins was brief. It ended with, "… And if you can't put a smile on your face when visitors come in, we can arrange for an early retirement."

But Labor Day weekend was coming. That meant for two days the wooden leg had to be in the downstairs hallway, adjacent to the large sailing ship model, *The Nauticus*. The board insisted the leg be made more accessible for viewing during this important weekend of visitation. It would be vulnerable to children's fingers, errant wheelchairs, and large women. Mr. Tompkins had yet to figure out a way to totally secure it. One afternoon, he had threatened a group of youngsters by waving his large umbrella. They all scattered, but he quickly recognized that was no solution. What to do? What to do? He would say his customary goodnight to the wooden leg and then walk down the street to his one-bedroom efficiency apartment that he rented from the widow Ruenzel. Maybe something would come to him on the way home.

That it did. As he walked past Hoover Drive, Thaddeus had a bit of inspiration. He would get Ben Turnbow to lend his son to the museum for the weekend to act as sort of a security assistant. Ben was a dependable friend to the museum. He always saw to it that the museum's parking lot got plowed out in winter before he swung downtown to do the main streets. Ben's son, Johnny, hung around the museum whenever he could. The lad would probably consider it a privilege to help. Being stationed in the hallway, he could help with visitor traffic flow while keeping an eye on the wooden leg. Then Thaddeus could make his other rounds without too much worry. Why hadn't he thought of this before? Suddenly, he was not so worried. A smile crossed his lips. Maybe he would have supper after all. Had Thaddeus known what Thursday would bring, the smile would have quickly disappeared.

* * * * * * *

Chief Olsen picked up the phone on the third ring.

"Well, finally! For a moment I thought you had fired all of your secretaries, Olsen," the voice on the other end said icily. "I've got a real disaster on my hands here, and you are probably sucking coffee and eating doughnuts!"

The chief rolled his eyes. "Is that you, Tompkins? What is it now? The ghost show up again?" Detective Shaw, one desk away, chortled in the background.

"Don't you begin with the ghost, Olsen. I saw what I saw. No, it's not the ghost, you witless bumbler," continued Mr. Tompkins. "The leg is gone! I'm telling you, it's really gone. You need to get your men down here immediately!"

"Settle down, Mr. Tompkins," said the chief in a consoling voice. "When did you notice it missing?" If Chief Olsen had been offended by Mr. Tompkins' insults, he hid it well.

"This morning. During my morning inspection," replied Thaddeus, softening some. "But when can you get down here? I can answer all of your questions while you begin your investigation," he said anxiously.

"Okay, okay, Mr. Tompkins. We'll do it your way. See you in five."

With that, Chief Olsen motioned to Detective Shaw to grab his coat, and they both scurried out of the office to the squad car parked in front of the police department.

Mr. Tompkins' grand plan for Labor Day weekend had been dashed on Thursday morning when he entered the museum's front door and, after hanging up his coat and stashing his umbrella, glanced up the stairway to where the wooden leg usually stood. Staring back at Thaddeus was an empty museum case. He rushed up the stairs as fast as his arthritic knees would allow. To his surprise, there was no broken glass on the floor and no evidence of forced entry. In defiance of all logic, the wooden leg seemed to have vanished into thin air. Collecting his thoughts, Mr. Tompkins surveyed the storage rooms on the second floor. He checked the custodian's closet—even the restrooms. Nothing.

Next, with little hope of finding anything, Thaddeus cased the first floor. He did find the pen missing from the information desk (how did it get on the window ledge?), but no wooden leg. He also completed a survey of the grounds. Neither effort yielded the missing artifact. At that point, the obvious thing to do was call Chief Olsen. The dilemma for Mr. Tompkins, however, was to find a way to buy some time so the public would be unaware of the theft before Saturday morning, thereby having limited effect on the weekend attendance.

As he prepared to pick up the phone, Thaddeus reviewed over in his mind how strange things had been happening ever since last Christmas. No one would listen to him, though, as Webster's residents thought him strange and eccentric to begin with. Chief Olsen brushed him off as an imagining old fool. Perhaps now someone would pay attention to his reports. Still, the disappearance could not have come at a worse time.

*   *   *   *   *   *   *

Chief Olsen was on the huge side. And yes, he did like doughnuts. But his obesity was more the result of Mrs. Olsen's pies, brownies, and overall excellent cooking than any morning pastries. The chief waddled more than he walked. When he strapped himself into his allocated patrol car, the seat belt barely covered his girth. He now specially ordered any uniform items. In his defense, Mrs. Olsen was quick to point out to her cronies at the Webster Quilt Society, "… Harold's weight does not make him any less of a policeman. His mind is still sharp as a tack, and who was it that broke up the gambling ring at Eddie's Pool Hall two years ago? Hmm?"

The chief was continually frustrated by his small police force, inadequate maintenance budget, and most of all, the fact he did not have a department secretary or computer. The police chiefs in Redstone and Watkins Pond had both. Well, he had only five years until retirement, and then he wouldn't need a secretary. To be honest, Webster police work was largely made up of petty incidents. Clare Hodge's dogs got out (again), people were double-parked in front of the barber shop (again), and the Washington children were truant (again). Deep down, Chief

Olsen knew things in the police department would likely never change (at least in his lifetime). To make matters even less tolerable, he had to put up with Thaddeus Tompkins, the museum's curator.

It was always something. Last month, Thaddeus claimed there was a strange animal stalking the grounds. In June, he claimed there were funny lights coming from the adjacent park. The previous Christmas holiday, Chief Olsen got no less than five calls regarding ghosts roaming the museum's hallways. One of those calls interrupted the chief's Christmas dinner!

The chief pulled up in front of the museum and turned off the ignition. "Well, detective, are you ready for some action?"

Detective Shaw just smiled and replied, "It could be worse, Chief; we could be on escort duty for Mayor Balducci."

Chief Olsen could only shake his head. "Not like those television detective shows, is it, Sam?"

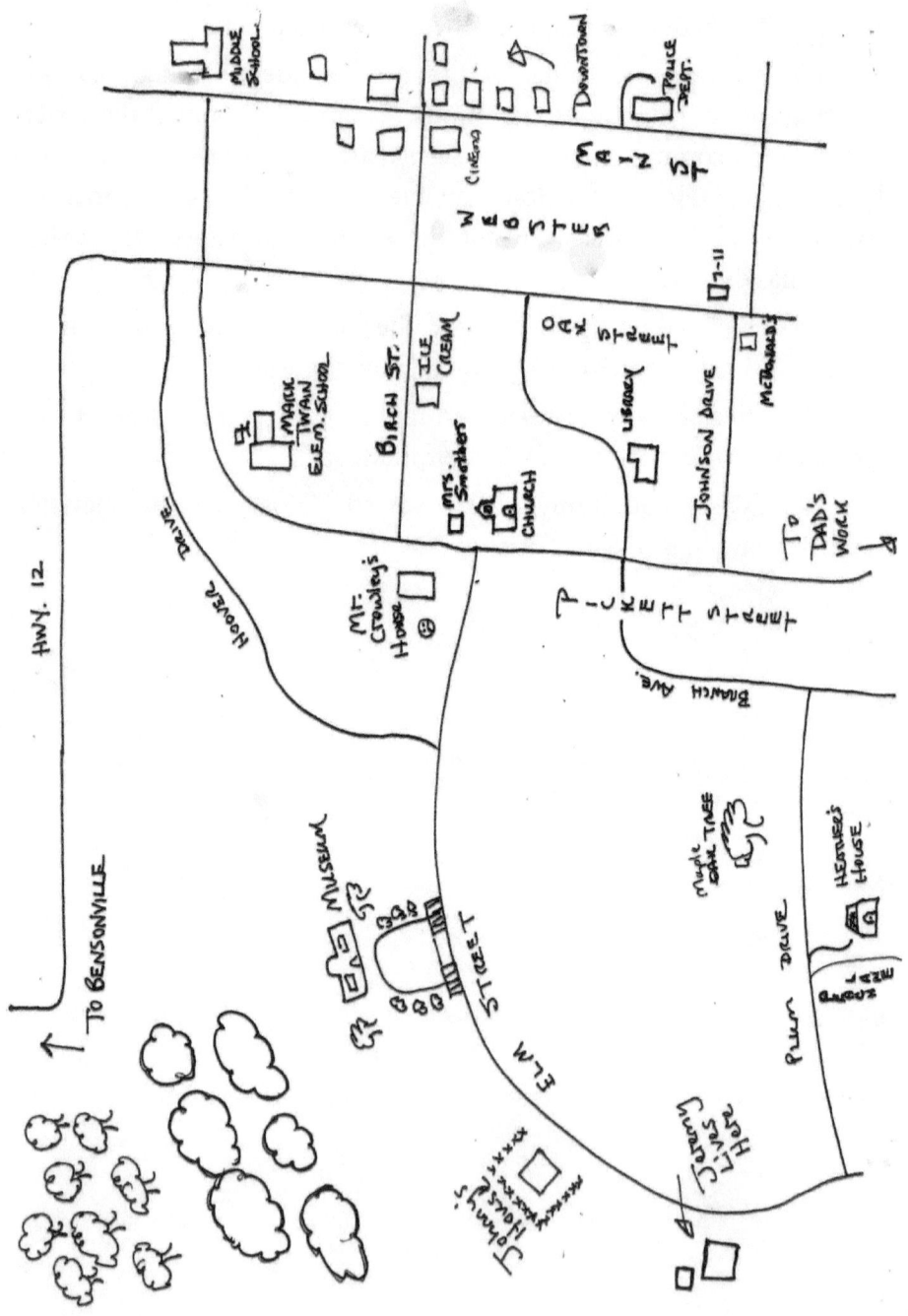

The Plot Thickens

Johnny looked at Jeremy with his mouth hung open. Jeremy responded with an equally astonished face. As Johnny turned to run into the house, he shouted to Jeremy over his shoulder, "I'll call you later. Promise!"

As Johnny approached the living room, he could see his mother and father in animated conversation. "I am not making this up, Jenny," Ben said, noting her look of incredulity. "Frank shared with me what he saw earlier at noon when he brought the dump truck back to the yard. Chief Olsen was putting up the police tape himself."

Before he could continue, Jenny asked quizzically, "But why would they close the museum before Labor Day weekend—the busiest weekend of the year?"

"I'm going to tell you, Jenny. Just listen," pleaded Mr. Turnbow.

Just then, Johnny, more intent on what was being said than where he was going, stumbled over the hassock and found himself on all fours staring up at his parents. "Ah, sorry, Dad…I couldn't help but hear…"

"No matter, Johnny," said his father while motioning his son to sit down somewhere. Johnny chose the green overstuffed chair because it was the closest. He didn't want to interfere any further with the conversation.

"Well, after Frank told me they were closing the museum, I decided to run up to the main office and see what I could find out. I was just turning up the stairs, and guess who I ran into?"

Mrs. Turnbow shrugged her shoulders and said, "Whom?"

"Officer Kraus. He was in quite a hurry and almost ran right by me. I grabbed his arm and tried to pick his brain, but he waved me off. He said to me, 'Sorry, Ben, no time to chat. Chief just radioed me to pick up some tools and get over to the museum right away…seems there has been a robbery, but don't say anything, okay? Chief doesn't want a lot of rumors going around town.' And with that, Jenny, he was gone. Oh, yeah, he was carrying a sign board."

Mr. Turnbow stroked his chin and said thoughtfully, "Did it ever occur to you that Officer Kraus has the same mannerisms as the scarecrow in *The Wizard of Oz*?"

Johnny's mother gave a look of exasperation. "And that's it, Ben? You don't know what's been taken?"

Brought back out of his reverie, Mr. Turnbow replied somewhat apologetically, "No, no, I don't know. But it had to be pretty significant for the chief to shut it down."

With that, his thoughts turned to the rumbling in his stomach and supper. "Is that fried chicken I smell, Jenny?" He proceeded into the kitchen, Mrs. Turnbow not far behind.

Johnny sat dumbfounded with this new information. So, Jeremy was right. The museum was closed due to robbery. What in the collection would be so important that its disappearance would lead to closing before Labor Day weekend? Few knew the museum exhibits as well as Johnny Turnbow. He began to take a mental tour of the museum, following the route he had taken on so many Saturday afternoons. It could be one of the thick old books Mr. Tompkins kept under lock and key. There was a tall glass cabinet in the corner of the local history room that was off limits to most everyone. Or maybe it was the Delaware Indian statue he so favored (along with everyone else in Webster). But it was pretty heavy; you would need several husky men to get it out the door, and Johnny was not sure it would fit. The only other artifact worth theft, in his "expert" opinion, was the wooden leg.

Johnny had ventured up to the second-floor landing on a couple of occasions, feeling Mr. Tompkins' eyes riveted on his back the entire time. While Johnny had felt a certain strangeness about the leg, he couldn't quite understand why Mr. Tompkins was so sensitive about it. Even if the leg had belonged to Blackbeard or some other notorious pirate, it was just a wooden leg. There was nothing else to give any further idea of what its owner looked like...no belt or waistcoat, or even a boot. A sword would have been more than neat. Jeremy, who had once set foot in the high school biology lab, indicated his preference for a real leg pickled in alcohol. Johnny attributed such weird notions to the fact Jeremy was allowed to watch *Night of Horrors* movies on Channel 56 on Friday nights.

Moving the wooden leg presented its own challenges. Encased in thick glass and bolted to the floor, Johnny had no clue how it could be moved without doing major damage to the landing floor. This mystery might require the help of Jeremy's cousin, Heather. Though Jeremy would never admit it, Heather was one of the smartest girls Johnny had ever met. She would be entering eighth grade this fall, only one year behind Johnny's brother, Buddy. Jeremy liked to yank on her long, amber ponytail but was careful to not tug too hard; Heather could take care of herself. She had taken karate since third grade and could outrun most of the boys in her class. Unfortunately for Johnny, Heather kept holding him up to Jeremy as some kind of role model.

"Why can't you be more like Johnny?" she would say loud enough for all of her friends to hear. "Do you ever see him chasing girls?" What Heather didn't know was that Johnny avoided girls like the plague— except for his sister, of course. They always made him tongue-tied and do the dumbest things. It was one of the reasons Johnny secretly wanted to be an astronaut and spend most of his life exploring planets.

Later, when Heather was out of earshot, Jeremy would turn to him and say, "Way to make me look bad, Turnbow!" Jeremy only called him by his last name after Johnny had done something to irritate him. Yup, as much as he would've preferred not to, they would have to bring Heather into the picture if they were going to get to the bottom of the robbery.

After supper that Thursday, Johnny asked permission to go over to Jeremy's house. His mother could not understand why he would need to see Jeremy again after spending all afternoon with him. "Oh, let the boy go, Jenny," said Mr. Turnbow. "School will come soon enough." He dropped his evening paper for a moment and said to Johnny, "Just be home before sundown, okay, Son?"

Johnny wasn't going to hang around for any further debate. He buzzed out the door and ran toward Jeremy's house. To his surprise, Jeremy was coming at him from the opposite direction. "Whoa, buster, what's up?" shouted Johnny. Jeremy stopped dead in his tracks. He motioned over to Johnny to meet him at the huge, spreading maple tree adjacent to Jeremy's house.

Once they caught their respective breaths, Jeremy began, "Well, my dad was hauling a load of gravel over to the street repair at Hoover and Oak when he saw Chief Olsen's squad car parked in the museum's lot. On the return trip, he stopped by the museum, but the chief had left. However, he did notice the 'closed' sign. Not only that, but when he walked up to the front door, he saw Mr. Tompkins pacing up and down in the lobby. Because the front window was open, he could hear Mr. Tompkins talking to himself. 'Who would take it? Who would want it? Why now?'" Jeremy stopped to take a breath.

"Did he hear anything else?" Johnny could hardly wait to hear more.

"Yes, there's more," replied Jeremy. "My dad was real curious, so he knocked at the door. When Mr. Tompkins answered, he would only open the door a crack. He was not happy to see him, my dad said. He was quite agitated and wanted to know what my dad was doing there. Well, my dad kind of faked it and said he had seen the 'closed' sign and was just checking it out. Mr. Tompkins told him it was none of his business and just a security issue. Then he slammed the door in my dad's face!"

Johnny felt deflated. He had hoped that Mr. Murkowski would have provided a better clue of what was stolen.

"But listen to this, Johnny," continued Jeremy. "My dad did get a peek at the stairway behind Mr. Tompkins, and the more he thought about it, he could not remember seeing the wooden leg in its usual place."

"He told you all that?" questioned Johnny.

"Nah, you know better than that," smiled Jeremy. "I had my ear to my parents' bedroom door. Buddy was listening, too, but he just sloughed it off as much ado about nothing. You know Buddy. If it has nothing to do with football, he isn't interested."

That sealed it for Johnny. They had to share all they knew with Heather and then find a way to check out the museum.[*] "Jeremy, what's Heather up to these days?"

"What kind of question is that?" retorted Jeremy. "Like I keep up with that know-it-all. She's probably gotten her textbooks early and has read half of them by now." Not that Jeremy wasn't a good student and didn't do his own share of reading, but Heather was the epitome of self-righteous scholarship. Was there anything that girl was not good at?

"We have got to get help," blurted Johnny.

Jeremy winced. Not again. Every time they had a particularly difficult puzzle to solve, Johnny had to drag Heather into it. "Are you absolutely sure we can't do this without Heather? You know she drives me nuts," complained Jeremy. Yes, he had to admit she was helpful. But she took such delight in bailing them out. It was more painful than sticking your tongue to an icy stop sign.

"There is no way we can break into the museum without Heather," stated Johnny matter-of-factly.

"Are you crazy?!" exclaimed Jeremy. "Where did that idea come from? 'Checking out' does not translate into 'breaking into.' If we are found snooping around inside the museum, Mr. Tompkins will have us for lunch!"

Johnny was distracted by the fact he could see Hans Murkowski walking up the street toward them.

"Hey!" shouted Hans in that squeaky voice of his. "Mom says you are to get home and take out the garbage, Jeremy."

Jeremy did not move. "You'd better hurry," continued Hans. "She is in one of those m-o-o-d-s again." He put special emphasis on the *os* in "mood."

Jeremy threw his bike around in disgust. "Don't do anything yet, Turnbow. I don't want to wake up tomorrow with Her Highness Heather

---

[*] *The past two summers the three friends had been involved in other "mysteries," so checking out the museum was not as unusual as it may seem.*

pounding on my door." But as Jeremy took off in high gear, Johnny was already thinking just how he was going to break this to Heather. This close to school, she might not want to get involved. She did always enjoy a good mystery, and that was his only hope.

He could see her closing one eye, pursing her lips, then saying, "Hmm, Johnny boy. It seems you have uncovered another tasty dilemma. I'm in."

*　*　*　*　*　*　*

As the sun set over Webster, twelve miles away in a valley adjacent to Bensonville, there was an old farmstead that had seen better days. The barn had more open spaces than wood. It gave one the distinct impression that a decent wind could flatten it in minutes. An old barn owl flew out of the roof toward the immense red oval disappearing behind the thick oak forest only one field away. Other than that, there was little evidence of life. If any farm animals did occupy the outbuildings, they were pretty quiet. A mangy spotted dog could be seen crawling underneath the porch of the two-story farmhouse. A few birds were settling within the cottonwood trees lining a dirt driveway…but that was it.

To the left of the farmhouse was a machine shed with a rusted tractor half inside. To the right was a collapsed chicken coop, and in the direction of the forest stood the barn. A surprisingly sturdy outhouse was only a few yards from the farmhouse's back door. The entire farmstead was a good quarter mile from the county road, hardly discernible with the fading light. Anyone driving by would not have given the place a second thought but for a weak bit of light steaming onto the lawn below from an upper-story window.

The small metal lamp—actually doing a bad imitation of a lantern—sat on a rickety end table at the side of a small bed. On the bed's thin mattress sat a huddled figure who was trying to read a crumpled bit of paper in the dim light. His hair was matted, and the jacket he was wearing had seen better days. The accompanying jeans had holes in both knees and his feet were bare. A pair of muddy boots stood all alone in a corner of the room. The man was intensely concentrating on the words before him.

"Five miles south to the..." What was that word? It looked like "page" but had too many letters. He continued on. "Turn left at the crossroads. Bear right past the oak tree..." The next word was actually a number, but he could not tell if it began with an "eight" or a "three." Before he could make it out, however, his concentration was broken by the opening of the bedroom door.

"So, there you are, Mad Dog. I kinda thought you would be looking to take a load off. Have you become reacquainted with the directions yet?"

Heather Comes On Board

Chief Olsen was in earlier than usual on Friday morning. As he surveyed the stacks of papers on his desk, on top of the file cabinet, and even those on the floor along the wall, he was forced to admit they contained very little of anything regarding the county museum's collections. That was part of the reason he had not slept very well.

Another was that Mayor Balducci had called him Thursday night just as he had fallen asleep. It was obvious that Mr. Tompkins had lobbied the mayor to lend his weight for keeping the museum open over the weekend. The mayor was not pleased that Chief Olsen had already decided to close the museum to facilitate the investigation.

As the chief reviewed the facts, it only made him more depressed. The initial investigation had yielded little. The case formerly holding the wooden leg was still completely intact. It remained bolted to the floor. Made of sturdy mahogany, the case was very solid. Six feet high, the front side exhibited a one-inch sheet of glass inserted into side grooves. There was a square trap door on top that was secured with a huge padlock. Strangely, no part of the case displayed any damage. No scratches, no indentations, no splinters—not to mention broken glass. There was a small amount of mud on the floor, but it probably came from Mr. Tompkin's own shoes (at least that was Detective Shaw's opinion). There had been a couple of decent thundershowers last week, and the museum grounds were still moist.

To complicate things even further, the chief and Detective Shaw could find no evidence of forced entry. As he said to the detective, "Sam, it's like the wooden leg vanished into thin air!"

No other museum objects appeared to be missing. Just in case, Chief Olsen asked Officer Kraus to inventory every artifact. He felt a little guilty about that. Eight hours with Thaddeus Tompkins was something he wished on no one, but it had to be done. In addition, Detective Shaw had walked the museum grounds but reported nothing unusual. The footpath to the neglected old gazebo was undisturbed. By the time they left the museum, all the chief and the detective had to show for their efforts was a heap full of ranting and raving contributed free of charge by a red-faced Mr. Tompkins.

The chief's meditations were interrupted by the sound of stomps coming up the stairs. His office was on the second floor, right next door to the large room used for public meetings—the Kiwanis monthly luncheon and an occasional press conference if the mayor wanted a larger crowd.

"Chief, you in there?"

Chief Olsen sighed. "Yes, Herb; door's open." He had hoped that time had stopped to catch its breath. The chief was not looking forward to today.

"Chief, I thought I would get an early start. You don't know by any chance where that old magnifying glass went to, do ya?" asked Officer Kraus.

The chief had not seen it in ages. "You might look in the bottom drawer of the file cabinet. If it's not there, I likely loaned it to Mr. James for his science class."

Officer Kraus seemed very determined to find it. After about five minutes of digging and making quite a mess of things, he held up the magnifying glass in triumph. "Ah-ha! Thought you could evade the searching of Officer Herbert J. Kraus, did you?"

Chief Olsen looked up at the ceiling and reflected, *And to think I had the chance to hire Sergeant Bowie from Muncie.* Of course, he would never say anything to hurt Officer Kraus' feelings. He really was a good chap. Officer Kraus could best be compared to Barney Fife of *The Andy Griffith Show.* His thin waist barely held up his holster. The chief often wondered how he made it through the police academy. You couldn't fault his sunny disposition, however. His hat often sat back over his thick black hair, and when he smiled, his entire face seemed to light up. Officer Kraus had the habit of lifting his massive eyebrows up and down when listening intently to any conversation. It made him appear Muppet-like.

"I'm off now, Chief. Still think I should get holiday pay for having to spend a day with Mr. Tompkins." With that, he opened the door, but before leaving, he turned with a big grin and said, "But you'll remember this at bonus time, right, Chief?"

Chief Olsen threw his staple remover at the door, barely missing Officer Kraus's left ear. That sent him scampering down the stairs and into the waiting squad car. But he went laughing all the way. That brought a smile to the chief's face, but it quickly disappeared as he returned to the business of the day.

*   *   *   *   *   *   *

Heather Stippich was standing in front of the bathroom mirror combing her hair. No pigtails today; a single ponytail would do. As she looked upon her reflection, she was greeted by a broad smile. School started next Tuesday, and it had been long in coming. Heather had been ready to return to school two weeks ago. She was entering the eighth grade, and it was going to be fantastic—she just knew it! High school would be okay, but Heather suspected it would be a different world.

For one thing, eighth grade meant another year with Mr. James—this time studying earth science. Mrs. Costello had promised her she would be placed in honors math. The rest of her courses were tolerable, and she managed straight A's. Heather thought there would be nothing better in life than to be a forensic pathologist. Since nobody ever knew what that meant, she just told people she wanted to be a science detective. That seemed to satisfy the boys and silence the girls.

That thought reminded her that there had been no decent mysteries this summer. Johnny Turnbow usually had something interesting he needed help on. Heather would never admit it, but her investigations with Johnny and Jeremy were really something she looked forward to. It had all started two summers ago when Johnny became an involuntary witness regarding the gas station holdup (it is amazing what you can overhear in a men's restroom). The efforts of the three friends led to the arrest of Tom Sylvester who was home on leave from the army. The following summer, Johnny and Jeremy uncovered a scam at the county fair when they mistakenly walked into the wrong tent and heard the confessions of the snake lady.

This summer, things had been very quiet. Some days, she just moped around and pretended to be perusing her beetle collection. Now, it was true Johnny and Jeremy were two grades lower than she was, but at least they would listen to her with a degree of respect as she spouted off on any number of subjects. There were times Jeremy became impatient with her, but she knew deep down he trusted her judgment. He did tell her to "put a lid on it" occasionally, not to mention the pigtail pulling was an irritant. Still, it was a whole lot better than listening to Michelle or Jasmin go on and on about what new clothes they were getting for school. Heather never did seem to please the fashion police, but that did not matter when you were on the honor roll every semester, president of the chess club, the best swimmer in your class, being tutored in French, and basically a teacher's pet. Heather had her choice of friends.

As she left the bathroom and skipped down the stairs, the doorbell rang. It was a little early for Michelle. She usually did not get up early on vacation mornings. The clock in the hallway said 9:35 a.m.

Her mom got to the door before Heather. "Well, what a surprise. We haven't seen much of you this summer, Johnny," said Mrs. Stippich as she invited him in.

"Sorry about that, Mrs. Stippich, but after Katie sprained her ankle, Mom needed me around the house a little more." That was Johnny's poor attempt at an excuse, and he was glad to see Heather walk up behind her mom.

"Hi, Heather," was all Johnny could muster.

"Nice to see you, Johnny. Missed you at the county swim meet," replied Heather a little too politely.

"Do you have time to, uh, talk?" fumbled Johnny.

Heather recognized the look. Johnny had a mystery in his pocket. He needed assistance. She had to restrain herself from appearing too interested. "Sure. Michelle's not due for another hour."

Heather gave her mom a look, and Mrs. Stippich retreated into the kitchen. "If you want a chocolate chip cookie, Johnny, I'll have some done when you get back," she said over her shoulder. Mrs. Stippich knew from experience that when Heather and Johnny "talked," they would be occupied for a while, and the conversation would not be taking place in her living room.

As they walked down the porch steps, they made an automatic turn down Plum Drive and headed east as if going to the library. That was not to be their immediate destination, however, as on the way stood a huge silver maple tree that had gigantic roots spreading in all directions. At five foot one, Heather was five inches taller than Johnny. Her long legs magnified the difference between them. As her ponytail bobbed behind her, it appeared only a matter of time before it would graze Johnny's red hair.

The maple tree stood in the middle of a vacant lot between Betty's Beauty Shop and a nondescript duplex. The tree offered the advantage of a place to sit down and, more importantly, privacy. Upon reaching the ancient maple, Heather plopped down on one of the more inviting roots, while Johnny just sat in the grass. "Okay, Johnny, what's up?" she probed. "You've been avoiding me all summer, and now with classes around the corner, you come knocking on my door. This has to be good."

After what seemed to be forever, Johnny finally replied, "Have you heard about the museum?"

Heather had not. Actually, the museum had been furthest from her mind. Since Heather had not heard the news, Johnny filled her in on all of the details. She interrupted from time to time to ask a question and then just listened attentively. "You say Jeremy's dad thinks the leg was taken?" Heather queried. Johnny barely stopped to answer, and when he had finished his story, he was quite out of breath. Heather did not immediately comment but stared back him with eyebrows furrowed.

Finally, she began to summarize what she had heard, as if talking to herself. "If I understand correctly, old man Tompkins left work on Wednesday night, and when he returned on Thursday, the leg was gone. He was preoccupied with the coming weekend and may have been less attentive than usual. Wonder if anyone has thought to question the cleaning lady."

Johnny was paying close attention, waiting for her to come to some revealing conclusion. Instead, Heather abruptly stood up and said, "Johnny, Michelle and your cookie will have to wait. We have to pay a visit to the library, and then I think we need to see what Mrs. Smothers has been up to. We'll call Jeremy and tell him to meet us at the library." When Johnny did not move, Heather waved him on and exclaimed, "Well, let's go. I hope you had a good breakfast."

Fortunately, they reached Jeremy with one call, and after muttering something about "Miss Know-it-All is at it again," he promised to be at the library in about fifteen minutes. Michelle was more easily dispatched. The library was not too far from Heather's house on Peach Lane. It was a matter of navigating Plum Drive to Branch Avenue, crossing Pickett Street, and then traveling a mere two blocks to the library—total distance being maybe a half mile. Heather and Johnny walked, while Jeremy, who had a bit further to go, rode his bike. They all arrived at the same time, just as the huge round clock above the library's entrance registered 10:30 a.m.

"Shouldn't we be looking around the museum while we have daylight?" questioned Jeremy. "The library does stay open until 8 p.m., you know."

Heather sighed and replied, "It won't do us much good if we don't know what we are looking for, Jeremy."

Jeremy and Johnny exchanged quizzical looks. It was then Johnny who said, "Heather, what do you hope to find in Webster Library? You complained all last year about how it didn't have the books you needed. How do you expect to acquire any evidence to solve a mystery?"

At this point, Heather knew she would have to take a moment to explain her logic, as the boys were clueless. She stopped in front of the entrance, swung around with her hands on hips, and proceeded to enlighten her younger friends. "My dear crime-solving partners, it is obvious that if Mr. Murkowski is right, the wooden leg did not get up and walk out of the museum by itself. In fact, to remove it from the second-floor landing during the night means this has to be a professional job. Putting those two facts together tells me it might be wise to check the newspaper file and see if anyone was released from the county jail recently."

Ah, Johnny thought, *the beauty of the daily police blotter.* Whatever deficiencies *The Reporter* had, they did not include the paper's dedication to reporting anything remotely connected with crime and police activity. Johnny's dad was heard to remark at times that he thought Chief Olsen paid the newspaper for such diligent reporting in order to keep a high profile before the public.

Heather strode confidently up to the checkout desk. Waiting to greet them was Emma Lord. "Miss Emma," as the students called her, was a kind soul behind a stern exterior. She always wore her hair in a bun and peered out at library patrons over her black-framed reading glasses. The fact she was on the tall side made her an even more imposing presence. However, she was always happy to see Heather, a promising young scholar. Had Emma Lord not become a librarian, she would have gone on to further study, perhaps becoming a professor. When her mother became ill, she switched to a terminal master's program, leading to employment at the Webster Library. Emma and Margaret Lord (aged seventy-five), shared a two-bedroom apartment on the far east side of town. In Heather, Emma saw herself and encouraged her in any way she could.

"Could we take a look at the newspaper microfilm, Miss Emma?" asked Heather.

"Of course, dear. You will be careful not to refile what you have already looked at, won't you?" As Emma spoke, she looked directly at Johnny and Jeremy, who she doubted were responsible enough to handle the microfilm on their own.

Guessing Miss Emma's apprehension, Heather jumped to their defense. "Oh, we won't, Miss Emma. All of us have done this before." Heather then winked at Johnny.

The threesome must have spent almost two hours poring over every police blotter from the past three years. As they were about to throw in the towel, Jeremy suddenly shouted, "There! I remember him!" That brought a loud, "Ssshhh!" from the vigilant librarian.

"He's the one who ran the truck into bank," Jeremy whispered. The caption below the picture read, "Bolton Gang Released Early from State Penitentiary."

Mr. Tompkins Makes Discoveries

Normally, Mrs. Smothers worked at the museum until noon, unless there were additional tasks that needed to get done. On Friday morning, after Mr. Tompkins arrived, she shared with the curator that she was not feeling well. Actually, Yvetlana Smothers got the impression Mr. Tompkins would rather she not be at the museum anyway.

"That is not a problem," he responded distantly, while pondering over a pile of papers. "You go home and get some rest. I'll need you healthy in case we open the museum this weekend." Mr. Tompkins had shared with her the bare essentials regarding the disappearance of the wooden leg. Never looking up, he threw her a faint wave. Mrs. Smothers gathered her things and proceeded to leave.

"Oh, Mrs. Smothers," added Mr. Tompkins, suddenly looking up. She tried to hide the worried look on her face. "I will give you a call tonight to let you know about any weekend hours." Flashing him a weak smile, Mrs. Smothers headed out the back door. As Boris had demanded, Yvetlana retrieved the silver key and placed it securely in the right-hand pocket of the wool coat she had worn to work—partially for that purpose. She only knew of its existence because once, when cleaning the curator's office, Yvetlana had knocked the small box containing it on the floor. As far as she knew, Mr. Tompkins had never seen fit to use it. Breathing a sigh of relief, she moved steadily across the parking lot.

Officer Kraus arrived at the museum Friday morning in time to see Thaddeus Tompkins walk up and unlock the front door. As he parked the squad car on Elm Street and gathered his supplies needed for the day's investigation, he could not help but think that he was not going to discover much. Years as a police officer told him that there was something very strange about this case. Normal police procedure was probably not going to crack the mystery. That didn't mean he was going to disobey Chief Olsen and cut out early, but it did mean he was going to keep an eye open for anything unusual.

As he proceeded to jump over the gate to the right of the entrance, out of the corner of his eye, he noticed Mrs. Smothers appear out of nowhere, ambling across the parking lot. Her head was covered with a scarf, and she wore a blue woolen coat as if it were October, not early September. In one hand, she held the handles of a paper bag with protruding articles of clothing. Mrs. Smothers stared down at the ground as she moved, giving the impression of not being aware of anything around her.

Moving to the walkway, Officer Kraus simultaneously waved and shouted out, "Good morning, Mrs. Smothers!" The last thing the poor lady expected was to be hailed by Officer Kraus. This caused her to jump as if scared out of her wits. Already nervous about taking the key—surely Mr. Tompkins would notice it missing at some point—Yvetlana dropped her bags on the ground and let out a shriek.

"Didn't mean to startle you, Mrs. Smothers," Officer Kraus responded. "Can I give you a ride somewhere?"

Sensing Officer Kraus was moving toward her to help, Yvetlana made a herculean effort to bend over and restore the bag's contents. In the process, her coat pockets rose, exposing the silver key to the air. Yvetlana's pocketbook had fallen a little farther away than the rest of the items. It was her stretch to pick it up that caused the key to somersault to the pavement. She was now breathing heavily and scurried to finish reorganizing her things.

Mr. Tompkins strode up behind the officer. "What are you doing, Kraus? Trying to give my custodian a heart attack?" he said gruffly. Mr. Tompkins moved to help her, but Mrs. Smothers motioned for him to stay away.

"No, I'm fine," she responded weakly. Her bag once more in tow, the frazzled custodian launched off in a trot, resuming her previous focus.

Mr. Tompkins stiffened and said, "Let her be, Kraus; you have more important things to attend to." The officer then turned and followed Thaddeus into the museum. Yvetlana threw them a furtive glance to make sure neither was going to follow her and then disappeared down Elm Street. If any of them had taken a moment to gaze out at the rising sun beaming down on the parking lot, they would have seen a reflective gleam stemming from a long silver key—the old kind that opened the doors of your grandmother's house. It just laid on the asphalt pavement as if waiting to be discovered. The small shining object, miniscule as it was, seemed destined for more important things than reflecting rays from the sun.

Once inside, Mr. Tompkins resumed shuffling through some papers while Officer Kraus pondered where to begin his investigation. Standing behind the information desk, Thaddeus looked quite anxious. He did not appear to have gotten much sleep.

"When would you like to begin going through the inventory?" asked Officer Kraus as he peered over the desk.

Mr. Tompkins raised his head slowly while holding tightly to two sheets of paper. He glared before speaking. Through pursed lips, he retorted, "Why don't you begin by doing what normal policemen initially do? Have a look around and give me a moment to finish my sorting." The curator continued with his fixed stare until Officer Kraus turned and moved into the local history room. His stern demeanor quickly morphed into an evolving smile, however, as he held up a particular piece of paper. "Ah, yes, here it is," he muttered, speaking to no one in particular. Mr. Tompkins' head jolted up as he directed his voice to the local history room. "Come look at this, Kraus. You should find this interesting."

The officer had been studying the Delaware Indian statue but quickly returned to the information desk. Mr. Tompkins shoved a piece of paper in front of him. "Read this, Officer Kraus. The shipping bill for the wooden leg." Thaddeus' long pointed finger was fixed over a stamped statement, somewhat smudged.

Officer Kraus looked it over carefully and then read aloud, "Property of HMS *Bountiful*. For safe delivery to home office. Transfer rights unallowed this voyage." Underneath was an illegibly scrawled signature, but below that was the identified owner: Captain A.S. Adams, Her Majesty's Royal Navy. Officer Kraus then removed his cap and proceeded to scratch his head. "Not sure what this means, Mr. Tompkins," he said, puzzled.

"Of course you don't, you half-wit." Mr. Tompkins snatched the bill away and explained, "I found this with the wooden leg years ago but never paid much attention to it. With a little examination, you would see the date reads December 10th, 1773. You would also see that there is a skull and crossbones in the corner with the annotation '3,000 pound sterling.' Plus, if you hold the document up to the light, you would also see someone tried to copy a map on the back." Mr. Tompkins stopped and stared intently at Officer Kraus as if expecting some reply. There being none, he continued.

"There is more to this leg than meets the eye. It would seem another visit to Dr. McDougal is in order. Wait here, Kraus, while I see if the professor is in." With that, he moved to his office down the hall to make a phone call. After what seemed like ages, Mr. Tompkins returned. He maneuvered around the desk and plopped a worn folder into Officer Kraus' hands. "Take this inventory list and make sure nothing else is missing. I trust you can find your way around the museum. Though, like I said before, it probably will be a waste of time." Thaddeus grabbed his hat and cane and made ready to leave.

"But you won't be back before I leave, Mr. Tompkins," said Officer Kraus worriedly. "Don't you want me to lock up?"

Mr. Tompkins just glared at him and placed two keys in his hand. "Make sure you double bolt the door, Kraus. Then stop by my place on your way home and leave the keys with Widow Ruenzel." Leaving the officer to contemplate his tasks, he then proceeded to his old Ford parked behind the museum in his designated stall. The sun had risen higher in the sky during the intervening minutes between Officer Kraus' arrival and Mr. Tompkins' departure. Its rays caused the silver key on the pavement to send out a beam of light toward the east wall of the museum. That beam caught Thaddeus' eye before he could reach down to open the car door. He shielded his right eye and tried to make out where the bright light was coming from. It seemed to be emanating from the middle of the parking lot. Moving slowly toward the light's source, he began to make out the silhouette of a key. *Now, what would a key be doing in the middle of nowhere*, he thought.

Mr. Tompkins bent over the object, giving the impression he was examining something living, not inanimate. He felt he should be familiar with it. Eventually, he lifted the key from the ground. Upon reflection, he remembered Mrs. Smothers crossing the parking lot earlier and deduced it had to have fallen from her coat pocket. Well, no time to be that concerned with it now. He would return it to her when he saw her next.

Officer Kraus came out on the landing in time to see Mr. Tompkins drive off. *Fossils—both of them*, he thought. He doubted the Ford station wagon could make it to the university and back.

✳   ✳   ✳   ✳   ✳   ✳   ✳

After Johnny, Jeremy, and Heather had made the startling discovery that the Bolton gang had been released early from prison a few months ago, they debated what to do next. It was almost 1:00 p.m., and no one had had lunch or even much breakfast, for that matter. Heather wanted to proceed to the museum immediately, but the boys did not relish investigating on an empty stomach. Jeremy pointed out they were only two blocks from the McDonald's on the corner of Johnson Drive and Highway 12. Of course, there was the matter of who had money. Jeremy had received his allowance that Friday morning; Johnny had sixty-three cents to contribute to the cause.

Heather rolled her eyes and said, "I suppose it is up to me to make up the difference. Again." She stomped off, exasperated, telling them, "I'll just pay for it. Come on. Time's a wastin."

Heather ordered a shake and did most of the talking as Johnny and Jeremy wolfed down their double cheeseburgers. "I'm sure that Chief

Olsen is in the early stages of his investigation, and we are really lucky the museum will not stay open this weekend. There still may be clues to find. We can survey the museum grounds easily enough, but how can we get inside? And what if Mr. Tompkins is somewhere around?" Heather seemed to be asking the question of herself. Suddenly, she turned to Johnny. "Remember when you were locked inside the museum last year after Mr. Tompkins closed early and thought everyone was gone?" Johnny nodded.

Jeremy appeared not to be listening. "You going to finish those fries?" he asked Johnny. Heather gave him a perturbed look.

She turned back to Johnny. "Didn't you crawl out a basement window?"

Johnny shoved his remaining fries at Jeremy. Then he answered, "I remembered that one of the windows was ajar, the latch broken. Mr. Tompkins had previously sent me down to the basement with a broken lamp he was going to repair. As I walked down the stairs, I felt this breeze coming down on my head. I hoped it had not been fixed. As it was, I was still barely able to crawl through it."

"What are the odds that Mr. Tompkins has had it repaired?" asked Heather.

Johnny thought for a moment. "Not likely. He has had bigger maintenance fish to fry this summer."

"You can say that again." Suddenly Jeremy was paying attention. "The air conditioning was out most of the summer. I only went once. It was like an oven in there."

"Well, that will be our plan then," noted Heather. Her blue eyes sparkled with excitement. "What time is it?" As if on cue, they all turned and looked at the round wall clock. It read half past two. She continued, "We can be over by the museum in a half hour or so. We'll check the grounds first, then see if the basement window is still accessible."

"Just a minute, Sherlock," countered Jeremy. "I don't know about Johnny, but I have to be home by four."

"We're not going *inside* this afternoon, silly," replied Heather.

"If we wait, we can operate under the cover of darkness. We'll meet at the museum again after the sun sets."

Johnny and Jeremy looked at each other in disbelief. "Do you realize what you are saying, Heather?" asked Johnny. "Our parents will kill us if they find out we have sneaked out of the house. I am still in trouble from the night we spent downtown trailing that old beggar you thought was a burglar."

"You got that right, bub," chimed in Jeremy.

Heather put on one of her miffed looks. "Well, I suppose if you children cannot make it, I'll just have to make this an individual investigation."

Johnny knew this was just her way of bullying them into going with her. He saw Jeremy's face redden and knew what was coming.

"Who are you calling 'children'?" exclaimed Jeremy. He said it a little too loudly, and now everyone was staring at them.

"Come on," said Johnny. "Let's get over to the museum. We can work this out along the way. We need to case that window." With that, they left McDonald's and proceeded up Johnson Street.

They did not know it, but at that very moment, Officer Kraus was ending his inventory early. He had had enough of stuffed owls and dusty bookcases. Besides, the wind was making the whole building creak funnily, and it was giving him the creeps. Nothing else appeared missing, and maybe it had been a waste of time. As he stared at the second-floor landing one more time, for the life of him he could not figure how anyone could have removed the wooden leg without a trace. Hopefully, in a week this would all blow over, and Mr. Tompkins would just fill out the insurance papers and find something more intriguing to put in the leg's place. One thing was for sure: his weekend was wrecked, and he was not looking forward to telling the Mrs. the weekend vacation to the lake was off. Now he would have to stop by the doughnut shop on the way home and purchase several Boston Cremes to ease her pain.

Officer Kraus dutifully secured the museum doors and headed to his squad car. Suddenly, he stopped for one moment and looked back at the shadows enveloping the museum. He was almost certain the red-bricked structure was whispering to him, "Find the leg…find the leg." Officer Kraus did not wait around further. He made a note to himself to not skip lunch anymore.

*   *   *   *   *   *   *

At home, Mrs. Smothers only had the energy to sit at her kitchen table, her head in her hands, clothed in one of the two flower-patterned dresses she owned. *Please, Boris*, she petitioned in her heart, *get here soon and relieve me of this key.*

For some reason, she had this terrible premonition that Mr. Tompkins would come barging through the door at any moment screaming, "You thief, return that key at once!" Boris did not disappoint, because exactly at 3 p.m., he was knocking firmly on his mother's door.

"Open up, Mother dear," he said. "Time to deliver the goods."

Roused out of her musings, Yvetlana let Boris in.

"You got it, right? Where is it?" he bellowed.

Yvetlana walked to her coat hanging on the door. She reached into the left pocket and, to her astonishment, found nothing inside. She glanced back and forth at Boris who began to sense something was not right.

"Is there anything wrong?" he queried slowly, taking a step toward the door.

"It's…it's gone," his mother stammered. Shaking, she could only cling to the thick coat and look pleadingly at her son. "Boris, I swear that I put it in my coat pocket." Then her eyes got wider. "It must have dropped out. That's it. In the parking lot when I dropped my bag."

Boris now seized her shoulders. "Are you sure? Because if we can't find it, I am not responsible for you. Understand?!" His face only reflected rage. With lips still curled, Boris relaxed his grip. He paused a moment before speaking further. "I can't go back and look for it now. Can't afford to be spotted." Boris moved to the refrigerator. "Got anything yummy in here, Mrs. Smothers?"

Yvetlana did not know if she was safe for the moment or not. "Try the stew," she suggested, keeping her distance. "Here, I'll heat it up for you." They did not speak for the next several minutes. Boris devoured the stew.

Standing up, he looked his mother straight in the eye. "Pray I don't return tonight, Mother. If I do, it means I did not find the key...and I won't be alone." Tears welled up in her eyes. Yvetlana had only seen that menacing look once before in her life. It was just before a man died.

Things Hidden

Dr. McDougal slammed the receiver down, and in one full sweep, he flung most everything on his desk to the floor. "That meddling old fool!" he muttered through gritted teeth. His face reddened, and his double chin seemed to shake with rage. "He will be the death of me yet."

Emily Quig trembled in the corner of his office. The last thirty-six hours had been devastating for her. She now feared for her safety. Dressed in baggy sweats, her diminutive frame gave the impression she was going to melt away into the woodwork. "Oh, get a grip, Miss Quig," implored the professor. "I need you to have all of your wits about you today. Remember our agreement." Slowly rising, his bulky silhouette appeared even more menacing, and Emily let out a shriek. "Quiet, you sniveling novice. Let me make it perfectly clear to you: I will stop at nothing to achieve my purposes. If you cooperate and complete your tasks, you will be amply rewarded. Shirk from your duty, and you will not have to worry about your academic career!" With that, Dr. McDougal pounded his fist on the surface of his oak desk, causing the remaining stapler to flip on its side.

Emily slid to the floor and grew very pale. Dr. McDougal was now in a quandary. If he did not see Thaddeus Tompkins later today, it might raise too many questions. Things had to appear normal—at least for another day. On the other hand, if he took the time to meet with the curator, it would delay and complicate things. The last thing he wanted was to have his henchmen sitting around twiddling their thumbs. While he did not fear Mad Dog and his company, who knew what mischief they could cause if they got bored. His only hope was to dispatch Thaddeus as quickly as possible.

*   *   *   *   *   *   *

Mr. Tompkins maneuvered his car down Pickett Street to Johnson Drive and then turned south on Highway 12. It was a good hour to Bradford, and he never exceeded the speed limit. While the phrase "tingling with excitement" did not normally match Mr. Tompkins staid personality, he was looking forward to his meeting with Dr. McDougal with great anticipation. Why hadn't he paid attention to the bill of lading before? How could he be so clueless? What was worth three thousand pounds sterling?

As he passed McClure's grocery store and gas station at the intersection with County Road W, he felt the engine shutter but paid it no mind. Mr. Tompkins was halfway to Bradford City. He did decide to err on the side of caution, however, and reduced his speed to forty-five miles per hour. When he reached the K-Mart store on the outskirts of Bradford City, Thaddeus knew he was close to his destination. Bradford

State University was a sprawling campus on the northwest side of the city of twelve-thousand-plus residents. After a few wrong turns, the sputtering Ford stopped in front of Bluffton Hall. Fortunately, there was a vacant visitor's parking stall.

It had been a while. Striding through a misty drizzle, Mr. Tompkins approached the marble steps leading to the entrance. He had to dodge a couple swarms of students; classes had just let out. Bluffton Hall was one of those Romanesque structures of red brick and stone that dotted a few other campuses, rising four stories into the air. Consulting the faculty directory just past the entrance, Mr. Tompkins affirmed that Dr. McDougal's office was on the third floor. The elevator was a welcome sight.

The clock in the third-floor foyer revealed Friday morning was about gone. Dr. McDougal's office was in a corner of the east wing. Raising his cane, Mr. Tompkins used it to knock smartly on the door.

"Please enter," responded the voice inside.

Mr. Tompkins swung the door open and was greeted by Dr. McDougal at his desk. A young student was seated near him. "Come in, come in, Thaddeus. It has been way too long." The professor stood and warmly extended his hand. "Let me introduce Miss Quig, one of my archaeology students. We were just finishing our discussion, is that not right, Miss Quig?"

Emily Quig promptly exited the office, nodding in respect to Mr. Tompkins as she left. "Excuse the mess, my friend. Still trying to get organized for the fall term, you understand," apologized Dr. McDougal. "Now, I understand you had more questions about that wooden leg?"

Mr. Tompkins began to speak, almost in a whisper. "You have not likely heard about the theft, Professor. I came to work yesterday morning only to find the leg vacant from its case. There was no evidence of a break-in or any physical damage. It is an absolute mystery...totally befuddling."

"My sympathies, of course, Thaddeus, but what could I possibly do to help?" purred Dr. McDougal.

"Well, it occurred to me that there might be more to the artifact than I originally thought. After going through its file, I uncovered this bill of lading going back to 1773." With that, Mr. Tompkins pulled out the document and placed it on the desk. "I wonder if you might find it as interesting as I did."

Dr. McDougal slowly picked up the piece of paper and began to scrutinize its contents. "There also appears to be a map on the back," noted the curator. He was anxious for some response and noticeably wringing his hands. After what seemed an eternity, Dr. McDougal looked up over the bill and said seriously, "Combined with what I have told you previously, Thaddeus, this bill of lading could definitely increase the importance of the leg. But I would need more time to research its meaning. Could you leave it with me for a while?"

Mr. Tompkins stood up, agitated. "I really need for you to give it your immediate attention. It may help to explain why someone would steal the wooden leg." After a short pause, he continued, "Certainly the notation about the sterling must make you curious."

Dr. McDougal furrowed his brows and replied, "I wouldn't make too much of it. It might be referring to all the contents of the shipment, not just the leg." Mr. Tompkins appeared crestfallen. "As for the map, it looks to be a very crude drawing. I would need to compare it with other period maps to gain any idea of its relevance."

Sensing the curator's disappointment, Dr. McDougal moved from behind his desk and placed his arm around Mr. Tompkins' shoulder. "Now, Thaddeus, I can appreciate your interest and concern. But this is likely just some prank. School is starting soon. Perhaps some students wanted to end their summer vacation with something spectacular."

Mr. Tompkins threw up his hands. "You don't understand. This had to be the work of experts. The leg completely vanished. Vanished, I say. Somebody must know its true worth." Then his eyes grew larger, and with a look of astonishment he mouthed, "Perhaps there was something inside the leg."

If Dr. McDougal was taken aback, he did not show it. The professor began to move Mr. Tompkins out the door. "Let me borrow your document for at least a couple days. If I find something definite, I will notify you immediately." But Thaddeus seemed lost in thought. He had had an epiphany and mechanically left the building. As he plopped into the driver's seat of his car, he gazed into space and kept repeating, "Inside, inside..."

Mr. Tompkins could not have known that Emily Quig had made a stop on the way back to her dormitory. The Ford would not start again until a mechanic performed some magic.

*   *   *   *   *   *   *

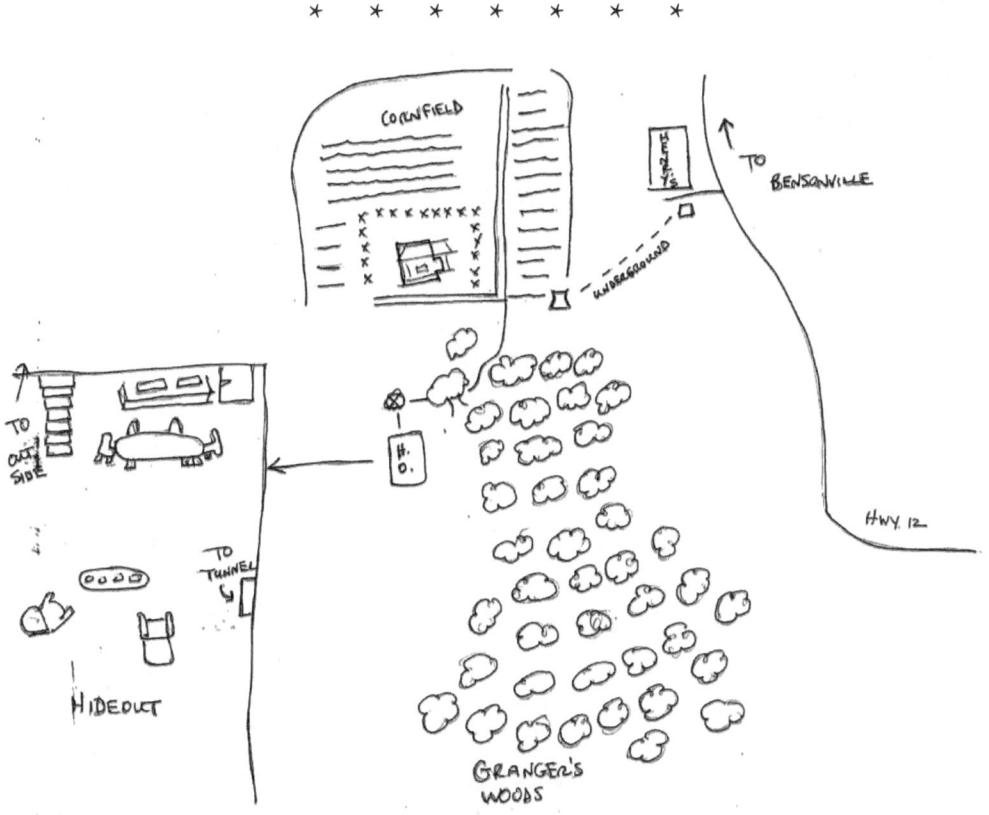

After giving up on trying to figure out the directions Thursday night, Mad Dog Scrima and Skippy Forrester awoke to the sun streaming through the farmhouse bedroom window Friday morning. As both were severely in need of a bath, and since there was no running water other than a hand pump in the backyard, they marched their way to a nearby pond. Even for an early September morning, the water was more cold than chilly.

Drying himself off with a towel he'd found in the farmhouse, Skippy posed a question to his friend, Harvey. "So, why all the secrecy? Why are we plunked in the middle of nowhere with no wheels?"

Mad Dog finished drying off his thick and undisciplined head of hair and then replied, "To my understanding, our boss has gone to a lot of trouble to pull off this heist. We are supposed to grab the leg tomorrow evening. I don't know all the particulars and don't care to. All we need to do is focus on the task ahead."

That seemed to quiet Skippy for the moment. Once back at the house, breakfast consisted of some beef jerky, warm beer, and a couple of Twinkies. Then they settled down to examine the directions in better light. There was a rough sketch of the farmhouse and its outbuildings. A squiggly line connected the farm to a square titled, "Henry's Auto Body." Above the line was written, "5 miles south to the garage." It was evident they had a healthy hike ahead of them. Near the square was a small rectangle marked with a cross. A dotted line then connected with another rectangle. Associated with that line were the words, "Turn left at the crossroads, bear right past the oak tree." Finally, there were three numbers in the corner of the paper: "8, 6, 3."

Since Mad Dog and Skippy could see dark clouds off in the distance to the south (the direction in which they were headed), they agreed further delay was not advisable. The squiggly line actually represented what seemed to be an old cow path. It kept them apart from the highway. The path was filled with summer growth, so there was a lot of tall grass to wade through. With every step, the two companions awakened a number of grasshoppers, which resembled a vanguard guiding them to their destination.

Skippy took longer strides, so Mad Dog made him walk behind him. They managed to cover the five miles in about an hour and a half. Neither had a watch, but by the sun, they surmised it had to be midday when they arrived at the garage. Mad Dog, hands on his hips, surveyed the vacated body shop and the surrounding terrain. "Skippy, what do you think that 'X' represents on the map?" In the past, Skippy had impressed him with his observational skills.

Skippy rubbed his unshaven chin and began to walk toward a phone booth off to the side. The door was half open, and the phone's receiver was dangling toward the slot where there should have been a phone book. Skippy walked in and stood silently. After a couple minutes, Mad Dog got impatient. "Hey, Skippy, are you waiting to be beamed up somewhere, or what?"

At about the same moment, Skippy tore a sheet of paper off the side of the booth. He then motioned to Mad Dog to quickly join him. Mad Dog quickly ran up to the booth. Pointing to a distant field, Skippy asked, "What do you see?"

Mad Dog peered through the glass panel. "I think I see a tree stump."

"Voilà! You win!" exclaimed Skippy.

He then showed the paper to Mad Dog. On it was written, "tree stump." "I think we should head there," suggested Skippy.

After about a thousand-foot walk, the duo halted at the huge stump. Mad Dog got out the map. "If you are correct, Skip, old boy, the crossroads is straight ahead."

Indeed, it was. On the right was a dirt road bisecting two fields. A caved-in barn sat directly to the west. To their left was what the locals called "Granger's Woods." Skippy followed Mad Dog to a large old oak tree. About halfway up the trunk was a lopsided sign that contained an arrow pointing into the woods. Below the arrow read, "Dunbar Tavern."

Mad Dog took out the directions again to look for enlightenment. Above the numbers (8, 6, 3) was written, "25 steps." Skippy started to pace off twenty-five lengths when Mad Dog placed his hand on his shoulder and indicated, "Stop." "Skippy," he grunted, "Let's use my legs."

So, after twenty-five shorter steps, they found themselves in front of a bush. They appeared to have reached a dead end. Skippy bent over to gain a closer look. Due to his height, he lost his balance, falling into the bush headfirst. "Ouch!" exclaimed Skippy.

Reaching into the bush, Mad Dog felt a small post. Together, they worked on the bush, eventually pulling it aside. Revealed was a three-foot post with a keypad on the top. Mad Dog and Skippy simultaneously smiled. Punching in the code 8-6-3, the post moved backward, revealing a trap door. It was obvious that the boss had gone to great lengths to prevent discovery.

Glancing around to make sure they were unobserved, Mad Dog and Skippy pulled on the trap door and descended down more stairs. The door automatically closed shut behind them. Clouds were now gathering, and the smell of rain was in the air.

Another
Investigation Begins

Johnny, Jeremy, and Heather arrived at the museum in record time. Officer Kraus was just pulling out onto Elm Street as they came up Pickett, but he did not notice them. He seemed to be in a hurry to get home.

Jeremy started to wave, but Heather quickly pulled his hand down. "Sure, that's just what we need. Officer Kraus bearing witness that we were seen near the museum late Friday afternoon."

Jeremy looked a little sheepish. "Well, we all can't be super sleuths like you, Heather. Excuse me for trying to be friendly."

Johnny reminded them of the fact that Officer Kraus leaving was a good thing. Now they only had to determine if Mr. Tompkins was getting ready to leave. "Maybe Mr. Tompkins will leave a little early today. After all, the museum isn't open." He was trying to be encouraging.

"The shades are down," observed Heather. "He might already be gone. Let's go see if his car is parked on the other side of the building." The clouds that had floated in, accompanied by a light rain, made it darker than it should have been. There was no light emanating from behind the shades, providing additional evidence that the museum was vacant. Moving cautiously to the north end of the parking lot, they knelt down in the knee-high grass bordering it. Nothing was moving either in or outside of the museum. Actually, the entire scene was rather eerie.

Johnny finally broke the silence. "If you look a little to the left, near the ground is the window I escaped from. You guys wait here. I'm going to check and see if it's still open."

"Be careful," said Heather and Jeremy in unison. Johnny slowly moved toward the giant willow tree shadowing the parking lot. He paused for a moment as he thought he saw something move across the window. It was soon evident that it was nothing more than a sparrow flying from the tree to the museum's roof and back again.

Johnny got down on his belly to cover the remaining distance to the museum wall. It had rained long enough that the ground was moist. He felt his T-shirt getting wet, so he zipped up his lightweight jacket. Now he would have to think up an alibi to satisfy his mother's inquiring mind. The closer he inched to the window, the more certain he was that there was a small crack between the basement window and the top of the sill.

Johnny had only a little way to go. He looked back and could make out Heather and Jeremy gazing on in anticipation. Johnny stretched out his arm as far as he could, allowing his stubby fingers to grab the end of the window glass. *Excellent*, he thought to himself. The window was open. Rising to his knees, he reached behind it. Johnny felt confident he could still squeeze through the available space.

Seeing no one around, Johnny took off at a low trot back to his friends. "The window is still open. I think I can get into the basement," he reported.

Heather gave him a thumbs up. "Okay, here's what we'll do. What time do your families turn in?" she asked the boys.

"My parents are trying to get us all to sleep earlier so we won't moan so much when school starts," contributed Jeremy.

"Yeah, lights are out at my house by 9 p.m.," added Johnny.

"Good," replied Heather. "Once you are sure your parents have gone to bed, sneak out and meet me back at this exact spot. I can get here earlier because I am supposed to have a sleepover with Megan. I'll have a flashlight to signal you once I see you approaching."

Jeremy rolled his eyes in disbelief. "Easy for you to say, Heather. I bunk with my little brother, and he's a very light sleeper. Not to mention my parents installed new locks on the front and back doors. I will have to mimic Houdini to get out!"

Johnny ruffled through his bushy red hair and appeared to be hatching an idea. "You got something you want to share, Johnny?" queried Heather, moving closer.

"Jeremy, do you remember we asked our moms if we could have an overnight before school started?" posited Johnny. Jeremy nodded his head. "Well, why should Heather be the only one to get a sleepover? When we each get to our houses, we will explain that we have been invited over to the other's to spend the night. Then, shortly after 9:00 p.m., we can set off for the museum. In the morning, we can return to our homes before breakfast. No one will know the better."

Heather had a broad smile on her face. "Johnny, you make me so proud when you talk like that."

Jeremy kept shaking his head. "This has disaster written all over it, Turnbow." But in the end, they all agreed it was the best plan they could come up with. So, with the sun beginning to lower, they all headed home to lay the groundwork for a nocturnal return.

*   *   *   *   *   *   *

Yvetlana Moscavlovich Smolanesky (known to Webster residents as Mrs. Smothers) came to the United States at the age of ten during the middle of World War II, disguised as a bag of rice. She was never to see her parents again, and it was a miracle she made it at all. Surviving on a diet of molasses, flour, and cornmeal, Yvetlana somehow managed the two-month voyage aboard a Greek freighter. Scared, cold, and twenty pounds lighter, she was discovered by a crewman when the boat docked in Boston. It was her good fortune that Mr. Long Ears (as she named him) spoke both Russian and Greek. That enabled him to understand her, and it also meant he could plead her case with the Fathers of St. John's (a Greek Orthodox Church) on the outskirts of the city. A small adjacent orphanage was to be her home for the next seven years. To her benefit, Yvetlana learned Greek and English and was able to make a living as a maid and cook in the neighborhoods of Brookline. At the age of twenty, she met an Italian baker and they had two sons before he died in a Thanksgiving Day car accident on the Summer Street bridge.

Stuck with two young sons and very little income, Mrs. Balducci (her married name) found herself in desperate straits. At her husband's funeral, she met a cousin of his who convinced her to move west to

Indiana and serve as a maid and nanny to prominent businessmen. In this manner, Yvetlana had a home in which to raise her sons, provide them with playmates, and manage a small income. The cousin was Alfonso Balducci, whose son Stephen would later become Webster's mayor. As a result, when her sons were old enough to leave home, she secured the custodian's job at the county museum. At the age of fifty, dusting off museum artifacts was a fine substitute for cleaning, cooking, and washing clothes. When Yvetlana arrived in Webster, she had her name changed to Smothers—it was easier to pronounce and spell than Smolanesky. She dared not use her married name; she did not want to make known her relationship to the mayor. Yvetlana took up residence in a basement apartment on Pickett Street.

Mrs. Smothers was never quite sure of Mr. Tompkins. He acted strangely at times and gave her penetrating stares, as if he expected she was going to carry off one of the "precious" museum objects. Every time she would climb the stairs to the second floor to clean the glass case that housed the wooden leg, Mr. Tompkins would find a reason to leave his office and do "second floor work." Coming up the stairs, he reminded Yvetlana of Ebenezer Scrooge walking up to his lodgings on Christmas Eve. Mr. Tompkins always seemed to wear a perpetual frown, and his untrimmed eyebrows hung over his beady eyes.

What would I want with a wooden leg? she used to ask herself. Certainly, she was not going to break the glass. For that and other reasons, Mrs. Smothers pretended to know only the barest of English. She had no desire for any extended conversations with Mr. Tompkins.

Now, Yvetlana's two sons did not amount to much. Whether that was because they had no father or substantial economic standings, no one would ever really know. They certainly ate well and always had a clean, if not extensive, wardrobe. Yvetlana sacrificed her own needs when they wanted the latest basketball shoes. Plus, she paid for movies, pizza, and even dental work that she could ill afford. Still, Boris and Iggy (short for Ignatius) were usually up to no good. They were the poorest of students and only graduated from high school because Principal Hart was tired of all the fights they caused.

Had the boys an ounce of consideration, they would have found steady work after high school. Their mother certainly deserved help in improving the family's situation. Extra income would have allowed a move to a roomier dwelling. However, they were unable to hold down jobs for more than a couple months at a time. The boys continued to eat their mother out of house and home. The only time they showed up was when they needed clothes washed or a good meal. Then they would disappear for days at a time. Poor Mrs. Smothers deserved a better fate.

Boris and Iggy hit rock bottom when they hooked up with the Bolton gang—Jarvis and Tommy Bolton and their partners Skippy Forrester and Harvey "Mad Dog" Scrima. Making a quick buck always appealed to the Smothers brothers. Still, until they met the Bolton gang, they usually restricted their efforts to cheating at cards or hustling pool. The Boltons had moved on to real crimes like robbery, auto theft, and credit card scams. When the First Bank of Indiana robbery went sour, the Bolton gang (including Boris and Iggy) were all captured and easily convicted. The Smothers brothers received a lesser sentence and were out on probation in three years. The others were in for quite a bit longer.

While in the state penitentiary, the Boltons and the Smothers had ample time to plan their next job. Now Yvetlana, the saint that she was, did not give up on her sons, but would visit them every month and bring them some of her culinary treats. At first, the sons were their normal ungracious selves. They laughed at her brownies, cakes, and cookies. But after a while, Boris and Iggy seemed anxious for her visits. In particular, they had many questions about the museum. Yvetlana was pleased. If only she had known what role she was to play down the road.

On Friday morning, as she left early for work, Yvetlana was met by Boris standing in her doorway. Boris was short but built like a wrestler. His muscular arms blocked her way. "Mother dear," he drooled. "What's the hurry? No time for a little conversation with your favorite son?"

Yvetlana jumped, a little startled. "Boris, what are you doing here at this hour?"

"I need a little favor," Boris answered. *When don't you need a favor,* she thought. Boris continued, "When you go to work today, in the men's restroom on top of the toilet is a box containing a silver key. Bring it home with you. It would mean a lot to Iggy and me."

"What would you be wanting with a silver key from the museum, Boris? The museum was closed yesterday. Who would have left it?" She had that mother's incredulous voice.

"Nothing you need to be concerned with, Mother," said Boris, his voice rising. "Just get it!"

Yvetlana knew better than to ask any more questions. "I'll…I'll look for it," she stammered.

"You had better do more than look, Mother dear," threatened Boris. Then his voice fell. "You do this for us, Mother, and we'll take you out for a real nice dinner." Their eyes met with understanding. Boris let his mother pass. As she scurried up the sidewalk, her rotund form wobbling as she went, Boris yelled after her: "No need to mention any of this to Mr. Tompkins, okay?"

Friday Intrigue

Mr. Tompkins could think of nothing else to do but return to Professor McDougal's office and use his phone to call for a tow truck. Thaddeus was so unhinged that he walked right through the building without stopping. When he came to the concourse lawn, he only then realized he had by passed the elevator. Retracing his steps, Mr. Tompkins once again found himself face to face with the professor's office door. This time it was ajar. After gently knocking to no response, he peeked around the door to find the office vacant. Mr. Tompkins surveyed the room; cluttered bookshelves took up three sides with more books stacked on the floor. Either Dr. McDougal was reorganizing his office, or he was getting ready to move some things out, as half-filled boxes were strewn about. There was barely room to walk. Funny, Thaddeus had not noticed any of this before.

On the desk's surface lay some unfurled maps and charts. There was a file to one side entitled, "Notes on Wooden Leg." Looking to his right and left, followed by a glance down the hallway, Mr. Tompkins made sure he was alone. He slowly lowered himself into the soft leather chair and began perusing what lay before him.

While he did so, he could not help but recall the word he had seen on the wooden leg—"death." And then there were the skull and crossbones—both on the leg itself and the bill of lading. Certainly, the leg had come from another part of the world. Maybe it came with its own built-in secret. Perhaps, as had occurred to him earlier, it was what was inside the leg that made it attractive to steal.

The residents of Webster knew that their curator could go off on tangents. They would have not been surprised at Mr. Tompkins' theorizing. It would not be the first time he was found grasping at straws to explain something mysterious. After all, it had not been too long ago when Thaddeus claimed he saw ghosts on the upper landing of the museum. But finally the curator may have found the evidence he was looking for.

Turning over the map on top of the pile, he found a more detailed inventory of what may have been placed on the HMS *Bountiful*. While outside, the wind had played havoc with his unkempt graying hair. Now, he had to keep pushing the hair out of his eyes to read the list. With his long bony finger, Mr. Tompkins scrolled through each item. At the very bottom were the words, "Gem-encrusted dagger...16 bags of doubloons...Timur Ruby."

He let out an audible gasp. "Timur Ruby!" The two words rattled around in his brain.

Dr. McDougal could come back at any minute. Thaddeus had to act quickly. He picked up the adjacent phone and dialed for the operator. "Get me a towing garage and hurry." Something in the tone of his voice must have prompted action, because in a matter of seconds he heard on the other end, "Joe's Towing and Repair." Mr. Tompkins summed up his situation and provided his vehicle's location. "Thank you, thank you," he said before hanging up the receiver. Gathering his wits about him, Mr. Tompkins rolled up the map and grabbed the folder. He scrawled a note to the professor: "Will return map and folder after the weekend. -T. T."

For a man who exhibited trouble navigating his way almost anywhere, Thaddeus Tompkins actually hustled to the elevator and, with a pounding heart, jumped through its opening doors and pressed the level one button. He was the only occupant—to his relief. He did not bother worrying about being discovered as he fled down the halls and out to his parked Ford. Throwing the "borrowed" items into the back, he slid into the driver's seat and took a deep breath. The pulsating lights of the tow truck were only a couple blocks away.

Once at the garage, though impatient to get back to the museum, Mr. Tompkins awaited the verdict on his dead car. He had only enough energy to just sit slouched in the waiting room chair, frazzled and somewhat wet from the drizzle. Soon a mechanic approached him. "Somebody poured some sugar into your gas tank, Mr. Tompkins. You got any enemies on campus?"

Thaddeus merely shrugged and shook his head in the negative. "Well, we will have to drain the gas tank, flush it out, and refuel the car. Should have it for you in a couple of hours." With that, the mechanic turned away, leaving his customer to close his eyes and take a most needed nap.

✳   ✳   ✳   ✳   ✳   ✳   ✳

Johnny and his friends could not know that both Mr. Tompkins and Boris Smothers would have reason to return to the museum on Friday evening. Each of the trio was surprised how smoothly their portion of the plan to return to the museum worked. Heather's parents had tickets to a symphony concert in Indianapolis and were in a rush to get out the door, so they didn't even bother to check with Megan's parents. The Murkowskis were involved in a bowling tournament at Joe's Pin Emporium, leaving Buddy to babysit. Jeremy's mother, Mary, once reminded of his overnight at the Turnbow's, only bothered to turn to Buddy and say, "Make sure your brother does not take the pajamas with the hole in the knee."

That left only Johnny to figure out a way to escape from his house. His greatest fear was that his parents would come up with some activity that would require the family to go somewhere together. However, the exact opposite was the case. Ben Turnbow turned to Jenny and remarked, "This has been quite a week. How about we lay back and make some popcorn after dinner and watch one of your favorite movies." (Ben prided himself on his VHS collection).

"That sounds like an excellent idea," she replied, giving him a big hug. Jenny turned to stir the spaghetti sauce on the stove. With her back to her husband, she added, "I do have to run over to Mrs. Matthews' first, though. Remember she sprained her ankle on Monday?" Jenny looked over her shoulder at Ben as he kind of shrugged. "Anyway, I promised her some supper so she wouldn't have to cook. It's tough when you are all by yourself."

Johnny suddenly saw an opening. He strode into the kitchen and blurted out, "Hey, Mom, you wouldn't mind dropping me off at Jeremy's on the way, would you?" When Mrs. Turnbow reacted with a quizzical look, Johnny was quick to say, "You said I could have one more overnight with Jeremy before school starts, remember?"

"Are you sure it is okay with Mrs. Murkowski?" Jenny Turnbow asked.

"Definitely," Johnny responded with confidence. "In fact, it was her idea."

"I'll confirm, Jenny," noted Ben as he dialed the Murkowski household. "Buddy, can I have your mom for a moment?" After a short pause, Johnny heard his dad say, "No, no message...thanks anyway." Ben Turnbow then explained to them, "Murkowskis have already left for a night of bowling." Turning to Johnny, he said, "You make sure you are a help and not a hindrance, understand?"

The only tricky part was when Johnny's mom dropped him off at the Murkowski residence. He was thinking of something clever to say at the door, but it suddenly burst open, and out jumped Jeremy. Each let out a shriek of surprise as they almost knocked each other over.

"Jeez, Turnbow, scare the heck out of someone, why don't you!" complained Jeremy as he adjusted his hooded sweatshirt. "What are you doing here, anyways? I thought we all were supposed to meet up at the museum."

"Hey, give me some credit, Jeremy," appealed Johnny. "I had a chance to escape and I did. When I learned my mom was headed out on an errand, I just asked for a ride."

Jeremy scratched the back of his head. "It is not like you live that far away. Normally we walk or bike to each other's houses."

"Yeah, yeah, I know," replied Johnny. "It gave me a chance to remind her of our overnight." He winked as he said it.

"Well, let's get going," said Jeremy, grabbing Johnny's arm. "Let's not give Buddy an opportunity to get suspicious."

What with daylight savings time still in effect, at 7:00 p.m., the sun still had a way to go before it set. The boys, therefore, decided to hide out in the Murkowski garage for an hour or so. The garage was an older frame structure with room for only one car. Frank Murkowski had his tool collection hanging on one side. There was a narrow shelf that extended along the back wall, and underneath it was a variety of paint and stain containers. Conveniently, there were a couple of fat logs they could sit on. Johnny hardly used his, though, as he kept pacing up and down, thinking about how the evening at the museum would go. Jeremy resigned himself, head in hands, to resting while he could. He was preparing for a long night.

When the sun did begin to set, a bird flying high in the sky would have seen three small figures head toward the museum from two different directions, along with Mr. Tompkins' yellow Ford pulling into the museum parking lot. What the bird would not have seen was Boris Smothers lurking in the woods north of the lot. How curious it was that all would play a part in a simple silver key reaching its destiny.

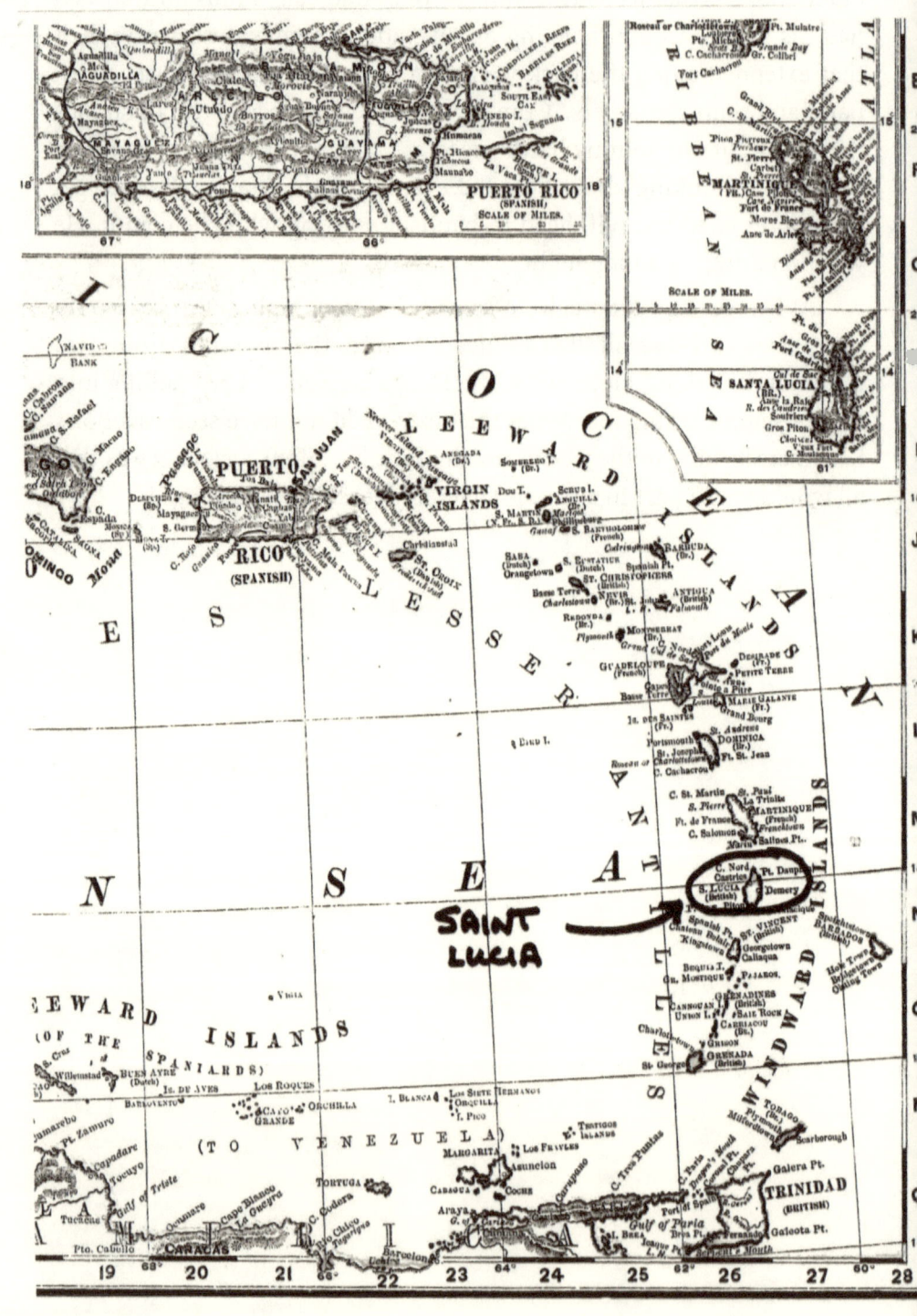

SAINT LUCIA

A Privateer's Story

Indeed, the sun was low in the sky as Mr. Tompkins pulled into the museum parking lot, for which he was grateful. After a grueling day, all he wanted to do was to get into the museum unnoticed. Other than the family of starlings hovering over the top of the adjacent woods, the scene was quite tranquil. There were a few puddles in the parking lot, but the rain had stopped; now the less humid air had that refreshing fragrance Thaddeus associated with clean sheets fresh from drying on the line in his boyhood backyard. With the rolled-up map under one arm and the folder held in his right hand, he plunged forward to the rear entrance.

Mr. Tompkins went immediately to his office and made room to scrutinize what he had borrowed. Maneuvering his desk lamp so it simultaneously zoomed in on the folder's contents and minimized the light showing forth from his small window, he anxiously sat down and began to read. The first page was simply titled, "Background Information: Wooden Leg." The next three pages were handwritten on unlined paper. They revealed the following:

> To be honest, there were very few characters from history who actually wore a peg leg. Peter Stuyvesant, the Dutch Governor of New York, was one. And even fewer pirates. However, there was one French privateer by the name of Francis Le Clerc, nicknamed Pie de Palo (Peg Leg) by the Spanish, who wore such a wooden leg.
>
> He functioned as a corsair during the mid-16th century. A corsair was a seaman or privateer who was not a true pirate. Such men had a special license (letter of marques) from a nation's

government. If caught by the enemy, however, they were treated like pirates, which usually meant hanging by the neck.

Francis Le Clerc assumed overall command of seven pirate craft, as well as three royal warships in 1553 for France. He specifically took command of one of the warships, while Jacques Sores and Robert Blondell commanded the two others. That year he raided a city in Puerto Rico and looted ports in Hispaniola, capturing hides and cannon. In 1554, he returned to the West Indies with eight large ships and 300 soldiers. He took Santiago de Cuba by surprise, occupying it for a month, eventually leaving with 80,000 pesos. Later on, Le Clerc was the first European to settle in St. Lucia and attacked passing Spanish vessels from Pigeon Island.

While Le Clerc finally returned to France, he did not bring any booty with him. Robert Blondell, under threat of death by Henry II of England, revealed that Le Clerc had a cache of coins and jewels in St. Lucia. After Le Clerc died in Paris of a sudden illness (1563), the French government took possession of all of his property, but no agents ever found anything of worth, other than his fort on 200 acres. During the 17th and 18th centuries, various English Captains visited St. Lucia. Some knew of the rumor handed down over the years of hidden wealth belonging to a French corsair. But nothing was ever found.

Until 1773, that is, when Captain A.S. Adams, commander of a decent-sized British warship, the H.M.S. Bountiful, ventured into the port of St. Lucia. Although he had studied at Oxford and was well on his way to becoming a doctor, his uncle, a barrister in London, secured for him a naval commission upon the death of the Captain's father. With little money for further study, a military career was a respectable option. Captain Adams had a special fondness for collecting. He normally brought back any number of specimens (both plant and animal) from his journeys. After arriving in St. Lucia in the spring, the Captain was particularly captivated by the birds nesting on the island's cliffs. He procured the help of several of the local natives to gain access into the numerous caves pocketing their sides.

If his journal is to be believed, Captain Adams sought rest in one of the higher caves after a strenuous day of investigation. He noticed that a particular cave seemed to extend deeper into the cliff than the others he had frequented. Motioning for his guides to wait, he struck a torch and walked cautiously back into it. Not too far inside, he heard the sound of rushing water. To his surprise, the cave led into a giant chamber. He could not believe his eyes. All around the chamber were piled chests of coins and jewels. There was some gold. It took him two weeks with the assistance of his crew and 60 natives to move the booty to his ship. Captain Adams declared his finds as the property of King George III and carefully inventoried everything he found.

One item, however, he kept for himself, as he considered it a curiosity—a wooden leg with strange markings. According to his journal, set off to one side from the bulk of the chests in a dark recess of the cave, the leg was wrapped in brown leather and tied carefully. He recorded, upon returning to his cabin, that he examined the leg more carefully. The skull and crossbones on the bottom of the leg were something he had seen before. It usually meant the item so marked was pirate property. What confused him was the word, "death," etched on the side. To take it meant death?

Captain Adams did not record any more details on the wooden leg. After landing back in England, it took up a position next to his hearth and became a matter of conversation to inquiring visitors. There was no evidence it ever left the house.

In 1818, he left all of his possessions, including the wooden leg, to his daughter, Elizabeth. Elizabeth married Captain Cornelius Stamford the following year. In their country mansion, not far from Portsmouth, the leg apparently lay stashed in an attic. Rumor had it that Elizabeth actually spent considerable time in the attic, contributing to the local impression she was a bit "mad". In fact, that is where they found her dead body in 1829. Captain Stamford had no use for the wooden leg and donated it to the Royal Archaeology Society where it gathered dust amidst their collections until 1927.

1927 was the year the Society hosted a meeting for archaeologists from around the world. Attending the meeting was Captain Robert Tompkins, fresh from a tour of the Orient. An American, Captain Tompkins was representing several American museums. He brought back with him several items from the Society on permanent loan. Those the Captain found less significant, he saved for display at the Benson County Museum in Indiana. Included was the wooden leg. To this day it has resided there.

With arms stretched out on both sides of his desk, Thaddeus Tompkins continued to stare at the document. He could not discern whether or not it had been written by Dr. McDougal. Lacking any date, all he could surmise was perhaps (not too long ago) someone had attempted to summarize what was known about the wooden leg. It certainly offered no evidence that those in a position to know regarded the wooden leg as anything special. And for his thought of something being hidden inside of it—the Timur Ruby, perhaps? No clue.

The rest of the folder's contents contained several pieces of correspondence. Evidently, Dr. McDougal had made some inquiries with the Society and other individuals in England about the leg. The letters revealed little. Why could he not connect the dots? Three thousand pounds sterling in 1773, by his own calculations, had to be a tremendous amount of money in the eighteenth century. Perhaps equivalent to <u>at least</u> a quarter of a million dollars in 1982. There was absolutely nothing about the wooden leg that would link it to that kind of worth. The

Timur Ruby, on the other hand, was not unknown to gemologists. Mr. Tompkins recalled reading an article several years ago about its history and disappearance. It was a huge gem and certainly would have been worth a lot. "Blast it all, man," he said to himself, clenching his hands. "What *is* the connection?"

About this time, Mr. Tompkins thought he heard a noise coming from the outside of the museum. He turned his head one direction and then another. The entire theft affair had left him feeling jittery and nervous. Rapidly he rose, striding toward the back door.

*　　*　　*　　*　　*　　*　　*

Once again, the three friends found themselves congregating in the tall grass on the east side of the museum parking lot. The ground was still moist, and now with the sun down, one could sense fog was not far from forming. To their surprise, Mr. Tompkins' old Ford was still in the parking lot, and there was a dim light coming from a rear window. Johnny, Jeremy, and Heather all looked at each other as if to say, "Now what?"

After a few moments of silence, Johnny interjected, "I don't see why this has to change our plans much. I'll get into the basement, and once Mr. Tompkins leaves, I'll come upstairs and let you all in."

"Too risky, Johnny," replied Jeremy, shaking his head.

Heather pursed her lips before adding her two cents worth. She let out a big sigh and added, "There is something to be said for taking advantage of that bit of light falling on the ground near the window."

Jeremy suddenly stared at Heather with his mouth wide open. "You forgot the flashlight, didn't you! There was no signal from you tonight."

Heather dropped her head and said softly, "Ah, left it in my other backpack." Johnny and Jeremy had come to expect perfection from Heather, and now it was Johnny with his mouth agape.

After a few seconds, Johnny broke the silence. "Well, that settles it, then. We move in now." As he spoke, Johnny ran his hand through his thick hair, betraying an element of doubt.

Jeremy placed his right hand on Johnny's shoulder. "Listen, we don't have to do this. We can leave it to Chief Olsen and Officer Kraus. It's just a dumb old wooden leg."

Heather moved between both of them. She peered at them intently. "Have we ever been known to walk away from a mystery? Only a few hours ago we were all together on this." Jeremy threw her a frown, indicating his commitment was perhaps less. "Honestly, this should not take that long. We get in and we get out."

Jeremy seemed to relish playing the devil's advocate. "You are leaving out one little possibility, Heather. What if that old geezer decides to make a night of it? I mean, it's not like he has anything to go home to."

Now it was Heather's turn to put her hand on Jeremy's shoulder. "I have a backup plan. You know how Mr. Tompkins still thinks ghosts haunt his museum, right?" Jeremy and Johnny nodded. "Well," she continued, "Jeremy and I might have to transform ourselves into a couple of discontented spirits." Heather winked at them as she said it.

Jeremy could only throw up his hands and fall on his back (he got up quickly, as the grass was still wet). "Is that all you have? Ghosts?"

"I kind of like it, Jeremy," responded Johnny. "Mr. Tompkins gets creeped out easily. Besides, I don't think he will stay that long. Even with the museum being closed tomorrow, Mr. Tompkins will have to get up early to assist with any investigation and ward off visitors."

With that, Johnny repeated his actions earlier in the day, moving cautiously to the willow tree and then on to the basement window. This time, under cover of darkness, he could accomplish the trek in a crouching position. Johnny knelt down before the window. He then pulled down on its frame to create as wide an opening as possible. Before crawling in, he took a glance back to his partners in crime, giving them a thumbs up. They were both waving at him frantically. What was their problem? Johnny could just make out Jeremy pointing to the right. But before he could turn his head, he felt large hands clasped around his legs and lifting him into a wheelbarrow position. Those same hands thrust him through the window, at the same time dislodging the window frame and breaking the pane. Down Johnny went into the basement, accompanied by pieces of glass. Good fortune was his companion, as he landed in a basket of rags.

Johnny was able to roll over onto the dirty basement floor, quickly picking himself up. It did take a while for his eyes to adjust to the dim conditions and his heart to stop pounding. Outside, Heather and Jeremy could only witness the entire episode in horror. The perpetrator of the deed was a short muscular man. Jeremy had started to run to Johnny's aid, but Heather pulled him down.

"No, no," she whispered firmly. "He'll catch you, too. Stay down and don't make a peep…Look! He's running off!" It was soon evident why. The back door of the museum had burst open, and they could see Mr. Tompkins looking both left and right for the source of the commotion.

"You! You there," he shouted. "Stop! Stop, I say!" At that point, Mr. Tompkins clutched his chest and fell back from the door.

By this time, Heather and Jeremy were lying prone on the ground, peeking up as they could. Mr. Tompkins' interruption brought them mixed feelings. The man had run off, it was true. But now Johnny was in danger of being discovered. They both stayed very still until Mr. Tompkins shut the back door. Heather said in a low voice, "Let's move to the willow tree. We have to figure out a way to warn Johnny."

While they made their way to the tree, Johnny was trying to figure out what had just happened. Surveying the damage to his person, he found only a small scratch on his neck. The blood was already drying. His shirt was a mess, though, and he could only imagine how much allowance money it would cost him. If he lived to get another allowance, that is. Somebody had not been happy to see him.

As Johnny's eyes adjusted to the darkness, it was now apparent to him he had avoided serious injury. There was glass all over the stone floor. The bag of rags (now on its side) rested up against a wooden post. It was that post that had deflected the glass away from Johnny. Having carried boxes down into the basement for Mr. Tompkins, Johnny knew there were two separate sections to the basement. A stairwell divided them, taking up a twelve-foot passageway. Mr. Tompkins was known for having a hard time turning down any donation, and as a result, the entire basement was filled with boxes and various artifacts. There were also a couple of cabinets, two desks, and an old diving suit. With the broken window to his back, the stairs were to his right. Johnny assessed his route to get to them. It would mean maneuvering around some rusty tools.

After several minutes of no sign of life from inside the museum, Heather and Jeremy moved swiftly from the tree to the broken window. "Johnny, are you all right in there?" Johnny could faintly make out Heather's voice. Looking up, he could see their silhouettes. Johnny moved to the base of the window but knew he would need something to stand on to get up high enough to escape. He signaled to his two friends by holding up his index finger to say, "Give me a minute."

Johnny managed to find three similarly sized boxes and struggled to put them in place. It did not help that one of the boxes was filled with half-empty paint cans. After what seemed an eternity, Johnny climbed up to about a foot below the opening.

"Can you pull yourself up?" asked Jeremy anxiously.

"I will need another box," responded Johnny. However, he was doing an interesting balancing act, and it was doubtful he could add another box to the stack.

Sensing the risk in doing so, Heather cautioned, "You had better wait until Mr. Tompkins leaves, Johnny." Heather and Jeremy then tried to relate what they had seen from their vantage point. After a few more minutes of animated discussion, they all agreed that Johnny would stay low until it was absolutely safe—but only after Jeremy had been assured that Johnny's injuries were minimal.

At one point, Jeremy pleaded, "Well, if I can't go home for help, let's just turn ourselves in to Mr. Tompkins. He'll be happy we can back up his story on the old vagrant, and I am sure he will realize it was not Johnny's fault he fell into the basement."

Heather could only scowl at Jeremy and declare, "Look, Mr. Tompkins will leave soon, and we can have our look around. Johnny is already inside and can let us in."

Jeremy was looking around, half expecting whoever it was that pushed Johnny to return. Sensing his concern, Heather added, "We can hide underneath the tarps next to the steps in case that man returns." She pointed to the stack of tarps that Mr. Tompkins had ordered for use during the weekend. Before they turned to leave, Heather said to Johnny, "I think we interrupted something. And I wouldn't be surprised if Mr. Tompkins is in danger."

If he had heard Heather say it, Mr. Tompkins would probably have agreed with her. He did not feel like sticking around to meet up with any intruder. Part of him wanted to call Chief Olsen and report the incident. The other part just wanted to skedaddle and get to the safety of his home, safeguarding the map and folder. So, it was without further delay that he began to gather his things up.

That would have been the end of it if Thaddeus had not heard a bunch of clatter coming from the basement. He began to sweat profusely, and his hands were shaking so badly that he could hardly hold the map. The chest pains he had experienced at the back door began to come back and he had to sit down. Gradually, he caught his breath. There was no further noise. It was probably just another rodent seeking shelter.

Mr. Tompkins took the keys from his desk and shoved them into his right coat pocket. Time to go. It was then he rediscovered the silver key he had met up with earlier in the day. Reexamining it, he sighed and set it down next to the phone. Another mystery for another day. And off the old man went, shuffling as quickly as his old bones would allow.

Johnny was still nursing his bruised shin when he heard a car start and pull away. For a while, after running into a heavy hoe, he thought for sure Mr. Tompkins would find him out. The hoe had collided with an assemblage of other tools, creating enough noise to awaken the dead. Limping as he went, Johnny ascended the stairs and prepared to let Heather and Jeremy into the museum. More than anything, he just wanted to let Heather do her thing and get back home.

Dr. McDougal's Dilemmas

Boris Smothers knew the boss would not be pleased (not that he knew who the boss was). Mad Dog would not be happy, and that meant the boss would not be happy. Friday had not been a good day for Boris. First, his mother had lost the silver key. He was not exactly sure, but he figured the key had something to do with access to their hideout. It did not help that Boris and Iggy were at the bottom of the food chain when it came to the Bolton gang. Mad Dog kept telling them information was shared only on a "need to know" basis. All Boris needed to know was that Mad Dog wanted him to retrieve the silver key.

Worse yet, Boris had scoured the parking lot, and there was no key to be found. So, if his mother had indeed dropped it there, someone or something had picked it up. The rain that had fallen was not of the downpour variety, so it was doubtful the key had been washed away into the grass. Plus, Boris had surveyed the adjacent grounds and came up with nothing.

Mad Dog carried a pager with him at all times. Members of the gang were instructed to use it as necessary (with emphasis on the "necessary"). So, it was with great reluctance that Boris had called in Friday afternoon. Though Mad Dog's pager was only one way, it was capable of receiving voice messages. Boris' message said, "Mad Dog, this is Boris. Key is lost—repeat—key is lost. Headed to rendezvous point."

*　　*　　*　　*　　*　　*　　*

What was supposed to have been a short department meeting turned into an hour-long harangue about assigned parking spots! Dr. McDougal was already in a bad mood when he returned to his office. Now, as he approached his desk, it was immediately clear that the map and folder were gone. The professor walked around to his chair and saw the note left by Mr. Tompkins. After reading it, Dr. McDougal crumpled it up and threw it across the room. He was shaking with rage. "Thaddeus Tompkins, you bumbling idiot!" he muttered. "You have no one else to blame now but yourself."

Dr. McDougal surmised what had happened. The plan had been for Tompkins' car to get a few blocks down the road before stalling. How much sugar did Miss Quig put in that gas tank? A full bag? So, of course, Thaddeus would've returned to McDougal's office to get assistance. Dr. McDougal lowered his head and sighed. *The best laid plans…* he thought. The professor then dialed a number he used in times of emergency.

"Joe's Pizza, where large pepperoni pizzas are half price this week," answered a peppy clerk.

"Let me speak to Marvin, please."

"Sure, just a sec. He's loading the cooler."

Dr. McDougal waited patiently. A few minutes went by.

"This is Marvin. What can I do for ya?"

"Do you have any deliveries going out to the west side of town, Marvin?" queried the professor.

"Oh, Dr. McDougal. Haven't heard from you in a while. I've got an order going out to the VFW Hall around 6 p.m. Will that work?" Marvin waited for the response and then confirmed, "Sure enough. Drop it off here, and we'll put it in your mother's mailbox."

Dr. McDougal's mother had died five years ago, but her vacant home provided a good place to work in private and receive deliveries. After writing out some explicit instructions, he sealed them in an envelope and placed them in his briefcase. Then Dr. McDougal put on his overcoat, locked his office, and proceeded to Joe's Pizza. He didn't need to drive, as the pizzeria was only three blocks from campus. An added advantage was his Cape Cod two-story home was only an additional three blocks from there. He would need to page Mad Dog before supper that another pickup was required.

Dr. McDougal had gone to great lengths to disassociate himself from Mad Dog and the Bolton gang. They only knew him from messages and printed instructions. In the end, they would take the fall for everything.

He smiled every time he thought of how flawless his plan was. Yes, there would be a few individuals sacrificed in the process, but he could have no living witnesses. It had taken the professor two years to put it all in place. He did not want to raise any questions or draw attention to himself.

The hideaway in rural Bensonville had taken the most preparation. Thanks to a couple of John Birch Society members who did not raise any eyebrows when he mentioned he was looking to build an underground shelter, he had managed to procure a crew of men to do the job. The tunnel to the museum was another story. Fortunately, there was a dried-out riverbed that snuck underground. It was then just a matter of finding some seasonal migrant workers who were anxious to earn some decent money and would not be sticking around Webster.

The hidden entrance to the shelter was Dr. McDougal's doing, taking up just a few weekends of his time. When the old Franklin farm had gone up for sale, the professor got it for a song, as the house and outbuildings on the property were in terrible shape. Besides, dairy farms were becoming a thing of the past. Old man Franklin had three kids, but they had no interest in farming and moved away from town as quickly as they could after high school graduation. It helped that Dr. McDougal was from Bradford. Not many knew him in Webster. He could come and go without drawing much attention.

Unfortunately, he now had to move on to his alternative plan. Thanks to the interference from the museum curator, he would be delayed a day from saying goodbye to Indiana. Just as he opened his front door, he heard the phone ringing. Dr. McDougal threw his coat on the couch and picked up the phone from the small table next to his reading chair.

"I told you never to call here unless you had a dire emergency!" he shouted. "What the blazes is the problem?"

Mad Dog coughed on the other end and spoke slowly and in a hushed tone. "The silver key is lost. I assume we can't move the leg without it."

Dr. McDougal grew pale and sat down in the chair. After gathering himself, he asked Mad Dog for details. Once he had the facts at hand, the professor pulled himself together and responded, "This may work out in the end. Thanks to Mr. Tompkins, Boris is going to have to make a return trip to the museum, anyway. I have a hunch he will find the key in the curator's office."

Dr. McDougal then indicated instructions were to be picked up from his mother's mailbox immediately. When the conversation ended, Mad Dog was clear on a couple of matters. First, the plan would have to be extended one day, and second, if the gang did not find the silver key, they would not be paid.

*　　*　　*　　*　　*　　*　　*

Mrs. Smothers was not at all confident Boris would find the key when he returned to the museum parking lot. She had not liked his demeanor the past couple of days. To put it bluntly, she was very scared. Earlier in the week, her house had been filled with gang members. They had a large piece of paper on her coffee table that resembled a map of some kind. But every time she moved closer to the group, they began to speak in hushed tones. She did not like the men Boris and Iggy had struck up with. Mad Dog Scrima was plain mean. The only one who showed her any degree of kindness was Skippy Forrester. He seemed decent enough but did everything Mad Dog told him to do. Skippy loved the cabbage stew Yvetlana had made on Monday evening. As he was the last one seated at the table, she was able to gain a few pieces of information from him.

For the longest while, Mrs. Smothers could not figure out what was so special about the wooden leg. Why the gang was going to such length to steal it was beyond her. But then Skippy let it slip that the leg contained a valuable jewel of some kind, worth more money than anybody could imagine. Skippy's eyes grew big as saucers when he proclaimed, "I cannot wait until I get my share. No more anyone telling Skippy what to do, no sir." He then went on to tell her how there was this island he knew of where he planned to buy a cottage and hire the local natives to serve him hand and foot. Yvetlana figured that based on his height, goatee, and bald head, the natives would think Skippy a god.

Plus, when he opened his mouth, there were three teeth missing. Skippy could have been a poster child for Halloween.

Putting two and two together, it did not take her long to realize that if Skippy were telling the truth, the gang would do anything to make sure they completed their mission. The silver key was obviously critical to their success. The fact she lost it, combined with the fact she could identify all of the gang, made her rather expendable. Mrs. Smothers literally shook as she tidied up the kitchen. Tears began to roll down her fat cheeks. She knew what she had to do. Yvetlana put the last bowl away and went to her tiny bedroom. She dug through the bottom of the closet and pulled out a flower-patterned satchel. In it she stuffed what belongings she could. Wrapping a scarf around her head and putting on her coat, Mrs. Smothers fled out the backdoor and headed north toward Bensonville to where her sister lived. She went cross-country, avoiding any roads and using the woods for cover.

By the time Officer Kraus had left and before Mr. Tompkins had returned to the museum (and while the three juvenile detectives returned home), Mrs. Smothers made her escape. She wanted nothing more to do with the gang, her sons, and the wooden leg. As the afternoon waned, from afar this poor mistreated mother resembled a bobbing pigeon following a country path and fading into the tall grass.

* * * * * * *

It did not help that Mad Dog and Skippy were seven miles from Webster. From the page sent from Boris, it meant he was headed to Ma's Diner (a.k.a. the rendezvous point). The diner was on the west side of Webster off of Highway 67. Basically, Boris had panicked. He was heading to the diner earlier than planned.

"That boy is a complete idiot," grumbled Mad Dog. "Does he think we can simply beam up and over to the diner?" Turning to Skippy, he asked, "How far do you think we may be from the diner?"

"Well," said Skippy thoughtfully, "the diner is on the west side of town. As the crow flies, maybe five to six miles. But I figure you do not want to mess with the woods. Probably twice that much."

The instructions to the gang said to be at the diner by 4:00 p.m. At the meeting, they were to be told where to go and when. Mad Dog had kept a lid on sharing information. Boris Smothers had been given the specific task to bring the silver key. Evidently, he had failed miserably. Now Boris headed to the diner after leaving Mad Dog his message. Mad Dog's dilemma was that if they did not link up with Boris before the meeting, who knows what he might blab all over the restaurant. *Loose lips sink ships*, thought Mad Dog. The need to get to Ma's Diner quickly put Mad Dog and Skippy in a real quandary. Mad Dog and Skippy ascended out of the hideout and surveyed the situation.

"Harvey, you still know how to ride a horse?" The words came out of the blue from Skippy, as if he were in another world.

"Do I look like I was born on a farm? When have you ever known me to get on a horse?" There were times when Mad Dog wondered if he was working with an alien.

"Don't you remember telling me that as a boy you helped out this jockey at the track, taking care of his horse and all?" Skippy replied with a kind of far-off gaze.

"First of all, that was ages ago, and second, what does feeding hay to a horse have to do with riding one?" said Mad Dog, getting more irritated.

Skippy rubbed his goatee and said matter-of-factly, "Well, just thought you might be interested in the horses that are grazing in the field this morning." Mad Dog squinted. Skippy had his attention. He continued, "Beats walking, you know."

Skippy turned and pointed. Five hundred yards or so to the west were several horses out grazing. Their owners did not seem anywhere nearby. Upon approaching the animals, it was apparent to Mad Dog that these were stock horses—agile and intelligent. Certainly a better ride than a huge draft horse. Evidently, the farm raised cattle, not milk cows. Mad Dog had to use all of his old instincts to gain the horse's confidence. Skippy should have had the easier mount, but he kept sliding over his horse's back like something one might see from a clown in a rodeo.

Mad Dog, with his short legs and compact physique, needed Skippy's assistance. With their arms clasped tightly around the horses' necks, off they went. Once they crossed the field and met up with a dirt road leading to Highway P, Mad Dog knew the rest of the way. The trick was to stay off the road so as not to attract any attention. By letting the horses trot along the road, they were not quite so conspicuous. One car passenger did lean out the window and shout out, "You boys having fun?" Other than that, traffic was light, and soon they could see Ma's Diner in the distance. Mad Dog and Skippy dismounted, and with a slap to their hindquarters, the horses headed back to their home. According to Skippy's pocket watch, it was 3:30 p.m. Soon Mad Dog would learn the details behind the loss of the silver key. He was not looking forward to the conversation.

Upon entering the diner, they saw Boris sitting off in a corner booth. They saddled into the seat across from him, and after ordering two coffees, Mad Dog grunted, "Well, what?"

With beads of sweat forming on his bald head, Boris leaned forward with his hands clasped and elbows on the table. Sighing as he spoke, Boris tried to explain. "My mother found the key, just where you said it was. And she made off with it without the old bugger knowing a thing. But…"

Now Mad Dog leaned forward. "But what?" He tried to keep his voice from rising. Ma's Diner was not a place that invited privacy. Still, the patrons were mostly truck drivers and poor locals. So as long as they didn't get in a ruckus…

"The way she described it, Mad Dog, was that Officer Kraus gave her quite a scare. She dropped all of her things, and that is, err, when the key must have fallen out of her coat pocket." Boris began talking faster. "I went back to the parking lot where it should have been, but I found nothing."

Mad Dog reached across the booth and grabbed Boris' shirt collar. "Are you sure your ma is not double-crossing us?"

"No, no, not a chance," stammered Boris.

Mad Dog then relaxed his grip and sat back down. Talking as much to himself as to the others, he murmured, "Tompkins must have it. He probably saw it in the parking lot." Seconds went by with no one saying anything. Then Mad Dog stood up. "Wait here while I go make a phone call."

Mad Dog could foresee that calling the boss would not make him happy. But this required a change in plans. All along, the boss had instructed Mad Dog to go easy on Mr. Tompkins and leave him alone, if at all possible. Now, Mad Dog did not see how he could. As expected, the boss was furious with the call. However, it appeared that Mr. Tompkins had made a second "mistake." Granted, his picking up the silver key was still in question. That did not matter much to the boss, however. Cutting the conversation short, the boss instructed Mad Dog to proceed to the mailbox drop for new guidance. Boris' evening was about to get more interesting.

Mad Dog walked directly back to the restaurant table, plopped some bills down to cover Boris' coffee, and glared at his round, bald head. Skippy could tell from Mad Dog's face that things had just gotten serious. Boris sat up straight and felt he was being addressed by a vampire. "Boris, we are going for a ride," spoke Mad Dog through gritted teeth. "We have work to do." Mad Dog then surveyed the diner and saw Tommy and Jarvis Bolton had arrived; they were sitting with Iggy Smothers in a booth at the far end. Turning to Skippy, he said, "Skippy, gather up the gang and move them to the hideout. Phase two of this operation has just begun."

Disappearing Acts

The plan to investigate the museum by Heather, Johnny, and Jeremy late Friday evening might have gone off without a hitch if Melody Stippich hadn't called Megan's mother during the symphony's intermission and asked her to remind Heather she had a dental appointment Saturday afternoon. Learning Heather had never shown up at the Larsen home sent things unraveling quickly.

Mrs. Stippich was on the frail side but known to become excitable quite easily—Heather was their only child, and Heather was…well… Heather. Mrs. Stippich reached out to Jenny Turnbow first, since Johnny had been with Heather earlier in the day. Ben almost did not hear the phone ring as the family was intently viewing *Back to the Future Part III*. He barely avoided tripping over their cat, Daisy, while lunging for the phone.

"No, not here…Really?…Well, Johnny is sleeping over at Jeremy's tonight…Yes, we will call right away." Ben hung up, and with concern written all over his face, he turned on the living room lights. Pausing the movie, he announced, "Heather Stippich did not show up at Megan Larsen's tonight for her sleepover. I need to check with Johnny to see what he may know."

Jenny was way ahead of him. Heather missing triggered speculation in her mind, and now she wanted assurance that Johnny was with Jeremy. "Hello. Is this Buddy? Can I speak to Johnny, please?" Quickly it became apparent to the Turnbows that both Johnny and Jeremy were not having a sleepover at the Murkowski's. Ben did not lose a moment in flying out the door and pulling on his white jacket as he went. Joe's Pin Emporium was only a ten-minute drive away, and it was not long before Mr. Turnbow and Frank and Mary Murkowski were racing to their cars.

*   *   *   *   *   *   *

Chief Olsen, Detective Shaw, Officer Kraus, the Turnbows, and the Murkowskis all sat in the Turnbow living room. Jenny Turnbow had shuffled Katie off to bed amidst a fair amount of groaning and complaining. She then put on a pot of coffee and some hot chocolate. Mr. and Mrs. Stippich were on the way, but they were an hour out.

Chief Olsen felt he was going backwards with the case. Things just kept on getting more and more mysterious. It was after 10:00 p.m. on Friday, and no one had any idea where the threesome had gone. A new library book left on the stairs led to a phone call to Emma Lord. Fortunately, she was at home watching the news. Emma confirmed all three had been at the library that afternoon. She added that they had been searching through newspaper microfilm. "I should have known they were up to something," she confessed.

The group was all deep in thought. The chief sat in the overstuffed chair, his double chin resting in his hands and hat still on his head. Officer Kraus rested on the arm of the chair with his back to the chief. His hands sat squarely on his knees, and every so often, he would shake his head.

Mrs. Turnbow clung to her husband's arm and quietly cried, never bothering to push her long brown hair out of her eyes. Mr. Turnbow's countenance was more thoughtful then overwrought. His reading glasses had slipped down his nose, but he did not seem to be aware of it.

Frank Murkowski had the build of a steelworker. He possessed a no-nonsense demeanor while he periodically stood up and paced the floor. At the moment, his massive head lay back against the couch and his eyes were closed. Mary Murkowski had grown up on a farm and had a dark, ruddy complexion, at least partially due to a lot of time in the sun. She was big boned, and with her arms crossed, she resembled a diminutive Buddha. Scowling, she appeared to be thinking about what punishment she would administer to Jeremy when she caught up with him.

Detective Shaw was in plain clothes—a blue sweater and grey slacks. He had been standing the entire time, and it was he who finally broke the silence. "Well, this is what we know. It is obvious, Ben, that your son met with Heather and got her mind rolling on the museum theft. Otherwise, why would three kids be wasting their time in a library on the last Friday before school starts? Some of us know how much they like a mystery. I'm telling you, they must have decided to get personally involved."

With that statement, Ben Turnbow winced, Jenny covered her mouth (uttering a small gasp), and the Murkowskis simultaneously stood up. Officer Kraus quickly rose and moved to the center of the room.

"Now, let's not get everyone more worked up than they need be, Sam," he interjected. "We've got every patrol car in the county keeping a lookout. I know that Heather is a smart one, and I'm sure they are safe." Waving his arms for effect, he continued. "Didn't all of you used to do some crazy things the last few days before school?" He surveyed the room but was not getting much of a positive reaction.

Mr. Murkowski sat down, turned to Chief Olsen, and said, "Chief, I think you should haul Thaddeus Tompkins in right now and make him tell us what he knows. He's always seemed a tad odd to me, and he definitely is hiding something. Otherwise, why would he go down to see his professor friend after confessing to Officer Kraus here that he had found some interesting paperwork on the wooden leg?"

Officer Kraus chimed in, "Yeah, and he let Mrs. Smothers go home early. Since when did he get so amenable?"

Chief Olsen raised his hands to stop the conversation. "Look, folks. We have a squad car parked outside his house as we speak, and if he tries to do anything suspicious, I'll pull him in pronto. But I don't want to tip our hand just yet. Tomorrow morning, the university police are going to make a call on Professor McDougal to see what light he can shed on our curator's visit. I suggest you all—"

Before he could finish, Mr. Murkowski was in his face: "So, you think it might be an inside job, Chief?"

Exasperated, the chief threw his arms in the air. "I'm not saying anything! We have a theft at the museum. We have no real leads. All we can do right now is put some solid police work into action. We might get lucky." He continued after taking a deep breath and calming down. "Just go home, get some sleep, and let us keep tabs on things until morning. If Johnny and company turn up, we'll let you know immediately."

It was Mrs. Turnbow's turn to stand up. With clenched fists at her side, she mustered all her strength and said between tears, "Get some sleep? That's easy for you to say, Chief. And why aren't we waiting for Heather's parents to arrive?"

Ben Turnbow put his arm around his wife's shoulders and tried to provide a calming voice to the conversation. "Jenny, the chief's right. No need for everyone to stick around here. We can wait for Mr. and Mrs. Stippich if that will make you feel better." Then turning to Frank and Mary, he said, "Listen, you know our kids. They could turn up at any minute. Frank, take Mary home. Maybe you could take a couple of swings around town—you might run into them."

Frank patted Ben on the shoulder and gave him a weak smile. Then he and his wife headed out the door. Chief Olsen and Officer Kraus followed close behind. "Don't worry, Ben…Jenny," added Detective Shaw. "Things will turn out all right." With that, he too was gone. Mr. and Mrs. Turnbow were left to their pondering and prayers.

*   *   *   *   *   *   *

After the meeting at Ma's Diner, Boris drove Mad Dog to Bradford in the beat-up pickup truck that had been, at times, his second home. Their destination, a small A-Frame house on a quiet cul-de-sac, almost appeared to exist in a world of its own. Two huge oak trees lined a dirt driveway that suffered from disuse. The house's exterior was in dire need of a paint job. Its front window had a long crack running diagonally across it, and the modest chimney was missing several bricks. The adjacent homes were blocked from view by huge hedges and gnarled vines.

Boris maneuvered his truck close to the tilted mailbox. Mad Dog opened the flap and pulled out an envelope. As the pickup sputtered off, he carefully read the instructions inside. Pursing his lips, Mad Dog turned to Boris and muttered, "There better be a bonus in this for us."

After dropping Mad Dog off at the hideout, Boris made his way back to the museum. It was darker now, and his movements would not be as observable. The elimination of Mr. Tompkins had now become an urgent priority. As important was the retrieval of the silver key, which Mad Dog felt was back inside the museum.

There was a service road not far from the museum entrance that led to an abandoned shed. It was not used much anymore, so the ride across the field was a bit rocky. That actually was to Boris' advantage. No one would be looking for him, and there was ample space behind the shed to hide the truck. The old machine shed was right at the foliage line. Boris could lurk in the bushes and choose the right moment to go in and deal with Mr. Tompkins. What Boris did not appreciate were the wet leaves that kept dripping on his leather jacket and his bald head. Unlike Skippy, he did not wear a hat.

Boris had begun to make his way to the rear entrance of the museum when he discovered he was not the only one trying to get inside. Because Boris was much better at following orders than giving them, he was at his wits' end on what to do. Mad Dog had not prepared him for this contingency. The hazy figure he observed seemed intent on breaking into the museum through the basement. *Well, perhaps I can help the lad*, Boris thought. His logic was if he could push him into the basement, the fall would likely injure the intruder. Then Boris would be free to complete his mission.

Being low to the ground, Boris was able to scamper quickly across the field, skirt the parking lot, and catch his breath behind the singular evergreen tree on the northwest corner of the museum. He could see Johnny clearer now. *This will not be a problem*, he surmised. What he could not know was that Jeremy and Heather were paying close attention to Johnny's every move.

Something occurred which did not work in Boris's favor, however. When he charged forward to shove Johnny through the basement window, Johnny made more noise than Boris anticipated while falling into the basement. That led to Thaddeus Tompkins throwing open the backdoor to figure out where the noise was coming from. Boris had to retreat from whence he came. Soon thereafter, Mr. Tompkins left the museum.

With his plan gone awry, Boris began to contemplate his punishment if he returned to Mad Dog with empty hands. He rubbed the top of his head and kept mumbling to himself, "He'll kill me. Mad Dog will kill me." Before he could garner up sufficient courage to return to the museum, there was its curator getting into his car and leaving. Boris' heart was in his stomach. The assignment to kidnap Mr. Tompkins had gone very badly. He thought it might be better not to return to the gang at all. It was then he caught the movement of two more youngsters emerging from underneath the tarps. Though Boris did not know he had been seen by them, it was a moot point. Maybe he could salvage something from the evening, after all.

When Heather and Jeremy stopped at the door with their backs to Boris, he seized the opportunity to run to the evergreen. Then, ever so slowly, he inched closer and closer to the stairs. The two comrades were so intent on listening for Johnny to come up from the basement that they never heard Boris coming. With a final lurch, Boris seized their hoodies, causing both to shriek.

"Quiet, you burglars," said Boris sternly. "One more word out of you and your friend inside will not be in condition to start school. Got it?"

Jeremy was shaking so hard, all he could do was nod his bouncing head. Heather was scared but still had some wits about her. "Seems to me *you're* the burglar...or should I say kidnapper?"

"Don't matter what I am, does it? You're under my supervision now. Keep your mouths shut and start moving." Boris tightened his grip on them both and headed across the field toward his truck. In his mind, he now had something to barter with to save his hide. But he did not have Thaddeus Tompkins, nor did he have the silver key. In truth, the odds were still not with Boris Smothers.

*　　*　　*　　*　　*　　*　　*

Who did have the silver key was Johnny. Once he heard the door slam above, he knew he could make his move. Gingerly, he maneuvered around the tools. Still slightly dazed, Johnny almost ran into a lantern hanging from the ceiling. He slowly climbed the stairs, cautiously opened the basement door, and peeked into the darkness. Whereas the basement darkness was initially impenetrable, its hallway counterpart was punctuated with tiny glowing lights on the floor. If they had been installed for security purposes, the lights sure failed miserably in regard to the wooden leg.

Johnny thought he would start with Mr. Tompkins' office first. It was the second door on the right. While pondering how he would gain entry, he was most surprised to find it unlocked. Mr. Tompkins definitely must have been in a hurry. Fortunately, there was a small ornamental desk lamp on the sturdy walnut desk. That allowed Johnny to avoid turning on the ceiling fluorescent lights. Johnny checked out everything—desktop and drawers, bookshelves, the closet, and even the wastebasket. There was nothing providing any link to the leg. The three-drawer file cabinet was locked, but its key lay right on top. The cabinet was stuffed with files on everything from artifact care to W-2 forms. There were no specific files on the wooden leg, and Johnny found that curious. Every other object had its own provenance folder, but under *L* the only file with "leg" was a reference to a Victorian table. Johnny even checked under *W* (to no avail).

As he turned to reenter the hallway, his eyes fell upon a key—a silver key—slightly rusted, but still shiny in part. It sat on the corner of the desk. Johnny had not seen it before. Mr. Tompkins had entrusted Johnny to put things away for him at times, so Johnny was aware of separate keys for the attic, rare book hutch in the local history room, and tiny wine cellar that was supposed to be a secret. This key was different in that it was heavier, longer, and, of course, silver.

Johnny decided to put the key in his pocket and share his new find with Heather and Jeremy, but when he opened the backdoor, they were nowhere to be found. Perhaps he should have looked for them sooner. He called out their names, and when that did not work, he began surveying the immediate outside area. Under the tarp should have been a perfect hiding place, but the two were not there. There was an empty candy bar wrapper near the porch. Johnny sat down on the porch steps, head in hands. Where could they have gone? He did know he was getting very tired. Johnny recalled that in the second-floor meeting room, there were some rather ornate sofas. Perhaps he could lie down for just a minute before finishing his casing of the museum. Johnny Turnbow no longer had the wherewithal to solve any more mysteries. When he woke up, his two companions might be back. He could only hope.

Saturday Morning: Curator Meets the Cops

For the majority of Webster's residents, there was nothing unusual about the beginning of the weekend. Those driving on Elm Street Saturday morning may have been surprised to see their museum closed, but other priorities were in play: preparations for school, putting gardens to bed, grocery shopping, and the like.

That was not the case for those associated with the missing wooden leg. Thaddeus Tompkins was up early. He had a crook in his neck from having fallen asleep at the table, but even that did not dampen his excitement. As he made himself a cup of tea, he hummed to himself and even appeared to be wearing a slight smile. Thaddeus returned to the table and gazed at the map, reminding himself of his nocturnal discoveries.

Brushing his mangled white locks off his face, Thaddeus again reviewed each item on the reverse side of the map with his long, bony index finger. He confirmed that at the bottom of the page was listed, "The Timur Ruby." The ruby was the only item with a proper name; it was written in capital letters and underlined. Mr. Tompkins fancied himself somewhat of an expert on valuable jewels of the world and had recognized it right away. The general story was that the Timur Ruby had worked its way to England via India and the Near East. That did not mesh with a Caribbean origin. But more to the point, it could not have been in the inventory given to King George by Captain Adams, as the ruby's appearance would have caused a great deal of excitement, and its history would have been better documented. Somehow, Captain Adams either kept it for himself or left it behind on St. Lucia, which made no sense whatsoever.

Assuming Captain Adams had it in his possession, why had he done nothing with it? Perhaps both Captain Le Clerc and Captain Adams found the wooden leg a convenient storage place for the ruby. Still, even if Captain Adams chose to keep the Timur Ruby a secret during his lifetime, certainly he would have informed his daughter of its existence and value before he died. The only thing Thaddeus could come up with was that possession of the ruby brought with it a curse. Why else would the word "death" have been etched on the leg? It was almost as if Captain Adams elected to be its custodian and protector.

Taking that theory as truth (which, admittedly, took a giant leap of faith), Thaddeus was stuck with figuring out how anyone could have known the ruby was hidden in the leg. If he, the museum curator, did not have a clue, how would anyone else? But then he started to put two and two together. Professor McDougal had the map and other documents. The professor was a student of anthropology and archaeology. The fact that he always feigned to have much interest in the wooden leg could have just been a ruse.

Thaddeus Tompkins was now anxious to prove his theory. He would need to return to his office and examine all of the documentation in detail. In addition, he was more curious than ever about the silver key. He was certain it tied into the mystery somehow. Thaddeus just knew it was going to be a wonderful day. Putting on his hat and scarf, he opened the front door; looking into the rising sun, he saw a gigantic ruby. Simultaneously, he broke into a grin from ear to ear. The sad thing was that no one witnessed it. The deputy parked across the street was dozing and never saw Tompkins walk briskly toward the museum.

* * * * * * *

Johnny woke up feeling a little stiff. The small oval window at the far end of the meeting room evidenced just the smallest glimmer of light. He pulled himself up into a sitting position with his hands resting on his knees. Facing him directly across the room was a portrait of Dr. Reuben Tompkins, grandfather of Thaddeus Tompkins. The portrait portrayed a dignified man with sharp features. Johnny felt his dark eyes penetrating his very being.

What do you know of this whole affair, Dr. Tompkins? he thought. Rubbing his eyes, Johnny stood up and pondered his next move. It had been a strange evening. He was hungry and thirsty. The museum did not have a kitchen, but there was a pantry of sorts next to Mr. Tompkins' office. He recalled seeing some food supplies on the shelves, but that was quite a while ago. Before Johnny sauntered down the stairs, though, he paused to stare at the empty case once housing the wooden leg. Sure enough, still gone, as if it had vanished into thin air. No visible damage to the case. Even in his half-awake condition, he had to admit that was indeed curious.

Opening the pantry door, he immediately spotted a small icebox in the corner. *Oh, please,* thought Johnny, *some juice or fruit, please.* It was not to be. Alone within the icebox was a sandwich that had seen better days. Johnny carefully unwrapped the wax paper. Limp lettuce clung to what Johnny thought was bologna on crusty rye bread. He held the sandwich to his nose, and when he perceived it had not gone totally bad, he took a bite. It would do. There was only a coffee maker on the counter, so he grabbed a plastic cup and settled for water. At least it was cold.

Then it was on to more important things. Johnny peered out several windows and then proceeded to the back porch. He could not see too far in the dim light, but it was obvious several people had been near the stairs. The grass had been matted down. Johnny thought he could make out footprints belonging to Heather and Jeremy. But there were some larger prints that appeared "adult". He walked into the grass and was able to make out their trail leading to the parking lot. However, the ground fog kept Johnny from pursuing things further. Not to mention that Mr. Tompkins could decide to show up early at the museum. Better to case the museum and see what he could find. Then there was the matter of the silver key.

Johnny got serious and returned to Mr. Tompkins' office. The natural light beginning to stream in from the window was a vast improvement from the night before. Though Johnny had not the benefit of knowing Mr. Tompkins' whereabouts on Friday (nor of his discoveries on the leg's history), he did know a messy office when he saw one. Funny, things did not look so strewn about the night before. Mr. Tompkins obviously left in a hurry on Friday evening. All the commotion must have spooked him, which got Johnny to thinking that his push through the basement window, Mr. Tompkins' hasty departure, and his friends' disappearance were likely related.

Johnny was beginning to think clearer, and he began to realize he may not have much time to investigate further. He began to focus on the silver key. Now Johnny, being no stranger to the museum, knew the location of the doors within its walls. The key was of the older variety, the type that might open an old closet door or a cupboard. There was a drawer under the reception desk that could be a possibility. Johnny tried that first. However, the key jammed as he tried to withdraw it, and it fell to the floor. Upon retrieving the key, Johnny's eyes fell to a business card on the floor: "Dr. Winston McDougal, Professor of Anthropology." Johnny wrinkled his eyes and thought for a moment. If Mr. Tompkins had thoughts to consult with Dr. McDougal over the wooden leg's disappearance, that would not be a surprise.

Johnny's intellectual reverie did not last long, however. A vehicle had just pulled into the parking lot, and its lights shined upon the museum's exterior. Trying not to panic, Johnny did the only sensible thing he could think of—retreat to the basement. He almost fell a couple of times when scrambling down the stairs. As he tried to get to the back basement wall, he slammed straight into a Civil War mannequin and toppled over some empty crates.

Great, Turnbow, thought Johnny. *Is there anything else you could do to let people know you are in the basement?* He brushed off his pants and straightened his flannel shirt. He should have worn his hooded sweatshirt like Heather and Jeremy. It might have padded his fall. Johnny listened hard for any sounds from above. He cautiously moved against the wall dividing the sections of the basement. There were sounds of walking, and he thought he made out a voice similar to Chief Olsen's.

Johnny did a slide walk along the wall until he reached the end of the basement. The cobwebs that kept attacking his face almost made him sneeze. Brushing them aside, Johnny managed not to trip over anything else in his way. He did stub his toe against a metal box that caused him to wince, but he managed to keep still. So, there he stood in the corner. If he had possessed the power to beam himself up to the first floor, he would have come out into the local history room. At least the noises upstairs were to the back of the museum.

Placing his hands in his pockets to keep them warm, Johnny was reminded of the presence of the silver key. Leaning backwards, he was also made aware of a small doorknob sticking into the small of his back. Now that he thought of it, Mr. Tompkins had alluded to the existence of a tiny storage room in the basement. Slowly turning around to face the knob, he indeed saw a small door, barely the height of Johnny himself. There are times in life it seems when fate intervenes to put folks into the places they need to be. This was one of those occasions. His eyes widening, Johnny moved the key toward the lock.

He had to keep from letting out a gasp as the silver key actually fit the opening. It turned a little hard, but a punctuated click was proof the door was now open. The door had not been used for a long time, it seemed. Johnny had to tug to get it open. To his surprise, upon walking through the doorway, what he found was not a closet at all. Instead, he had discovered a tunnel. Even though it was very dark, Johnny backed into the passageway and gently closed the door behind him. Groping the sides of the tunnel, he estimated it was about six feet wide. The ceiling was a few feet higher than Johnny was tall. Light had to be entering the tunnel at some point, because once Johnny's eyes were accustomed to the dark, he could make out a torch hanging upwards and to his right. Oh, what he wouldn't give for a match and some lighting fluid.

Part of Johnny wanted to stay put and wait until the persons upstairs left. The other part was most curious about the tunnel and where it led. Could it have something to do with the wooden leg's disappearance? Could the tunnel have provided an escape route? Or was it just a road to nowhere?

Well, it couldn't hurt to follow the tunnel a little ways, reasoned Johnny. *Certainly better than staying stationary and brushing off spiders!*

*　*　*　*　*　*　*

Indeed, Johnny had heard Chief Olsen's voice. He and Officer Kraus had slept very little after leaving the Turnbow residence the night before. It was bad enough they had no real leads on the missing wooden leg, but now three kids were missing, too. Together with Detective Shaw, they had put together an action plan for Saturday. It took several cups of coffee, but they agreed on a three-pronged approach. First, Chief Olsen and Officer Kraus would have a heart-to-heart talk with Mr. Tompkins. They particularly wanted to discern what he had learned from his meeting with Professor McDougal. The chief had a hunch Thaddeus knew more than he was letting on. Still, knowing the curator's penchant for cracked-up theories, he was trying not to get too optimistic. Another search of the museum and grounds was also in order. There was a good chance that Johnny, Jeremy, and Heather had headed to the museum at some point.

Second, Detective Shaw would link up with the university police at Bradford State University and pay a visit to the professor. In the detective's mind, it would be most interesting to discover what would be so attractive about stealing an artifact that had been sitting around for years garnishing very little interest. Certainly, an anthropologist with Dr. McDougal's reputation should have some opinion on the matter. It would be a nice change of pace to discuss the matter with a saner mind.

Finally, they would have George Kostov, part-time security guard, fend off any visitors to the museum. He could turn on the bubble light on the squad car and feel important. George, age sixty-three, had worked several years for the Bank of Indiana in town as one of their security guards. He had lost a stop or two but was useful for minor assignments that usually freed up the chief and Officer Kraus for other more important tasks.

Chief Olsen was none too happy with George, however, as on the way over to the museum, they found him snoozing in the squad car in front of Mr. Tompkins' lodgings. Rapping on the driver's window, the chief yelled, "Wake up, you bumble head! You were supposed to keep tabs on Mr. Tompkins. And there he is—headed to the museum. Don't expect to get paid for this assignment, Kostov!"

Far ahead down Elm Street, they could just make out the cragged figure of Mr. Tompkins. After the chief jumped back in the car, Officer Kraus gunned the engine and sped forward to catch Mr. Tompkins before he entered the museum. Mr. Kostov followed in his car, feeling a little sheepish and irrelevant.

Thaddeus Tompkins was aggravated to be greeted by Webster's finest before he could even set foot in the door of the museum. Moving as quickly as his rotund body would allow, Chief Olsen burst out onto the lawn. "Mr. Tompkins!" hailed Chief Olsen. "You are up bright and early this morning! And you seem to have some interesting items with you."

"I thought you had a mystery to solve," snarled Thaddeus. He increased his gait up to the museum's entrance.

"That is exactly why we are here," replied the chief. "We are curious as to what you discovered from meeting with Professor McDougal."

As Mr. Tompkins unlocked the front door, Officer Kraus and Chief Olsen tailed right behind him. Moving quickly to his office, Mr. Tompkins threw the charts on a chair and hung up his coat in the closet. He turned to confront his visitors.

"Now, what the blazes is so urgent that you had to barge up here at the crack of dawn?" said the curator tersely, his lips quivering.

"As I was saying, sir, we are most interested in learning if the professor could shine any light on the disappearance of the leg." Chief Olsen tried to sound official. "Officer Kraus shared with me that you were quite excited to find the bill of lading for the wooden leg. There seemed to be some value attributed to it. Perhaps enough value to make it worth stealing?" The chief's eyebrows lifted, and he tilted his head in such a position as to encourage an answer.

Mr. Tompkins thought carefully before he answered. How much did he want to share with these so-called officers of the law? If he brought the ruby into question, his hopes of retrieving it were lessened. While he wanted the wooden leg found, he was not yet ready to discuss the real prize.

Thaddeus was taking too long to respond for Chief Olsen's liking, so he interjected, "As we speak, Mr. Tompkins, you should know that a couple of policeman from the university are on their way over to interview Professor McDougal. We hope your story matches his." The chief stated this firmly so that it left no doubt in the curator's mind that telling the truth was in his best interest.

"Actually, Chief Olsen, the professor was unable or unwilling to shed much light on the subject," responded Mr. Tompkins in a softened tone. "He asked for more time to examine the shipping bill. I would have returned much sooner, but I had some mechanical problems with my car." He then turned to Officer Kraus and said, "By the way, Officer, thanks for dropping the key off with Widow Ruenzel."

Chief Olsen put on his perturbed face. "That doesn't answer why you are here so early carrying some charts or drawings." The chief nodded toward the rolled documents.

"Oh, those," said Mr. Tompkins slyly. "I borrowed those from the professor. More out of curiosity than anything else. Would you like to look at them?"

By giving the impression they were of little value to the case, Chief Olsen was thrown off. "Maybe later, Tompkins. Right now, we are more interested in what happened to Johnny Turnbow, Jeremy Murkowski, and Heather Stippich!" His voice rose as he stated their names.

If the chief was expecting a reaction, he did not get much of one. Mr. Tompkins merely looked surprised, somewhat baffled. "What would I know of their circumstances, Chief Olsen?"

Officer Kraus moved forward toward the curator. "Look here, Mr. Tompkins. We think those kids were investigating the wooden leg's disappearance on their own. Now they are gone themselves, perhaps in some kind of trouble. If you saw them Friday, you need to fess up!"

Chief Olsen had to hold his assistant back from lunging at Thaddeus.

"We're going to look around," added Chief Olsen. "Are you sure you have nothing to say on their whereabouts?"

Mr. Tompkins thought about the disturbance at the back door Friday night. Just in case there was any evidence that might incriminate him, he decided to offer up what happened.

"The only thing I can tell you is that before I left the museum last night, I thought I heard a ruckus out back. When I opened the door, I could see nothing. I left shortly thereafter. You can understand if there was a prowler around—what, with the theft of the leg and all—I did not want to hang around to become a victim."

Chief Olsen and Officer Kraus did not respond but moved quickly out the backdoor to survey the grounds. They could see the grass had been trampled on. The tarp next to the stairs seemed to have been dislodged. Officer Kraus then yelled out, "Come here, Chief! A window has been broken!"

While the officers were outside, Thaddeus took the opportunity to recover the silver key before they returned. Unfortunately, to his chagrin, it was gone. Someone had been in his office. Those kids? He scratched his head. Nothing else seemed disturbed. Could the perpetrator of the crime have returned for the key? Mr. Tompkins clenched his fist. He feared an opportunity lost.

Soon Chief Olsen and Officer Kraus came running through the door and scurried down to the basement. Mr. Tompkins decided it was in his best interests to follow.

As they all reached the basement, Chief Olsen announced, "Mr. Tompkins, we seem to have evidence of a forced entry. Glass is scattered all over, and things are in disarray. Are you sure you saw no one?"

Mr. Tompkins was now shaking slightly. "No, no one," he stammered. He did not know what to think.

"Well, Chief, it had to be someone on the small side to get through that window," offered Officer Kraus.

Chief Olsen surveyed the basement from side to side, a task made easier when Mr. Tompkins turned on the basement lights. "Whoever they were, they are gone now," he concluded. "Kraus, I want you and Kostov to go over this basement with a fine-toothed comb. I am going to check out the rest of the museum. When you are done, do the same with the grounds and parking lot. When I am done with my survey, I am going to call Detective Shaw and see what he has found out. My gut tells me one of those amateur detectives was here last night."

Boris (Almost) Makes A Delivery

When Mad Dog Scrima and Skippy Forrester descended into the hideout on Friday afternoon, after their eyes adjusted to the dim light, they could only stand in amazement at what they saw. This even went beyond the preparation that had been made for them to get to the hideout. Mad Dog covered his monkey face with his hairy paws, and Skippy removed his hat and scratched his bald head. An underground bungalow had been carved out of the earth as if by magic. The room they were standing in measured about nine by twelve feet, and the walls, though made of dirt, were smooth and straight. The floor was also even. The construction had probably been aided by the heavy clay content of the soil. To their left was an old brown couch kept company by a coffee table that appeared to be one stop away from collapsing. The facing wall had a long burlap curtain. Skippy slowly approached it and cautiously pulled the curtain back. Revealed was a long, dark, damp corridor.

While Skippy was investigating the curtain, Mad Dog surveyed the right-hand side of the room. There were several chairs of the straight-back variety. With chipped paint, they appeared to be recent residents of an antique store. There was an open entrance into a smaller room that obviously was meant to serve as a kitchen and eating area. A square wooden table painted light green was flanked by makeshift shelving. There was no stove; in fact, there was no electricity of any kind. The light in the room came from an oil lamp that had to be refilled. However, a corded wall phone had been installed above the kitchen table. It was obvious to Mad Dog that the hideout had a transitory purpose. Still, quite an impressive bit of work, all the same.

Skippy and Mad Dog both glanced toward the wall opposite the curtain at about the same time. Skippy's jaw dropped while Mad Dog exhibited a worried look. A grated door in the shape of a half circle, no more than four feet high, guarded the contents inside a hollowed-out storage room. It was those contents, not the door, that caused them both surprise and concern. Several wooden crates, clearly marked, "Danger! Explosives!" resided therein. Though Mad Dog knew there had to be some kind of getaway plan, he had not been told any details. What he did know was the gang had to move the wooden leg from its hiding place as soon as the boss gave the word. Mad Dog also knew the silver key was important to the leg's retrieval.

"I ain't no good with explosives, Harvey," offered Skippy sincerely.

Mad Dog placed his hairy hand on Skippy's shoulder. "And you won't have to be, my friend."

Mad Dog looked Skippy square in the eye and uttered the words in a rare moment of compassion. The two had been through much together. No matter what, they had the other's back.

"I'm sure someone in our talented band has played with dynamite," added Mad Dog.

They did not have much time to contemplate use of the explosives further before Boris' voice message came in.

*   *   *   *   *   *   *

What a difference a few hours could make. Boris had started his day on Friday by instructing his mother to get the key. Having failed her mission, Boris tried to retrieve the key from the parking lot. Not finding it, he contacted Mad Dog, met at the rendezvous point, drove Mad Dog to Bradford to pick instructions from the boss, and then returned to the museum with orders to snatch both Mr. Tompkins and the key. He had failed miserably. Still, perhaps all was not lost. He had the two kids. Maybe they would provide bargaining power.

Boris was further hindered by Heather's and Jeremy's combined resistance. When Boris and his human bounty left the museum, he had to drag them through the wet grass as Heather and Jeremy would not walk of their own accord. Yanking on Heather's ponytail was the only way Boris could get her to move forward. Once at the truck, he tied them up with some rope and threw them into the back of the pickup.

"Maybe a nice drive in the rain will improve your disposition," growled Boris. He had to have been quite intimidating to the two young detectives. Tall and burly, his mother was quite right: he did resemble a professional wrestler. Boris was slightly shorter than his brother, Iggy, but twice as menacing. Too bad he did not have a brain to match.

As the truck rattled north on Highway 12, the clouds began to break up and a full moon pierced through jagged openings. Heather and Jeremy were wet and cold. The shock of being kidnapped was beginning to wear off, however.

"Heather Stippich, this is some mess you have gotten us into," moaned Jeremy.

"Put a lid on it, beans for brains," retorted Heather. "This is no one's fault. How were we to know that the intruder would come back? If you want my opinion, Mr. Tompkins may have stepped in it big time himself."

Actually, Jeremy was not really interested in opinions. He wondered where they were being taken, not to mention if he would live to see another day. He found himself second-guessing the decision to hide under the tarp. In the time it had taken Mr. Tompkins to leave the museum, their kidnapper must have had to time to regroup. They should have made themselves known to the curator.

"Admit it, Heather. We took a risk. And now we are paying the price. I only hope that Johnny has the good sense to get out of the museum and contact Chief Olsen." With that, he squiggled his nose, trying to get rid of an itch.

Heather had no reply. Her lip quivering, she could only begin to guess what the remainder of the night would hold.

It was late in the evening when Boris arrived at the hideout. Even with the directions Mad Dog had given him, it was no easy task following them in the dark. Plus, it had started drizzling again. The directions did, however, enable Boris to find his way over the field behind Henry's Garage to the tree stump near Granger's Woods. There he parked the truck and led his captives to the bush and the keypad. Punching in the code, the trap door was revealed, and Boris (with great trepidation) pulled it open.

Though Heather and Jeremy could not use their arms and hands, they did have the use of their feet. So, as Boris bent over to open the door, momentarily letting go of the rope he had been using to drag his captives, the duo bolted. Boris was further handicapped by the light emanating from the hideout, which temporarily blinded his sight. Heather and Jeremy scampered into the nearby woods. Jumping shrubs and boulders and dodging tree branches, they worked their way into the sylvan darkness.

"Hey, you two! *Stop!*" screamed Boris. With that, he was overrun by the occupants below. Tripping over each other, they ran in the direction of Boris' outstretched arm. But it was to no avail. What moonlight there was did not penetrate the dense woods nearly enough to let the gang members make out any shapes or forms. Iggy, Skippy, and Tommy Bolton returned to confront Boris. Their hands and arms agitated, they exclaimed in unison, "What the hell have you been up to, Boris?"

✳ ✳ ✳ ✳ ✳ ✳ ✳

Detective Samuel Shaw had served on the Webster police force for sixteen years. He graduated from Webster High School and had always wanted to be a police officer. After passing the required tests and a physical exam, Sam had begun working with Chief Phineas Gordon before his twenty-fifth birthday. Five years into his assignment, Chief Gordon resigned due to poor health, and Chief Olsen came on board. Sam and the chief hit it off immediately. The chief was quite a few pounds lighter in those days, and they would go to the gym early every morning. Detective Shaw prided himself on his appearance and was the sharpest officer Webster had ever seen. He soon made detective when his predecessor retired.

For one reason or another, Sam had never married. His devotion to the job and caring for his elderly mother seemed to be the primary reasons. Long-time residents claimed Sam had had a girlfriend from Louisville who'd died from cancer. On the surface, it was strange he had never left Webster and gone to a larger police department, but truth be known, Sam really loved Webster. Most of Webster's citizens understood that Detective Shaw was the real power behind the throne. Chief Olsen ran a good department, for sure, but he rarely made a decision without consulting the talented detective first.

With his close-cut black hair and handsome features, Detective Shaw could have been a department store model. Whenever he stopped by the doughnut shop for coffee, the waitresses fought to serve him. And it really was Sam who solved the bank robbery case (with an assist from Johnny Turnbow and friends). The missing wooden leg did not, at first glance, seem to compare with the seriousness of that robbery. In fact, Sam initially figured the theft to be a prank. But as he began to think about it, his gut told him there was something very odd about the entire affair. He could not help but wonder if the theft had anything to do with his running into Iggy and Boris Smothers twice in the previous month.

While Chief Olsen and Officer Kraus were concentrating on Mr. Tompkins and the museum, Detective Shaw made a few phone calls and spoke with some of Webster's residents. Mr. Grant noted that the brothers had begun to come into his service station once a week after the advent of summer. George Franks, First Bank of Indiana president, informed Sam that Boris had opened a bank account on July 1st. In addition, Cora Swift, who clerked at the hardware store, said Iggy had come in and purchased a number of tools. Boris and Iggy Smothers were well-known to locals. Their renewed presence in Webster was not exactly welcome.

Even though Boris and Iggy had been out on probation for a while, initially they laid low. They located an old, abandoned hunter's shack a couple of counties away and made do with the basics. Mad Dog said it was best if they did not establish any associations back in Webster. This new job the Bolton gang latched onto only required Boris and Iggy to make regular contact with those still in jail until everyone was out.

Saturday morning, on the way to Bradford, Detective Shaw swung by Mrs. Smothers' lodgings on Pickett Street. No one was there, but he did see new tire tracks in the driveway. In addition, there was a slew of footprints around the back door. The detective wondered if the recently released members of the Bolton gang were up to something. They could have been using Boris and Iggy as their stooges this past summer.

But Sam had to move his mind to the morning's assignment—drive down to Bradford State University and pick Dr. McDougal's brain. He had only been in the professor's presence twice before. The first time was when Bradford State University was celebrating its centennial. Sam had been invited to a formal faculty reception due to his connection with the School of Business (his cousin, Virginia, was the dean's secretary). The second occasion was more circumstantial. The detective had been called in to assist with an antique store break-in in north Bradford. Dr. McDougal was there, sharing his expertise on Asian porcelain. In both cases, they had hardly spoken more than a few sentences to each other.

"Hello," answered the professor when called Friday evening at his home.

"Dr. McDougal, this is Detective Shaw from the Webster Police Department," said the detective by way of introduction. "Might I have a few moments of your time tomorrow morning? You were visited today, I believe, by Thaddeus Tompkins, our museum curator, regarding the missing wooden leg from the museum's collection."

There was a rather lengthy pause, followed by a cautionary response.

"Yes, Thaddeus did come by for a visit. He seemed rather overwrought about the missing artifact. I am afraid I could offer him only limited assistance," responded the professor. "I am not sure what help I could provide, Detective Shaw," he added.

"We are just trying to pull together a few loose ends, professor," Sam assured him. "I think I will only need an hour of your time—max."

The professor could hardly say no, but the request was most inconvenient. Dr. McDougal had a lot of loose ends to tie up himself.

He did not know if the kidnapping mission of Thaddeus Tompkins had been successful. He did not know if the silver key had been retrieved so the wooden leg could be moved. Worst of all, he did not know the status of the police investigation, such as it was. Time was of the essence. The professor was not pleased that it was Detective Sam Shaw who would be doing the questioning. He probably was the only competent member of the Webster Police Department.

"I would appreciate your expediting the interview, Detective Shaw," replied Dr. McDougal. "I have a sick mother to tend to tomorrow morning."

With that, they set the meeting for 9:00 a.m. on Saturday. Now, Sam was enjoying the scenery along Highway 12. The trees were full of foliage with only a hint of changing colors. He never tired of the Indiana landscape donning plenty of green growth, succulent streams, and intermittent ponds. The land exhibited just enough undulation to keep driving over it from getting monotonous.

Detective Shaw arrived at the professor's office five minutes early.

"Thank you for your promptness," welcomed Dr. McDougal. "Please, have a seat." The professor had straightened things up considerably since Friday. "Fire away, Detective. I will do what I can to help."

Sam began. "Chief Olsen and I are curious as to why Mr. Tompkins seems on the verge of an epiphany regarding the wooden leg. Certain documentation has gotten him worked up about something. What was the purpose of his visit to your office?"

"He wanted to make a mountain out of a molehill, to be honest," surmised the professor, twirling a pencil in his hand as he spoke. "You see, he brought me this shipping bill and thought it made a connection to the value of the wooden leg. As usual, our good museum curator has once again boarded the train of speculation. I did sympathize with the leg's disappearance, knowing how fastidious Thaddeus has always been with the museum's inventory. But to build a case on one piece of paper— even if it is from 1773—well, it is definitely jumping the gun."

With that, Dr. McDougal leaned forward and placed both of his large hands on his desk. "Detective Shaw," he pronounced sternly, "that wooden leg has from its arrival at the museum been given an importance way beyond its provenance. If the wooden leg was stolen—and I rather doubt that—it has nothing to do with its perceived value."

The resident anthropologist then sat back up and waited for a response.

"We are perplexed, Professor, as to how it has disappeared from its case on the second floor of the museum without any sign of disturbance. It just smacks of a professional job. The fact it could be of considerable value makes that assessment more credible," offered up the detective.

Rising up, Dr. McDougal threw up his hands. "I truly wish I could say with some certainty that this wooden leg was a valuable object, but the evidence just does not support that conclusion." After a pause, he went on. "I did tell Thaddeus, and I offer you the same, that I will go through my files one more time and see if there is something I have missed from previous investigation. To be honest, though, this whole wooden leg fixation on the part of Mr. Tompkins is getting a little tiring."

Detective Shaw ended his querying with some questions on the professor's whereabouts the past few days, along with his previous associations with Mr. Tompkins. Sam left his card in case Dr. McDougal came across anything interesting. Just as he was about to leave, a young female student appeared at the office entrance. This seemed to disturb the professor greatly.

"Miss Quig," he said, rushing toward her. "You must have gotten our appointment wrong. As you can see, I have a visitor. Please come back at ten as we arranged." With that, he escorted Emily out the door. She started to protest, but the professor literally pushed her down the hallway.

"She could have stayed," remarked Detective Shaw. "We are really done with our interview."

"Actually, Detective, I need to prepare her makeup test. It isn't ready for her to take," Dr. McDougal was sweating and tried to act unconcerned as he showed the detective out of his office. Detective Sam Shaw thought this rather odd and referenced the experience for further reflection.

Reaching his vehicle, he heard his car phone ringing. "Yes, this is Sam...Okay...Got it. No, he didn't have much to offer. He seems to think Mr. Tompkins has gone off the deep end again. See you at the museum."

The entire drive back to Webster, Detective Shaw could not help but think he was missing something. Maybe after meeting with his comrades at the museum, the mystery would begin to make more sense.

Granger's Woods

The thick woods that extended from the southern fringes of rural Bensonville in Shiloh County, directly south into Benson County, forming a parallel line to that county's western border, were full of red maples, shagbark hickories, tulips, and other deciduous trees. Though only its northern portion was actually on land originally owned by Simeon Granger, an early farmer of the area, the entire woods were known as Granger's Woods.

Fortunately, Shiloh County had not been a hotbed of development like other parts of Indiana, so the woods were not threatened. The tri-county planning board had even designated the woods as a "critical watershed" requiring environmental studies be completed before any building permits could be issued.

It was into Granger's Woods that Heather and Jeremy fled late Friday evening. There was no discernable path, but having loosened their ropes, the two companions groped and clawed their way deeper and deeper into the forest. By the time they found a small clearing, giving them some space to catch their breath, they looked a sight. Heather's ponytail was totally disassembled, and her amber locks were decorated with various leaves and twigs. Both she and Jeremy had several scratches along their necks and hands. Jeremy's red hooded sweatshirt was torn in several places, while Heather's hand-knit pullover had totally lost its form. Pieces of yarn dangled from her body, giving the impression she was wearing a coat of worms. Burrs had managed to attach themselves to Heather's jeans and Jeremy's sweatpants.

Heather and Jeremy collapsed on an old log that was (thankfully) not wet. Breathing deeply, their words came out in spurts.

"Have...we...lost...them...you think?" stammered Jeremy.

Heather pushed back her hair. "I think we're safe until it gets light out," she offered.

A stream of the moon's light fell into the clearing and clouds could be seen racing across the sky. The two looked at each other. At the same time, they pointed their arms and exclaimed, "Oh, my god!"

That caused them to break out laughing, as much from shock as from their appearances. The loosened ropes dangled like spaghetti noodles over their chests and arms. Together with their torn clothes, disheveled hair, and burr-covered legs, the loose rope contributed to a look that could only be described as wood elves having a bad day. Heather's mirth quickly turned to tears, and she buried her head in her hands. Jeremy moved closer and put his arm around her shoulders.

"Hey, Heather, we escaped that goon. We'll get out of this, you'll see," he said encouragingly.

"I was sure we were goners," she sobbed.

Jeremy stood up and surveyed the surroundings as best he could.

"Not tonight we're not." Jeremy paused. "But I think we should keep going. If we can get to the other side of the woods before dawn, we've got a good chance of escape."

Now it was Heather's turn to stand. She put her outstretched hands on Jeremy's shoulders. "We have to get back to Webster. We know too much. Do you know who captured us?"

Jeremy shrugged. "I could not get a good look at him."

Dropping her arms, Heather started pacing around. "I am almost certain it was one of the Smothers brothers. He was taking us to a hideout, I'll bet. As we ran away, I think I heard other voices."

She turned and stated emphatically for anything in listening range, "Jeremy, we were right. The Bolton gang is back!"

With that, they began to clean themselves up, picking the foliage from their garments. Jeremy found a small pool of water off to the side. That allowed them to wipe off their dried blood. Since Heather's backpack had been left in the truck, they had nothing to collect water in. Instead, against all they had been taught, they gorged themselves on the cool water from the puddle.

"I might get sick, but at least I won't die of thirst," ventured Jeremy.

To gain some sense of direction, they looked up at the bright moon. It had moved slightly to the right since they had arrived at the clearing.

"East must be straight ahead." Heather's voice was less than confident.

"I don't have a better answer," replied Jeremy.

Without further delay, they began to carefully navigate their way among the bushes and trees. Every so often, they could hear something moving in the darkness. That, combined with tree limbs swaying in the breeze, resembling arms poised to grasp anything near, motivated them not to dally. High above, an owl surveyed their progress. The nocturnal animals were watching. No further harm would befall Heather and Jeremy that Friday night.

*   *   *   *   *   *   *

Iggy Smothers, Skippy Forrester, and Tommy Bolton escorted Boris Smothers down the stairs to the main room of the hideout. Boris studied the room. To his left, seated on the old brown couch, was Jarvis Bolton, his brown leather boots resting on the coffee table. He was tossing an apple up and down in the air, a smirk on his face. Jarvis had thick black hair that had not seen a comb in some time. He was distinguishable from his brother by the scar on his right cheek—evidence of a knife fight from long ago. Directly in front of Boris was Harvey "Mad Dog" Scrima, arms folded. His face was a total scowl.

Iggy moved to stand next to his brother. Tommy and Skippy moved to the chairs on the right side of the room and sat down. In a menacing tone, Mad Dog began to speak—or, more accurately, growl.

"You are alone, Boris. Perhaps you have something to report on the whereabouts of one Thaddeus Tompkins. Perhaps you're preparing to reach in your pocket and produce the silver key. I await your report with bated breath."

As he spoke, he moved closer to Boris. Both were 5' 4" tall, so Mad Dog could look at him square in the eye. In the dim light, Mad Dog, with his bushy eyebrows, dark eyes, matted hair, and a mouth quivering with controlled rage, appeared to Boris as one of the devil's agents. Boris could hardly think how to respond.

"I was interrupted by some dang kids…they loused everything up. I lost the element of surprise…You gotta believe me, Mad Dog."

Mad Dog had now pulled out a huge knife and held it poised in front of Boris' trembling face. "So, you let Tompkins get away? But you did go in and retrieve the key, right?"

Boris stepped back against the wall, his eyes getting larger. "No, no, all I could think was to poach the two kids hiding near the porch. I brought 'em back here…"

Before Boris could finish, Mad Dog had placed his knife directly under the gang member's chin. "No Tompkins, no key, and now you tell me you brought two urchins back to the hideout?" Mad Dog's voice was rising as he spoke. No one in the room dared move.

"So, where are these prizes you bring as booty? What possible value did you think they had?" snarled Mad Dog.

"They ran off, Mad Dog," interjected Iggy. "We was all blinded by the light coming out of the room. But they'll never survive the night in the woods." His pleading, however, fell on deaf ears.

Mad Dog pulled on Boris' right collar. "I never should have let you back in this gang." With gritted teeth, he continued. "Smothers, you and your mother have failed me miserably. Thanks to your bumbling, the key is not in our hands, and Tompkins is still at large. Now we have to clean up after the mess you have made, and we only have a few hours to do so."

Iggy tried to intercede, but was quickly pulled back to the couch by Jarvis.

"Please, please, Boss, I can make up for this. Give me another…" Those were the last words Boris Smothers uttered. With a swift movement of the knife, left to right, Mad Dog sliced his neck, causing Boris to slump to the floor. Everyone stood as they witnessed Boris clutch his throat. Soon he was gone.

Mad Dog wiped his knife off on Boris' shirt. Then he turned to Skippy. "Skippy, you and the boys take this poor excuse for a human being outside. Find a proper burial site for him."

Iggy could only stand with his body quivering. Tears were streaming down his face. Mad Dog strode over to him.

"You want to end up the same as your brother?" Mad Dog asked in a quiet but stern voice.

"No, sir," replied Iggy. He could only stare at the floor.

"Well, here is what you are going to do, Iggy. I am going to give you a chance to live another day." With that, Mad Dog thrust the cleaned knife into his left hand. "You take this knife, you hightail it into those woods, and you track down those two kids. And then you kill them. Do you understand?"

Iggy could only nod his head.

"Make sure you dispose of them properly. Then you come back here, and we'll discuss your future. Got it?" declared Mad Dog. Iggy was still standing motionless. "Well, move it, you sloth!" yelled Mad Dog.

Iggy ran up the stairs and fled into the darkness. Mad Dog sat down in a chair and set his head in his hands. With everyone now at the hideout, the professor would be leaving him a message in the morning at the appointed time. The message would include instructions concerning movement of the wooden leg and a planned diversion. Mad Dog was not looking forward to that conversation.

*   *   *   *   *   *   *

Johnny gradually made his way down the tunnel. Its sides were a little moist, but the ground seemed firm enough. When he reached the torch, he got down on both knees and felt around the floor. To find a match would be a miracle. To his disappointment, no miracle was forthcoming.

The good news, however, was the tunnel was pretty straight, and there were no impediments to moving forward. So, onward Johnny trod. Step by step. Until he came across a puddle. *Where would the water come from?* he thought. His question was soon answered as a small stream of light broke through the tunnel's ceiling. It was not much illumination, but it did allow Johnny to see farther down the tunnel. It seemed to go on forever. *How far should I go?* Johnny pondered. To be honest, there was no turning back.

The long walk also allowed Johnny to contemplate what they knew. He and his friends had definitely interrupted something. Since Mr. Tompkins had been still at the museum, it was probable the curator was the target of something sinister. *He must be in possession of something they need.* It was at that moment he began to put some pieces together. He was in a tunnel because he had found a key. Could it be too much of a stretch to think the key may have been the object of the intruder's interest? Was the tunnel integral to the theft? If someone thought Mr. Tompkins possessed the key, could he have been in danger?

Johnny was confused, though, why the thieves would need to return to the museum at all if they had the wooden leg. They should all be long gone by now. Johnny, Jeremy, and Heather also were not privy to Mr. Tompkins' visit to Professor McDougal. Therefore, Johnny did not suspect the curator knew anything of value that could make him a person of interest.

It was Johnny's hope that the end of the tunnel would provide some answers. Little did he know, his wish would be granted. Sometimes, however, one should be careful what he wishes for.

Searching For Answers

There was a ruckus emanating from Elm Street in front of the museum. Mr. Kostov was trying to straddle the right gate leading up to the entrance. Even though the gate was locked, he seemed to believe the threatening group in front of him would scale it at any moment. The police tape circumventing the entire periphery of the museum's grounds was having no deterring effect. Confronting the security guard were three sets of angry parents.

"Get out of our way, Kostov!" shouted Fred Murkowski. He had his brawny hands placed on George's chest.

"Let us through!" screamed the others.

Chief Olsen and Officer Kraus had been conferring at the information desk when they heard all the noise. The chief plopped his hat on his head and headed out the door with his deputy hot on his heels. Running toward George, both men were waving their arms, trying to gain the group's attention. Chief Olsen collapsed on the gate, slightly out of breath, and addressed the Murkowskis, Turnbows, and Stippiches.

"Folks, no need to get excited." Then, turning to George Kostov, he said, "George, let them pass. Herb, get the key from George and let them in."

Everyone became suddenly subdued and waited for the gate to open.

"We're here to get an update, Chief," stated Mr. Turnbow.

It was obvious to Chief Olsen that none of the party had slept much on Friday night. In fact, the Murkowskis and Turnbows were wearing the same clothing they had on previously. Bill and Melody Stippich, in contrast, seemed stylishly out of place. Mr. Stippich had on a corduroy sports coat with slacks. Mrs. Stippich wore a scarf wrapped around her white blouse. Her high-end skirt was silk. What the group did share, however, were doleful faces, and in the case of the mothers, reddened eyes and tear-stained cheeks.

Chief Olsen tried to cheer them all up by saying, "Well, your timing is excellent. Officer Kraus and I were just going over the findings of this morning's investigations. Detective Shaw arrived minutes ago from his visit to Dr. McDougal. Let us go in, and you can hear what we know."

He then turned to Officer Kraus and asked him to put on another pot of coffee. The parents, mustering what energy they could, followed the chief into the museum, where he directed them into the History wing. Extra chairs were brought in from the meeting room on the second floor.

Once seated, Frank Murkowski queried in a surly tone, "Where is that overpaid curator? I'd like a few answers from his sorry ass."

"He is sequestered in his office for the moment," replied the chief. "Herb here can read you the statement he gave us, if that would be of interest." Since no one responded, the chief continued. "It does not appear that Mr. Tompkins has had any connection to the disappearance of your children. He does seem to have come up with some fanciful theories on the importance of the stolen leg, but he is no closer to coming up with answers to this mystery than we are."

Noting the crestfallen faces of his audience, Chief Olsen quickly added, "But let me share with you what we have uncovered that sheds some light on things. Before I begin, let me warn the ladies present that the information is not all positive. Still, we have some leads, and all of us must keep a stiff upper lip."

The chief waited a moment while Officer Kraus distributed the coffee to everyone and then began. "First off, there was a break-in, as the basement window of the museum was broken in back. We think someone or something fell into the basement. Officer Kraus found some broken artifacts right below the window. He and Mr. Kostov performed a detailed search of the basement. There was evidence of footprints around the stairwell, but there is no way of knowing how recent they were, since all of the clutter on the floor made for a very muddled scene."

Officer Kraus interrupted. "In speaking with Mr. Tompkins, we learned he heard noises outside, but when he opened the back door, he could see nothing. He did not stick around to find out."

"That figures," responded Ben and Frank in unison.

"Herb," continued Chief Olsen, "why don't you share with everyone what you discovered out back?"

"Well, some of the credit should go to Mr. Kostov, Chief," replied Officer Kraus. It almost seemed like he was trying to put the security-guard-turned-detective in a better light. "He noticed that the wet grass leading to the adjacent service road was disturbed. We both agreed someone must have been dragging a heavy load. More importantly, we found this."

Officer Kraus then pulled out a candy bar wrapper from his right pocket. "Do you know of anyone who likes Milky Way bars?"

Mary Murkowski let out a shriek. "That is my Jeremy's favorite candy bar!" Frank had to hold her to keep her from falling off her chair. The rest of the parents threw her looks of concern.

The officer glanced at the chief as he continued. "We thought it a possibility there could be a connection. Mr. Kostov and I walked back farther to the service road and noticed recent tracks likely belonging to a pickup truck." Officer Kraus then stopped. Chief Olsen was giving him a silent signal that he preferred to make the summation.

"Thanks to this discovery, folks, we are almost certain that one or more of your amateur detectives have been kidnapped," interjected Chief Olsen. You could have dropped a bomb in the room and had the same effect. Jenny Turnbow fell on her knees, Mary Murkowski began sobbing, and Melody Stippich fainted. As their husbands tended to them, the chief tried to put a positive spin on things.

"It is our theory that Johnny, Jeremy, and Heather interrupted this break-in. Whether it relates to the missing leg or not, we have no evidence. If it is any consolation, they may have saved Mr. Tompkins from physical harm."

"It is no consolation!" bellowed Frank. "Let me have a piece of Tompkins' hide. I'll get the truth out of him!"

As Frank made strides toward the curator's office, Officer Kraus stepped in and tried to settle him down.

"We don't think they were looking for Thaddeus Tompkins, Frank," he stated. "If this has something to do with the theft of the wooden leg, they perhaps were coming back for something."

Frank Murkowski slumped back into his chair. At this point, Detective Shaw walked into the room. "Things are getting more complicated," he announced. "My interview with the professor did not yield much, but there was something funny about his behavior. He did claim Mr. Tompkins was off on another wild goose chase. As we investigate further, I have asked Chief Olsen's permission to set up a twenty-four-hour watch of the museum. We will need to deputize a few citizens."

Immediately, three hands went up. "Excellent, excellent. Officer Kraus will swear you in and issue you your weapons."

Jenny clutched her husband's arm and gave him a concerned glance.

"Don't worry, Jenny," assured Ben Turnbow. "We will all be careful."

Detective Shaw continued. "In addition, we have put an all-points search out for the kids. As we speak, the police from adjacent counties are looking for any suspicious pickup trucks."

When he finished, it was agreed there was nothing more the mothers could do by sticking around the museum, so after several hugs, they left for home. Jenny and Mary promised they would return with a substantial lunch and dinner. Ben, Frank, and Bill began to get their instructions from Officer Kraus. Chief Olsen and Sam Shaw walked out on the back porch to pick each other's brains.

* * * * * * *

Thaddeus Tompkins sat at his office desk staring into space. Chief Olsen told him he was under protective custody. It felt more like house arrest. No matter what you called it, he knew he would not be free to move about. He would not be free to pursue the mystery of the wooden leg. Therefore, the Timur Ruby, which Thaddeus truly believed existed, was beyond his grasp.

Mr. Tompkins had few options. He could tell the police everything he knew and suspected. That meant advising the chief to bring in the professor for more questioning. It also meant turning over the maps and charts. In addition, he would have to mention the silver key. Bottom line: it would be the reasonable thing to do, considering the reality of his situation.

Yet, the more he thought about it, the more he warmed up to the idea of taking an unreasonable approach. Mr. Tompkins believed he knew how to get to the leg and the ruby. Whoever attempted to break into the museum on Friday night wanted the silver key. He cared far less about what happened to the kids. They had no business snooping around, anyway. Served them right to get poached. Mr. Tompkins felt there were two uncontestable facts. One, the silver key was required to get to the wooden leg, and two, whoever planned to retrieve the leg did not have the key. So, if he could get to the key first, the prize could be his.

However, Mr. Tompkins could not blow his nose without drawing attention. How was he going to be able to search the museum for the key if he couldn't even leave his office? So, yes, Thaddeus sat despondently, trying to cook up a workable plan.

His reverie was interrupted by Detective Shaw. "Mr. Tompkins, how would you like to serve as bait?"

"You think whoever tried to break in last night will try again tonight?" asked the museum curator.

Sam Shaw sat down in the small chair facing the office desk and put his hands on his knees. "We don't think it, Mr. Tompkins. We expect it. There is something in the museum that is essential to the thief's plan of action. Personally, I think it has something to do with the missing artifact. Chief Olsen is not so sure. But a petty thief does not kidnap children. You and the children have gotten in the way of a sophisticated scheme."

Mr. Tompkins scratched his chin. "So, all I have to do is sit here like a guinea pig, waiting to get kidnapped, too?" he replied sarcastically.

"You have nothing to fear, my friend," stated the detective. "Officer Kraus and I will be waiting in the wings for their arrival; he will be stationed outside, and I will be inside."

With a wicked smile, Thaddeus responded, "Perhaps you underestimate those who you are dealing with, Detective. There might be more at stake here than meets the eye."

"On that point, I could not agree with you more." Detective Shaw stood up. "Your professor friend is involved in this somehow. He acted strangely today when I visited him. Dr. McDougal was too emphatic about the importance of the wooden leg being overblown. Strangely enough, Mr. Tompkins, your continual optimistic assessment of the leg's worth these past many years may prove most accurate."

Sam paused for a moment, then turned before leaving. "We'll see where tonight leads us. But I have a good friend in Bradford City who is going to keep an eye on the professor." Then he winked and left.

Drat! thought Thaddeus. *He is onto something. I have got to find that key!* With those thoughts in mind, he got down on his hands and knees and began to scour the floor. Anyone watching would have attributed his actions to his everyday eccentricity.

* * * * * * *

Professor McDougal, after dispatching Miss Quig and showing Detective Shaw the door, plumped down in his chair and reached into the right-hand drawer for a couple of aspirin. Saturday night, the wooden leg was supposed to be transferred from its location in the museum through the tunnel and then transported by the gang to the county airport. Things were not going according to plan. With much more delay, the professor would be forced to cover his tracks and abort his departure.

First item of business was to contact Mr. Scrima and find out if his instructions had been carried out. An appointed time had been set for the call, so the gang leader was expected to answer. The phone seemed to ring forever. Finally, a voice could be heard: "This is Harvey Scrima."

"Mr. Scrima, I trust you have good news for me." The professor spoke in a soothing tone, masking his true concern.

"About that, Boss..." Mad Dog had made, but never received, a direct call from the boss. His forehead quickly became sweaty. "Thanks to Boris Smothers and his bumbling, we have neither the key nor Mr. Tompkins."

When there was no reply, Mad Dog continued. "He paid for his failure with his life, if that means anything. The boys finished burying him early this morning. Don't worry...no one will find him."

Dr. McDougal slammed his fist on his desk. "Look here, Mr. Scrima. Do I personally have to come down to that hideout and take charge of the operation?"

Harvey "Mad Dog" Scrima was not a man easily intimidated by anyone, but the boss was an exception. He replied, "No, sir. No, sir. I will have that key for you before sundown." Mad Dog thought better of even mentioning the two kids who had been kidnapped and got away.

"We don't have until sundown, Mr. Scrima!" shouted the professor. "This morning, I was visited by Detective Shaw, who I think suspects something. My guess is that asinine Tompkins is already spilling his guts to the police about his theories when he shouldn't even be around to say diddly squat!" His voice started low, but continued to rise as he spoke.

"Not only that, but he absconded with some of my maps and charts. Even that idiot chief may start putting two and two together if he gets his hands on them. I need action *now!*"

Before Mad Dog could reply, all eyes focused on the tunnel entrance. A boy had appeared. All he could say was, "Boss, I have to get back to you. An unexpected guest has arrived."

*　*　*　*　*　*　*

Johnny had spent all morning walking down the tunnel. It had seemed to go on forever. Parts of the tunnel were narrower, and his clothing kept rubbing against its walls. Therefore, there was little of him that was not muddy. Occasionally, a worm or creepy critter had made its presence known. Plus, there had been more puddles here and there. What freaked out Johnny the most, however, was a good portion of tunnel just got darker. It was a good thing he was not claustrophobic.

Johnny had to stop and sit down at one point. Had he discovered a road to nowhere? Perhaps this was a vacated passage that had long ago become rendered useless. He might get to the end and find it abruptly stopped. Hunger and thirst were setting in. Johnny had not thought about the need for a snack, and now it had to be close to lunch. For a moment, our intrepid explorer thought about going back. What was the worst that could happen to him? Heather would explain it all to Mr. Tompkins, Chief Olsen, and the parents. After being grounded for a week, things would get back to normal. School would start, and they could move on from this mystery.

They say curiosity can kill the cat. And it was curiosity that kept Johnny plodding forward. Eventually, he could see some light far off in the distance. He thought he could even make out some voices. "You are beginning to imagine things, Johnny Turnbow," he said to himself. "Just like a mirage in a desert." The light got brighter, though. The noises he heard seemed to get louder. Then, he rounded a bend—and there it was. A curtain covering an entrance.

"Iggy better have found those kids," said Tommy Bolton.

"Where do we go from here, Harvey?" probed Skippy. He ignored Tommy.

"We are in a world of hurt. That is all I know," replied Mad Dog. "We have no key…we have no curator."

Johnny could make out some of the words, but not enough to put any sinister meaning into any of them. Time to find out whether he had uncovered friend or foe. So, mustering up every ounce of bravery he could, Johnny walked through the curtain. His eyes grew wide. Everybody just stared at each other. After hanging up the phone, Mad Dog walked up to Johnny and uttered, "You looking for something, kid?"

Discovery and Escape

Johnny did not know how to respond. He ran his fingers through his mussed-up hair, loosening a few pieces of mud in the process.

"I got lost," was all he could manage. Standing in front of him were four intimidating men. On his far left was a tall, lanky character with a fisherman's hat and a toothy grin. Directly in front of him was a much shorter person resembling a monkey. It was hard to see his face due to the hair sprouting from all directions. The guy looked menacing, and his heavy eyebrows were drawn close to his dark eyes. Not anyone to be fooled with. The other two looked similar enough to be brothers. One wore his hair short, but each bore an earring in his right ear. The fella on the right wore a white muscle shirt and baggy jeans. His arms were covered with tattoos. Next to him was a slightly shorter specimen who wore a red flannel shirt and army camouflage pants. On his head was a Chicago Cubs baseball hat. The two had very round faces that could have been used for plates.

The hairy one nodded to the two on his left, and before Johnny could move to run back into the tunnel, they both lunged at him, grabbing his arms. The Bolton brothers then flipped Johnny over and shook him violently.

"Hey, knock...it...off!" sputtered Johnny.

After a couple minutes, all of the contents of Johnny's pockets were lying on the earthen floor. Tommy Bolton, the flannel-shirted one, then dragged Johnny over to the couch and plopped him down.

"Those are my things!" protested Johnny. He attempted to stand up, but Tommy pushed him back down.

"You'll stay there, you twerp, if yous know what's good for ya," growled Tommy.

"Ah, what do we have here?" Mad Dog said, his eyes widening.

Amidst candy wrappers, a small wallet, and smatterings of mud lay the silver key. "Skippy, come take a look. This should make the boss happy."

Skippy sauntered over and bent down to scrutinize the key. "Too bad Boris is not here to verify if it is the same key he had his mom pick up," he observed.

"Well, how many silver keys do you think are wandering around Webster, you dolt—a couple dozen?" responded Mad Dog. "Appears I have some good news to report for a change." Tommy and Jarvis Bolton jumped up from the rumpled sofa and started clapping.

With that, Mad Dog strode into the kitchen and dialed the professor. Perhaps he would live to see another day after all.

* * * * * * *

Iggy Smothers flung himself into the woods that drizzly Friday night. For a while, he ran on, flinging back branches as he went. But it was not long before he realized there was no evidence of a fresh trail. The odds were good he had deviated from the path the two kids had taken. Iggy gazed down at the knife in his right hand and realized the precariousness of his position. He had a couple of choices. He could use the nocturnal hours to search the immense woods (with no flashlight, by the way), or he could plot his escape. For a minute, Iggy thought about turning himself in and reporting his brother's murder. Since he did not savor the return to prison, however, Iggy decided he would save that option as a last resort.

By his reckoning, Iggy figured if he turned to his left, he would be heading north—towards Bensonville. Then he remembered Boris had slipped him the truck keys as they walked down into the hideout... evidence that Boris did not feel the odds of him surviving the night were good. So, Iggy backtracked toward the hideout. By the time he reached the trail, no one was around. Boris' body had likely been already buried. It was only a matter of minutes before he located the truck and wheeled out of the field. With any luck, he could be in Fort Wayne before sunrise.

* * * * * * *

It was inevitable that Heather and Jeremy would eventually run out of energy. Even though their adrenaline was flowing and they figured one or more of the gang were on their trail, they had to stop.

"Heather, I can't go any farther," gasped Jeremy. "Let's aim for that grove of trees up ahead and take a break."

With her hands on her knees, Heather nodded in agreement. The grove was protected by a ring of bushes. Fortunately, the evening's rain had not penetrated very far into the grove. Lying down against the poplar trees, neither of the amateur detectives could be seen from a distance. Even though there was nothing but bark to act as a pillow, Heather and Jeremy were soon fast asleep.

Dawn was breaking, and the myriad of birds were chirping before the two woke up.

"My gosh, I am so sore," moaned Jeremy. He tried to move his body around for a bit of relief.

"We may be sore, Jeremy," responded Heather, "but we are alive."

"Point taken, Heather," Jeremy said in agreement.

They both surveyed their surroundings, being careful to not make much noise. The woods were reasonably thick, and they felt somewhat safe. The question was where to go from there. Hungry, damp, and with less than a full night's sleep, Heather and Jeremy summoned what strength they could muster and pressed forward. There seemed to be branches on the forest floor everywhere they stepped. Adding insult to injury, the tree leaves were still dripping water whenever jostled. When Jeremy stepped into a muddy puddle, Heather had to lunge at him to muffle his shout. Buzzing flies and the occasional mosquito made matters worse.

Just when they thought there would be no end to the woods, they stepped out into a field from where hay had recently been removed. There was no evidence of Webster. On the far side of the field was a farmhouse and several outbuildings. As it was early in the morning, there did not appear to be any signs of human activity. Still, Heather and Jeremy were hesitant to barge out into the open. Only after several minutes did they resolve to cross the field and seek help from the farm's residents.

Jeremy suggested they may want to crawl across the field on their stomachs to avoid attention. Heather tilted her head and gave him "the look."

"Hey, I just do not want to become breakfast for any of the gang," explained Jeremy.

"Actually, Jeremy, it seems too quiet," Heather commented further. "If any of those thieves were hot on our trail, the birds would let us know."

With that, they both started out. In some ways, it felt like being in the eye of a hurricane. It took them about twenty minutes to reach the farm. Just as they were about to knock on the farmhouse door, it burst open, and a tall, elderly gentleman in bib overalls stepped out. It was difficult to tell who was more surprised.

"Whoa, what brings you tadpoles to the farm this early in the morning?" greeted the farmer.

Heather and Jeremy both started talking at once.

The farmer interrupted, "Hey, hey, one at a time, young'uns. Where did you come from?" Jeremy pointed to the woods.

"We really need to get to Webster, mister," pleaded Heather. "We really have uncovered some bad shit." She immediately wanted to retrieve the word as she said it. Jeremy stared at her with his mouth open.

The farmer, whose white locks protruded from his straw hat, raised his eyebrows. "So, you are in some kind of trouble, I take it?"

"Have you heard of the museum theft, sir?" asked Jeremy?

"Can't say I have," the farmer responded, stepping down the porch stairs. "Follow me out to the barn. I have to milk Mrs. Peepers before she gets too restless."

Heather dutifully followed the farmer to the barn without saying anything else. "What would you have to do with a museum theft?" queried the farmer.

Jeremy looked at Heather, silently encouraging her to explain.

"You see, sir…"

"Call me Mr. Tom," said the farmer.

"Mr. Tom," continued Heather, "my friends Johnny and Jeremy and I think we know who did it; we just escaped being kidnapped. We've spent all night in those woods." Heather pointed toward the trees that were now beginning to sway in the wind.

Tom Barlow had farmed for over forty years. He and his wife, Edna, raised three boys and a girl. They had twelve grandchildren. He knew something about kids. Tom said nothing while he finished milking Mrs. Peepers. Jeremy wanted to jump in and say something, but Heather put her finger to her lips indicating for him to wait.

Mr. Tom then walked over to the farmhouse door, opened it, and said in a loud voice, "Mother, I'm taking the truck into town on a short errand. Lock the doors and do not open up for anyone. The shotgun is in the closet." He then motioned for his two visitors to move to the truck and get in. Heather did not know why she did it, but when they all were seated, she reached for Jeremy's hand and held it tight. Then she fought back tears of relief.

*   *   *   *   *   *   *

Emily Quig was the youngest of nine children. She grew up in Fort Wayne, Indiana, where her father was a prominent corporate lawyer. Her mother ran a flower shop, and Emily had learned at a young age to hate Valentine's Day. If the term "runt of the litter" could be applied to humans, it would have applied to Emily. Not only had she inherited all of the short genes in the family, but Emily caught every cold, flu, and sore throat that came along. It did not help that her mother felt the need to protect her from every perceived danger. Result? Emily, up until her enrollment at Bradford State University, had led a very sheltered life.

Emily saw college as a way out of her shell. She was so anxious to finally have a life. In fact, the day her mother drove away from the dormitory, Emily wept tears of joy. Her course load for the first semester as a freshman was the minimum twelve credit hours (her mother had insisted she take a light load). Besides English, American history, and psychology, Emily had received permission to enroll in the Principles of Archaeology class. She loved archaeology and devoured up anything she could find on the subject, whether it was a PBS special or a *National Geographic* magazine.

On the first day of class, she learned the professor originally slated to teach the class, Dr. Benjamin Olsen, had taken medical leave. It was obvious that his replacement, Dr. Winston McDougal, was not happy about stepping in. Further, it became obvious to Miss Quig that Dr. McDougal was going to make the class much harder than it needed to be. The first quiz she took in the class yielded her a score of 62%. Since Emily was determined to pass all of her classes—staying in college was not a priority for her, but a necessity—she garnished up the courage to meet with the good professor. Little did she know that it would be her undoing.

It did not help that the tiny Emily Quig had to confront the larger-than-life Professor McDougal. When given the opportunity to help with the professor's museum "project," she thought it would be a wonderful opportunity. The next two weeks, however, turned out to be a nightmare. Emily soon realized she was to be a pawn in a sinister affair. The obvious thing to do would have been to visit the dean's office. In her mind, however, she kept thinking that her part would be a small one. When asked to put sugar in Mr. Tompkins' gas tank, it was easy enough to do, though Emily certainly did not feel good about it. Now, though, her roommate had given her a note to report to Dr. McDougal's office… on a Saturday, to boot. He was an evil man; she was sure of it. Therefore, mousy, 4'11" Emily Quig decided to make a stand. She would inform Dr. McDougal she was no longer interested in his plots and schemes. Flunk her, if he must. Before she left her room, though, she paused.

Turning to Doris, she said with a determined look, "Roomie, if I do not return in an hour, contact university security and tell them to go to the Anthropology Department."

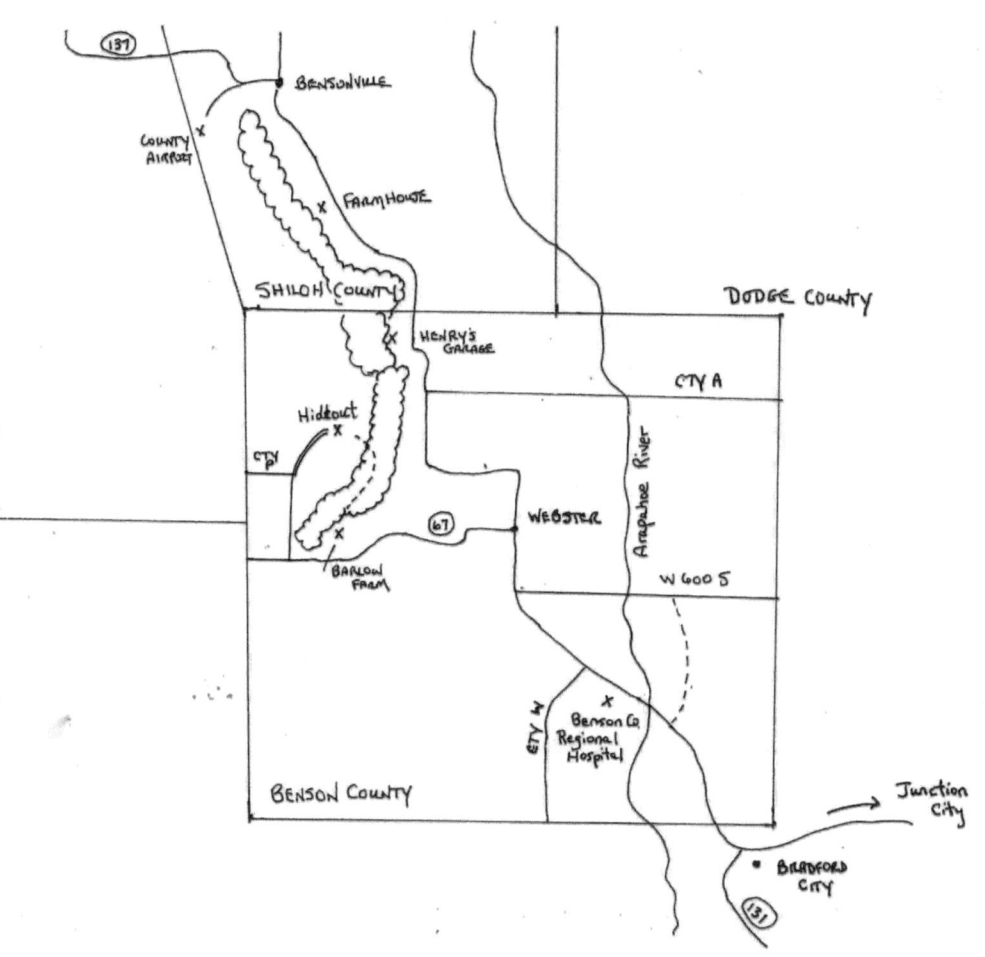

The Calm
Before The Storm

Certainly, it was not usual to see a new, shiny black Cadillac with a chauffeur inside cruising down Highway 137. The idyllic countryside was more accustomed to local tractors, worn pickup trucks, and an occasional remodeled Chevrolet. Highway 137 more or less paralleled the stretch of interstate recently repaved between Washington and La

Croix, Indiana. Anyone in a hurry would avoid it. Too many curves with tiny hamlets to pass through. However, for someone who was trying to work their way over to Bensonville with little notice, it was an ideal route.

Mr. St. George, as the professor was prone to call him, was the perfect man for the assignment. He did not ask questions, and better yet, he could remember very little when others asked <u>him</u> questions. Mr. St. George had been a family friend for many years. Now retired from his limousine service, Mr. St. George took on special assignments; the kind that earned good money for the hours worked. On this late summer Saturday, his orders were to show up before sundown at a vacant farmhouse north of Webster, park inside the lonesome old barn on the property, and wait for Dr. McDougal.

The good professor had given thought to changing the arrangements with Mr. St. George, but with Saturday's developments, he thought better of it. Feeling the heat from several directions, Dr. McDougal decided he had to move the leg as scheduled. Now he had caught a break. The silver key had not only been located but was in the possession of his henchmen. Yes, there were still a few loose ends. The Webster police were likely watching the museum, there were two kids on the loose who would be anxious to tell their story given the opportunity (the professor had little confidence that Iggy Smothers had carried out his mission), Thaddeus Tompkins could not be trusted, and then there was the newspaper. In Saturday morning's paper, on page two, there was a small column:

WEBSTER YOUTHS MISSING

According to authorities, three Webster youths, Heather Stippich, Johnny Turnbow, and Jeremy Murkowski, were reported missing by their parents. They were last seen Friday afternoon at the public library; there is a possibility they were trying to investigate the museum theft reported previously. If anyone has word of their whereabouts, please contact Detective Sam Shaw at 317-203-8999.

Dr. McDougal did know the whereabouts of one of those missing, but he was not about to call Detective Shaw. If the professor's plan were successful, Johnny Turnbow would truly be missing very soon. Dr. McDougal was just beginning to put together his strategy for the evening when there was a knock on his door. He figured it must be Miss Quig responding to his summons.

"Professor, could I have a word?"

Ah, it indeed was the diminutive Miss Quig, but she appeared more confident than usual. "Miss Quig, you are a little early," the professor said smoothly.

"I have thought things over, Dr. McDougal, and I know you will probably flunk me, but I can no longer be a part of your schemes," stated Emily with all the conviction she could muster. She paused to await an answer, but none was forthcoming.

Dr. McDougal merely smiled wistfully and opened his desk drawer. Holding up a remote device, he punched the center button, which immediately closed and locked his office door.

"That is unfortunate, Miss Quig, but I am not sure at this point you have a choice. Even though I am sure there is someone who knows you are here—perhaps your roommate—it will be to no avail. I foresaw this possibility, and right now, there is an associate of mine parked near your parents' house. If you choose to continue to be obstinate and stymie my plans for this evening, one phone call will lead to their demise."

Emily's eyes grew big as she realized she was into something far more foreboding than she had previously thought. She could barely utter a sound.

"Is there a phone call you would like to make?" asked the professor. He then handed her the phone.

Slowly, Emily moved to receive it. Her eyes blinked steadily as she dialed her roommate. "Doris? ...Don't worry about me; I have some group study tonight. May get in late."

Emily struggled as she spoke and hoped Doris understood her alibi. Then she slowly returned the phone to the professor and just stood, completely crestfallen. The energy had been sapped out of her. Dr. McDougal moved toward her and placed his arm around her shoulder.

"You have nothing to fear, Miss Quig. Once you have completed your mission, you will be free to go," he said, but not convincingly. "I wish I could offer you more comfortable accommodations in this office," Dr. McDougal added, "but I am afraid you will have to stay here until we depart together early this evening. But do have a chair."

Emily resigned herself to the inevitable and sat down. She found a table to rest her head on. Suddenly, Emily felt very tired and promptly fell asleep. Dr. McDougal quickly got going on putting all the pieces together for the evening's festivities.

*   *   *   *   *   *   *

It was about nine miles into town. Tom Barlow did not say much while he was driving, and Heather and Jeremy were content to wait quietly. The only thing he asked about was the kidnapper himself. From the kids' description, it was not someone he recognized. He was really not familiar with the museum situation; in fact, he had never visited the county museum. Edna had taken the grandkids there once but had returned unimpressed. That part of the kids' story he would let the police sort out.

Tom was just coming around the turn past the Lawrence farm when the truck gave a jolt, and he felt the left front tire go wobbly. Christmas, not again! He'd had the tire plugged just a month ago. Tom maneuvered his truck over to the shoulder the best he could.

"Stay inside, kids," Tom directed. Heather and Jeremy looked at each other as if to say, "Now what?"

Bending over with hands on knees, Tom surveyed the damage. There would be no plugging the leak this time. The tire was totally blown. He stood up and let out a big sigh. Tom then went over to the passenger door and opened it.

"Out you go, urchins. We have to take a little walk and see if the Lawrences are home," he explained.

Heather and Jeremy dutifully jumped out and followed Tom's long strides toward the white, two-story farmhouse. The prior evening's rain made the dirt entrance road a little muddy with a few puddles. Half a dozen chickens were out and about, crossing the road here and there. There stood a barn and the usual outbuildings in the distance, but otherwise, there was no sign of life.

Tom marched up to the porch door, opened it, and proceeded to the inside door. He knocked firmly, shouting out, "Henry, Gladys, you home?"

After waiting a few moments, Tom repeated his query, but there was no response. "Well, kids, they might be out working. Let's take a look around."

It was over ten minutes before they all saw a figure out in the distance on a tractor taking up the last of the hay. Tom waved enthusiastically toward the tractor. Then he whistled. "Henry! Tom Barlow, here. Need some help," he proclaimed loudly.

The thin, gangly man bounced off the tractor and headed their way. After a warm greeting, Henry Lawrence asked what brought them out that time of day (it was close to 9:00 a.m.). After hearing Tom's brief report, Henry invited them all in for some breakfast.

"These poor kids must be starving by now. Don't suppose you bothered to feed them, Tom?" Henry said with a wink. "Gladys ain't home—off tending to her mother. But I can still make some mean bacon and eggs."

There was no immediate rush. The truck was going nowhere, and Tom was happy to get Henry's reaction to the kids' story.

"You say your names are Heather Stippich and Jeremy Murkowski?" asked Henry. "Knew a Murkowski once. Ran an auto body shop outside of Terre Haute."

Henry scrutinized their faces. "Tell me again from the top what happened to you last night."

In between gobbling down their food, Heather and Jeremy took turns relating everything that had happened. Henry nodded from time to time and evidenced sincere concern for their plight.

"We don't have much bad stuff happen around these parts. Would you agree, Tom?" Tom nodded in agreement. Henry stood up.

"Excuse us for a moment, young'uns," Henry declared. "Mr. Tom and I need to have a chat. Why don't you have a walk around outside and say hello to our pigs in the far shed." He then pointed in the direction of a pig pen.

Jeremy actually seemed excited about seeing some pigs up close, but Heather just walked with her head down, wondering if they ever were going to get to Webster. She was not even sure Mr. Tom or Mr. Henry believed their story. Heather did feel safe, however, and was so very relieved to have escaped the gang. *Patience, Heather*, she told herself. *This will all work out in the end.*

"Tom, let me ring the Webster Police Department," Henry began. "Gladys has the car, and my boys went fishing last night over beyond Summit Lake. Don't know when they will return. We have got to get word to the authorities. Then we will get to work changing that tire."

Tom Barlow rubbed his unshaven face. "Good idea, Henry. The sooner I get back to Edna the better. There are some strange things going on, and who knows what or who will come out of my woods next."

After several rings with no answer, Henry and Tom agreed they should tackle the tire problem and try to call again later. The sun was coming up nicely to the east of the farmhouse. It was to be a warm day. Heather and Jeremy were ready for all the warmth they could get after their nocturnal trials.

*   *   *   *   *   *   *

As Saturday morning came to a close, most of Webster was taking care of business. For those associated with the museum theft, there was reason for optimism on a variety of fronts, though obviously involving conflicting agendas.

The museum was under watch with Mr. Tompkins as unwilling bait, Heather and Jeremy were awaiting transport to Webster, and Dr. McDougal's gang had possession of the silver key. Chief Olsen and

Detective Shaw were confident they were on the verge of breaking open the case. Jenny Turnbow, Melody Stippich, and Mary Murkowski just knew in their hearts their children would turn up soon.

The one individual who was losing hope was Johnny Turnbow. Tied to a chair with a box of dynamite at his feet, he could see no possible means of escape. And that was indeed a pity, because Johnny was beginning to put together the pieces to the mystery of the wooden leg. Granted, he didn't have Heather's sage advice to guide him, but some things were obvious. The Bolton Gang was connected to the disappearance of the wooden leg. Assessing the occupants of what was obviously a hideout, he did not think any of the four were the mastermind behind the operation, however. Certainly not the Bolton brothers, who had proved their ineptness during the bank robbery. The Smothers brothers were conspicuous by their absence, but they were too low on the food chain to be in charge of much beyond showing up when ordered. Initially, he thought the scary hairy one going by the name of Mad Dog could be the leader. But then he caught snippets of the conversation that Mad Dog had with someone else (no name surfaced).

"Boss, Dame Fortune has blessed us with an unanticipated development," reported Mad Dog into the phone. "The silver key has been delivered into our hands."

Mad Dog then went on to explain Johnny's arrival. Shaking his head affirmatively throughout most of the conversation, Mad Dog spoke in short syllables.

"Understand…Back on schedule…Right…Tonight? Got it," was all Johnny could make out. Still, it was plain to him his delivering of the key had set events in motion that perhaps had been put on hold. Well, the key opened the door to the tunnel. The tunnel led to the hideout. It only made sense that wherever the missing leg was, it was either to be transported down the tunnel or stashed somewhere while the gang made their escape down the tunnel. The numerous boxes of dynamite indicated the gang was going to blow up something. The museum? The tunnel? The hideout? Johnny's mind was going in several directions at once.

Johnny realized he had no cards to play. He had no idea where Heather and Jeremy had gone off to. Did they go to get help? Had they alerted either Chief Olsen or Mr. Tompkins to his predicament? Maybe he should have trudged upstairs from the museum's basement and revealed himself. Maybe his friends were among the group who arrived this morning. Why wasn't he thinking clearer before heading down the tunnel?

Johnny's musings were interrupted by Tommy Bolton who thrust his hand into Johnny's face. "You like Snickers bars, kid?" Tommy taunted. "You gotta be starving by now…Here, have a bite."

And with that, Tommy shoved half of the candy bar into Johnny's mouth. "I know who you are," sneered Tommy. "You are that Turnbow brat that interfered with our bank heist. You and your two buddies. Well, you'll…"

That was where Jarvis pulled on his arm and interjected, "Watch what you say, brother." Jarvis gave Tommy a look that reminded him it might be best if nothing was said about the other kids.

Tommy Bolton just threw down his hand and walked away muttering, "Just forget it."

At that point, Mad Dog and Skippy, who had been consulting in the kitchen, walked toward the brothers. "Tommy, you come with me," instructed Mad Dog. "We're going to take a little walk down the tunnel and make sure this key works. Jarvis, you go check on that truck Boris drove here. Skippy is going to keep our new buddy company."

The only thing Johnny could think to do was to utter a silent prayer, petitioning for angelic interference. He couldn't imagine anyone showing up to deliver him from his quandary. His thoughts turned to his mother, and he mouthed, "Sorry, Mom."

The Door of Opportunity Swings Both Ways

Thaddeus Tompkins could be accused of many things, but being an idiot was not one of them. With no evidence of the key in his office, he sat down at his desk to assess things once again. To tell the truth, he had made some conclusions regarding the wooden leg surpassing the progress of Chief Olsen and his associates. Thaddeus had correctly identified why the wooden leg was of value. He was more convinced than Detective Shaw concerning Dr. McDougal's involvement. A second look at the professor's folder seemed to be in order.

Now, peering over every sheet of paper, it became even more obvious to him that the good professor had had more than a passing interest in the wooden leg and its contents. There was one piece of correspondence in particular that caught his attention. It was dated March 25th, 1982. The letter was addressed to Century Flight Company and read:

Dear Sirs:

After reviewing the material you sent to me, I would like to arrange for a private Charter flight at the end of August. It will involve using a small municipal Airfield between Webster and Bensonville, Indiana.

My business card is enclosed. Call me at my office and we can work out the details.

Cordially yours,

Winston S. McDougal, Ph.D.
Department of Anthropology
Bradford State University

143

"...The end of August," indeed. Why would Dr. McDougal need a charter flight at an inconspicuous airfield around the time of the theft of the wooden leg? Thaddeus' suspicions—at least in his mind—were now confirmed. He laid back in his chair, gazing up at the ceiling, his bushy white eyebrows occasionally twitching.

"So, Dr. McDougal, you need a key to get to the wooden leg," he surmised. The fact someone had been prowling around Friday night meant they 1. did not have the key and thought he did, 2. thought the key was in the museum, or 3. had a key that was to be used. The first premise meant Detective Shaw was correct in considering Thaddeus bait. Mr. Tompkins hoped the second premise was not true, since trying to find the silver key in the museum would be a severe challenge. However, if the third premise were true, it was just a matter of finding what door it would open. Thaddeus had a smirk on his face as he considered the word "just." Thaddeus ran over in his mind all the doors and entryways in the museum. Obviously, without the key, he could not try it on anything. However, perhaps by the process of elimination, Thaddeus *could* determine what it might open.

Almost leaping to his feet, the museum director gathered up all of his keys and decided it was time to find out what they did not open. Yes, he could not leave the museum per his instruction from Chief Olsen, but he was not restricted to his office. Therefore, in the early afternoon, Thaddeus Tompkins began his inventory of every door within the museum's walls.

With his large ring of keys in hand, Thaddeus turned right out of his office and maneuvered around the circular hallway. He double-checked every door and closet to ensure there was a matching key assigned. While to the uninitiated this would have appeared unnecessary (how many years had Mr. Tompkins worked at the museum?), Thaddeus was leaving nothing to chance. Perhaps a lock had been changed in his absence. When he reached the stairs to the second story, Thaddeus glanced over to the local history room and noticed Detective Shaw engrossed in one of its selections. The detective seemed quite preoccupied as he sat at one of the round tables with his back to the room's entrance. Thaddeus was able to quietly ascend the staircase without being noticed, though a squeaky step almost gave him away.

While Officer Kraus monitored the museum grounds outside, working in Thaddeus Tompkins's favor was that the newly deputized "three musketeers" had been sent to check out Mrs. Smothers' residence. Their first task was to see how she was feeling, and the second was to see if she could ascertain the whereabouts of her sons. As a result, Thaddeus had a window to pursue his investigation.

Once on the upstairs landing, he thoroughly checked out the meeting room and two adjacent closets. Nothing unusual was apparent; that did not surprise the museum curator. Thaddeus did stand for several minutes gazing at the empty display case. It was as if he was staring at a two-way mirror, wondering if the wooden leg was staring back at him. But, of course, that was impossible, so he tiptoed down the stairs and entered the natural history room. There were no doors to check, but Thaddeus walked up to the case displaying several small mammals. He reached around to the back of the case and pushed a button. The case promptly swung open. Thaddeus looked to his right and left to make sure no one was watching. Beads of sweat were forming above his eyebrows. He then slipped behind the case, closing it behind him. Known to no one but himself, there was a secret stairwell leading down into the basement.

It was fortunate Mr. Tompkins was a thin, bony man. The stairwell resembled that found in the manor house at Mount Vernon, Virginia. Steep and narrow. In the basement, it came out in the northeast corner. Upon discovering the stairwell years ago, Thaddeus had piled a number of boxes in a semicircle to both protect and hide the entrance. As he made his way into the basement proper, even in the mid-afternoon, not a lot of light streamed through the windows (that should have been cleaned long ago). The broken panel that someone had fallen through did send a ribbon of light across the basement floor, though. Still, that was on the opposite end from where he'd descended. Thaddeus was able to survey the east half of the basement with some ability.

Thaddeus never did like the basement. Without adequate climate controls, thanks to what he perceived as a stingy museum board and an equally parsimonious Supervisor Higgins, nothing of great value could be stored. The only artifacts in the basement were items that had to be kept because of donor requirements. It was impossible to get any kind of a decent collection. Therefore, Mr. Tompkins relied on loan agreements to occasionally spice up the museum's exhibits.

Artifacts were not his main concern that Saturday afternoon, however. Thaddeus made his way around the musty, damp surroundings to reach each of three small doors he recalled once seeing. Surprisingly, the two doors on the west side of the museum each opened with a pair of rusty keys. Upon opening the first, a small bird flew out, giving the impression it had been trying to escape for some time. Thaddeus wiped away the cobwebs and, with the aid of a pocket flashlight, could only make out a dirt floor and a few wood planks. The second room was also tiny, perhaps 3x4 feet in size. It was similar to the first but housed a pile of bricks.

At the very end of the west wall (southwest corner) was one final door. Like Johnny, he had to navigate the Civil War mannequin and various crates to reach it. Thaddeus could not remember when he had last come near this door. Since none of his main keys had fit its lock, he basically ignored its presence. Now the moment of truth: did he currently hold the correct key? With each succeeding key failing to turn the lock, Thaddeus Tompkins became more anxious. Now he was down to the last key. It also failed. Thaddeus placed his hands against the door and said to himself, "What secrets do you hold, my wooden friend?" At that very moment, the door suddenly opened—he had to catch himself from falling down at the base of the door. Thaddeus found himself face to face with Mad Dog Scrima and Skippy Forrester. He let out a squawk before Skippy covered his mouth and muffled any further sounds.

* * * * * * *

Ben Turnbow, Frank Murkowski, and Bill Stippich took their deputy assignments seriously. When asked to check out the status of

Mrs. Smothers, they immediately scurried to Frank's Dodge pickup (they were not allowed the use of a squad car) and hustled off to Pickett Street. Making a right turn off of Elm Street, Mrs. Smothers' modest home sat adjacent to St. Patrick's Church on the east side of the street. Overgrown rose bushes lined the screened-in porch. A dirt driveway had been unused for some time, and weeds had filled in the former tire tracks.

A more diverse trio would have been hard to find. There was Frank with his muscular steelworker image; Ben, lanky with a pipe hanging from the side of his mouth, resembled a schoolteacher, not a Department of Public Works employee; and Bill was still distinguished even though he now wore a hooded sweatshirt. Pulling in front of the house, each cased a different side of the residence, looking for any sign of life. It was quite quiet, and only two kids passing by on bikes broke the silence.

"Gentlemen," began Ben, "it is time to see if Mrs. Smothers is inside." The porch's flimsy door was unlocked. Ben then proceeded to the front door and knocked assertively. After repeated knocking, he shouted, "Mrs. Smothers, are you home?" Nothing.

The three then walked around to the back entrance facing a short stoop. Empty milk bottles were strewn about. Ben tried more knocking and more shouting to no avail.

"You don't think this would be a time where breaking and entering would be allowed, do ya?" barked Frank.

"Well, this is an important case of missing persons, theft, and who knows what," Bill chimed in.

Before he could continue, Ben began to play with one of the back windows, resulting in the screen falling to the ground. To his surprise, the window could be pulled open.

"Frank, Bill, give me a hand here," he said. "Hoist me up. I think I can get through the window."

Minutes later, they were all inside surveying the furnishings. Though the kitchen looked neat and orderly, the house definitely gave the impression that Mrs. Smothers had left things unfinished. The living room was disorganized with unfolded clothes strewn everywhere. Bill reported from the bedroom that the bed was unmade. Frank noticed towels on the floor in the bathroom.

"Someone seems to have left in a hurry, and I am not sure they are returning," postulated Ben.

"Do you think Mrs. Smothers was kidnapped, too?" asked Frank.

Ben shook his head. "No, Frank. Don't think so. No sign of any struggle or breakage...she could have gone off with her sons, I suppose."

Bill reminded them that it had only been a day, after all, since Mrs. Smothers had left the museum for home. She could be on an errand.

"Didn't she have a sister who lives out of town?" Frank remarked.

"Regardless, Frank, she cannot shed any light on things in her absence," noted Ben.

In the interests of solid policework, the three deputies surveyed the house in detail and walked the backyard looking for clues. They came up with nothing and eventually returned to the museum. As they pulled into the museum's parking lot, they could see Chief Olsen and Officer Kraus having an animated conversation.

"Chief, I'm telling you—we have a reached a dead end," declared Officer Kraus. "This sitting around is driving me nuts. Kostov and I looked over the entirety of the basement. Only way out of that dusty pit is up the stairs. No sign of any kids being there. Tompkins says he didn't see them. Maybe they did break a window. Who knows?" Officer Kraus waved his hands over his head.

"The point is that they are gone. Probably taken," Kraus continued. "There has been no report of any suspicious truck. We won't get any word back from the state lab on the tire tracks until early next week—if we are lucky!"

"Well, what would you have me do, Herb?" responded the chief. "Sam says to have patience. The assailants will be back. He believes things will crack tonight."

Before Officer Kraus could protest, the three deputized citizens walked up with their report.

"Sorry to interrupt, Chief," apologized Ben Turnbow. Checked out the Smothers place; managed to get inside and found it vacant. Most of the house was in disarray. We think Mrs. Smothers left in a hurry. In any case, there was no one around to question." Frank and Bill nodded in agreement.

Now Officer Kraus began to screech. "Another disappearance! Are you kidding me?" His eyes began to bulge. "Who's next, Chief? Have you seen Sam lately? Huh? Huh?"

Officer Kraus now stood toe to toe with Chief Olsen, who just rolled his eyes. At that moment, Detective Shaw came out the front door of the museum.

"Hey, what's all the ruckus out here? You interrupted some serious reading, you know," queried the detective.

"Sam, Herb here is only getting a little frustrated," replied the chief.

"Frustrated?" yelled Officer Kraus. "I'll give you frustrated. How about I bring some worried mothers over here, and they can read you the riot act!"

Everyone was now in a circle around Officer Kraus. Chief Olsen explained to Detective Shaw that Mrs. Smothers also seemed to be missing.

"That does not necessarily surprise me, Chief," commented the detective. "She could be off with one of her sons. She did leave early from work yesterday...not feeling well, I understand?" Detective Shaw surveyed the group.

Officer Kraus was beginning to calm down. "Maybe you're right, Sam. But it still smells. Just smells."

With impeccable timing, the Turnbow's sedan pulled up in front of the museum, and Jenny Turnbow stepped out with a basket full of what appeared to be an early supper.

"How are the guardians of the museum?" she greeted.

"Ready to eat a horse," replied her husband. Frank and Bill were right behind him as they scurried toward the ladies.

Jenny waved to the three remaining and said invitingly, "There's enough for all of you, you know. Get on over here, guys."

The group then moved in unison to the museum to see what delightful refreshment Jenny, Melody, and Mary had conjured up. They decided to convene and eat in Mr. Tompkins' office. To their surprise, he was not there.

The chief looked quizzically at his astute detective. "Sam, you've been here all afternoon. Where is Mr. Tompkins?"

"He was in his office when I went to read in the history room," Detective Shaw said with a concerned look. He then stepped into the hallway and shouted out, "Mr. Tompkins, where are you? We have some supper here."

Leaving the baskets of food on the curator's desk, everyone began to search the entire museum for the missing Thaddeus Tompkins. After every corner had been investigated, one by one, the group members returned to the first floor, perplexed and even more confused. Detective Shaw's gambit had backfired. Either the perpetrators had successfully managed to steal Mr. Tompkins right from under their noses, or Thaddeus had escaped on his own. The end result was that the bait was gone.

Rubbing his chin, Detective Shaw struck a meditative pose.

"Well, if the thieves do not know he is gone, they could still show up at some point to retrieve him," he speculated.

Officer Kraus was exasperated beyond explanation. "Maybe Mr. Tompkins was right all along!" he shouted, his thin arms flailing accompanied by frantic pacing. "This place is haunted! We are fighting ghosts. What chance do we have?"

Most of the group looked at each other with great concern as they watched Officer Kraus become unhinged. Only Mary Murkowski walked up to the deputy and grabbed his arm.

"Ghosts? Do you really think so officer?" she asked.

"Herb, get a grip," responded Chief Olsen.

Frank gathered up his wife, and the group of parents decided to go sit down and eat in the local history room. Chief Olsen, Officer Kraus, and Detective Shaw remained in a tight circle by the information desk. At that very moment, they heard a vehicle pull up in front of the museum.

In a matter of moments, a deep voice bellowed, "Chief Olsen, you in there? I have a couple of youngsters you may want to see."

ℬetter ℒate ℐhan 𝒩ever

Jarvis Bolton was not a man to mess with. He took his assignments seriously and was the polar opposite of Boris Smothers. With his tattoos, earrings, muscle shirt, black leather boots, and studded black leather vest, Jarvis could easily have been mistaken for a biker. Though he had a nice head of black hair, he was not an attractive man, but certainly an imposing one.

When Jarvis reached the place where the truck should have been, he squinted and put his hands on his hips and stared intently into the distance for several minutes. Jarvis was nobody's fool, and when no truck keys were found on Boris' person, he immediately decided that Iggy Smothers had them. He also was very sure that Iggy would not succeed in finding the two kids. That led to his final conclusion that Iggy would flee and do it via the truck. It appeared he was right on all counts.

"You know how to hot start an engine, Jarvis," Mad Dog had instructed. "Do what you have to do to get that truck started. We are going to have some hot property to transport this evening."

Now, hot starting an engine would be the least of Jarvis' challenges. And he was right. In the time he had spent walking over to the spot where he was to find the truck, Jarvis had come up with a plan. Henry's Auto Body had gone out of business, evidently some time ago. A "closed" sign hung diagonally over the front door. The large garage door had two windows with broken panes. The entire shop was in need of a good paint job. Weeds grew in abundance and had about covered where there had been a driveway. The phone booth stood off to one side and actually looked more functional than anything else on the property.

In all of this, Jarvis saw an opportunity. A rusted Toyota rested alongside the garage. He proceeded to push the vehicle out in front toward the highway. A lesser man, or men, would not have attempted it, but Jarvis had won the strong man contest at more than one county fair in his time. He grunted and growled, slowly inching the sedan to where those driving by could easily see it. Jarvis was aided in his plan by the fact the left front tire was flat, even though it made it more difficult to push.

County Highway 12 was a reasonably traveled road between Bensonville and Webster. Jarvis counted on the fact this was a Saturday and more of the area's county residents might have headed to either city to do some shopping or visiting. It was now later in the afternoon, and he figured someone would be heading home. Jarvis' expectations soon came to pass.

Ambling down the highway, proceeding at five miles below the speed limit, was an older couple in a stake truck. Jarvis moved out into the path of the truck, waving his arms frantically. He had to be an intimidating figure to the couple. The elderly man slammed on his brakes and came to a complete stop. The window on the passenger side slowly came down.

"You in some kind of trouble, mister?" asked the woman.

"My car here got a flat, and I need to get into town to get some help," responded Jarvis.

The man then rolled his window down and stuck his head out. "You some kind of heavy metal fan, are you?" he questioned. "Don't get many of you types out here."

When Jarvis moved closer to the truck, the man pushed on the accelerator and sped off, causing Jarvis to fall over backwards. Jarvis spewed out several obscenities and waited for another opportunity. It was not long in coming.

Next to approach in the southbound lane was a young man in a bright yellow Chevy Corvette. He was driving alone. Jarvis once again sprung into the road. With the radio blaring, the driver screeched to a halt and swerved off the road.

"Dang, you trying to get yourself killed?!" he yelled.

"Sorry about that," responded Jarvis. "I've had a flat. Need to get into Webster pronto. Can you give me a hand?" Jarvis motioned him over to the Toyota.

The young man, with hands in his jean pockets, strolled over to where Jarvis had knelt down by the blown tire. Just as he got near him, Jarvis leapt up, holding a large wrench. Before the innocent victim had time to react, Jarvis clobbered him alongside the head, causing his body to crumple to the ground. The young man was out cold and probably would be for quite a while. It was an easy matter for Jarvis to drag him into the garage and stuff his body underneath several old tires. Some blood from the young man's skull had settled on the ground. Jarvis covered all of it with loose dirt. Then he moved the Corvette off the road and drove it toward the woods. Soon Jarvis had the vehicle camouflaged with tree limbs. True, it was not a truck, but the car would meet the need.

Smiling, Jarvis strolled back to the hideout. There were days he amazed himself.

*   *   *   *   *   *   *

All Mad Dog Scrima could do was muffle a laugh. The look on Mr. Tompkins' face was priceless.

"Look what we have here, Mad Dog," announced Tommy.

"This must be the infamous Mr. Tompkins," replied Mad Dog. Putting his finger on Thaddeus' forehead, he continued, "You are a very wanted individual, sir. Did you know that?"

All the curator could do was wiggle and squirm.

"He's definitely a live one," added Tommy.

Mad Dog turned serious. "I'm going to make sure this key works. Then we'll take this unexpected arrival back to the hideout." He then paused before looking at Tommy and noted, "You know, this whole caper may work out yet."

Indeed, the key did work, and they went swiftly back down the tunnel, dragging Thaddeus Tompkins most of the way. Mr. Tompkins was a muddy mess before they reached the dangling curtain. When they arrived, Jarvis had already returned. Skippy was throwing some old miniature marshmallows at Johnny's mouth. He had more securely tied up Johnny to one of the straight back chairs.

"Skippy, Jarvis, help Tommy tie up our new guest," ordered Mad Dog. "I'm going to alert the boss." As he entered the kitchen, he announced to the group, "We are now going to be able to get this operation back on target. I'll be back with specifics in a minute."

Needless to say, the professor was most pleased. He had been struggling with how he was going to get his hands on his "friend" Thaddeus. With any luck, the fact that Mr. Tompkins had been lurking around the museum basement meant he had not jumped in with both feet to aid the police. Now the pesty curator could be eliminated and Miss Quig could be put in place to complete her assignment.

"Mr. Scrima, you need to get Mr. Tompkins over to the farmstead," said Dr. McDougal. I will meet you there. Eliminate any signs of your presence and prepare to blow the hideout. Make sure the lad is adequately secured in the kitchen. He will be a casualty of his own curiosity. Also, make sure your dynamite man knows the signal and is not premature in lighting the explosives. As I shared with you before, that individual is to hightail it down the tunnel, getting as far as he can before all hell breaks loose. Everyone must be at the rendezvous point by 7:00 p.m. Do I make myself clear, Mr. Scrima?"

After assuring the professor he indeed understood the drill, Dr. McDougal ended the conversation. Mad Dog gathered his gang around him.

"Skippy, move Johnny boy and the curator into the kitchen so they do not hear all the details of what I am going to share," instructed Mad Dog.

Johnny began to show new signs of life, but there was nothing he could do as Skippy lifted him and the chair he was sitting in toward the kitchen. Mr. Tompkins sat helplessly by, securely tied. Shortly, he was in the kitchen adjacent to Johnny. Mad Dog moved to the couch and began to speak in a low voice.

"Boys, the time has come for the rubber to meet the road. If you all carry out your assignments, your patience will be rewarded. Jarvis, did you find the truck?"

Jarvis kind of smirked and rubbed one of his earrings. "Well, Boss, let's say we have a vehicle and leave it at that."

Mad Dog scrutinized Jarvis and then moved on. "As long as we can get old man Tompkins and the rest of us to the farmhouse, you can spare me the details. Tommy, you got the explosives. You remember what the signal will be?"

Tommy nodded his head. "No problem, Boss. When I'm through, nothing will be left of this joint."

Tommy resembled a Marine gone rogue. You could say he played at being the Terminator all year long. Whereas Jarvis looked pretty tough, Tommy just looked mean and crazy. To be honest, Mad Dog figured Tommy could blow at any time.

"You just make sure to not dilly dally around after you light the fuses. It will be up to you to get down the tunnel on your own. Got it?" Mad Dog said emphatically.

"Okay, then," he continued. "Jarvis, you will drive the rest of us up to the farmhouse, where I will deliver Tompkins as asked. The professor will meet us there with the girl. We'll get the rest of our instructions there."

After a few parting words, Skippy and Jarvis retrieved Mr. Tompkins, and they all high-fived each other before splitting up. Had Johnny and Mr. Tompkins not been gagged, they could have had a nice conversation about how each got to the hideout. Instead, all Johnny could do was look at Mr. Tompkins and wonder how they each got themselves into such a pickle. Johnny was not stupid. He knew it likely was the last he would see of the gang. Tommy Bolton was there to use the dynamite he saw earlier. He had no doubt of it. Tears welled up in his eyes, as he could see no way out of his situation. *No one should die without getting to say goodbye to his friends*, he thought. Johnny offered a silent prayer. He could only hope angels were listening.

*   *   *   *   *   *   *

Dr. Winston McDougal put the phone down and reflected on how Madame Fortune had smiled down on him. Only a few hours ago, things looked very bleak. Years of preparation and hard work seemed about to go up in flames. And irony of all irony, Thaddeus Tompkins delivered himself into the gang's hands. The professor could only shake his head and grin. He now held all of the cards. Next, it was just a matter of executing the plan.

"Wake up, Miss Quig. It is time to leave," he announced.

Emily roused herself and tried to shake off her hazy condition. It was time for her to muster what courage she could. This meant playing her role and not giving Dr. McDougal any hint of her betrayal. What the professor did not know was when Emily had called her roommate, Doris, she had built in some predetermined code words. Use of those words told Doris that she was indeed in trouble but not to act immediately. Though Emily had never considered the professor would use her parents as a bargaining chip, she had foreseen that Dr. McDougal might have something up his sleeve to deter her from bailing out on their agreement.

Dr. McDougal came over to her and placed his two forefingers under her chin. Looking her in the eyes, he said, "We are at a critical phase, Miss Quig. You must follow every direction that flows from my lips."

After giving her pause to nod in the affirmative, the professor continued.

"It is probable we are being watched as we speak. My car is in the east lot. Detective Shaw is a bright man. We cannot leave unnoticed. So, it should not surprise you I have an alternative departure in mind."

Emily tried not to be too curious. Dr. McDougal then moved to a small closet on the far side of his office (it was a miracle he could get to it). Speaking as he opened its door, he shared, "I am going to adjust my wardrobe, and we will leave out the north door of this building to an awaiting pizza truck. In that it is Saturday and late in the day, I doubt we will be meeting many students. That being said, Miss Quig, you will not engage in conversation with anyone."

Dr. McDougal then covered his large frame with a flowered dress, that in some quarters may have been mistaken for a tablecloth. He covered his head with a dark brown wig and then donned a small hat holding a tiny flower. No one could accuse the professor of mirroring an attractive woman. When he turned to Emily, she let out a shriek.

"Calm yourself, Miss Quig. I will be back to my normal, charming self in a short time," he purred.

Dr. McDougal surveyed his office before they left. Yes, there were parts of his academic life he would miss. To leave his library was difficult. Once he walked down the third-floor corridor, there was no looking back. However, he had had this discussion with himself many times before. The professor would not miss the department politics nor the teaching load. He found most of the university students undeserving of his intellect. There was much of the last five years of his life he felt wasted. Procuring the ruby would heal a lot of wounds. Dr. McDougal was ready to be the master of his own destiny.

As Emily and the professor slowly walked from one end of the building to another, their eyes were fixed on the stairwell ahead. They did not see peeking out from behind the ladies' room door a young lady with long black hair and a narrow face. Doris Guice had correctly interpreted the coded message and moved quickly to spy on the professor's office. She had been patiently waiting a long time. Finally, she saw Emily, and in contrast, an overwhelming female figure moving toward her. Doris did not know what to make of them. Emily, in roomy sweats, exhibited a zombie-like appearance. The woman was focused, and there was no conversation between them. Doris waited until they had passed and begun to descend the stairwell. She then moved swiftly to Dr. McDougal's office door. It was locked, and Doris could hear no noises inside.

Presuming it was vacant, Doris made tracks to the stairwell. Cautiously reaching the second-floor entrance, she peered out an oval window to observe Emily and her companion entering a Joe's Pizza truck. Though Doris was not yet sure who the woman was, the entire scene was plain weird. If Emily were in danger, she knew she had to act quickly. But whom to contact? The campus police, Emily's mother, the FBI? Doris paused a moment to collect her thoughts. She could also get ahold of her boyfriend, Daryl, and they could follow the pizza truck in his modified VW. Doris decided on the last option and dashed away to her dorm room.

A Partial Reunion

As you might expect, there was a range of emotion exhibited by the museum's occupants as they rushed out on the porch. Standing before them was the imposing figure of Tom Barlow with each of his large farmer hands resting on a shoulder of Heather and Jeremy. The two junior detectives still presented a rather ragged look. Even though they had managed to dislodge the burrs, twigs, and leaves from themselves, their torn clothing, unkempt hair, and numerous scratches were very evident.

"Oh, my god," exclaimed Melody Stippich, her small hands covering her cheeks. After the initial shock, she and Bill slowly ran forward toward their damaged daughter.

Heather could only stand with outstretched arms, tears streaming down her face. Jeremy did not have much time to react before Frank and Mary Murkowski were covering him with hugs and kisses.

"Mom, Dad, you're smothering me," he gasped.

Mary was too busy crying to say much, but Frank was heard to utter, "Thank God you're safe."

Chief Olsen, Detective Shaw, and Officer Kraus were each relieved at this unexpected development. They tactfully gave the families room to reacquaint themselves. Herb could be seen wiping a tear from his eye. Sam Shaw's face carried a faint smile, and the chief kept clapping his hands in a punctuated manner to express approval.

Not so elated at the scene before them were Ben and Jenny Turnbow. Though they refrained from interrupting the reunion, Jenny could be seen saying quietly, "But where is Johnny? Where's my Johnny?" Ben's lip was quivering slightly as he wrapped his arm around Jenny's shoulder.

Chief Olsen stepped forward. "Folks, I know you are happy to have your kids safe and sound, but where is Johnny?"

The Stippiches and Murkowskis turned and gathered themselves. Melody Stippich then faced Heather, and while stroking her hair, she asked, "Yes, dear, do you or Jeremy know where Johnny is?"

For a moment, no one spoke, and it was as if the whole world waited for an answer. Though the museum itself could not answer the question, the edifice seemed to let out a sigh, but to the uninitiated, it was a small breeze coming from the woods.

After what seemed an eternity, Heather tried to respond. "We don't…we just don't know," she sputtered. "The last we saw of Johnny was when he was pushed into the basement."

Everyone looked at each other, but Detective Shaw rose to the occasion to rescue an awkward situation. "Let's not stand outside," he encouraged. "Come, everyone; let's go inside to take some refreshment and get these children fed." Looking toward Mr. Barlow, he added, "Sir, you are welcome to join us. I did not catch your name."

"Well, I did not have an opportunity to offer it," chuckled Tom. Moving toward Detective Shaw, he held out his hand and said, "You'll likely be wanting a statement from me."

Chief Olsen and Officer Kraus shepherded the group into the museum, and everyone found a seat in the local history room. Poor Jenny Turnbow was beside herself and could not speak. The other parents restrained their elation out of respect for the Turnbow's disconcertion. Ben Turnbow stood beside his wife and listened attentively as Heather and Jeremy told their story.

"Have to be honest, everyone. We figured we were goners. The guy who kidnapped us was beyond scary. It was like he stepped out of a World Wrestling Federation video," remarked Jeremy.

Heather nodded. "We tried to resist, but he dragged us across the grass to his truck." The parents all winced.

"But how did you manage to escape?" questioned Mary Murkowski.

Heather and Jeremy gave each other a glance as if to say, "Do you want to tell them?" Finally, Jeremy started.

"The man parked his truck off of some highway. We walked a bit past a field. When we stopped, some guys came out of the ground and seemed really anxious to see our kidnapper. That's when we bolted."

"I've never run so fast in my entire life," Heather said with emphasis. "Mom, I am so grateful you got me involved in swimming early on. Without the conditioning it has brought me, I am not sure I could have made it far enough before running out of steam."

"You reached some woods then, am I right?" asked Chief Olsen.

"Yup," they both replied.

Jeremy went on. "I think because it was dark and rainy, we were able to get away. Plus, they seemed to be arguing as we fled. I don't think they were happy with our captor."

Officer Kraus, who had left the room, returned with some county highway maps. He laid them out on the floor of the room. "Best I can figure is that the kidnapper had to have driven north on Highway 12. There are a lot of woods on the west side of the highway, practically all the way to Bensonville. I say we get some dogs and start checking out some possible stopping points. Perhaps the kids could help us."

That suggestion received a prompt, "Over my dead body!" from Frank Murkowski. He stood up when he said it, his face shaking.

Detective Shaw intervened. "The sun will be setting in a few hours. Skies have pretty much cleared, but it will be a tough search at night. And we should probably continue staking out the museum."

"I'll go," exclaimed Ben Turnbow. "We've got a son still missing. Time is precious." Jenny squeezed his hand.

It was then Chief Olsen's turn to stand up. "We have enough to do both, I think. Herb, why don't you and Mr. Turnbow arrange to meet the Shiloh County officers at the Sinclair station halfway to Bensonville. Try to determine where the truck may have left the road. Report back on the half hour."

Continuing, the chief added, "Sam, have you heard anything from your man at the college?"

Detective Shaw shook his head in the negative. Chief Olsen stroked his chin, perplexed. Mr. Tompkins had disappeared. Dr. McDougal had not made his move (if he had one to make). Johnny was still missing.

Yvetlana was nowhere to be found. There was a gang out there plotting something. Maybe it was time to bring in the feds.

In the end, it was decided to let Heather and Jeremy go home to get cleaned up and rest. Their parents were all too willing to take them. Detective Shaw and Chief Olsen would spend Saturday night at the museum. Officer Kraus and Ben Turnbow would search the countryside—all night, if necessary—with the help of other law enforcement. Chief Olsen also made one call. He managed to track down his sister, Hazel, and have her man the phones at the police station in case of any unexpected calls. George Kostov was to be stationed near the Smothers house in case Yveltana (or any of her sons) returned. That seemed the best they could do with the information they had.

It was going on 3:00 p.m. There was much to do before the sun went down. There was no time to waste.

*   *   *   *   *   *   *

There were some advantages to being on the school's women's track team. Doris covered the distance between Bluffton Hall and the Student Union in record time. It was a matter of crossing the quad and making a hard left. That is where her boyfriend, Daryl, worked on Saturday afternoons; he manned the information desk.

"Daryl," she gasped. "You have to leave now. It's an emergency!"

Daryl did not respond immediately. He had never seen Doris so anguished. Daryl had known Doris since high school, though they were not an item until the summer after graduation. They became good friends by working at the same camp for disadvantaged children in Brown County.

Whereas Daryl could be a little high strung, Doris was the epidemy of calm. Though Daryl was not actually done until 5:00 p.m., he did not see where leaving ten minutes early would be a big deal.

"Hey, Joey!" Daryl shouted to a passing frat brother. "Be a good boy and sit here for ten minutes. I gotta run!"

Then they were off. Daryl Rasmussen and Doris Guice both were around 5'8" tall, and thin, and they were both on the track teams.

"Where is your car parked?" Doris asked.

"Behind the Union. I drove to work," Daryl responded.

Daryl had no time to ask questions as Doris took off running to the parking lot. His powder blue Volkswagen showed spots of rust that he was trying to remove. It stood out easily from the rest of the cars in the lot, but it being Saturday afternoon, the lot was only half full, anyway.

While Daryl fumbled for his keys, Doris yelled out, "Go, go! This could be a matter of life and death!"

Daryl spun the VW out of the lot. "Where to?" he asked.

"Drive to the north side of Bluffton Hall," Doris instructed. "We are looking for a Joe's Pizza truck. We should be able to catch up with it. I think they have just a few minutes' head start."

As they drove, Doris filled Daryl in on Emily's predicament. Doris did not have a lot of specifics, but she knew her roomie was in trouble.

"You know, I told Emily to avoid that Principles of Archaeology class," stated Doris, her arms gesticulating. "Those anthro professors are all weird."

"But you said she left with an elderly woman," noted Daryl, just a bit confused.

"Yes, that was too curious. Are you at all familiar with Professor McDougal?" continued Doris.

Daryl was a sophomore and a declared political science major. He'd had a class last term in Bluffton Hall. "Only saw him once at a retirement luncheon for Dr. Jones last April. Rather large man with heavy eyebrows and a strange smile."

"That could match up," Doris mused. "But why would Dr. McDougal be in drag? Why a disguise?"

Before Daryl could offer a response, they spotted the pizza truck getting gas at the Shell station just off campus.

"Pull over and park, Daryl, but not too close…did I tell you what an angel you are to help out on short notice?" Doris flashed one of her endearing smiles that reminded Daryl why he was smitten with her.

The driver pumping the gas was a pizza delivery guy they recognized, though they did not know him by name. It was hard to make out who was in the front passenger seat. The good news was the truck was in their sights.

Daryl and Doris wondered where the truck would head next. The campus was bordered by two north-south streets, McGregor on the west and Lewis on the east. Running right through it was Allen Boulevard. The truck had headed out on McGregor, and the gas station was on the corner adjacent to Maple Street. If the driver stayed north on McGregor Street, he would come to Highway 12. Going left took one to Webster; going right took one to Junction City.

The pizza truck, once filled with gas, did head north on McGregor and turned left at the light. Daryl had to buzz through a yellow light to stay close. When the truck did not turn off on Stewart Drive nor State Road 131, it became obvious this was not to be a normal pizza delivery.

"I'll bet he is heading to Webster," predicted Doris.

Everything was going fine until five miles down the highway when the pizza truck turned abruptly onto a dirt road. Daryl tried to stop but missed the turnoff. By the time he could turn around and get on the truck's trail again, it had disappeared.

"Crap!" exclaimed Doris. She dropped her face into her hands. After a minute, Doris raised her head and gave Daryl a thoughtful stare. "Time to get to Webster and report all this to the police."

Daryl needed no further direction, and he soon was speeding down Highway 12. Really didn't matter if the cops pulled him over or not. The couple was looking for them, anyway.

*   *   *   *   *   *   *

Dr. McDougal was not happy they had to stop for gas. He was anxious to get out of Bradford as soon as possible. He became less happy when Marvin, the pizza truck driver, turned to him and said, "Doc, I think we are being followed."

The professor looked out his rear-view mirror.

"See that blue VW bug two cars behind us? He was behind us when we left the gas station. When I have slowed down, he has refused to pass me," Marvin explained. Marvin was known to have excellent observational skills, which Dr. McDougal valued.

"Okay, we'll move to our discussed alternate route, Marvin," instructed the professor.

Marvin understood that to be a dirt road a mile or so ahead. It cut over a hill and linked up with W 600 S, which led back to Highway 12, but much farther down the road.

Dr. McDougal could not be sure if the driver of the VW were one of Detective Shaw's associates or not. But he would take no chances. Since the link up at the farm was not scheduled until 7 p.m., he had some wiggle room. They would cool it for an hour and then head through Webster.

"Marvin, how much more do I need to compensate you for removing the pizza logo from the side of your van?" the professor asked.

Marvin exhibited a silly grin and then answered, "Oh, throw in a couple hundred more clams, and I think I could be persuaded to take on a new identity." Then he and the professor each laughed.

"Miss Quig, you are welcome to stretch your legs if you would like. Marvin has some maintenance to accomplish. But do not get any strange ideas of leaving us. It could affect your parent's health," the professor reminded Emily.

Dr. McDougal and Emily Quig then found a large oak tree to sit down next to. "This could actually prove beneficial, Miss Quig. It will give us a chance to review your role in the recovery of the wooden leg. Why don't you share with me what you will do once we get to the museum."

Emily swallowed hard. If she came out of this escapade in one piece, she was going to go live with her aunt in Chicago. "Once the coast is clear, I and a couple of your hired hands will proceed to the information desk. We will then proceed up the stairs to the glass case. I am to squeeze myself into the space between the case and wall. Then I insert this key (she held it up) into the sliding door lock and open the glass panel in front of me. I then reach in and pull out a wooden leg. I extend it out until one of the men can grab it. After that, I re-lock the glass panel and extricate myself from behind the case." Emily recited all of the instructions in monotone.

"Excellent, Miss Quig," Dr. McDougal said ecstatically.

Turning toward the professor and looking him straight in the eye, she asked, "Why don't you just break the glass case and take the leg out from the front? Why all of this extra work?"

Dr. McDougal gave her a knowing smile and replied, "Ah, but you miss the entire point, dear Miss Quig. No one can see the wooden leg presently because of a hologram I installed a little while back. Mr. Tompkins, and anyone else paying attention, thinks it is missing. We do not want to do anything that would do away with that impression. Not to mention that there would be no reason for your employment. That would be a shame, would it not?"

At that point, he gave his best impression of a Cheshire cat right out of *Alice's Adventures in Wonderland*. Emily was correct; it was an elaborate scheme. Unfortunately, she now knew too much and would have to be dealt with. Well, first things first. Mr. Tompkins was at the head of the line.

Soon Marvin could be heard shouting, "All taken care of, Doc. Ready to roll if you are." Evening was beginning when the truck pulled into the farmstead's driveway. The car driven by Jarvis Bolton had arrived several minutes before. All the pieces were in place for a most interesting evening.

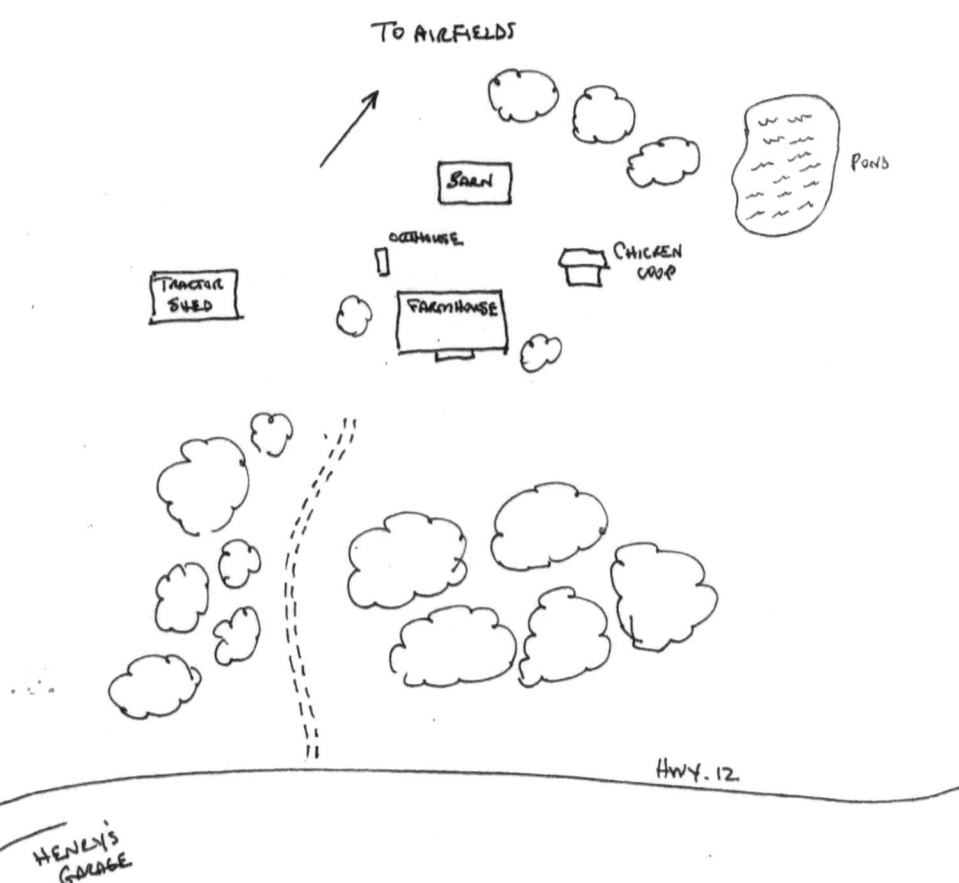

Exploding Developments

Marvin slowly pulled the pizza van onto the dirt road leading up to the farmhouse. Dr. McDougal held up his hand, and Marvin brought the vehicle to a halt.

"Marvin, be a good man," petitioned the professor, "and give this note to that short hairy individual standing on the porch." Simultaneously, he pointed to Mad Dog Scrima.

Mad Dog had gathered his team on the farmhouse's front porch. As it got closer to 7:00 p.m., they collectively focused on the highway with a mixture of emotions. Mad Dog himself, though not easily intimidated, was slightly anxious about meeting his employer. When he contracted to do the job, Mad Dog had not figured it would get so complicated. Had the key and the museum curator not suddenly fallen into their hands, the impending meeting could have taken on an entirely different flavor. Now, Mad Dog could only hope to finish the entire affair. While the remuneration was substantial, he feared the entire team was at personal risk if they failed. The boss would likely just as easily eliminate them as Mad Dog had Boris Smothers.

There was also the nagging question about what happened to the two kids who had escaped into the woods. At some point, Mad Dog assumed they would find their way back to Webster. It likely would not matter once Tommy Bolton lit the fuse, but it placed another variable into the leg recovery operation.

Skippy Forester kept removing his hat and scratching his head, as if perplexed. To be truthful, he had complete faith in Mad Dog. Over the years, they had been through many scrapes together. Even though they had never retrieved that pot of gold at the end of the rainbow, they had done well enough. Managed to eat and drink well most of the time. Yes, the prison time due to the botched bank job was indeed their low point, but Skippy was confident this heist was going to put them on easy street. It should be noted Skippy viewed life through a glass half-full.

Leaning on the porch rail that had seen better days, Jarvis was pleased with his Friday contributions. Not only had he salvaged the transportation arrangements to the farmhouse, but it also turned out his bludgeoning of the innocent passerby pleased Mad Dog. All Mad Dog would say to Jarvis was, "This young man's body may come in handy." The man still had a faint pulse but appeared to have gone into a coma. Maybe an added bonus for his "foresight"? Jarvis was never fond of the Smothers duo, and now with them out of the picture, there would be greater shares for the rest of them. So, the fact Jarvis had a cunning smile on his face was understandable.

Thaddeus Tompkins was not on the porch. He sat inside in what loosely could be called a living room. Mad Dog had dared him to try and escape. "Please give me a reason to kill you, you old fart," he had snarled. Actually, Mr. Tompkins was hoping he could negotiate his way out of his predicament.

Marvin carried the note to Mad Dog Scrima. Surveying the three men on the porch, Marvin thought to himself, *The Professor has outdone himself this time.*

After Mad Dog read the note's contents, he grinned. Turning to Skippy, he directed, "Escort Tompkins up to the back bedroom. Tie him securely to the bedpost. Then come down and assist Jarvis with taking our guest in the trunk also to the bedroom. You can lay him down on the bed. When you are finished, go take five in the machine shed while the boss and I make some preparations for the remainder of this evening."

Dr. McDougal waited patiently for his instructions to be carried out. He raised his eyebrows with surprise when he saw the prone body being carried from the car to the farmhouse. If he harbored any concern regarding the missing truck, Dr. McDougal did not show it. The professor had asked Mr. Scrima to provide a volunteer for the evening. He had no idea that a warm body had been stashed just to fulfill the assignment. This caused him to laugh out loud and Emily Quig to give him a look of foreboding. Emily was *so* anxious to get her role in this morbid affair over with.

Once Dr. McDougal was sure he was alone with Mr. Scrima, he told the pizza driver, "Pull the van around to the back of the farmhouse. There you will find a black Cadillac parked inside the barn. Position the van so it cannot be seen from the road. Keep your eye on the girl and await my further orders. And oh, yes, Marvin, your assistance has been more than appreciated." The Professor stared directly at Marvin, smiled, and winked. Marvin reciprocated with a smile. His payday was coming.

∗ ∗ ∗ ∗ ∗ ∗ ∗

Dr. McDougal had no desire to deal with anyone but Harvey Scrima. He had planned for his identity to be revealed to as few people as possible. The professor had no concern about Marvin nor Mr. St. George. They were trusted confidants. Each would play his role and keep his mouth shut. The gang was another matter. Mr. Tompkins and

Emily Quig…well, they would not be around to share their involvement with anyone.

Mad Dog did not know what to think of the man vacating the van. At first glance, it appeared the boss was a woman. But as Dr. McDougal drew closer to Mad Dog, he pulled off his wig. Mad Dog let out a sigh of relief.

"Concerned I was a member of the weaker sex, Mr. Scrima?" teased the professor.

Mad Dog gave a nod. "I have had little experience working with dames," he replied.

"Well, here I am," announced the professor, his arms outstretched. That provided Mad Dog with a full view of his immense frame. The professor wrapped his arm around Mad Dog's shoulders.

"Let's go pay Mr. Tompkins a visit, shall we? It is time we eliminate this curatorial thorn in our side," he said with some satisfaction.

Marvin drove off, and Dr. McDougal and Harvey Scrima entered the farmhouse. With the sun low in the sky, an eerie glow enveloped the entire farmyard. The two large oak trees abutting the farmhouse flickered their leaves, as if to warn all passersby to stay away. Shadows streamed across the grass, and two ground squirrels scurried underneath the front porch. A barn owl's lament could be heard in the distance. With the evening's participants all in their assigned places, a quiet dread pervaded the air. There are times when Mother Nature perceives the immediate future with uncanny accuracy. This was one of those moments.

As Mad Dog and the professor slowly mounted the stairs leading to the bedrooms, Thaddeus Tompkins sat tied to the bedpost, quivering. He knew he had to pull himself together. By now, his worst fears had been realized. Indeed, Dr. McDougal was the mastermind behind the wooden leg's theft. But there seemed to be a lot more to the whole affair than the perceptive Thaddeus had deduced. Could he negotiate his way out of this predicament?

At that moment, the door to the bedroom opened, and there, bigger than life, was the professor. The image of Mad Dog by his side filled Mr. Tompkins with foreboding.

"Professor, whatever little I know of this affair has not been shared with the police, I assure you," he said with all the confidence he could muster.

"Shhh," responded Dr. McDougal. "Thaddeus, your fixation on the wooden leg over the years has grown from modest irritation to irksome meddling. In fact," he continued, "you came oh-so-close to ruining all of my hard efforts." With that, Mr. Tompkins flinched.

"I do appreciate the fact you 'chose' to show up before Mr. Scrima, in a timely manner," acknowledged Dr. McDougal.

"And I know I can be of assistance to you," Mr. Tompkins said enthusiastically.

"More than you can imagine," snickered the professor. He then reached behind the curtain window and pulled out what appeared to be the wooden leg.

"You have it! You have it!" shrieked Mr. Tompkins.

"Not quite, Thaddeus," Dr. McDougal replied. "Not quite. However, you have improved my confidence that those who find it will think it is the real one. Of course, someone has to get credit for its theft, agreed, Thaddeus?" Dr. McDougal gave Mr. Tompkins a wicked smile.

Continuing, Dr. McDougal said, "When the authorities find it in damaged condition, they also will find you." He then turned and pointed to the body Mad Dog had concurrently pulled out from under the bed. "Of course, you had an accomplice. I can only imagine that the police will put their heads together and consider it a plan gone bad."

"What do you mean, 'damaged condition'?" asked Mr. Tompkins.

Dr. McDougal flipped his hand and answered, "It won't matter to you, Thaddeus. I have a surprise for you. I have decided to make your demise almost painless."

With that, Mr. Tompkins' eyes grew very wide. He watched Dr. McDougal pull a tied white bag from the purse he was using with his disguise. The professor moved over to the bed and held the bag up for Mr. Tompkins to see.

"Now watch closely, Thaddeus, and try to restrain your reaction." He turned to Mad Dog and motioned him over closer to where Mr. Tompkins was sitting.

In one fell swoop, Dr. McDougal loosened the bag and threw its contents into the air. Before Mr. Tompkins could muster more than a high-pitched squeak, his face found itself the recipient of a multicolored coral snake. The snake bit his forehead, and the implanted venom began to induce numbness. Mr. Tompkins tried to speak, but only a muffled, "No, no, no," was heard. Mad Dog lurched back as the snake slithered to safety under the bed. The gang leader was speechless.

Dr. McDougal proceeded to remove his dress and moved toward the clothes closet where he had a change of attire at hand. In a matter of minutes, he was once again himself in suit and tie.

"Mr. Scrima, this is now how we will proceed," the professor announced. "Lay Mr. Tompkins on the bed and move our other guest into the stuffed chair in the corner. Place this wooden leg at the foot of the bed. My watch tells me it is after 7:30 p.m. Gather your team and prepare to head toward the museum. Before you go, give the signal to your man at the hideout. As soon as you hear the explosion, hit the road. And I do not mean Highway 12." Dr. McDougal then winked at Mad Dog.

The professor was taking great delight in seeing the final stages of his plan unfold. Now to check on the plane.

*   *   *   *   *   *   *

Saturday night activity in downtown Webster was usually centered around the cinema near Birch and Main Streets, a small bar and grill that featured a country western band, and Phil's 76 gas station that stayed open until 9:00 p.m. Chief Olsen and Officer Kraus took turns working weekend evenings at the police station, but on this particular evening, it was just the chief's sister, Hazel Wendland, who sat at the desk to man the phone.

As Daryl came to a screeching halt in front of the police station, Doris leapt from the car and ran to the front door. She had no way of knowing the doors were locked after 6:00 p.m. Doris rattled the door handle, then pounded on the door. Daryl ran up from behind, read a sign on the door, and yelled, "Push the red button!"

After what seemed an eternity, a heavyset woman came limping up to the solid steel doors. Hazel peered out at the two and wondered what might have brought them to the station. She had been briefed by Chief Olsen to relay any incoming informational traffic to him immediately. So, against her better judgement (the girl was jumping up and down waving her hands), Hazel cracked the door and stated officiously, "The police officers are all out on a case. What do you need?"

Trying to contain her excitement, Doris replied, "We think we have been witnesses to a kidnapping. I am certain my roommate is in trouble!"

"It is really urgent we speak to a police officer," interjected Daryl.

"Well, you may as well come in, but I am not sure what I can do." Hazel did not mind answering the phones, but she was not prepared to handle any visitors. After escorting Daryl and Doris to the chief's office, Hazel pointed to two chairs. "Have a seat and give me some specifics."

Doris spoke a mile a minute, reviewing the events of the afternoon. Hazel had to ask her to slow down more than once. When Doris had finished, though, Hazel felt her story was suspicious enough that she should alert her brother. Getting on the police radio, Hazel began with the call sign, "Echo One, this is base calling. Echo One, do you read me?"

After a few moments, the radio crackled, and a voice could be heard. "This is Echo One. Come in, base."

"Hey, big brother, I got a couple of live ones here. Look like college kids. Claim they witnessed a kidnapping. Over," reported Hazel in her low voice.

Chief Olsen could be heard sighing on the other end. "Can you get a statement from them? My Form 6Bs are in the second drawer of the file cabinet under 'Pending Cases.'"

It was apparent Doris was getting more and more agitated. Daryl put his hand on her left shoulder and interrupted. "Ma'am, we don't mean to be disrespectful, but we don't have a lot of time to act. The kidnappers ditched us, and they need to be pursued *now*!"

Daryl shouted the last word and Hazel looked up, putting her hand over the receiver. Hazel silently stared directly at Daryl. Then she continued her conversation with the chief.

"Bernie, I'll complete the report, but couldn't you send Herb over with the squad car? This might require more immediate attention." Doris squeezed Daryl's hand and gave Hazel a weak smile.

Sounding exasperated, Chief Olsen blurted, "I'm up to my neck with that wooden leg case at the moment, Sis. Herb is out on the road trying to track down some kidnappers of our own. Johnny Turnbow is still missing, and now the museum curator has gone off and disappeared. Detective Shaw and I are stationed at the museum, as we expect something sinister to happen here tonight. Get some more details and get back to me! Echo One out."

Hazel just rolled her eyes. "Base out."

"Okay, you can see you have come at a bad time. Now you," she said, directing her finger at Daryl, "tell me again why the urgency, and keep your companion here from interrupting." Hazel shot Doris a 'Keep your mouth shut' look.

"Look," replied Daryl, "all I know is the pizza van gave us the slip and went off on a dirt road that was headed toward some woods." He paused a moment to gaze toward Doris. "I know she seems a little frazzled at the moment…(Doris frowned)…but she is pretty levelheaded. Really." Daryl added the last word for emphasis.

"If this professor was in drag, as she suspects, he took her roommate into a pizza van," he continued.

"Name of roommate?" asked Hazel.

"Emily Quig," Doris interjected. That caused Hazel to frown.

"Go on," Hazel directed.

"Emily had given Doris a code word to alert her if she was in trouble," Daryl went on.

"And why would Miss Quig be in trouble?" asked Hazel.

Doris jumped in. "May I explain, please? Daryl is not that acquainted with what has been going on."

Doris then explained that Emily had been working with Dr. McDougal, her Principles of Archaeology instructor, on a special project. Doris did not know all of the details, but she felt Emily may have gotten in over her head.

"Could the police at least put an alert out on this pizza van?" Doris pleaded. She then turned toward Daryl. "You got the license number, right, Daryl?"

Daryl scrambled around in his pockets and pulled out a scrap of paper.

"I did get part of it, at least," he replied. Daryl handed over the paper to Hazel.

Hazel read the numbers out loud, "YZ667…you seem to have one number missing."

Daryl nodded in agreement. "He sped off before I could make it out. It was either an eight or a nine, I think."

After Hazel pinned down a more exact location of where Doris and Daryl thought the van turned off, she got back on the police radio. "Echo Two, this is base calling. Echo Two, come in."

"Echo Two here, base. Come back to me." Hazel recognized Officer Kraus' high-pitched voice. "Herb, we got a possible 671 involving a pizza van with Indiana license YZ667 headed toward Bensonville from Webster. Where you at?"

"That you, Hazel? Well, I'll be darned. Chief did say he was going to ask you to come in. It's been a while. Glad to hear your voice," Officer Kraus said rather enthusiastically.

"Don't have time for the chitchat, Herb. Tell me exactly where you are right now," continued Hazel.

Officer Kraus pulled the squad car into a farmyard driveway and consulted his wrinkled Indiana roadmap. Ben Turnbow leaned over to see if he could help. Ben pointed his finger on the juncture of County Road A and Highway 12. Officer Kraus nodded.

"Hazel, I'd say we just passed County A about six miles out of Webster on Highway 12. We've been making periodic stops to check out possible exit points," Officer Kraus answered.

"Herb, these kids say the pizza van went off Highway 12 out of Bradford about four miles. Do you still carry the county plat map around with you?" queried Hazel.

"Yeah, I got it somewhere," he replied. Officer Kraus pointed to the glove box, and Mr. Turnbow started rifling through it. He finally found the multi-folded, ear-worn map underneath some Snickers wrappers. "Okay, we have it," Officer Kraus acknowledged.

"See if you can find a road that would connect back over to Highway 12," instructed Hazel. If there was one thing Hazel was good at, it was maps. An avid hiker as a girl, Hazel knew the tri-county area very well. She was acting on a hunch.

"From what I can tell, Hazel," reported Officer Kraus, "there are two possibilities—Edson Road and W 600 S."

"Wouldn't be Edson Road, Herb," noted Hazel. "Bridge went out a month ago. Won't get one to Highway 12. Has to be W 600 S. That is still south of Highway 12. It is possible the van these kids are referring to might be coming your way. Not to tell you how to do your job, but could you sit tight for a few minutes and keep a lookout?"

"Roger that, base. I'm turning around now. Will plant myself on Highway A behind the tree on the corner," said Officer Kraus dutifully. "Echo Two over and out."

The conversation over, Doris and Daryl headed over to the McDonald's for some supper. At 6:30 p.m., as the two college students sat down to their double cheeseburgers, the pizza van, now labeled "Ace Cleaners," was speeding out of Webster toward the farmhouse. Because Ben Turnbow and Officer Kraus were looking for a pizza van, when Dr. McDougal sped by in the modified vehicle, they only gave it passing notice. It did not help that Officer Kraus was regaling Ben with former investigative exploits. At 7:15 p.m., they decided to move back out to Highway 12.

A half hour later, Officer Kraus pulled into the Sinclair gas station.

At the museum, Chief Olsen and Detective Shaw were debating how the most recent kidnapping report might connect with events to date. At the Murkowski and Stippich households, Jeremy and Heather were already in their pajamas and preparing for bed after an exhausting day. Jenny Turnbow sat on her living room couch next to the phone, dabbing her eyes. George Kostov sat in his car just down the street from Mrs. Smothers' house, trying not to nod off. Mad Dog Scrima, his sidekick Skippy, Emily Quig, and Jarvis Bolton all sat in the yellow Corvette alongside the highway, waiting for the "big surprise."

The explosion was a tribute to the incendiary talents of Tommy Bolton. The noise was so loud that as it reverberated throughout the towns of Webster and Bensonville, anyone for miles around could hear it. The red and orange flames accompanied by hissing smoke rose high above the trees of Granger Woods. Birds took off from their arboreal hiding places for safety, and all kinds of forest animals could be seen fleeing to the surrounding fields. While the world stopped for a moment in suspended shock, Mad Dog grinned and slammed his foot on the accelerator.

A Dirty Business

As he drove west on Highway 67 back to his farm, Tom Barlow reflected on the events of the day. He thought about his kids; some were scattered around the country, and he didn't see his grandkids often enough. Heather and Jeremy reminded him of his granddaughter, Sara, and grandson, Franklin. Would a stranger have helped them in a similar situation? What was really doing a number on his brain, however, was the fact another kid was still missing. From what he could gather from Detective Shaw, there was a boy named Johnny who had accompanied Heather and Jeremy to the museum. That fact he fell into the museum's basement and had not been heard from since was more than strange. If his two sidekicks had been abducted into the countryside, was there the possibility this Johnny was at the same destination?

If anyone knew Granger's Woods, it was farmer Barlow. The eighty acres he managed had been his father's (and his grandfather's before that). Corn crops had transitioned into soybeans, but the farmland contiguous to the woods had always been Tom's world. Whether it was hunting deer, ducks, and rabbits or fishing in the small pond in the southwest corner of the property, Tom Barlow loved the outdoors. On Sunday afternoons when his dad was napping, Tom would hike off into the woods with his brother Isaac to see what they could find. As a result, there was little of the woods he had not traversed adjacent to the farm.

It was near suppertime when Tom pulled into the circular dirt driveway near his farmhouse. He moved out of his truck and walked around to the west side of the house. With hands on his hips, he stood and gazed out over the field in the direction of where the kids had come from. Tom scratched his head and scrutinized the woods. It probably would not take much to determine where Heather and Jeremy had exited. Tom then turned his head to the declining sun. With a little determination, he just might be able to reach the other side of woods before sunset.

"Pappa, you gonna come in for supper or just stand out there contemplating life?" questioned Irma.

"Do me a favor, Ma, and keep my meal warm. I'm going to look in the woods a bit," Tom replied.

Irma rolled her eyes. "You want your gun?"

Tom nodded his head. "Yes."

Irma retrieved the 10-gauge shotgun from the closet. Handing it to her husband, she asked, "You want Bobby and Arnie to join you?" She had surmised something out of the ordinary was going on. Two of their sons lived a short way away, farming the acreage to the south on the other side of Highway 67.

"Best call them over, Mother. I'll give them a few minutes, and then I am heading out," Tom responded.

It did not take long for the trio to unite and head toward the woods. The ground was still moist from Friday night's rain. Bobby and Arnie were as tall as their father and had strapping figures. From a distance, the three appeared as mythological heroes on their way to yet another quest (even if they each wore bib overalls).

Granger's Woods was a mixed forest. The pine trees, which grew quickly, greeted all visitors entering the woods. Dead branches littered the forest floor, and the Barlows surveyed the surroundings to see if they could identify any freshly broken branches. It did not take long before Bobby reached up and pulled down a disturbed limb from a red oak tree.

"Dad, someone or some animal has been here recently," he announced. "The fact this small branch is broken outward suggests whatever it was came from inside the forest."

Tom and Arnie agreed with him. "Looks like the urchins came stumbling out to our field right about here," remarked Tom. "In fact, their trail appears pretty obvious."

The Barlows were all good trackers, and they made decent progress moving farther into the forest. It was not long before they came to the glade where Heather and Jeremy had rested. Puddles of standing water surrounded a fallen log.

"Boys, take a seat for a moment," directed Tom. "This might be a dangerous mission we're on. Those kids were running away from some dangerous dudes. Not sure what we will find on the other side of the forest. If you want to return home, I won't hold it against you."

Bobby and Arnie kind of smirked. Like they'd ever run away from trouble before. Arnie stood up and put his arm around his father's shoulder.

"Now, Pops, you wouldn't be trying to cut us out of all the fun, would you?"

Tom replied, "Yeah, I know we have been through some scrapes together before, but there is something sinister going on here."

Tom then shared with his sons what he was able to garnish from the conversations he'd had at the museum and his talk with Detective Shaw. People and the wooden leg had both disappeared. He did not think it was a matter of a simple theft. Professional thieves were involved. Kidnapping kids, and perhaps others, was in play. If the youth's abductor indeed took them to a meeting place near Granger's Woods, they could find several other ruffians there. Tom did not think any potential gang members would be happy to see them.

"Well, Dad, we are armed, and we know how to use these shotguns. Plus, we have the element of surprise," offered Bobby.

"Both Bobby and I have worked part-time security before," added Arnie. "It's not as if we have never had to deal with bad guys."

Tom looked down on the ground and clenched his teeth. "I know that, but these could be real hoodlums." After a pause, he looked his sons straight in the eyes and said, "Okay, then. But let's be careful and smart. Bobby, you take my left flank, and Arnie, you take my right. Let's move slowly and try not to create a racket."

*　*　*　*　*　*　*

The Stippich and Murkowski families had the same reaction to the explosion; they collectively ran out onto their porches and looked into the western sky. The air in the distance was a reddish-orange smoky haze as plumes of fiery debris hung above the trees. With mouths agape, they could only wonder about the source of the conflagration.

Heather and Jeremy flew out of their bedrooms, simultaneously recognizing that the location of the blast had to be around the same area where they'd escaped their captors. Instinctively, they also had the same thought: *Johnny is in danger.*

Heather tugged on her mother's arm. "Mom, I think I know where Johnny went. I think he's been hurt!"

Bill and Melody Stippich gave each other worried glances.

"Do you think it has something to do with that explosion?" asked Bill.

"Daddy, that is in the same direction that Jeremy and I escaped from!" Heather exclaimed. "Now that I think about it, I can remember some other men coming out of the ground—like from an underground chamber."

Heather began to pace back and forth. "If Johnny had been taken there, too…" she thought aloud to herself, "…if he were a prisoner." With that, she became more agitated.

Grabbing her parents' arms, she began to pull them toward their garage. "Hurry, we have to go!" Heather shouted.

"Whoa, whoa," replied her father. "And where we would be going? It's already getting dark."

"We can't just sit here," bemoaned Heather. "Johnny could be dead by now!" With that, she collapsed on their fenced porch and started to sob.

Both Bill and Melody pulled her up.

"Well, I tell you what we can do," offered Bill. "Let's head over to the museum and see how Chief Olsen is responding."

With resignation, Heather followed her parents to their car and accepted the hoodie her mother had grabbed for her. After all she had been through, the initial elation of having been rescued from almost certain disaster was now turning to dread that on this Saturday, she may have lost a very good friend.

* * * * * * *

Frank Murkowski was more of a man of action. As he looked at his son's expression, he dragged his hand across his closely cropped hair and asked, "Jeremy, is what we are seeing near where you and Heather were taken?"

Jeremy nodded his head in the affirmative. Frank, unlike Bill Stippich, knew the county very well and was already determining in his mind which roads would take him and Jeremy close to the source of the explosion.

Knowing in advance the reaction he might get, Frank announced, "Mary, Jeremy and I are going to check things out."

Mary gasped, and her hand flew over her mouth. Hans and Katie started jumping up and down. "Can we go, too, Daddy?" they exclaimed.

Buddy stepped in as the oldest and noted, "No, guys, this is something Dad and Jeremy have to do." Jeremy almost fell over in shock, as Buddy rarely came to his defense. Buddy then grabbed his mom's waist and whispered in her ear, "It will be alright. Dad has a plan."

"Jeremy," directed Frank, "go get a coat and some gloves. I don't want you getting cold. Besides, you can sleep on the way." Frank then went to their one-car garage, retrieved his hunting rifle, and picked up some extra ammunition.

Jeremy was out of the house in a flash, and it was not long before the Dodge truck was headed west out of town on Highway 67.

* * * * * * *

Chief Olsen and Detective Shaw strode out to the entrance of the museum at the sound of explosion and strained to see its source. Not happy with their view of things, they ran up to the second floor and into the board room. They threw up the west-facing window.

"Foul play at work, Sam," the chief said softly.

"You want me to link up with Herb and take charge of the investigation?" Detective Shaw knew from past experience how excitable Officer Kraus could get.

"You read my mind, Sam," replied the chief. "Put together a task force in conjunction with the Shiloh County officers. Why do I have this bad taste in my mouth that this entire case will end badly?"

Sam Shaw could only offer a meek smile. In his own mind, he perceived the explosion as somebody covering their tracks. The frustrating part to Detective Shaw was he and the other authorities seemed to continually be a day late and a dollar short. So, what would be the next step? If he were coordinating the actions of a bunch of professional thieves, what would be their escape route? Yet, in the back of his mind, he could not help but think there was some unfinished business to take place at the museum.

"Chief," Sam suggested, "I think you should stay at the museum. You've got Hazel at headquarters. Summon George to hightail it up here. We can stay in contact through our radios."

"I tend to agree with you, Sam, but we are going to have every fire station within fifty miles wanting to know what is going on. I've got to handle all the traffic, and I cannot do that with one radio from here," countered the chief.

"Well, at least get George up here, then," Detective Shaw said with some exasperation. "And what about your new deputies? Get Frank Murkowsi and Bill Stippich back over here."

As Detective Shaw readied to leave, up pulled Mr. and Mrs. Stippich.

Bill stepped out of his green Oldsmobile Delta 88 and opened the door for his wife. Heather bounded up to the museum's entrance. She singled out Chief Olsen.

"Chief Olsen, I am so afraid that Johnny was near that explosion," she gasped. "We have to get there immediately!" Tugging on his arm, she added, "Can we take your squad car?"

The chief put his hand on Heather's shoulder. "Detective Shaw was just leaving and will link up with Officer Kraus and Mr. Turnbow to check things out."

Heather looked back at her parents and then to the chief and Detective Shaw. "Can I please go, too? The waiting will kill me. I have to know if Johnny is okay."

Bill Stippich nodded his head in approval. Chief Olsen and Detective Shaw stared at each other. Detective Shaw broke the silence.

"I don't see any harm, Chief. Heather could help with locating the hideout." Sam did not add that he now wondered if any hideout still existed.

"Okay, then. Off with you," directed Chief Olsen. He then turned to Mr. Stippich. "Bill, you think you could handle things here at the museum with George while I head back to the office to coordinate the investigation?"

Melody Stippich grabbed her husband's arm and said, "You do that, and I'll head over to Turnbow's to stay with Jenny. She will definitely need some comforting at this point."

So, with things decided, Bill moved inside the museum, and Chief Olsen headed to his office. The sun had set, so any discoveries relating to the case and Johnny's safety would have to be made at night.

*   *   *   *   *   *   *

Officer Kraus and Ben Turnbow were standing in front of the Sinclair station, conversing with Officers Sheridan and Plank of the Shiloh County police force. In stark contrast to Herb's thin profile, the two men were in great physical shape, both about 5' 10". Officer Plank wore his hair short, and his face seemed a little small for his body. Officer Sheridan had brown, wavy hair, and aviator sunglasses highlighted his tan Grecian features. The explosion sent a shockwave through their startled bodies.

The only thing they could say in response was, "Oh, my god."

Without any discussion, the officers leapt into their respective squad cars and flew off down Highway 12 with sirens and flashing lights ablaze. When they neared Henry's abandoned garage, both cars pulled off the highway. They could not believe their eyes. The south side of the garage was plastered with dirt, and the immediate foreground was littered with branches and rocks. Even from a distance, the men could make out a large crater adjacent to Granger's Woods. A path of littered trees pointed toward the site of the calamity.

Officer Krause turned to Officers Sheridan and Plank and asked, "You got anything like a shovel in your trunk?"

Looking around, Officer Sheridan replied, "No, but it appears there are some tools over beside the garage."

Officer Sheridan then proceeded to retrieve a shovel resting on the ground in front of what was once a service bay. As he got closer, Officer Sheridan stopped abruptly. Pointing to his left, he exclaimed, "Gentleman, there appears to be some tracks ahead."

The group strode up to the former parking spot of the yellow Chevy that Jarvis Bolton had camouflaged from view. It was obvious to all of them that the tracks were fresh.

"Let's take a cast of these tire tracks, Gus," said Officer Plank to his companion. "I'd guess the car that was here was a small sedan."

Doing a reconnaissance of the garage's periphery, it appeared they could discern further tracks, though fainter, headed toward the woods behind the garage. Officer Kraus took an officious stance and addressed the group. "I think this discovery warrants a look inside."

Quickly, they noticed blood on the floor next to the counter. "It has not been here that long," offered Ben Turnbow. "The blood is still bright, though dried."

Ben and the officers squatted down to get a closer look. They could not be sure, but based on the way dust had been scattered, a body might have lain on the cracked tile surface.

"I think we should call in some backup," announced Officer Kraus.

Before he could say much more, Herb heard the mobile phone go off in his car. He swiftly went to retrieve the call.

"Echo Two here…yeah…okay, got it. When can you be here? We pulled off at the old Henry's Auto Body. I'll send Officers Sheridan and Plank to look ahead while we wait for you. Light is about gone. Make sure you have the search lamp."

Officer Kraus reported back to the group. Detective Shaw and Heather Stippich were heading their way. Detective Shaw would be taking over the investigation. "Gus and Frankie, why don't you proceed to check out that big hole out there? See if you can find any evidence of survivors or victims. Mr. Turnbow and I will wait for the detective. Take a flare with you and shoot it up if you find something."

Officers Sheridan and Plank could not imagine anything human surviving such an explosion. It was not a long walk, though they had to dodge rocks of all sizes, not to mention the multitude of tree branches. Piles of dirt were strewn in every direction, giving the impression of a prairie dog convention gone bad. Coming up to the huge cavern in the ground, they could make out a few pieces of furniture thrown here and there. Without more light, the officers could not find evidence of any bodies.

Gus Sheridan commented, "Whoever it was that set this off did not skimp on the explosives."

They began to turn back when they heard a shout. "Hey, over here! We have men down. Please hurry!"

The Beginnings of a Rescue

No one ever accused Skippy Forrester of being a man of great intellect. In fact, he was a bit of a Pollyanna, always figuring that if you could just turn the corner, things would turn out alright. He was a sinner without guile, a criminal without contempt. Skippy never looked at what he did as breaking the law so much as just getting a piece of the pie. Harvey Scrima knew this and never assigned Skippy to the sinister aspects of any job they undertook.

But now, even Skippy was beginning to see some holes in the plan to abscond with the wooden leg. The more he thought about the evening ahead, the more questions he had. As Mad Dog took several back roads (some of which only qualified as trails), Skippy was piling up questions in his head. Finally, one slipped out.

"Harvey, I've been thinking, and something doesn't make sense," he blurted out.

"Be careful what you say, my friend," responded Mad Dog. "Little pitchers have big ears."

Mad Dog was referring to Miss Quig and Jarvis Bolton sitting in the backseat of the Corvette.

Skippy pressed on. "Why are we going to all the trouble of retrieving the leg and then heading down the tunnel to the hideout that has been blown up and surely attracted a lot of attention? We do have to get back to the farmhouse, right?"

Mad Dog let out a big sigh. He felt bad that he had sworn to the professor that he would not share the details of the heist with any of the gang members until it became absolutely necessary (and then only on a need-to-know basis).

"Skippy," Mad Dog replied in a whisper, "we will not exactly be going back to the former hideout. Rest assured, we will meet up again at the farmhouse. Leave the details to me. You just keep being my right-hand man, okay, buddy? Things will make sense to you real soon."

Skippy slid down in the front passenger seat and gave Mad Dog a whimsical smile. He moved his fisherman's hat over his eyes and decided to concentrate on what he would do with his share of the loot.

Dr. McDougal had banked on Chief Olsen mobilizing his forces and sending them all to the site of the explosion. If anyone were at the museum when the team arrived, he figured it would only be a skeleton force—one easily overcome. He did expect there would be a lot of traffic on Highway 12 as the local citizenry tried to satisfy their curiosity. As a result, he deliberately had Mr. Scrima take a roundabout route to the vicinity of the museum. Under the cover of darkness, he had no doubt the team could carry out its mission.

Though the theft itself was not bothersome, there were three hurdles to the evening's agenda that concerned him. For one, the explosives expert (a.k.a. Tommy Bolton), after triggering the explosion, was to backtrack about halfway to the tunnel's entrance. There, he was to locate what looked like a manhole cover in the earthen ceiling. Removing the cover would allow the team to escape on the east side of Granger's Woods. It was critical the cover be found.

For another, they would not return to reunite with the car. Instead, everyone except Miss Quig would mount up on three saddled horses that were explicitly placed in an adjoining field. There was a small creek that flowed underneath a bridge on Highway 12 that they would follow until it was safe to head northwest to the farmhouse. Everything was ready, but Dr. McDougal was aware that Mr. Scrima was not fond of riding horses.[†] Speed was of the essence. Horses were absolutely necessary. He needed Mr. Scrima to suck it up and ride.

Finally, there was also the matter of disposing of Miss Quig. The professor liked Jarvis Bolton. He had style. How he'd handled acquiring a vehicle to transport everyone to the farmhouse was pure genius. Maybe the professor would retain Mr. Bolton's services after all. Therefore, the professor had entrusted Mr. Bolton with a syringe to drug Miss Quig. Unknown to Jarvis, she was not to wake up. Hopefully, this surprise insertion into the getaway would not upset Mr. Scrima.

Of course, Dr. McDougal had not dealt with Jarvis directly. But this time, the assignment went through Mr. Fish, his driver. By midnight, he intended to be on a plane to Canada. Yes, the professor realized that there would be cops up and down Highway 12 all night. Yes, he knew there would be roadblocks. Still, a dark, old abandoned farmhouse tucked away off the road should not be the focus of anyone's attention. He was counting on it.

*   *   *   *   *   *   *

[†] *The professor was unaware of Mad Dog's horse ride to Ma's Diner.*

Daryl and Doris had just about finished their supper when the explosion rocked the sky. Both jumped up from their booth at McDonald's, and Daryl stated softly, "It looks like July 4th all over again!" The couple's first inclination was to jump in the VW and head out of town to the explosion's source. Then Doris hesitated and turned to Daryl.

"Let's get back to the police station rather than head off willy-nilly with the rest of Webster's population," she said.

That they did, and they almost beat Chief Olsen back to his office. They caught him moving swiftly up to the station's entrance.

"Sir, Mr. Policeman, sir," hailed Doris.

Chief Olsen tried to wave them away.

"We are the ones who reported the kidnapping. Maybe we can help with some clues," they pleaded in unison.

Chief Olsen continued to the door as he replied, "Okay, come on in, but stay out of the way until you're spoken to."

The phones were rattling off the hook, and poor Hazel was at her wits' end.

"Thank goodness you are here," was her greeting to the chief. "That explosion has released all of the whackos within fifty miles. Some think they just saw a UFO, others are wondering what gas line has been hit, and then we have those asking if you are forming a posse!" Hazel threw up her hands and headed to the ladies' room.

Chief Olsen signaled to Daryl and Doris. "You two get in here. Help me handle these phones and take down information. Tell everyone we're gathering up all the cops in Benson and Shiloh Counties and will get word to Channel 6 as soon as we have something."

"Oh, Chief," noted Doris in a worried tone, "I think you have reporters here already."

Sure enough, the Channel 6 mobile van was parked out on the street, and a reporter was speaking into a microphone in front of a gathering crowd. The entire periphery of the station was lit up like a Christmas tree. Chief Olsen could only wipe his brow and head outside. He would have to make a statement, no matter how brief.

✶   ✶   ✶   ✶   ✶   ✶   ✶

Tom, Bobby, and Arnie Barlow made their way steadily through Granger's Woods. Tom had told his sons to hold off using their hunter pen lights until absolutely necessary. He did not want to alert any undesirables of their presence. As they neared the western edge of the woods, Tom waved his arms, indicating they needed to stop. He placed his index finger to his lips. Tom thought he heard something. They all crouched down and strained to see through the dimming light. There were sounds of twigs snapping about five hundred feet to their left.

"Probably just a deer, Pops," whispered Arnie. Though Tom's first inclination was to follow the sounds into the forest, his gut said to press ahead.

Bobby saw it first. "Pops! Ahead at one o'clock," he exclaimed.

As they simultaneously entered the clearing housing the hideout, standing open was some kind of trap door.

"Looks like someone got a little careless," concluded Arnie.

"Shhh, I hear something," responded Papa Barlow. They all stopped to listen.

In the bowels of the hideout, Johnny Turnbow was trying to make whatever sound he could from behind the rags gagging his mouth. He even tried to rattle his chair, even though he could not tell if that would make the fuse move quicker or disturb the vials of liquid surrounding him. If you could call it a blessing, the fuse must have been a good thirty feet, snaked around the room. Tommy Bolton took great care to make sure he had time to put distance between him and the hideout. Tommy had been meticulous in his preparation. Beneath Johnny's chair were a dozen neatly stacked sticks of dynamite. In a semicircle around the chair, Tommy had placed several vials of nitro. Though he was sure the dynamite would do the job, why take chances?

"Don't be getting fidgety now, kid," Tommy advised Johnny, carrying a sinister smile as he said it. "We don't want any premature fireworks."

Johnny was tempted to take them both out, but back in the recesses of his mind, he held onto faint hope someone would come to his rescue like in *The Lone Ranger*. Johnny could not believe he was not feeling more panicked. His eyes were getting bigger, however. Sweat was beginning to trickle down his brow and make his skin itch. If not for his heavy head of red hair, the sweating could have been worse.

Tommy put the finishing touches on his preparations and checked his watch. "Ah, just about ten minutes until showtime," he shared. Turning to Johnny, he took off his Cubs hat, wiped his brow, and said, "If you have a god to pray to, I would start now."

With that, Tommy Bolton leaned over, causing his camouflage pants to expose his butt crack. He lit the fuse and moved toward the curtain.

"Great to get to know you, kid," Tommy said insincerely and let out a deep belly laugh. Then he disappeared down the tunnel.

That is when Johnny began to try to make noise, and that is what Tom Barlow heard from above.

It soon became apparent to the farmer that the hideout had been vacated. Tom led the way down the stairway but stopped halfway down, extending his arm back to stop the progress of his sons. Before him was a young boy tied to a chair that covered sticks of dynamite and several other boxes of the explosives strewn around. There was a lit fuse moving ever so steadily toward the chair. Scaring him more were what looked like little test tubes from a chemistry lab also surrounding the chair.

Tom pushed his hand out firmly toward the youth. "Stop moving!" he rasped.

Tom was no expert on incendiary devices, but he knew any sudden movement might set off the liquid. If he rushed to stamp out the fuse, any spark could send them all to the promised land. The fuse was now halfway to the kid in the chair. Tom figured they might have about five minutes.

Tom then turned to his two boys. "Okay, this is what we are going to do. I am going to move slowly toward the kid. I will untie him and then carry him over to you. You grab him and rush into the woods. I will not be far behind."

Bobby and Arnie did not question their father, but they knew this was going to be close…very close. They could only watch as their dad walked delicately toward the chair. Flawlessly, he untied the rope and removed the gag from Johnny's mouth, immediately replacing it with his large hand. Bobby grabbed one arm, Arnie the other. They swung Johnny around (who was in shock by this time) and scrambled up the stairs.

Tom Barlow was right behind them but then clutched his chest. There was a sharp pain, and he could hardly breathe, much less move. Tom stumbled upward, and once outside, he had taken a few steps toward the woods when the ground shook and all hell broke loose. His boys and Johnny fared a little better. They were shielded by a buffer of trees when the explosives went off. The sound generated by the blast was so intense that they all suddenly lost their hearing. Fortunately, the brothers had the sense to keep running, as it was not long before secondary explosions took place. Wood was flying all around them, and a huge branch just about knocked Arnie's head off. Finally, it became too dangerous to run any farther, and they all fell to the forest floor. Blood was streaming from Bobby's ear, and Johnny was unconscious. They did not realize it, but they were not to see their father in one piece ever again.

*   *   *   *   *   *   *

Jeremy never had been witness to his dad speeding...maybe five miles above the speed limit, but that was it. Now, though, Frank Murkowski was approaching 70 mph in a 55 mph zone. When he turned his truck onto Highway P, debris was already strewn across the road. That did slow him down. In a couple of miles where Highway P took a sharp left, they found a dirt road leading to the source of the explosion. Unfortunately, it was not long until they could drive no farther.

"Jeremy, watch your step, now. We have to tread over a lot of debris," Frank counseled.

Just being near the woods again was bringing back bad memories. Jeremy felt his heart pound. It was not so much he felt unsafe, but more a foreboding of disaster and deep concern for his best friend. Jeremy wanted to think the best, but from everything they now saw, he could not see how anyone could have survived the explosion.

It seemed an eternity before they saw the crater ahead. Frank knew about war. His father had served in both the Pacific Theater in World War II and Korea. War movies were popular in his home when he grew up. So, when Frank turned to Jeremy and pronounced, "This is a war zone," he was not exaggerating.

Little by little, they picked their way over the mounds of dirt, scattered limbs, branches, and liberated rocks. As they mounted one particularly huge mountain of dirt, Frank quickly covered Jeremy's eyes. There was an arm without a hand and a solitary foot. Frank surveyed the scene in all directions but could not find evidence of more than one individual. The hole in the ground before him, however, made Petersburg, Virginia, of Civil War times, pale in comparison.

"Jeremy, we have a gruesome scene below. Try not to look around too much...but we have to see if there are any survivors." Frank tried to sound convincing, knowing deep down there could be no survivors.

Half sliding down the hill, Jeremy just about stepped on the torn arm.

"Ugh...I feel like I am in a horror movie!" he exclaimed. Looking around, he added, "This all looks familiar now. But whatever was below ground has been destroyed."

Both dad and son were thinking, *Maybe Johnny isn't here after all.* The arm and foot certainly did not belong to a boy. On the other side of the coin, there would be no more remains to be found, as anyone below ground would've been pulverized. Slowly, they moved toward the woods. Pieces of furniture were helter-skelter. A portion of an old couch was actually hanging from a tree.

As Jeremy scanned his former escape route, he thought he saw something moving. "Dad!" he shouted. Something was moving up ahead. Sure enough, a man was trying to crawl from the woods. He stretched out his arm to them.

Frank and Jeremy moved as fast as possible toward the figure in distress. Kneeling down, they could hear the wounded man say, "Help us...brother...boy...that way."

The man tried to throw his arm backward and point into the woods. It was then that Officers Sheridan and Plank arrived on the scene. Frank cried out to the officers as Jeremy suddenly realized what the man meant by "boy."

*   *   *   *   *   *   *

Iggy Smothers made his way north along Highway 12, his speed limited by the old farm truck's worn windshield wipers. Iggy had the window down on the driver's side to help him see. His long black hair swayed with every burst of wind. As he entered the Bensonville city limits, he thought of his mother, and for a moment, he felt a twinge of guilt. The right thing to do would be to let her know of Boris' demise. Of course, Iggy had no idea she was no longer at home. He did not realize he could have made a small detour and visited with her at her sister's house. No matter; any obligation Iggy felt to provide her information on her son's whereabouts quickly dissipated.

Iggy was not the brightest light bulb in the room, but he did perceive that the wooden leg operation was in trouble. The thought that Mad Dog and the gang may fail brought him some solace and balanced out any fear he had of being tracked down. And if they were successful, Iggy hoped the financial rewards would cloud Mad Dog's thirst for revenge. As he thought about it, the more he concluded that Mad Dog had actually done him a favor. By being removed from the events of the weekend, Iggy had a decent chance at resurrecting his life. Sure, if the operation went down, his name could come up—and he would be sought for questioning. But if victorious, who would give a whip about Iggy Smothers, the low man on the totem pole?

Every so often, even in the mind of a dim-witted individual, inspiration makes its mark. It occurred to Iggy that if he tipped off the authorities about what was going down, it would remove any potential heat on him individually. Of course, he would want to make sure he was not premature in sharing information. Once he got himself settled in Fort Wayne, an anonymous phone call would be in order.

Steadily, Iggy made his way to Miami County. It was close to midnight when he passed the county marker. Suddenly, out of nowhere, a young doe bounded across the highway. Iggy swerved to avoid it and, in the process, skidded off the road. The ancient truck slid off the embankment and tipped over on its side. Iggy's head jerked toward the open window and slammed against the ground. It appeared for that evening, Iggy would be sleeping in the countryside. Out cold, he did not realize the truck's cab protected him from the rain. That would prove to be the only blessing he was to receive during his nocturnal journey.

As the sun rose on Saturday morning, Iggy had still not come to. Therefore, he did not know when an off-duty patrolman stopped by and discovered the accident. Iggy was still unconscious when the ambulance came and did not wake up when taken to the Fort Wayne Mercy Hospital. He lay prone in the emergency room bed all day, and at 4:00 p.m., he was officially declared to be brain dead.

Iggy Smothers had no way of knowing that the explosion went off as planned. In reality, the accident had moved Iggy to the sidelines, as far as the wooden leg heist was concerned. In fact, he would remain on the sidelines of life in general for the foreseeable future. Phone calls made to his mother's home went unanswered.

The bottom line was that Mad Dog and his gang had dodged a bullet and did not even know it. There would be no anonymous phone call to the police. Had Boris and Iggy Smothers known the fates to befall them, they might have elected to stay in jail.

Sentinel Stippich

William Haynesworth Stippich was a graduate of Amherst College (B.A. in Political Science/pre-Law), and later graduated cum laude from Yale Law School. He came from a long line of successful professional men. The Stippich name was well known in western Massachusetts. He'd met his future wife, Melody, while interning at Fritch-Gallows law firm in New York City; she was finishing an English literature degree at Columbia University. It was a fluke that brought them to central Indiana. Bill's uncle, Patrick Stippich, was teaching law at Indiana University, and there was an emergency vacancy among the law school's professor ranks. Bill took a sabbatical from his Boston law firm and never returned. One thing led to another, and eventually Bill took up practice in Indianapolis. He agreed to settle in Webster, as Melody wanted a more peaceful place to raise their daughter. As Melody put it, "Bill, you are rarely at home during the week, anyway. Why does it matter where we live if you have a reasonable commute?"

So it was on that Saturday evening that Bill Stippich found himself the sole guardian of the museum. It was perhaps an odd assignment for a lawyer such as himself, but then again, it never occurred to him he would be deputized, either. In any event, Bill did not give much importance to his custodial responsibility. All the action was west of town. He only hoped that Johnny would be found safe. His daughter really enjoyed the company of the young man, and it would decimate her if anything happened to him. Bill and Melody did not have much social connection with the Turnbows, but they seemed to be nice folks and did not deserve personal tragedy to intrude on their lives.

Bill stood on the porch and gazed at the flames licking the distant forest. What the explosion had to do with the disappearance of the wooden leg, the children, and Mr. Tompkins, he did not know. He only hoped for things to get back to normal before school started the upcoming week. Anyone observing Bill's silhouette from afar would have seen his shadowy countenance framed by an eerie light.

Mad Dog Scrima and Skippy Forrester were not concerned about the appearance of anyone residing at the museum Saturday evening. Their goal was to get Miss Quig into the museum as expeditiously as possible, retrieve the leg, and make their escape through the tunnel and back to the farmhouse—all without drawing attention to their party. They were prepared for any encounter that might pop up, but truthfully did not feel there would be much resistance to overcome at the museum. The professor had organized things perfectly. The local and county police would be directing all of their efforts to the location of the explosion. Their theft operation had not gone particularly smoothly, but except for a few casualties along the way, they had not been deterred from accomplishing the task at hand. They need only use their professional skillsets to complete the job.

As Dr. McDougal had suggested, Mad Dog made sure they took only local roads to return to the museum. They carefully avoided Highway 12, only crossing it once to connect with the dirt road that ended up near the museum's parking lot (the same road used by Boris during his aborted mission). In less than an hour, the yellow Corvette was positioned in the same spot Boris Smothers had parked his truck. What should have been a moonlit sky was instead filled with haze from the remnants of the explosion. In some respects, it provided a perfect visual screen for Mad Dog and his companions. Bill Stippich was doing them a favor by standing outside the front entrance of the museum.

Before exiting the car, Mad Dog gave some final instructions.

"Okay, gang, it's show time. Miss Quig, might I remind you that your cooperation will be to your and your family's advantage. Skippy, though it would appear the museum is empty of cops, I doubt Detective Shaw would leave the building unguarded. Be on your toes. Have your knife handy, but let's not take anyone out unless it is absolutely necessary. Let's move out."

With that, the team of four quietly exited the car and knelt down in the grass. Mad Dog waited until their eyes adjusted to the dark (eerily illuminated as it was) before moving forward. He had them all crouch down as they walked toward the back door.

Emily had a lot of mixed feelings at this juncture. She could call the professor's bluff and sabotage the entire operation. Perhaps the threat to her parents was just a ruse to get Emily to cooperate. If indeed somebody were inside the museum, maybe she could alert them to Mad Dog's presence. Of course, any attempt to escape on her part could lead to her demise or, at the very least, bodily injury. Emily felt the one card she had to play was the fact they could not get the leg without her help. That being said, they could make her completion of that assignment very uncomfortable. And she liked both her ears just the way they were, thank you.

In the end, there was no subterfuge on the part of Emily. She would play her role unless conditions drastically changed. One reoccurring thought did disturb her, however. Emily felt she now knew too much. Even if she did do as told, what guarantee did she have that Mad Dog would not eventually do her in?

While Skippy and Emily lurked beside the back porch, Mad Dog proceeded up to the door to see if it was open. Surprisingly, it was. Because its hinges had not been oiled in some time, Mad Dog had to carefully inch the door open bit by bit. He need not have been concerned, though, because Bill was still gazing out toward the burning forest. He had not heard a sound. Mad Dog motioned for Skippy and Emily to follow him inside. The only lit area they could see was the local history room. That was to their advantage.

Mad Dog pointed to the right hallway, indicating to Skippy that he should do a recon of the downstairs. He then led Emily and Jarvis behind the information desk to where they would wait for Skippy's report. Skippy moved stealthily around the curved hallway. As he neared the local history room, he became more cautious. Peering inside, he found it vacant. The foyer between the information desk and the front door was also empty. He did notice the front door was ajar, however. As Skippy moved to check out the other side of the hallway, he heard, "Psst…over here."

Skippy joined Mad Dog and Emily.

"Skip, there is nothing down the left side of the hallway," Mad Dog noted. "Are we clear otherwise?"

"The front door is slightly open, Boss. Not sure if we are alone," replied Skippy.

"Tell you what," said Mad Dog. "We'll give it ten minutes. If no one appears, you go around from the outside and determine if we are alone."

Nothing happened, and soon the ten minutes was over. For whatever reason, Bill did not see an immediate reason to go back inside the museum. Things were pretty quiet. It was obvious police work was not his forte.

Skippy decided to move around the west side of the building. This meant he had to scale the small iron fence that was part of the museum's periphery facing Elm Street—but it was not a major obstacle. As Skippy approached the porch, he laid face down on the ground. Slowly, he raised his head and looked up. Practically on top of him was Bill Stippich. Skippy pulled out his sturdy knife and got ready to pounce. Before Bill knew what hit him, he had a major gash in his right leg. Bill slumped onto the porch, which gave Skippy the opportunity to send his fist crashing into Bill's jaw. Bill was out for the count. Skippy then pulled Bill's body down to the ground. Pulling a large handkerchief from his pants pocket, Skippy gagged Bill's mouth. Next, Skippy kicked at the latticework hiding the crawlspace with his size twelve boot. It quickly caved in. Bill was not a small man, but Skippy was able to move him into the crawlspace without too much difficulty.

Skippy lurched out onto the porch and ran inside the front door.

"Found ourselves a lookout, Harvey," he reported. "Need a rope to tie him up. He's knocked out. Will get the one we threw in the trunk of the car."

With that, he scampered to the Corvette, retrieved the rope, and with Jarvis's help, he proceeded to tie up Bill before he came to. Skippy knew they now would have to move quickly.

Advancing up the stairs, restricted to the natural light available to them, Mad Dog, Skippy, and Emily made their way to the wooden leg's case. Jarvis kept watch at the front desk.

Skippy remembered the conversation he and Mad Dog had had in the farmhouse bedroom. "Hey, Boss, how about I take a look around for some things to nick while you and the miss retrieve the leg?" he posed.

"Normally, I would say go at it, Skip," replied Mad Dog, scratching his hairy neck. "But this operation does not feel right anymore. I want to get it and get out."

Emily shared Mad Dog's desire to put their association with the wooden leg behind them.

*   *   *   *   *   *   *

Chief Olsen came back into the station, pulling off his hat and wiping his brow. The phrase "put through the ringer" certainly applied to him. Plopping down in his desk chair, the chief let out a huge sigh.

"Whew," he exhaled. "Please tell me there will be no more sessions with the press tonight."

"Dream on, Brother," said Hazel, half laughing. "The three of us must have logged in a half dozen more requests from surrounding stations. You know you have a big story when Channel 13 in Indianapolis comes knocking."

"And that doesn't include every Tom, Dick, and Harry who have called in wondering whether we just got hit with a meteorite!" added Daryl. After a pause, he continued, "Seriously, Chief, we are really worried about our friend, Emily. Any new developments come in on the radio?"

"Thanks for reminding me," responded Chief Olsen. "Time for me to check in with Officer Kraus."

In the hour or so since Chief Olsen had spoken to Officer Kraus, there had been some major revelations—at least as far as the scene of the explosion was concerned. Detective Shaw and Ben Turnbow had arrived at Henry's Garage just about the time Officers Sheridan and Plank linked up with Frank and Jeremy Murkowski. Officer Kraus offered up a full report once contacted.

"Where have you been, Chief?" Herb exclaimed. "Been trying to get through for over thirty minutes!"

"Had to devote some time to Channel 6 and a few other reporters, Herb. Truly sorry for the delay. What have you got on your end?" Chief Olsen sounded genuinely apologetic.

Officer Kraus was anxious to report. "Some good news, Chief. Officers Sheridan and Plank ran into Frank and Jeremy who had discovered three survivors. One of them was Johnny Turnbow...yeah, his dad is with me. Johnny is still unconscious but breathing. Ambulance has been sent for and is on the way. There were two other men with him. Don't have their full names, but I believe the shared last name is Barlow. They have been injured, too, but not quite as severely."

Chief Olsen interrupted. "Barlow, you say? There was a farmer, Tom Barlow, who brought back Heather and Jeremy, remember?"

Officer Kraus acknowledged that he did. However, the name had not registered until Chief Olsen reminded him.

Kraus continued, "From what we can gather, Chief, these guys saved Johnny's life. There is evidence of one other person, but whoever it was, their body parts are strewn all over. Hell of a mess."

Chief Olsen wanted to know if fire departments had yet responded. Officer Kraus said the first truck had arrived. Webster's volunteer fire department (Station One) was the first on the scene, followed by Salem's only hook and ladder. The chief alerted him that Bensonville's two departments had trucks on the way. There were several other county units who were responding, and the Army National Guard from Bradford City had a chopper in the air that was to drop water from above.

The Benson County hospital was the nearest triage unit (located halfway between Webster and Bradford City), and it was the hospital providing the ambulance.

"Imagine Ben will want to ride with Johnny to the hospital," mused Chief Olsen. "Let me know when they leave. I want to meet them there."

After a short pause, he added, "Hey, have you seen Detective Shaw and the Stippich girl yet?"

Officer Kraus noted he had communicated with them on the radio, but he and Ben Turnbow had charged off to the site of the explosion before they had arrived. Chief Olsen said not to worry, as he would contact the detective directly.

*   *   *   *   *   *   *

Jeremy had trouble holding back tears as he knelt over Johnny's body.

Initially, he thought Johnny might be dead. But Jeremy felt a faint pulse from Johnny's wrist, and it was evident he was still alive. The two men adjacent to Johnny were conscious. One was leaning against a huge stump, and the other was being held up by two officers. He half heard their conversation.

Bobby Barlow's dark hair was matted to his skin where blood had collected. Though otherwise in one piece, the voices of the men kneeling next to him seemed to emanate from an echo chamber.

"Can you hear us, sir?" questioned Officer Sheridan.

"Don't try to speak," added Officer Plank. "Nod your head."

Bobby did just that. He could only manage to blurt out a few words at a time. "Dad...coming up...Couldn't see...Did he make it?"

Officers Sheridan and Plank stared at each other and then looked back over their shoulders at the body parts strewn around near the cavernous hole in the ground.

"Was your father with you?" asked Officer Plank.

Bobby shook his head in the affirmative and pointed toward the former hideout. At that point, Arnie, tried to explain things better. Arnie was holding his right leg. In stumbling forward, he had jammed his knee, and it was throbbing off and on.

"The three of us—Bobby, Dad, and I discovered the underground room. Dad managed to get the kid out before the explosion. There was

207

enough dynamite and nitro down there to take out half the county. We took the kid and started running toward these trees. Never saw where Dad ended up." Arnie had more of his faculties at the moment, and his eyes got wide as he looked toward the devastation.

In seeing what remained of an arm not far away, Arnie could only mouth, "Oh, my god, oh, my god." Tears began to stream down his face.

About then, Officer Kraus and Ben Turnbow arrived at the scene. Ben rushed to his son's side. Turning to Frank Murkowski, Ben beseeched, "Tell me, Frank—he's alive, right?"

Frank put his hand on Ben's right shoulder and noted, "We think he's got a chance, Ben. The ambulance is on the way as we speak."

In fact, they could all hear the sirens in the distance, growing ever closer. Fire trucks were now arriving, and the attack on the adjacent inferno had begun. Officer Kraus briefed Officers Sheridan and Plank on what was known about Tom Barlow and that it was likely his body parts that were scattered on the ground. They agreed that it was best that Shiloh County take charge of the site investigation going forward. Therefore, Gus and Frankie would conduct whatever interviews they could and collect evidence (to include gathering the remains of Tom Barlow). Herb would follow the ambulance back to the hospital.

Moving over to Ben, Frank, and Jeremy, he suggested, "Ben, why don't you ride with Johnny to the hospital?" (As if Ben Turnbow needed any prodding to do so.) "I'll follow behind you in the squad car. Anyone want to ride with me?"

It was then Frank Murkowski had a suggestion of his own. "Herb, if you could take Jeremy with you, I think I had better get back to the museum and make sure Bill Stippich has some support."

All concurred that that made sense. Officer Kraus noted he would inform Chief Olsen of their decisions. Shortly after their discussion, two men from the ambulance arrived and examined Johnny. They endorsed the assessment that Johnny was still breathing and alive, but time was of the essence.

✶   ✶   ✶   ✶   ✶   ✶   ✶

By the time everyone had gone their separate ways from the disaster scene, it was now close to 9:00 p.m. Conspicuous by their absences were Detective Shaw and Heather Stippich. That was the result of the conversation between the detective and Chief Olsen.

"Echo Three, do you read me? This is base calling," queried Chief Olsen. There were a few squawks from the radio, and then the familiar voice of Detective Shaw was heard.

"Base, this is Echo Three. Go ahead."

"Where are you now exactly, Sam?" asked the chief.

"I'm now at Henry's Garage, and I haven't been able to catch up with Herb and the Shiloh County officers. Every time I get to where they said they were, they're gone!" Detective Shaw's exasperation was equally due to not linking up with Kraus and his being out of the action. He was supposed to have taken charge of the investigation by now. Events had instead overtaken him.

"Sam, sorry about that. Officers Sheridan and Plank are coordinating the investigation now at the disaster scene. Herb, Ben Turnbow, and Jeremy are on their way to the hospital as we speak. Frank Murkowski is headed back to the museum to check on Bill Stippich…And yes, Johnny is alive."

When Heather heard that news, she covered her face with her hands and let out a sob.

Detective Shaw thought for a moment before saying anything. "Chief, the bottom line is that while we have managed to locate all of the kids, we are not any closer to zeroing in on those responsible for the theft or the explosion. Anything new on Mr. Tompkins?"

Chief Olsen indicated there was not.

"Well, have you heard from Bill? Any news from the museum?" Detective Shaw continued.

The chief had not had a moment to check in with Mr. Stippich with all of the phone and press traffic swarming him.

"You say Mr. Murkowski is on the way there?" continued Detective Shaw. Chief Olsen confirmed that. "Tell you what. I am going to stop by the museum and drop off Heather with her father. I'll relieve him and meet up with Frank."

Two hours had passed since the explosion. Sam Shaw was right. The three missing children had been found. Two had survived their ordeal. The jury was still out on Johnny Turnbow. Others had not fared so well. Tom Barlow was dead. Thaddeus Tompkins, Emily Quig, and Yvetlana Smothers were all unaccounted for. The missing leg was, well… still missing. Those behind the theft were still at large.

If Johnny could talk, he would've had a lot to say. Jeremy and Heather could somewhat identify their abductor, but unbeknownst to them, he was no longer alive. The vehicle he had used was totaled near Fort Wayne. In addition, Detective Shaw had heard nothing from the stakeout of Professor McDougal. Any clues they may have gathered from the hideout literally had gone up in smoke. As Detective Shaw drove back to the museum, he wondered if the night had any other helpful cards to play.

What a Difference a Few Hours Can Make

Dr. McDougal and Marvin Fish both sat on, or near, haystacks in the barn nearby the limousine and pizza truck. The professor's legs straddled the sides of his haystack, his body supported by his two mammoth arms reaching to the back of the stack. Mr. St. George was facing him, sitting sideways on the front seat of the limo with the driver's door open. Marvin's head was resting against another haystack as his body lay prone on the barn floor.

"Professor, how long do you think it will be before we can pull out and head to the airfield?" asked Mr. St. George.

Dr. McDougal had a thin smile on his lips. "With any kind of luck, my friend, Mad Dog and associates should have retrieved the leg by now. If everything goes according to plan, in about an hour, they should be here at the farmhouse."

"Are you really going to pay the gang their cut, Professor?" Marvin asked, his eyes playful.

Before Dr. McDougal replied, he stared at Marvin for a few moments. Then he said with a chuckle, "You know me too well, Mr. Fish."

"Actually," he continued, "you and Mr. St. George have cut into my profit margin enough as it is."

The professor arose and began to slowly pace around.

"Gentlemen, as you know, this operation has been in the planning stage for some time and involved severe logistical challenges. Some may say I have gone to too much trouble just for the theft of a precious gem. I would reply that they vastly undervalue the Timur Ruby. Once broken down, it will bring me millions. My devising my elaborate scheme was not so much about stealing the leg, but more to do with covering my tracks. Building the hideout and tunnel, installing the hologram, and hiring Mad Dog and the Bolton gang has been an elaborate ruse to throw off investigators. I did not count on, however, how difficult it would be to retrieve the silver key. Nor did I count on that idiot Tompkins putting two and two together. Not to mention we have that incessant Detective Shaw nosing around."

The professor continued. "Still, with your help, I may pull this off yet, and you will benefit with your own retirement funds." Dr. McDougal stopped to face his two assistants. "Now, let us be clear about our escape. Once the gang returns with the leg, I will be driven by Mr. St. George to the airdrome. Marvin, you will assist the gang in starting a small fire in the barn. But make sure you give me a twenty-minute head start. Then, distribute the sealed envelopes to each of the gang members. To avoid them getting suspicious, open one envelope with its stack of bills, and give it to Mad Dog. Remind them it's just a deposit, dependent upon our successful exit. You will then follow our route to the airdrome."

"With any luck, the planes will be in the air before authorities discover the fire. It probably won't matter, as they will soon discover Tompkins and his 'accomplice' on the second floor of the farmhouse. Even Shaw should be thrown off long enough for all of us to be long gone."

The professor paused and dropped his head for a moment before speaking again. He stepped closer to his relaxing driver and bent down. "Has the second plane been prepared?" he said in a whisper.

Marvin nodded his head in the affirmative.

"Good. Remember, both of you: after escorting the gang to the plane, give the pilot his share. Once they are airborne, drive directly west until you reach the small hole in the wall called Homer. Stash the van behind the vacant cement factory. Mr. St. George, no one will be looking for your vehicle. You don't have to rush to your final destination. Do you have the plane tickets I purchased for you?"

"That I do," replied the limo driver.

"The flight tomorrow afternoon will depart out of Chicago Midway International Airport," said the professor as a reminder. "I expect to see you in Toronto late Sunday afternoon."

With that, Marvin and Mr. St. George stood up, and they all joined hands. Unitedly, they felt a rush of excitement. The entire operation, five years in the making, was almost over.

*   *   *   *   *   *   *

Heather sat in the front seat next to Detective Shaw, her head swimming. The events of the last couple days were difficult to comprehend. Just a short time ago, she and the boys had been innocently plotting to investigate the disappearance of the wooden leg. Before she knew it, Johnny was in the museum's basement, and they were kidnapped. Then came the harried escape and their rescue by farmer Barlow. Following the reunion with their families, and just when she and Jeremy were ready for a well-earned, good night's sleep, there was the explosion and the revelation that Johnny was alive.

As a result, here she was, the night approaching 10:00 p.m. "Detective Shaw, I am trying to make sense of everything. With all that has happened, we are no closer to knowing who took the wooden leg. People keep disappearing, and then Johnny turns up after that horrific explosion. Does any of this make sense to you?"

"I can only say someone or some group has gone to an awful lot of trouble to not only steal the leg but also return to the museum," responded the detective. "The entire affair feels dark, that's for sure."

Detective Shaw did not want to share with Heather that he was beginning to think the explosion of the supposed hideout was to throw the authorities off track. Sam had a real sense of foreboding that they might not like what they found at the museum. As he pulled the squad car into the parking lot, he cut the lights. He motioned to Heather to stay in the car for a few minutes. When nothing seemed to be stirring, both walked around to the front door. All was dark inside. That seemed rather strange.

They both pounded on the door. There was no response. Sam paced around the porch.

"Wait," injected Heather. "I hear something." The sound seemed to be coming from underneath the porch.

Detective Shaw got down on all fours and put his ear to the porch floor. Turning his head to the left, he said, "Heather, I think the sound is coming from the far end over there." He pointed to the west edge of the porch.

Heather ran over and knelt down to try and listen for any noise. Just then, there was a muffled cry.

"Help me, help me…Someone please help me."

Heather jumped off the end of the porch, quickly followed by Sam. Peering under the porch, they could see a body. The detective motioned for her to stay put and inched his way under the porch.

The next thing Heather knew, Detective Shaw was pulling her father out by his feet.

"Daddy!" she screamed. "Are you alright?"

Together, she and the detective loosened the rope and freed Bill Stippich from his bondage. When propped up, his previous struggle to free himself was evident. There were scratches on his face, and his scarf was muddied and torn.

"Water...can I get some water?" Bill gasped.

The door was open, so Heather ran inside and retrieved a bottle of water from the pantry. Once he drained its contents, Bill began to speak.

"One minute I was on the porch, gazing at the fire, and the next thing I knew, my leg had been slashed and I fell down. A fist hit my jaw, and I blacked out. When I woke up, I found myself under the porch... don't know how long I was out."

Heather was hugging her father while Detective Shaw attended to Bill's leg. "Heather, I need to radio for some help. Your dad needs this wound attended to," he noted.

There would be no need to radio headquarters because Frank Murkowski was pulling up in his truck. "Over here, over here," shouted Sam.

Frank ran up to the porch. "What have we here, folks?" Frank asked.

It became evident to Frank that before him was a wounded Bill Stippich. He looked first at Detective Shaw, then Heather. "I had a premonition Bill was in need of help. That's why I sent Jeremy along with Officer Kraus to the hospital. Guess I was a little late to the game."

The threesome helped Bill Stippich to his feet, and with his arms draped around Sam and Frank, he limped to Frank's truck.

"Frank," he offered, "I think it's best we contact Melody and have her meet us here to take Bill to the hospital. I would like you to stay with me, and I am also going to call the chief."

Sam then turned to Heather. "The goal, young lady, was to get you connected to your family. Things have gotten a little more complicated, but perhaps you should go with your mother to the hospital, too."

Heather looked upward and reflected on this new development. "If it is alright with you, Detective Shaw, I would like to stay here. Everyone will be at the hospital. As much as I would like to check on Johnny, I am so angry I could spit. Johnny, Jeremy, I, and now my father have been physically attacked. I just want a piece of whomever is responsible for all of this!" With that, she threw a clenched fist into the air.

Under normal conditions, Detective Shaw would have protested, but this was no normal situation. "Okay, but don't go off on any tangents. You stay close to us and follow our lead."

Poor Melody Stippich. When Frank reached her at the Turnbow's, he thought she was going to come unglued over the phone. At that point, Jenny Turnbow stepped in and offered her assistance. In less than twenty minutes, she was on the scene with Melody, and they were whisking Bill away to the hospital.

In the meantime, Detective Shaw was contacting Chief Olsen. "The plot thickens, Chief. You had better get over to the museum immediately! Bill Stippich is down...Yes, he has been wounded and taken to the hospital. I'm going to carefully look around. Frank is with me." Sam was careful not to mention Heather's presence. He was not sure the chief would have agreed with his decision to let her stay.

*   *   *   *   *   *   *

At Benson County hospital, it felt like a mini reunion one more time. Officer Kraus and Jeremy followed the ambulance to the hospital and got there at the same time as Ben Turnbow and the still-unconscious Johnny. Johnny was immediately taken to intensive care, but only Ben was allowed to stay by his side.

From the air, the hospital resembled a poorly drawn half circle. Its east-facing side overlooked the Arapahoe River. Johnny's room was on the first floor. Officer Kraus and Jeremy were escorted to the south wing waiting room. A good half-hour went by.

"Do you think he will pull through?" Jeremy asked Officer Kraus in a hopeful tone.

Officer Kraus wanted to sound reassuring, but he was nervous about the whole thing himself. "Johnny is a tough kid. I think…I think it will just be a matter of time." With that, he moved to the water cooler.

Jeremy stood up with his hands in his pockets. "This is nothing like our other adventures. I think we got ourselves in over our heads." He continued, "At this moment, we all should probably be dead."

"You can't always tell where investigations are going to take you," responded Officer Kraus. He tried to sound official and knowledgeable. "That's why police work is not for everyone."

He would have continued, but at that moment, Jeremy saw Mrs. Stippich and Mrs. Turnbow wheeling Mr. Stippich into the emergency room entrance, which just happened to be in the same wing as intensive care. Jeremy took off to greet them. Officer Kraus then took the opportunity to call Chief Olsen.

"Chief, you said to call you when Johnny got to the hospital. Sorry I forgot to do that. But we're here."

"Maybe it is better you didn't call, Herb. Mayor Balducci has been on my back, plus I'm headed over to the museum. Seems Bill Stippich was attacked, and I just got a call telling me they found two bodies near the basement. I'm about ready to put the entire town on lockdown!" said an exasperated Chief Olsen.

"Well, roger that, Chief," confirmed Officer Kraus. "Jeremy and I just saw Mr. Stippich being wheeled into the emergency room. What time you got, Chief? I show us pushing a few minutes after ten."

"That's correct, Herb. This could be a late night," added Chief Olsen. "Listen, once things have settled down there, how about coming back to the station? We got a couple of volunteer kids on the phones, and Mary is pooped out. She needs some relief."

Officer Kraus agreed, and after checking with Melody Stippich and Jenny Turnbow, he headed back to Webster. As he turned to leave, he noted Jeremy curled up fast asleep in a chair. He retrieved a blanket from a nurse and covered Jeremy up. Sunday morning could not come soon enough.

*   *   *   *   *   *   *

Before Chief Olsen arrived, the trio at the museum did a search of the first two floors. There did not seem to be any disturbance. Heather noticed a little dirt on the stairs, but that was all. When the chief did arrive, they briefed him on what had come to pass. He was not ecstatic about Heather being there, but he did not make a big deal about it. Sam gave him a cautionary look.

All four then headed into the basement. "I got footprints here!" yelled Frank Murkowski. "They seem to be headed toward the back."

Detective Shaw threw his arms out to stop anyone from proceeding. "Hold on; let's not destroy the evidence," he exclaimed.

Upon closer examination, there appeared to be four sets of footprints leading to a small door at the very back of the basement. Three of the prints obviously belonged to adults, but one set seemed quite a bit smaller. Heather walked up to the door, which appeared locked. More out of curiosity than any expectation, she pushed against it, and it seemed to give a little.

"Hey, could I get a little help over here?" Heather pleaded.

Soon Frank Murkowski was giving the door his shoulder, and it caved in. Heather, Frank, Sam, and Chief Olsen stood side by side, gazing down the tunnel. Numerous footprints stretched into the darkness. The chief aimed his flashlight at the tunnel floor. He then motioned for Detective Shaw to case out the tunnel. After what seemed an eternity, Sam returned, panting heavily. "You are not going to believe this, Chief, but we have more bodies!" Detective Shaw announced.

Mad Dog Shows
a Softer Side

In the 1970s, the science of holography took off. In 1977, Fred Unterseher and others published the *Holography Handbook*, which was a guide to producing holograms at home. Dr. McDougal became fascinated early on with holograms and their potential use. Simultaneously, the professor discovered both the existence of the handbook and the Timur Ruby. As he pondered how he would get his hands on the ruby, he knew a simple theft of the wooden leg would not suffice. The existence of the ruby was unknown. The professor wanted to keep it that way. It was then he began to put the elements together for an elaborate scheme. The creation of a hologram became an important element of it. He grew absolutely committed to ensuring the theft would leave no trace of the leg and no surviving witnesses. As the months went by, his preparations began to border on madness. Any savings that Dr. McDougal had were exhausted by the construction of the hideout, the retention of Harvey Scrima and his gang, and, finally, the creation of the hologram.

The professor used the principles of dynamic holography to make the wooden leg "disappear," employing phased conjugate mirrors to make it appear like the leg's case was empty. Due to Mr. Tompkins' unique security system, the mirrors had to be installed on the outside of the case. He thought Thaddeus would never leave the Thursday evening of the hologram's activation. If anyone had been paying attention, they would have noticed a UPS truck parked behind the museum after midnight. But, of course, it was Webster. The activation took place remotely from the truck.

Dr. McDougal hoped the large remuneration to the gang would be enough incentive to guarantee perfection…not to mention the added share for Mad Dog himself. The worst scenario would see the professor disappearing and forging a new life in Canada. At least he would not have to put up with students who made a mockery of learning any longer.

*   *   *   *   *   *   *

Before the others began their descent from the second floor, Jarvis Bolton headed down to the basement and toward the tunnel. From afar, in the dim light, Jarvis could have been mistaken for a small bear ambling along in the dark. He was anxious to see if his brother Tommy had survived the explosion. He did not have to wait long.

"Yo, Brother, about time you showed up! I'll be a lot happier when we are back at the farmhouse," growled Tommy Bolton.

Tommy was standing at the tunnel's entrance, hands in his pockets. He still wore the same red flannel shirt. His camouflage pants, however, had turned decidedly brown from the dust and dirt that had descended upon him after the explosion.

"Did you find the opening?" asked Jarvis anxiously.

Tommy sighed and nodded his head up and down. "Yeah, I did. Almost suffocated from all the debris flying down the tunnel, though. Who planned this fiasco, anyway?"

"I did get a glimpse of the guy in charge before we left the farmhouse. Huge s.o.b.," shared Jarvis. "He sure went to a lot of trouble setting up this job. Guess it don't matter much to me, as long as we get our cut."

With that, Tommy led Jarvis back to the spot where they would leave the tunnel. Jarvis glanced up into the night sky and secretly hoped the horses would be in place. As he thought back to the events of the last couple of days, he could not remember being part of anything stranger. So far, the gang had not been found out, and things were certainly going smoother than the aborted bank heist. Still, the whole operation was more than creepy. The added assignment of eliminating the girl did not make him feel any better, though it did show confidence from the boss. In fact, Mad Dog had told him his contributions to date had impressed everyone.

Tommy and Jarvis returned to the entrance of the museum basement and stood fast. The waiting was killing them.

Meanwhile, at the top of the stairs, it was time for Emily Quig to complete her assigned mission. Mad Dog and Skippy stood with arms folded while Emily squeezed behind the case. She wondered how anyone larger than her could have fit in the tight space. Just as she had been told, there was a keyhole, and the key she held fit perfectly. The leg did not feel as heavy as Emily had expected. Carefully, she pulled the leg toward her.

"Easy, easy now," directed Mad Dog. Skippy moved closer to Emily in case there was a problem.

Soon the leg was out. Mad Dog wrapped it in a blanket he had produced from somewhere. Then he held up his hand.

"We mustn't dawdle on our way down to the tunnel," said Mad Dog in a very serious tone. "Miss, stay close behind me. Any false moves and my friend Skippy will take the appropriate action. Understood?"

Emily just nodded. Down they went, and soon they were making their way across the cluttered basement floor.

Mad Dog Scrima was not a man who embraced sentimentality. Perhaps the only warm spot that remained in his heart was for his sister Maude who had died at age six of a congenital heart problem. His parents worked several jobs, and he was raised primarily by an aunt. He was mostly ignored. At age thirteen, he had his first run-in with the law, and by age sixteen, he was in a juvenile detention center.

Yet, on this Saturday night, in the basement of a museum, he found himself feeling sorry for Miss Quig. The fact he was feeling sorry for someone at all bothered him. Why should he care what befell her? The professor had decided to use her as a means to an end. So what?

But it gnawed at him that a young girl, and a tiny one at that, should be brought into this affair. He certainly had no regrets about Johnny Turnbow. The kid had it coming after butting into the gang's business. And if he'd had any say or control in the matter, he would have taken care of the two brats who escaped into the woods. Miss Quig, on the other hand, had not voluntarily injected herself into the theft. Mad Dog was not privy to the agreement she'd made with Dr. McDougal, but in his mind, once the girl had played her role, she should be cut loose. Of course, they would have to stash her somewhere until the gang had made their escape; that was no small matter.

Now, as they approached the door to the tunnel, standing before them were the Bolton brothers, grinning like two Cheshire cats. Jarvis had his armed draped around Tommy.

"Mad Dog, Tommy located the trap door to the outside," reported Jarvis. "We are locked and loaded. Ready to get out of here."

Mad Dog surveyed the two. Then Skippy chimed in.

"Dang, Tommy, you look like you just came out of a dirt shower!"

Tommy scowled. "Well, you birdbrain, that is what happens when one sets off an explosion that could have taken down the White House. What am I supposed to look like, a telegram delivery boy?"

"No harm intended, friend," replied Skippy.

"Enough of the pleasantries, gentlemen," interrupted Mad Dog as he made his way past the Boltons and eased into the tunnel. "Let's get moving. The sooner I get back to the farmhouse, the better."

It was several minutes before they came to the place Tommy had marked. Mad Dog gathered everyone around him and laid out the order of ascending through the opening that resembled a manhole cover. Skippy was to go first and receive the wrapped leg from Mad Dog. Tommy would go next, followed by Miss Quig. Mad Dog was to be the fourth to go and Jarvis the last.

Hands were locked to support the feet of the one going up until there was enough ground to grip to reach the surface. All proceeded as directed until it was time for Emily to ascend.

Mad Dog clasped his hands and prepared to lift her up. As he looked to Jarvis, expecting him to do the same, he spotted Jarvis pulling a needle out of his boot. Several things quickly passed through Mad Dog's mind: One, Miss Quig was not to make it to the farmhouse—at least conscious. Two, he did not like this development. And three, though Jarvis Bolton and Mad Dog Scrima were about the same height, it would be foolhardy to confront Jarvis directly.

In a matter of seconds, Mad Dog pulled out his hands, shoved Miss Quig to the ground, and dove for Jarvis' knees. Jarvis buckled to the ground, dropping the needle. As Jarvis righted himself and prepared to charge at Mad Dog, the gang leader scooped up the needle. Then when Jarvis made his move, Mad Dog thrust the needle into his abdomen. Jarvis fell with all his weight on Mad Dog, and the latter let out a loud groan. Thanks, however, to the potency of the chemical concoction the professor had put together, the effects were immediate. Jarvis went limp and stopped breathing.

Emily sat aghast with mouth and eyes wide open. She did not know what surprised her most—the fact she was to be attacked before leaving the tunnel or that the hairy gang leader defended her. Recovering from her stupor, Emily moved to the two bodies and pushed on Jarvis with all of her might, rolling him off of Mad Dog. She did not take the opportunity to escape down the tunnel.

Soon, both Mad Dog and Emily sat staring at each other. Emily was the first to speak.

"Why…why didn't…you let him stick me?" she stammered.

Harvey Scrima thought hard before he replied. He was not entirely sure himself. There was no logical reason. It went against every grain of his thieving body.

"You shouldn't die," was all Mad Dog could come up with.

Then something happened that defied all odds. Emily Quig reached out and gave Mad Dog a huge hug. "Thank you, thank you," she whispered, tears streaming down her face.

Mad Dog slowly lifted his arms and returned her hug.

"Hey, what's going on down there?" said Skippy and Tommy in unison.

Due to the lack of light, they could not discern where anyone actually was. All that was apparent was that no one was standing. Mad Dog held his fingers to his mouth and whispered, "Shhh."

Mad Dog slowly stood up and walked up to the opening above him. "I'll explain in a minute, boys. I'm lifting Miss Quig up now. Then you will have to pull me up. There will be no help coming from Jarvis."

*   *   *   *   *   *   *

About the time Detective Shaw announced his discovery and Officer Kraus made his way back to headquarters, Officers Sheridan and Plank were finally getting their heads wrapped around the scene at the explosion. It had taken a while to cordon off the area of the explosion. It was hard enough to coordinate the various emergency and fire vehicles arriving at the scene. Then there was the matter of curious bystanders. When three teenagers had hopped into the hole that had housed the hideout, Gus Sheridan had had enough. He shot his pistol in the air three times.

"The next person to enter the crime scene will spend the rest of the night behind bars!" Gus announced.

Frankie Plank whisked the boys out of the newly made cavern and began pushing the thirty or so arrivals back into the field. Gus joined him. Once order had been restored, Gus made a couple more announcements.

"Folks, this is a dangerous place to be right now. Our firemen have enough on their hands with this blaze without having to worry about someone getting hurt. I suggest you return to your homes. You can hear all about this affair on the morning news."

"Skedaddle now," added Officer Plank.

And then, after the officers waved their arms and prodded with their nightsticks, the crowd began to disperse. They were assisted in their efforts by the newly arrived Bensonville police officers.

"Can you believe this, Frankie?" said Gus, shaking his head. He sat down on a stump that barely contained his squat posterior. "We are going to have to get a SWAT team out here in the morning when they can see something."

"Yeah," added Frankie. "By then, hopefully the fire in the woods will be extinguished and we can do a better survey of the area."

"I feel sorry for those Barlow boys, though," Gus reflected. "Their dad seems to have been blown to kingdom come." He paused. "That reminds me: we need to call the Webster Police Department so someone can go over to the hospital and get their statements tomorrow morning. Can't imagine we will get relieved here anytime soon."

With that, they returned to the action and began cleaning up the area.

✳   ✳   ✳   ✳   ✳   ✳   ✳

Doris Guice was fighting sleep, stroking her long black hair, while continuing to field phone calls. Fortunately, the number of calls had steadily decreased as the evening progressed. Daryl had been slugging down cans of Coke for a couple of hours now. The chief's sister, Hazel, should have been tired, but she kept plugging away. All three of them perked up when Officer Kraus came bursting through the doors bearing culinary offerings.

"Anyone for some pizza?" he proclaimed joyfully.

Daryl almost knocked over the file cabinet trying to get to the pizza.

Grabbing a big slab of the pie, he exclaimed, "Pepperoni, my favorite!"

"Ah, Daryl, my dear," cut in Doris. "I know you are not forgetting Hazel and I may like a piece, too."

Daryl stopped chewing, and with his other hand, he brought the box of pizza over to where they were sitting. Hazel waved him away, as she had chosen to exist on vending machine candy bars.

Officer Kraus attempted to bring them all up to speed as they ate.

"The good news is all the kids have now been accounted for. Johnny Turnbow will likely survive, thanks to the heroics of the Barlow family. He and Jeremy Murkowski are at the hospital with various family members. Guess the chief went to the museum. Any word from him?"

Hazel shook her head negatively.

After straightening some papers, she interjected, "This place has been a zoo. I think the media have finally taken a break, though the Channel 6 van is still parked in front of the station. With you here now, Kraus, I'm headed home. Call me in the morning if you need me."

And with a wave of her hand, Hazel strolled out of the station. Officer Kraus was about to protest, but he saw that it would have no effect. So, he grabbed a cup of coffee and plopped down at the desk. Doris' phone rang.

"Police headquarters, how may I help you?" Doris wearily answered. "…Yeah, sure."

Doris then handed the receiver over to Officer Kraus.

"You don't say, Chief," Herb replied. "Jarvis and Tommy Bolton?"

The thrust of the conversation confirmed that the Bolton gang was indeed involved, if not the prime mover behind the events of the past two days. Detective Shaw had found their slumped bodies on the tunnel floor. Unfortunately, he had not detected the opening in the tunnel ceiling. Still, Officer Kraus was instructed to put an all-points bulletin out on all the remaining members of the Bolton gang.

After several minutes, Doris stood up and walked over to Officer Kraus. "You say this Bolton gang is involved with today's events, including the explosion. But what about our friend Emily? Do you think the gang was behind abducting her? And for what reason?"

Officer Kraus scratched his head and gave her a strained smile. "It is possible, but we don't know where the rest of the gang members are presently. Certainly one of the gang attacked Mr. Stippich."

Officer Kraus began to pace the floor, trying to put the pieces together. "Your story about following your friend as she left campus raises a lot of questions. The gang must have needed her, that is for sure."

Daryl stopped wolfing down pizza to ask a question.

"But why hasn't anyone tried contacting Dr. McDougal? We know Emily was walking with some woman on the floor of his office. Emily had alerted Doris that she thought there was something fishy about her connection with the professor."

"We'll definitely follow up with him tomorrow," promised Officer Kraus.

Doris slammed her fist on the desk. "Tomorrow may be too late!" she screamed.

That caused Daryl to drop a piece of pizza on the floor. It also caused Officer Kraus to pick up the phone.

And Then There Were Two

Tommy Bolton, leaning over, peered into the tunnel. The wind had picked up, and his untucked flannel shirt waved up and down.

"I think I saw Jarvis move, Mad Dog," he exclaimed. "I'm going to jump down and get him out."

"Believe me, he's a goner," replied Mad Dog.

Mad Dog was intently examining the wooden leg. He motioned for Skippy to head off Tommy.

"How can you be so sure?" said Tommy, standing up. "Listen, he's my brother and I say I'm going in!"

Now it was Mad Dog who slowly stood up and faced Tommy.

"Let me try and explain it to you as best I can," he said patiently.

"We do not have time to reassure your sibling concerns. Unless you want to volunteer your portion of the heist, I suggest you put your butt in motion and follow us...*now!*"

Tommy was having a hard time controlling his anger. Neither men were about to give any ground. Mad Dog wiggled his ear, and Skippy understood what to do. In one fluid motion, Skippy pulled his trusty knife from his backside and flung it toward Tommy. The final Bolton brother let out a gasp and fell backward.

Emily covered her face with her hands. In a matter of minutes, she had seen two men go down. Mad Dog sauntered up to her and put his hand on her shoulder.

"Miss Quig, it was just a matter of time before we cut Tommy loose. You may not realize it, but you are not expected to show up at the farmhouse. The good professor must not have wanted you around to act as a potential witness to his scheme. Without sharing his plans with any of us, he evidently gave Jarvis an additional 'assignment.' Personally, I do not like surprises. Never have had problems taking people out as needed, as you have just seen. But killing *you*...even offends my idea of fairness. Besides, now I am beginning to wonder if the professor has plans for me and Skippy, too."

Emily released her hands, looked into Mad Dog's eyes, and softly said, "So now what?"

Mad Dog waved Skippy over to him. "Remove your knife from our friend's chest and shove him down into the tunnel. Let the authorities figure out why the Bolton brothers decided to die underground. I want to examine this leg just a little longer."

Mad Dog knew the ruby had to be in the leg somewhere. As he moved his hand up and down its surface, his mind was spinning. Explaining why the Bolton brothers did not return to the farmhouse was not the hard part. What to do with the girl was quite different. He was at the crossroads of a decision.

Every so often Skippy Forrester produced wise counsel beyond expectations. After he had disposed of Tommy, Skippy joined Mad Dog on the ground with the leg.

"Hey, Harvey, it seems our boss is using us. The way I see it, we are the ones who will be left holding the bag. Tompkins is dead. That innocent bystander is dead. Emily was supposed to be dead. We have taken all of the risks, and we may get our money, but you can't spend money behind bars."

Mad Dog just looked up at his long-time associate and smiled. "I could not agree with you more. We are going to deliver the leg as expected. But I'm going to make a minor adjustment, and the three of us are going to leave this party." After a pause, he glanced at Emily and said, "Come along, Miss Quig. You are going to live to see another day."

*   *   *   *   *   *   *

Dr. McDougal stood anxiously on the farmhouse porch. To his right could be seen fire and smoke, though it was obvious the flames were diminishing. Highway 12 running past the farmhouse was now empty of traffic. Had it not been for all the haze, numerous stars would've been twinkling down on the blackness below. There was tension in the air as the moment of truth was at hand. Either the mission would soon come to its successful conclusion, or the professor would be making an airborne escape—poorer and a fugitive.

In the distance, he began to make out three horses. "Ah, Mr. Scrima," he said aloud, "you have not disappointed me."

But the closer they came, it grew obvious that there were only two horses and two riders. There should have been four riders on three horses. Dr. McDougal sensed things had gone askew. He did let out a sigh of relief, though, when he saw the leg strapped to the side of one mare. As the horses crossed the highway and moved up the driveway, the professor recognized Mr. Scrima and his associate. Mad Dog and Skippy slid off their rides and ambled up to the porch.

"You had some casualties, Mr. Scrima?" inquired Dr. McDougal.

"You might say that, sir," answered Mad Dog.

Mad Dog placed the wrapped leg in the professor's hands. "The Bolton brothers decided they wanted a bigger share and were disrupting the operation. We left them dead in the tunnel."

Dr. McDougal at first was concerned about their demise, but then smiled slyly. This was actually a good thing. More for Detective Shaw to figure out. Plus, it would ensure there would be no attention directed to him until he was well gone.

"I am not interested in the details. You and your friend can have their shares. Matters little to me. The important thing is that you have delivered the goods," he said, pleased. "Let me see the leg," the professor demanded.

While Mad Dog and Skippy stood watching, the boss unwrapped the leg's covering. The professor then turned his back to them, and all they could hear was a small *click*. When Dr. McDougal turned around, he was beaming.

"Totally excellent, Mr. Scrima. Time for you to be paid. Follow me."

Soon, all three had joined Mr. St. George and Mr. Fish in the barn.

"Marvin," spoke Dr. McDougal, "I don't think we need to set the barn on fire just yet. Could you see about laying a delayed fuse?"

Marvin saluted his mentor and disappeared into the night.

"Now," the professor continued, "let's dispense with formalities. The Bolton gang seems to now be minus the Boltons and others. Therefore, Mr. Scrima, meet Mr. St. George, my driver. Mr. St. George, Mr. Scrima." He then turned to Mad Dog. "Do you want to introduce your friend?"

"Of course," answered Mad Dog. "This is my close associate, Skippy Forrester." Skippy doffed his hat.

"Good," noted the professor. "I will be brief. I have two planes ready. Mr. Scrima and Mr. Forrester, you will get in one, and I will get in the other. Mr. Fish, who just left, will provide you your share of this adventure as you board the plane."

Harvey Scrima interrupted. "I would feel better if you were with us when we boarded. Not that I don't trust you, but I would like to make sure our compensation is delivered directly. I don't know Mr. Fish."

Dr. McDougal curled his lips. "I don't think that is a big issue."

When Marvin returned, Dr. McDougal directed him to retrieve the package of bills reserved for Mad Dog and his gang.

"Let's give you your money right now, then," said the professor.

That being settled, Mad Dog was presented an envelope. He counted out the contents.

"Seems a little short, it would seem," observed Mad Dog.

"Certainly you don't think I am going to present you with all of your earnings before you get on the plane," Dr. McDougal said innocently.

It became clear that someone would have to blink. Mad Dog shrugged.

"Have it your way, Boss," he replied. "Skippy and I are ready. By the way," he added, "do we have a destination?"

"Let's just say, Mr. Scrima, you will be in a warmer climate. What you do after you land is your business."

Marvin, who had been witnessing the conversation, then chimed in.

"Chums, in the satchel I am carrying is the rest of your dough. Follow me to your plane."

While Mad Dog and Skippy walked with Mr. Fish to their waiting plane, Dr. McDougal got in his limo and sped off with Mr. St. George, leg in hand. Mad Dog winked at Skippy. What Marvin Fish did not know was that Emily Quig had been watching the group that entire time. She was aided by the blackness and was no more than 500 feet behind them.

In one evening, Emily had acquired confidence that surprised her. She no longer felt threatened. The hairy one they called Mad Dog no longer scared her. In fact, she felt safer than at any time during her abduction. When Mad Dog had laid out his plan to her, Emily not only supported it, but actually was excited to be a part of something so dangerous. The thought that Dr. McDougal would come out on the short end of the stick would make it all worth it.

So, grabbing a pitchfork from the barn, she moved quietly, slowly inching up to the three shadowy figures ahead of her. Emily waited for her opportunity and took slow breaths to maintain control of her emotions. When Mr. Fish had his back to her, and before Mad Dog and Skippy boarded the plane, she ran like a fairy, nimble and quick. Swinging the pitchfork, she slammed it into the back of Mr. Fish's head. Down he went in a lump.

Skippy clapped and Mad Dog gave her a hug. They all turned as they saw the professor's plane climb into the air. The pilot of their plane was heard to say, "Everything all right out there?"

"Yeah, keep your knickers on," Skippy yelled out.

Mad Dog tore open the satchel and shook his head from side to side, letting out a snicker. "That old dog does not disappoint. Nothing but paper."

Mad Dog then handed some bills from his envelope to Emily.

"Here, Miss Quig," he grunted. "You have earned this. Just do us a small favor and don't contact anyone until morning. But don't stick around, either. That limo driver will be coming back soon, I suspect. Perhaps you could hide in the farmhouse until things blow over."

Emily just shook her head and smiled. And then they were in the plane. Tears flowed down her cheeks. With moistened eyes and emotionally drained, she ran to the farmhouse, only looking back to see the plane take off. But before she opened the front door, it occurred to her that the professor had mentioned something about a fire. Perhaps she should pursue a safer refuge. Emily then started walking north alongside the highway. After about a mile, she came across an old outbuilding that had seen better days...but it had a roof and straw. That would do.

* * * * * * *

Tommy Bolton had gotten it right. His brother, Jarvis, was not dead.

As Detective Shaw, Chief Olsen, Frank Murkowski, and Heather bent over the discovered bodies, Sam checked Jarvis' pulse.

"I'm getting a faint heartbeat, Chief," Sam announced. "Help me lift him up." Frank and Chief Olsen got behind each shoulder and sat Jarvis up against the wall.

"Detective, there don't seem to be any wounds on his body," noted Frank in a puzzled voice. "Yet, his buddy bled like a stuck pig."

Heather jumped in. "Look here, in his stomach. It appears to have been punctured."

"Good observation, Heather," said the chief and detective unitedly.

"I saw these men in the newspaper we examined," Heather continued. "They are part of the Bolton gang."

Detective Shaw nodded his head in agreement. "You are right, Heather. Jarvis and Tommy Bolton, to be exact."

Heather stood over the brothers, moving her head from side to side causing her ponytail to sway. "They look like Harley-Davidson riders."

Detective Shaw ran his fingers through his black hair and mentally examined the possibilities. He reviewed in his mind the members of the gang and wondered why the four other members had left their companions for dead—or close to it. They were able to identify Tommy from his wallet. That meant Jarvis drew the long straw. Did someone get greedy? Were they deemed expendable? It was now obvious the tunnel connected the hideout and the museum's basement. The detective figured either Jarvis or Tommy had set the explosives and headed toward the museum to escape physical harm. Why the need to hang around the museum, though, if they already had the leg?

Detective Shaw was brought out of his reverie by Chief Olsen. "Do you think the three of us could get these bodies back to the museum?" he asked.

"What do you think I am? Chopped liver?" chimed in Heather. With her hands on her hips, it did not appear she was willing to be a bystander.

Frank tussled her hair. "You can have some of this action if you want, young lady." Everyone was smiling.

So, by hook or by crook, the team of four (with the assistance of a found wheelbarrow) managed to get Tommy and Jarvis up to the window that Johnny Turnbow had fallen through. Chief Olsen summoned an ambulance. More casualties for the hospital, but Tommy would head to the morgue.

Frank Murkowski began to vocalize what everyone was thinking.

"This group of thieves has gone to an awful lot of trouble to steal the wooden leg from the museum. From what I know of the bank heist, the Bolton gang would not seem to have enough smarts for this kind of elaborate scheme."

Detective Shaw snapped his fingers. "Right," he exclaimed. "Professor McDougal."

Chief Olsen had learned a long time ago not to question Sam's sixth sense. "You think he is the brains behind this caper, Sam?" the chief asked.

"It all makes sense. Mr. Tompkins makes a visit to the university and then disappears. Two kids get nabbed. Yvetlana Smothers goes home from work and has not been seen since. Appears people started getting in the way. Not to mention the Bolton boys. And, Chief, didn't Hazel call you about two students reporting their friend had been kidnapped?" questioned Detective Shaw.

"I'll have Dr. McDougal picked up for questioning, Sam," offered Chief Olsen.

"You won't find him, Chief," noted the detective. "I fear he may be long gone." Turning to Jarvis Bolton, who was still comatose, Detective Shaw added, "We may have to wait until Jarvis comes to before getting some answers."

The ambulance arrived, and Jarvis headed to see the doctor and Tommy the coroner. Chief Olsen and Detective Shaw drove back to the police station while Frank took Heather with him to the hospital to check on her friends.

Saturday night ended, and more people had perished. Johnny, Jeremy, and Heather had made it and could start school, but the Barlows had lost their father. It seemed in order for someone to live, someone had to die. The theft of the wooden leg had gotten way too complicated. Emily Quig should have been close to dead, but who knew Harvey Scrima had a heart after all. She was a member of the missing persons list that included Thaddeus Tompkins and Mrs. Smothers. There was a lot of tying up to do and many questions to answer—not to mention people to find. It was time for some sleep, though some would get more than others. On Sunday, several prayers would be uttered in Webster.

Unaware of much of what had gone on were Jeremy's siblings (Buddy, Hans, and Melinda) and Katie Turnbow. Their parents thought it best that they did not go to the Benson County hospital, so Katie had a sitter and Buddy was in charge at his house. They did know of the explosion and that Johnny was at the hospital, but as far as Buddy was concerned, the major impact of the day was that his brother was in a heap of trouble. His attitude would change, of course, but for the moment, he enjoyed not being the one getting yelled at.

Johnny Lives to See Another Day

The sun rose over Webster on Sunday morning, and there was no evidence of the excitement from the previous day. If anyone looked to the west, there was a warm glow from the flickering embers of a dying fire. A southerly wind had pushed most of the smoke up toward Bensonville. In fact, any local resident stepping out on their porch would have proclaimed Sunday to be a most excellent fall day.

To the intrepid participants of the mystery of the wooden leg, fatigue had finally overcome them. Chief Olsen, Detective Shaw, and Officer Kraus had all dozed off at the station; the chief was flung back in his desk chair with his tie undone. Herb Kraus was face down on an adjacent desktop. Sam Shaw had found a chair in the corner and propped his shoeless feet up on Herb's desk. Daryl and Doris were on the floor. Daryl had his back against the wall, and Doris used his lap as a pillow, curled up like a cat.

Doris had calmed down when Officer Kraus explained to her that Dr. McDougal had likely disappeared. Further searching for him would have to wait until morning.

Thankfully, the press had all gone home with the exception of a lone TV news van parked on the street. The driver was asleep behind the wheel.

Over near Granger's Woods, out of sight of the town, Officers Sheridan and Plank had pulled an all-nighter. Fire crews had all left just before dawn. All injured persons had been evacuated, and the officers had completed their inventory of the grounds. In the process, they'd reverently gathered the remains of Tom Barlow. The officers stood staring over the gigantic hole in the ground.

Gus Sheridan finally broke the reverie and spoke. "Christmas, Roger, have you ever seen such a hole?"

The chasm in the ground resembled half of a caved-in football field, something akin to an enormous sinkhole. Officer Plank shook his head from side to side. "Crap, Gus, they should fill this with water…make a small lake and stock it with perch."

Officer Sheridan rolled his eyes. "Just like you to be thinking of fishing at a time like this." After a moment, he continued. "Nothing left here to do, my friend. Let's pack it in and file our reports at the office. I would imagine Chief Olsen and his boys will be conducting a lot of interviews today. Don't know about you, but I'm going directly home after we're done and not waking up until Monday!"

With that, they walked over to their patrol car and slid into the front seats. Both officers seemed unaware of the amount of dirt they had accumulated, much of which was falling onto the upholstery. That would not make Superintendent Masters a happy camper. Pulling out on to Highway 12, they had the road all to themselves. When they had gone about five miles or so, however, they came upon a young woman in sweats wandering alongside the shoulder.

"Well, well," said Officer Plank, "what do we have here?" Officer Sheridan moved over to the right side of the road, and both officers got out of the car.

"Hey, miss, you need some help?" shouted Officer Sheridan.

Soon they were face to face with Emily Quig. Long ago, her ponytail had become unraveled. Her unkempt brown hair was all over the place. Emily stopped in front of them, and with hollow eyes and a monotone voice, she stated, "You may want to investigate a farmhouse not far down the road."

Her right arm pointed south. "Oh," she added, "and you may want to call for assistance. Some *bad* things happened there last night."

*　　*　　*　　*　　*　　*　　*

Johnny woke up to silence. His parents were asleep in wheelchairs provided by the nursing staff. They had spent the entire night in his room. The dim light led him to believe initially that he might still be underground. Then, as he glanced around, it was obvious he was in a new environment. First of all, things were too clean. Johnny tried to lift his head, but it felt like his cranium had turned to solid rock.

Straining, Johnny tried to reconstruct the prior events. Flashing through his mind were several images. A man laughed as he exited a room with earthen walls. Then there were hands untying him from a chair. Soon he was being carried up the stairs into the night air. Finally, a huge explosion in his ears…and then nothing.

As hard as he tried, he could not remember much before that. He had a terrible desire for soda—any flavor would do. Turning his head, he could see a table attached to where he lay. But all that was on it was a white plastic cup. He could not tell if it was filled. As he began to reach for it, he heard a voice.

"Hold on a sec, mister. Let me help you with that." A person in white had entered his room.

Suddenly, his bed was rising. Once propped up, he was handed the cup, and he tried to take a sip. Only water. "Coke…Could I have a Coke?" Johnny's voice was a little raspy, and the sound of it echoed in his head.

"I think that may be possible," replied the nurse. "Let me check with Dr. Morgan."

After what seemed an eternity, the nurse returned with a glass of dark liquid. Oh, it tasted so good. Johnny drained the glass's contents. Now elevated, he could see more, and he thought he recognized his parents.

"How are you feeling, young man?" asked the nurse.

"Head is very heavy. And there is this echo inside when I speak or listen. My body aches all over, but I don't feel anything broken." Johnny paused. "Are those my parents?" he asked.

"Johnny," replied the nurse, "you are in the hospital and have had quite a shock to your system. Your parents have been in your room all night, waiting for you to wake up."

His dad began to stir. Ben Turnbow sat up and rubbed his eyes. Looking straight at Johnny, he could see his son was awake. "Son, thank God you've come to."

Ben stood up and grabbed Johnny's hand. Then he gently aroused his wife, and upon her seeing Johnny awake, she began to cry. "Oh, Johnny," she sobbed, "we didn't know if you were going to make it."

The next several minutes were spent with the Turnbows reviewing the events of Saturday evening. As they spoke, Johnny's memory began to return. The entire ordeal in the hideout came back to him, followed by his time in the museum.

"Are Jeremy and Heather okay?" Johnny said with a real look of concern on his face.

"They are," said his dad. "They had some challenges of their own..."

Mr. Turnbow was going to continue, but his wife held her fingers to her mouth and whispered, "Shhh."

"...But we can share all of that with you later. Your breakfast has arrived, and you should really eat," he announced.

It was not long before Jeremy entered the room. "Boy, Johnny, you gave us a bloody scare."

Jeremy was soon followed by Heather, who wanted to give Johnny a big hug but was restrained by Mrs. Turnbow. "Later, dear, later," Jenny was heard to say.

"You made it, Johnny. Thank goodness you are alive!" exclaimed Heather.

Ben and Jenny Turnbow thought it wise to give some time for the kids to catch up. Besides, there were not supposed to be more than two people in an intensive care room at one time. The nurse was already giving them the evil eye.

Over the next hour, it was nonstop talking with Johnny being allowed to eat his oatmeal, applesauce, and toast. Comparing notes, Johnny was astounded to learn Jeremy and Heather had been kidnapped. His mouth got wider and wider as they recited their story. Heather had a hard time speaking about Mr. Barlow and his sons. Jeremy was as interested in her recollection of Saturday night as Johnny was. When all had been brought back up to speed, they took a moment to collect their thoughts.

Heather was the first to speak. "We probably bit off more than we could chew with this case," she mused. "Still, it sounds like we can identify most of the gang, and that counts for something."

"True," countered Jeremy. "However, the Bolton gang could not have devised such a complicated plan all by themselves."

"According to Detective Shaw, Dr. McDougal had a hand in it somehow," noted Heather. "Mr. Tompkins went to see him on Friday. Now, Johnny, you say Mr. Tompkins was underground with you and was taken out before the explosion. Mr. Tompkins must have gotten in the way of the operation. I fear for his life. Not to mention my poor father was attacked before we got to the museum."

The three agreed there were more questions than answers. Johnny and Jeremy were also puzzled as to why Jarvis and Tommy Bolton were found lying in the tunnel.

"Sounds like the gang began to unravel," summarized Johnny. "I know the one they called Mad Dog was awfully upset with the Smothers brothers."

The nurse returned with Dr. Morgan, and Jeremy and Heather had to leave the room. That gave them a chance to check on Mr. Stippich. It also gave them a chance to relate Johnny's story to all the adults. As everyone began to compare notes, certain elements of the case became clear.

To begin with, Mr. Tompkins was missing and definitely in trouble. Also, the gang members appeared to have had a falling out. Tommy Bolton was dead, his brother Jarvis was in bad shape, and Boris and Iggy Smothers remained a question mark. Johnny had reported to his companions that neither of the Smothers brothers were in the room when he'd walked through the curtain. Of the two remaining gang members, Johnny was sure the short, hairy one was calling the shots.

Heather recalled from their library research their names were Harvey Scrima and Skippy Forrester. She always seemed to have the ability to put things together…so when she suddenly stood up and began to speak, everyone listened.

"Assuming Dr. McDougal is the mastermind of this operation, he would not be stupid enough to work with the entire Bolton gang. So it is possible he communicated only with Mr. Scrima. If he was putting pressure on Mr. Scrima to deliver the wooden leg and complete the operation, it is not inconceivable that he became impatient with the Boltons and Smothers. Perhaps they became expendable, or maybe he wanted their share of the action," Heather paused for a moment. "I mean, the gang wouldn't be involved if the payoff wasn't substantial."

"I think you are on the right track," responded Frank Murkowski. "It just seems like if you were going to steal something, you would steal it and vamoose." He moved his hands together in a sweeping motion. "There is something that does not make sense here," Frank continued. "The fact the Bolton brothers were found in the tunnel leads me to believe the theft may not have been a done deal before Saturday evening."

"But, Frank," followed up Ben Turnbow, "the leg was definitely missing two days earlier."

"True," countered Frank, "but maybe they were unable to remove the leg from the museum itself until Saturday."

"Could they have stashed it somewhere?" asked Heather.

"Definitely a possibility," answered Frank.

Before the conversation could continue, Detective Shaw and Officer Kraus entered the reception area.

"Good morning, everyone," greeted the detective. "I hope you all are going to stick around for a while. Officer Kraus and I hope to get all of your statements."

Then Detective Shaw bounced up to the reception desk and asked about the condition of Jarvis Bolton. He was all smiles when the receptionist informed him that Mr. Bolton had come to and had to be fitted with restraining belts. It seemed Jarvis was not pleased to be in a hospital (although the being alive part was okay).

Jarvis Tries an Alibi

Officers Sheridan and Plank were not interested in doing anything but getting back to headquarters and handing off their passenger to the desk sergeant. They were supported in that decision by the fact that Emily Quig was fast asleep in the backseat. Of course, they were not aware of her being a person of interest, as Officer Kraus had only talked about looking for a van. He had not mentioned who might be <u>in</u> said van. The explosion had curtailed any conversation they would have had in that direction.

The Shiloh County sheriff's office and adjacent police academy were on the north side of Bensonville. It was still early morning when they pulled into the south parking area.

"Hey, miss," said Officer Plank as he shook her shoulder. "Time for you to come inside."

Emily slowly opened her eyes and realized she was in another unfamiliar place. When she'd begun hiking down Highway 12, mostly she'd just wanted to make her way back to the university and comfort of her dorm room. Emily, while she had a lot of information to share, had no clue about any of Saturday's events involving Johnny, Heather, and Jeremy. Nor did she know about the efforts of Chief Olsen and others to solve the mystery of the missing leg.

The transformed Miss Quig had made an executive decision before leaving the dilapidated shed that had been her night's shelter. Mr. Scrima had given her a wad of bills. While Emily did not mind telling her story about her involvement in this sordid affair, she did not relish having to explain what she was doing with so much money. She already had decided it would not be necessary to divulge the complex personality of Mr. Scrima. Upon finding a rusty shovel against the wall, Emily therefore began to dig a reasonably deep hole and bury her gift.

"Officers," she asked, "where are we exactly?"

As Officer Sheridan helped Emily out of the car, he answered, "Shiloh County police headquarters."

Well, at least she was with the good guys this time. It was not long before Emily was seated in the lobby. Unfortunately, she had to wait out a shift change, so it was a few minutes before an officer came to escort her to a side room.

"I'm Officer Dean," the female in uniform said, introducing herself. "Soon another officer will be in to take your statement. Is there anything I can get you while you wait? A doughnut, soda, or something?"

Emily instantly became aware she was starving. "I'll take anything you have, ma'am."

Officer Dean produced two frosted doughnuts, a banana, and a glass of cold milk. Emily devoured them. Then, she found herself staring at a rather tall policeman.

"Good morning; I'm Hugo," said the officer. "Let's talk about why you were wandering down the highway, yes?"

Emily, once seated at a small table, began, "I believe I have been a pawn in a rather bizarre theft involving Professor McDougal of Bradford State University." She blurted out her recollection of the past three days, barely taking a breath.

Officer Hugo Campbell did not react to any of her statement. He simply shuffled his notes, then finally pushed away from the table and said to Emily, "I'll be right back."

Officer Campbell went to confer with several other officers. "Hey, guys, you recall that missing person report we got yesterday about a student at Bradford State University?" All nodded. "I think she just showed up."

That led to the desk sergeant making a call to Chief Olsen. The ringing phone at the Webster police station abruptly woke everyone up.

"Yes, this is the Webster Police Department…We did issue the missing person report, yes…You don't say…Repeat that name again?… I'll send a car to pick her up." Chief Olsen hung up and turned to Daryl and Doris.

"This is your lucky day, amigos. Seems your friend was just delivered to the Shiloh County police station. How would you like to take a ride?"

The two students almost fell over each other scrambling to grab their things and follow Chief Olsen to his squad car. They took the rear entrance, as they did not want to alert the parked news van of their departure.

*   *   *   *   *   *   *

The only thing Jarvis Bolton wanted at that moment was a piece of Mad Dog Scrima. The last thing he remembered was Mad Dog sticking him with the injection that had been meant for the Quig girl. What should Mad Dog care about her anyway? It was a total rejection of gang ethics on the part of Mad Dog.

What bothered him more was that he was lying in a hospital bed. Tommy should have come to his rescue. Either Tommy tried and failed, or he did not try at all. The first scenario could mean Tommy had been taken out, or at best, injured and a prisoner of sorts. The second possibility would mean he was truly a patsy, perhaps set up by McDougal himself. That did not make a lot of sense to Jarvis, so he began to feel he might not see Tommy again.

In actuality, it was a moot point. The cops had found him, and he quickly had to figure out what his alibi would be. Because he did not know the whereabouts of his brother, he had to assume he was also in custody, in the hospital, or dead. Certainly, by now even that idiot Chief Olsen had connected him with the Bolton gang. But the ace up his sleeve was that they likely did not know where the rest of the gang was. Jarvis' challenge was to explain his presence in the tunnel resulting in the least amount of personal damage.

Jarvis did not have a lot of time to think. Soon, there was a plain clothes cop standing in front of him.

"Getting a little antsy, are we, Mr. Bolton?" greeted Detective Shaw. "It seems you must have gotten caught in the crosshairs with some members of your gang. Perhaps you would like to explain why we found you unconscious in the tunnel?"

Jarvis glared at the detective. Then he swallowed hard before saying anything. Fortunately for Sam Shaw, the nursing staff had cleaned him up before he came to. A few hours earlier, he had smelled like a dead raccoon.

"Listen, I just signed up to help with the museum heist. Mine was a bit part." Jarvis replied. "All I knew is I was to keep a watch on the girl. The boss wanted her kept safe for some reason."

Detective Shaw raised his eyebrows. "Jarvis, are you telling me the same man who almost strangled a bank guard to death was employed to babysit a young lady?"

Jarvis scowled. "It was more than that. I was Mad Dog's muscle. We didn't know who we would run into."

"Do you mean Harvey Scrima, the leader of your pack?" asked Detective Shaw.

"Yeah, he is the one you should be looking for. Guess he decided he wanted my share of the action," replied Jarvis. "Don't know why. Never did nothin' to him. One moment I was standing in the tunnel, and the next thing I knew, I was being stuck."

"Tell you what," said Detective Shaw. "Why don't you take it from the top and give me your version of what went down."

Jarvis gave it his best shot. He explained how he and Tommy were approached to help with a theft. Took his orders from Mad Dog Scrima and didn't know the details behind everything. When asked about the hideout and explosion, Jarvis said they were holed up underground until it was time to move.

"Hold up just a second, Mr. Bolton," interrupted Detective Shaw. "You make it sound as if the theft did not take place until Saturday night...but the wooden leg has been missing since Thursday."

Jarvis squinted and thought hard. "Wouldn't know about that. We were told the theft would occur last night."

"Let me summarize for a moment, Mr. Bolton," Sam continued. "You guys blow into town, sit in an underground hideout for a couple days, and then get ready to strike. You tie up a young boy and then explode the hideout before heading to the museum to steal—I am presuming—the wooden leg. Obviously, there was no concern for Johnny dying in the process. When you get to the museum, you or another gang member takes out Bill Stippich." The detective took a breath. "Let's say you are right. The wooden leg was still somewhere in the museum. But why would you need a girl to help you? And how many of the gang were at the museum last night?"

"I want to see a lawyer," Jarvis interjected. "I got my rights. Not saying nothin' more until I get a lawyer."

Sam Shaw moved up close to Jarvis until they were face to face.

"Let me tell you something, you scumbag. In the past couple of days, we have seen two kids kidnapped, one kid tied up to die, a museum curator go missing, the mother of the Smothers brothers off to god knows where, and a deputized citizen attacked. And the only member of the Bolton gang we have in custody is you. Are you prepared to take the fall for the rest of your cronies?"

The detective's voice rose as he spoke, and Jarvis flinched.

"You'll get a lawyer, Mr. Bolton," he stated, walking away. "But only after I get a statement from Johnny Turnbow. Something tells me you are leaving out a few things."

Jarvis once again yanked on his restraints. He began to sweat just a little. Suddenly, a plea bargain was beginning to look really good.

*　　*　　*　　*　　*　　*　　*

The Turnbows, Murkowskis, Melody Stippich, together with Heather and Jeremy, were hanging out in the south wing waiting room. They were the only occupants. Officer Kraus was busy taking statements from each of them. He, per his usual manner, was making it a more formal process than it needed to be.

Overall, the news had been good. Bill Stippich's leg gash was healing nicely, and Melody was told he could go home that evening. Johnny, fortunately, had not suffered any major injuries. Beside numerous scratches and a good-sized bump on his forehead, his only other concern was loss of hearing. Johnny reported to the doctor he'd noted some improvement after he had eaten a little breakfast. Ben and Jenny Turnbow were told Johnny would not be released for a couple days, mostly for observation.

Arnie Barlow had a sprained knee, and his brother, Bobby, had come away from the explosion unscathed. Frank promised them a steak dinner when they were back up to speed. He had developed an affection for the two heroes.

Everyone looked up as Detective Shaw entered the waiting room. Officer Kraus stopped his interview with Melody for a moment.

"Did he crack, Sam?" said Herb with excited anticipation. "Did he say where the rest of the gang is?"

Now everyone was focused on the detective. He thought for a moment, and when he spoke, his words were measured.

"I believe you all know that the Bolton gang has at least six members: Harvey Scrima, Skippy Forrester, Jarvis and Tommy Bolton, along with Boris and Iggy Smothers. I can account for four of them being in the tunnel after the blast. Jarvis claimed he was Harvey's, a.k.a. Mad Dog's, personal assistant. Said he and Tommy signed up for the theft but were just along for the ride. Guess that would make them a part of the Scrima gang. Part of his duties were to keep an eye on a girl they needed for the heist."

Officer Kraus interrupted. "Wait a minute...would that be the friend of those kids who were answering phones at the station?"

"Probably so, Herb," replied Detective Shaw. "Believe her name is Emily Quig. The strange thing is they appear to have returned to the museum to steal the leg, or should I say, to retrieve the leg. Very odd. Why would Miss Quig be needed?"

At this point, Detective Shaw had to stop and fill in the group on the missing person report received from Doris Guice and Daryl Rasmussen.

"Did he enlighten you on why there was an elaborate tunnel and hideout?" asked Mr. Turnbow.

"Never got that far, Ben," answered the detective. "I suspect it had to do with getting away with the theft unnoticed. Would have to agree that it does seem like a bit of overkill."

"Somehow, Mr. Tompkins must have gotten in the way or discovered something about their plans," surmised Heather. "The three of us ended up smack dab in the middle of it." She sighed.

"Before we go any further," added Detective Shaw, "I want to speak to Johnny when he is up to it. He was the one who discovered the tunnel. He was the one who was tied up in the hideout."

At that moment, a nurse entered the room and announced there was a phone call for Detective Shaw. Sam was gone ten or so minutes and returned. He motioned for the Turnbows and Murkowskis to come over.

"I need to ask a big favor. That was Chief Olsen. He just got a call from the Shiloh County police. They picked up Emily Quig on Highway 12 this morning on the way back to Bensonville. I would like to borrow Heather and Jeremy to run up to their headquarters. Believe it could be beneficial having the three youngsters there comparing notes." Detective Shaw then held his breath.

The two couples looked at each other and all nodded affirmably in unison.

Officer Kraus' curiosity got the better of him, and he joined the group.

"Hey, what's up, Sam?"

Turning toward Herb, Detective Shaw replied, "Looks like our college students were onto something. Emily Quig has been found by Officers Plank and Sheridan. The chief took Daryl and Doris with him to hear what she has to say. Evidently, Miss Quig already gave a statement."

"Well, let's get going, then," said Officer Kraus excitedly with arms waving. "This case is about to crack wide open!"

Detective Shaw put his arm around the officer's shoulders. "Actually, Herb, I need you to finish taking your statements. When you are done, the chief wants you to interview Johnny Turnbow. Are you up to it?"

Officer Kraus looked at Sam, then at Ben, Jenny, Frank, and Mary. "I suppose so," he replied. He looked a little crestfallen. "Guess interviewing Johnny is pretty critical, huh?"

"Definitely," responded Detective Shaw.

It had been a while since Officer Kraus had a chance to be part of a big case. And now he felt he was kind of a bystander. He began to itch his right ear (a typical behavior when he became perplexed).

"You go on then, Sam," Officer Kraus replied in his most dutiful voice. "I'll hold down the fort. We can compare notes later."

With that, he stood, hands on his hips, and announced in his high-pitched voice, "Okay, folks, here is how it is going to go down. I am going to finish getting my statements from you, and then I am going to speak with Johnny. I don't want anyone wandering off."

Detective Shaw just rolled his eyes and smiled. "Heather, Jeremy," he beckoned. "I am going to need your help. Are you willing to ride with me to Bensonville?"

The two companions jumped up and were soon at his side. "You can count on us," noted Heather. Not that either of them had slept that well.

Getting Away is Not Always Getting Away

The interesting thing about the theft of the wooden leg was that on Sunday morning, no one had all the information. Dr. McDougal left for Toronto, ignorant of the fact Emily Quig was not disposed of. He knew two more members of the gang had been killed but did not know the details. He was unaware that his right-hand man, Marvin, had been decked by a pitchfork and that Mr. Scrima and others were onto him.

None of this was of great importance to the professor because no matter how you cut it, he had the leg and the gem and had landed in Canada before the sun came up. In the morning, he would meet with his contacts to have the ruby cut and dispensed to the buyers. On Monday, his bank account would be a lot healthier, and Dr. McDougal would be on to his next destination.

Anyone who has ever had his heart slip into his stomach due to personal loss or disaster would have empathized with the good professor when he sat in his hotel room and opened the tiny compartment in the leg that housed the Timur Ruby. In the dark of the night, the ruby had felt like it should and appeared as it should. In the light of his hotel room, he realized something was seriously wrong. The stone he held was too light and obviously painted.

Dr. McDougal stood up, his entire six-foot frame trembling. He picked up the wooden leg and threw it across the room, shattering a lamp. Mr. Scrima must have swapped out the stones before reporting to the farmhouse. He did not know how that two-bit burglar figured it out, but he deeply resented being double-crossed. (No matter that he had cheated Mad Dog and Skippy out of what was due to them.) Looking down from his twentieth-floor balcony at the almost vacant streets below, Dr. McDougal reviewed his options.

*   *   *   *   *   *   *

Marvin Fish regained consciousness, greeted by a throbbing head. He began to make out the fatherly face of Mr. St. George. The limo driver was snapping his fingers.

"You have to get your wits about you, mate," he said. "We need to get moving. That fuse of yours is headed toward its destination." Mr. St. George nodded toward the farmhouse.

"What hit me? <u>Who</u> hit me?" asked Marvin.

"Can't say for sure," responded Mr. St. George. "I pulled up as the second plane took off."

With the help of his associate, Marvin stood up, albeit a bit wobbly. He noticed the pitchfork lying on the ground. "I think I see the weapon."

"They probably wanted the bag of money before they boarded the plane," reasoned Mr. St. George.

"Well, a lot of good it did them. Hope they weren't too disappointed with the contents," countered Marvin.

"It's beyond our pay grade, friend," noted Mr. St. George. "Let's just get a move on and blow this joint." He smiled. "Excuse the double entendre."

The two were soon on their way, unaware their boss had been double-crossed and that their payday would be delayed.

*   *   *   *   *   *   *

Mad Dog and Skippy crawled inside the Piper Cub.

"Buckle up," instructed the pilot.

"Where are we headed?" inquired Mad Dog.

"Someplace safe," responded the pilot.

They were soon airborne, and the smoldering fire and lonely farmhouse were far below. Skippy unbuckled his safety belt and moved closer to the pilot.

"I believe my friend asked you a question," said Skippy. "He'd like a more specific answer."

"You guys have nothing to worry about," replied the pilot. "Everything's taken care of. The boss has arranged for a safehouse. You lay low for a week or two, then you can go where you want."

Skippy pulled out his knife and held it against the pilot's throat.

"I'm going to ask you one more time, and if we do not get a proper response, there will be a new pilot flying this plane. Understand?"

The pilot took a huge gulp. This was not what he'd signed up for.

"St. Louis," he stammered. "We're headed to St. Louis."

Skippy turned to Mad Dog. "Does that sound like a warm climate to you?"

"No, Skippy, definitely not," Mad Dog responded. Addressing the pilot, he continued. "I presume there is a greeting party waiting for us?"

"I just know I am to land at Arrowhead Airport," said the pilot defensively.

Mad Dog put his hand on Skippy's shoulder. "Ya know, Skip., I never liked St. Louis. Ever since I got that parking ticket at a Cardinals game, I've not been a fan."

Mad Dog then moved in front of Skippy and whispered into the pilot's ear. "How about let's head to Texas."

"Afraid my hands are tied," said a shaky pilot. "Only enough fuel to get to St. Louis."

Mad Dog stroked his chin and thought for a moment. "Tell you what. How far can we get if we head south instead of west?"

After a lengthy pause, the pilot answered, "Probably Nashville or somewhere in Tennessee."

Mad Dog and Skippy plopped back in their seats.

"Okay, then," announced Mad Dog. "Here's our new plan. Turn south and head toward the Tennessee border. There's a landing strip outside of Cooksville. I'll settle for that."

When the pilot hesitated, Skippy drew out his knife one more time. Soon the plane was headed in a southerly direction.

*   *   *   *   *   *   *

On Sunday morning, as Chief Olsen and his crew headed to the Shiloh County police headquarters, Officer Kraus continued taking statements, while Officer Campbell typed up Emily's statement. The common understanding among all investigating the case was that the remaining members of the Bolton gang, Dr. McDougal, and his two henchmen had made their escape.

Things were not all rosy for the criminals, however. Dr. McDougal did not have the ruby, Mr. St. George and Mr. Fish were in for an unpleasant surprise, and Mad Dog and Skippy Forrester were stuck in Tennessee, literally not out of the woods. What none of them knew was the fuse Marvin lit had blown out twenty-seven feet away from the back of the farmhouse. All the extraordinary effort to turn attention to the building housing Mr. Tompkins and the unlucky young man was all for naught.

While their whereabouts were unknown to the authorities, another of the gang surfaced as a result of a police bulletin that came in on Sunday morning. George Kostov had been pulled off his stakeout of Mrs. Smothers' house and told to go home and get a good night's sleep on Saturday evening.

As a widower, with an apartment on the far east side of town, George arrived home, made a quick bowl of soup, and crashed on his couch with his television blaring. As a result, he did not hear the explosion and slept through the evening's excitement.

It was not until his phone rang early Sunday morning that George was rudely brought back to reality. George was a miniature version of Chief Olsen and wobbled his way over to the phone next to the television.

"This is George," he said weakly.

"George, I need you to roust yourself and get over to the station," barked the chief. "I am heading up to Shiloh County with the two students who were here all night."

"Chief, what's up? Has there been a break in the case?" asked Mr. Kostov.

"Where have you been, Kostov? La-la land?" screamed Chief Olsen. "I don't have time to bring you up to speed at the moment. Call me back from the station when you get there."

With that, the conversation ended and George ambled into the bathroom, mumbling something about getting a hobby.

It was not long before George was parking his aging sedan in a "For Official Use Only" spot. Things did not look all that different to him, apart from the news van parked in the street in front of the station. He retrieved the Sunday paper from the front stoop and could not help but notice the blaring headline: "**Explosion Rocks Granger's Woods.**"

There was not a lot of information, and everything had happened too late to make the Sunday edition. There was a caption under a picture, however, that read: "*Late last night, a huge explosion occurred several miles west of Webster. Adjacent woods were set ablaze. Many stations responded to the fire. It is not yet known if anyone was injured. The cause of the explosion is unknown. Chief Bartholomew Olsen and area police have launched a full-scale investigation.*"

Mr. Kostov scratched his head and wondered aloud if this had anything to do with the theft of the wooden leg. Once he had straightened things up somewhat (the office had looked like a pigsty when he'd arrived), George called Chief Olsen back.

The chief filled in George the best he could and was adamant that his volunteer cop was not to make any statements to the press, no matter how assertive they became. That did not give George warm fuzzies. He was not good at confrontation. Before they finished, George alerted the chief to something that had come over the wire.

"Chief, this just came in when I arrived. Do not know if it has anything to do with the case, but let me read it to you."

The bulletin stated, "*Ignatius Smothers, age 30, of Webster, Indiana, died today of wounds suffered in a truck accident on Friday, September 2nd. No known cause. Accident occurred seven miles south of Fort Wayne. No other passengers involved. Smothers was once a member of the Bolton gang and had been released from probation two years ago.*"

"You don't say, George," pondered Chief Olsen. "Hmm, one more member of the gang accounted for. Odd…very odd, indeed."

Little did the occupants of the two cars racing toward Bensonville know that Miss Quig was not the only person of interest they would want to speak with. Yvetlana Smothers had decided it was time to talk with the police.

*   *   *   *   *   *   *

Mrs. Smothers had arrived at her sister's house late Friday evening. It had been a long walk to Bensonville. In nine hours, she had covered twenty-three miles. Considering her age, physical condition, and the fact she was walking cross-country with only a few morsels to sustain her, it was a miracle she'd arrived at all. It was a tribute to her Russian constitution and a testament to what fear can motivate people to take on.

Marna Kopps (formerly Marna Smolanesky) had joined her sister in Webster several years after World War II. Four years younger, Marna had (amazingly) survived the war and moved with her family from town to town. Their father was a shoemaker and made just enough to keep them from starving. Finally, enough was enough, and Marna was put on a boat to America to join Yvetlana. Marna arrived in time to journey with Yvetlana and her sons to Indiana. She was placed in a foster home and actually did well for herself. After her high school graduation, she married her high school sweetheart, James Kopps, and they both secured jobs with Filson's Department Store in Bensonville. Marna was unable to have children, but they did love dogs; there always was a German Shepherd in the house.

Marna and Yvetlana kept up a communication of sorts. James and Marna had no use for Boris and Iggy, so the two families did not spend much time together. But Marna was always there for her older sister when needed. The Kopps lived on the east side of Bensonville in a small, two-story house. It was in a neighborhood of modest homes. Their house rested at the end of a cul-de-sac on Juniper Court.

When there was a knock on their door around midnight, Marna eased out of bed so as not to wake her husband (although he was a heavy sleeper). She was startled to see Yvetlana at the door.

"Sister!" she cried. "What brings you here at this hour?"

Observing Yvetlana from head to toe, Marna continued, "You look as though you have been through a tornado!"

Yvetlana then collapsed on the floor, and all Marna could do was drag her to the sofa and make her comfortable. Marna removed her scarf and coat and found some blankets to keep her warm. And there, Yvetlana rested well into Saturday morning.

Yvetlana, upon waking, and after some hot tea and biscuits, relayed her story to Marna, expressing both her concern for her sons and her fear of them.

"Don't worry, dear," said Marna. "You are safe here. James will be home from work around 5:00 p.m., and then we'll discuss what to do further."

Therefore, James was home when the three of them experienced the sound of the explosion.

"What in damnation was that?" exclaimed James, rising to his feet. They all rushed out onto the porch, and even though they were miles away, they could see the orange glow of flames in the distance to the south. Yvetlana started shaking, and it took some work to calm her down. Marna ended up getting her some sleeping pills and escorting her to the spare bedroom.

"Something is definitely not right, James," stated Marna, returning to the living room.

Like many others that evening, they stayed glued to their radio and eventually the local news at 10:00 p.m. After determining there was no more to be learned, James and Marna retired for the evening.

On Sunday morning, Yvetlana strolled into the kitchen and made an announcement. "I have to go see the police. My boys are in trouble; I know it." Then she sat down at the small table and wept.

An hour later, James, Marna, and Yvetlana were at the Bensonville Police Department. While Yvetlana was giving her story to an officer, Sergeant Bill Adams strolled into the room and asked, "Are you speaking to a Mrs. Smothers?"

That being determined in the affirmative, Sergeant Adams conferred with the officer, sharing with him the same bulletin that had appeared at the Shiloh County police station.

"Let's not upset Mrs. Smothers any more than she already is, but I was talking to Gus Sheridan this morning…he shared with me his and Frank's experience at the explosion site. Evidently, they are having some kind of confab with Chief Olsen this morning. I suggest we take Mrs. Smothers over there. She did say she worked at the museum, right?"

That being settled, soon Sergeant Adams, Officer Clooney, Yvetlana, and Marna were all in a squad car and heading to the northwest side of town. The bells of St. Thomas Catholic Church were ringing for the 11:00 a.m. service as they pulled into the county sheriff's parking lot. The bells seemed to be announcing, "Yvetlana is here! Yvetlana is here!"

You Can't Interview a Corpse

Anyone who had spent even a modest amount of time with Jarvis Bolton knew he had no problem doing what had to be done to complete a job. If that meant hurting people, so be it. If someone died in the process, so be it. The victim at Henry's garage was not his first. The amazing thing was that Jarvis had never been charged with murder. As a younger man, he had been arrested for throwing a patron through a bar window, but for the most part, Jarvis covered his tracks well.

When Dr. McDougal had initially approached him about harming Miss Quig, Jarvis (out of character) must have exhibited some apprehension. Therefore, the professor assured him, "Not to worry, my friend. She will eventually wake up."

Jarvis was not surprised, then, to wake up in the hospital. The same thing would have happened to Miss Quig had Mad Dog not turned the tables on him. He was surprised, though, when his body began to twitch about thirty minutes after Detective Shaw left his bedside. The twitching was followed by an increased heart rate. Next, Jarvis' right arm went numb. Finally, he began frothing at the mouth. There was no time to alert a nurse. The twitching evolved to convulsions, and soon Jarvis Bolton was no more.

Dr. McDougal knew very well he could not have Emily Quig alive to spill the beans on his involvement in the theft of the leg. So, he had lied to Jarvis. Unknowingly, Jarvis was supposed to be the executioner. By keeping the assignment secret, the professor meant to ensure there would be no interference.

The injection proved successful, but not on its intended victim. Emily Quig would live to name Dr. McDougal as the prime mover behind the theft. Even as Jarvis expired, many things would come to light at the Shiloh County police station. The jig was up. Still, a number of would-be witnesses had died. Not to mention that those of the gang still alive had escaped. Even if a nationwide manhunt was initiated, Dr. McDougal did not fear being caught.

To state it simply, the plan to steal the wooden leg had been executed. It had been a success. Unfortunately for the professor, he had crossed into the endzone without the football. Harvey Scrima had the ruby. Not only would his buyers in Toronto do a disappearing act, but Dr. McDougal was also left high and dry with no retirement fund.

It did not surprise Dr. McDougal when the pilot escorting Mr. Scrima and his buddy did not call him at the appointed time. Anyone capable of double-crossing him was certainly capable of hijacking a plane. Having calmed down from his immediate reaction, the professor knew he had to come up with another plan—this one to get the Timur Ruby back in his possession.

*   *   *   *   *   *   *

Officer Kraus was just about to begin his interview with Johnny when he turned to see nurses running down the hall. They were soon followed by two orderlies and a doctor.

"What the…?" said the officer, looking down the hallway.

A security officer came up to Officer Kraus and suggested they both head toward the activity.

"Johnny, I'll be right back. Don't go anywhere," instructed Officer Kraus, as if Johnny had any energy to get off his cot.

Ben and Jenny Turnbow waved Officer Kraus on. Herb could be such a nervous Nellie at times.

Upon arriving in Jarvis Bolton's room, the officers were greeted by Dr. Morgan. "Officer Kraus, Mr. Bolton is dead. I am almost certain he was poisoned. All signs point to organophosphate insecticide."

"Insecticide?" said Officer Kraus in disbelief. "How is that possible?"

"The strange thing," continued Dr. Morgan, pulling on his moustache, "is that we mainly find this kind of poisoning with suicides."

By now, Jarvis had lost all color. "I am sure you will want an autopsy on this one, right, Officer?" clarified Dr. Morgan.

"Yes, yes, of course," mumbled Herb.

An ambulance had already pulled up, and soon Jarvis was whisked off to the morgue. Officer Kraus went directly to his squad car and made a call to Chief Olsen.

"Chief," announced Officer Kraus, "we just lost another member of the gang. Bolton started foaming at the mouth and appears to have been poisoned. They're taking him to the morgue as we speak. Figured you would want an autopsy."

"Stay on top of it, Herb," replied Chief Olsen. "We are just about to begin having a group conversation up here in Bensonville. After you're done at the hospital, hustle on up here. I think we're close to putting a lot of pieces together. By the way, you should know Iggy Smothers was in a fatal vehicle accident south of Fort Wayne."

Officer Kraus returned to Johnny's room, and in his most officious voice, he said, "Folks, we need to get this interview with Johnny done ASAP. Ben, you and your wife try not to interrupt until I am done. I'm needed in Bensonville."

Johnny did the best he could, even though his mind was still a little fuzzy. He explained falling through the museum's basement window, retrieving the silver key, falling asleep in the board room, and then discovering the tunnel. Johnny trembled as he recalled his experience in the hideout.

"Officer Kraus, I should have been a goner. Who was it that saved me?"

"Heather and Jeremy probably didn't say anything about Mr. Barlow's sons when they mentioned the farmer to you," answered the officer. "Tom Barlow got Heather and Jeremy back to Webster and then he and his sons went out to search for you. They found you in the nick of time."

"When do I get the chance to thank him?" asked Johnny.

Officer Kraus pursed his lips and looked down at the floor for a minute. Raising his head, he said, "Well, you don't. He did not survive the explosion."

No one in the room said anything. Johnny's face grew pale, and it was a while before he spoke. "You know, Mr. Tompkins and I only saw four members of the gang. Two were obviously brothers. Both were just plain mean. They would periodically go over and kick Mr. Tompkins' chair to wake him up. One shoved a candy bar in my face. From what Heather told me, they were Tommy and Jarvis Bolton. The short, hairy one had to be the leader. They called him Mad Dog. His tall companion was as thin as the Bolton brothers were stout. He was called Skippy."

Johnny's voice then trailed off and it was obvious he needed to rest.

"You've done just fine, Johnny," said Officer Kraus, reaching over and rubbing Johnny's red mop. "We'll talk more later. Get some rest"

The Turnbows each gave Herb a hug (which made him uncomfortable) before he prepared to leave. Officer Kraus bumped into Dr. Morgan one more time in the lobby.

"You know, Officer, my mother volunteered at the county museum and got to know Mr. Tompkins pretty well. I hope he has come to no harm," offered the doctor.

Officer Kraus chose his words carefully. "He is still officially missing, but we have no evidence he has been harmed. I'll be sure to let you know when he turns up."

Then the good officer rushed to his car. He did not need any more probing questions from Dr. Morgan.

*   *   *   *   *   *   *

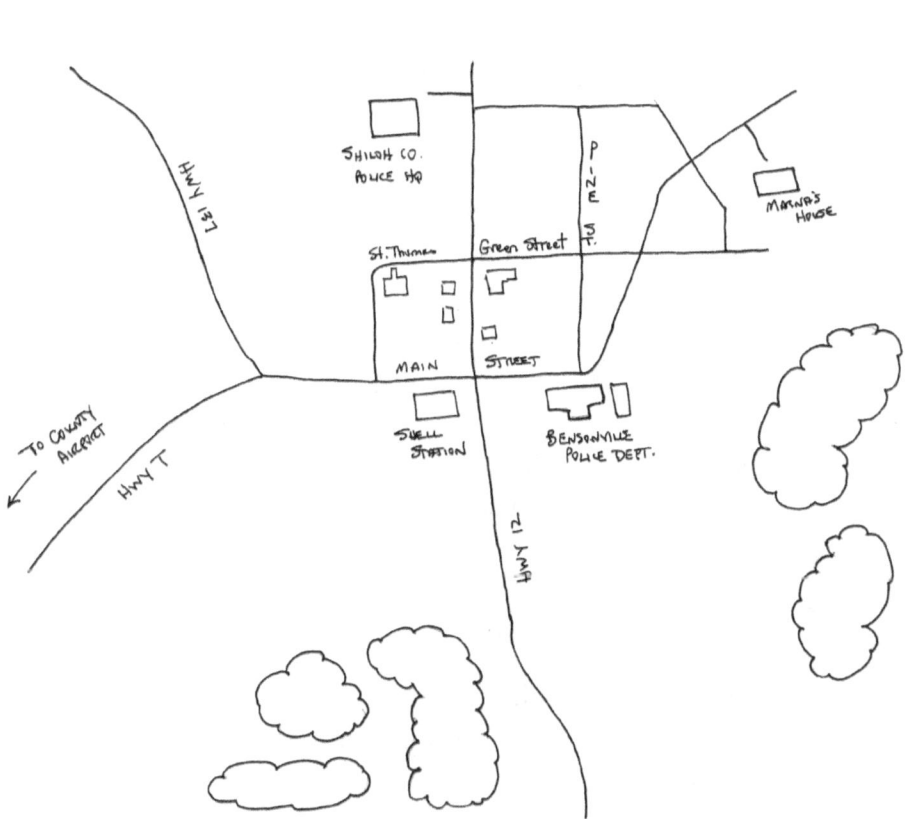

By the time Officer Kraus had traversed Highway 12 to Bensonville, it was almost noon. As he passed by the point on the highway nearest the explosion site, he could not help but notice several cars pulled off the road. Curious citizens walked as far as they could before confronting the roped-off area. Officer Kraus made a mental note to have a state trooper stop by. What they did not need right now was someone falling into the huge gaping hole.

When Officer Kraus entered the Shiloh County police headquarters, he was greeted by Officer Campbell.

"You must be Officer Kraus. The group is in the conference room. They have been waiting for you." With that, he quickly escorted Officer Kraus to the back of the building. Herb was taken aback by all those assembled. His jaw dropped.

Chief Olsen and Detective Shaw were in one corner of the room talking with who appeared to be Mrs. Smothers. The portly woman had her black hair wrapped in a big bun, and she periodically dabbed her eyes with a large white handkerchief. On the other side of the room, the two students, Daryl Rasmussen and Doris Guice, were chatting away nonstop with Emily.

They were laughing at each other's appearances. Daryl and Doris looked as if they had slept in their clothes (which they had). Emily bore the scars of having been in the tunnel, not to mention traversing through fields and forests and sleeping in a wooden shed. Her light blue hoodie was dotted with specks of brown and small leaves.

Heather and Jeremy sat on a small bench drinking their orange sodas. A small female officer called Spunky sat next to them with a bag of potato chips. Routinely, little hands dipped into the bag.

"I hear you kids have been through quite a lot. How are you holding up?" asked the officer.

Heather smiled and shook her head. "After all of this, going back to school will be a snap."

Jeremy chuckled and could only wonder how they had survived their ordeal. They were interrupted from their musings when Detective

Shaw turned and saw Officer Kraus in the room. He moved to the center of the room and began gesturing for all to gather around him.

"Listen up, everyone. We are unitedly going to get up to speed with what we know and have experienced. As they say in my world, it is as important to know what you don't know as it is to know what you know."

Sam turned to Officer Plank (who was still chafing about having to stick around the station). "Is there something I can stand on?"

Officer Plank carried a small bench over to the center of the room. "Have at it, Detective."

Detective Shaw was an impressive presence as he stood above everyone. Technically, Chief Olsen could have taken charge, but no one expressed any surprise that he did not. Sam, with his neatly trimmed black hair, white shirt and tie, and polished shoes resembled a leading man from a police drama.

"We are going to have each of you speak in the order you came into this affair," declared the detective. "First, we will hear from Mrs. Smothers. Heather and Jeremy, you will go next. Officer Kraus, you will then stand in for Johnny Turnbow. I will then read Miss Quig's statement. Miss Guice and Mr. Rasmussen will follow with anything they have to add. Officers Sheridan and Plank will review what they learned at the site of the explosion. Then I will sum up."

That being said, everyone took a seat. When it was their turn, each participant occupied the podium facing the chairs. Mrs. Smothers rose slowly and had to be helped to face the group.

Uprooting some stray hairs from her dark eyes, she began, "I have always loved my boys. But I also knew they could be mean and threatening. Still, I had never seen Boris both so angry and afraid at the same time."

Yvetlana wiped her eyes and continued. "I did not know why the key was so important, but I knew Boris would kill to get it. That is why I left."

"How did you walk all the way to Bensonville?" asked Chief Olsen.

Yvetlana sighed. "I have walked such distances before in the old country. Of course, I was a bit younger. It was walk or possibly die."

Then she looked the chief straight in the eye. "Tell me, what has happened to my boys?"

Chief Olsen bit his lip. "You had best sit down, Mrs. Smothers."

He then handed her the police bulletin detailing the accident near Fort Wayne. Yvetlana covered her face with her hands and intermittently sobbed. Her sister, who had been waiting in the lobby, was escorted in, and she bent down to comfort Yvetlana. Between sobs, Yvetlana posed the question, "And Boris, what about Boris?" she pleaded.

Officer Sheridan stood up and motioned to Detective Shaw to let him answer her.

"Ma'am," he began, "Officer Plank and I were at the explosion site all last night." He glanced at Officer Plank. "There were men who helped Johnny Turnbow to safety. One of them, a farmer named Tom Barlow, didn't make it out alive. At first, we thought it was just his body parts that were strewn over the ground. But early this morning, we found this."

With that, he moved over to Mrs. Smothers and handed her a damaged driver's license. The picture was blurred, but the last name could be read: "Smothers".

That was more than Yvetlana could handle. She collapsed on the floor as her sobs turned to wailing. Her sister struggled, even with the assistance of Officer Plank, to get Yvetlana up. Fortunately, there was a nurse on duty at the police headquarters, and she was summoned. A sedative was suggested and given. Marna, together with her husband, then managed to move Yvetlana to their car. For the near future, Mrs. Smothers would grieve in silence.

Group Think

— or —

Putting Two and Two Together

Before Heather and Jeremy could begin their summation, Chief Olsen stood up and added background to Yvetlana Smothers' story.

"So, you all know, Mrs. Smothers shared with us that her house served as a meeting place for the gang from time to time," noted the chief. "She fed them but did not engage with most of them. The only one that gave her the time of day, she reported, was the one they called Skippy. Mrs. Smothers was able to confirm that all the members of what we know as the Bolton gang were together."

The chief continued, "Mrs. Smothers only caught bits and pieces of their conversations, but she did figure they were trying to steal something. By the time Boris tasked her with retrieving the silver key, she surmised the museum was involved."

Officer Kraus jumped in. "Did she think Mr. Tompkins caught onto their caper?"

"Not particularly," replied the chief. "But Mrs. Smothers recalled he was always fixated on the wooden leg. The theft only seemed to make him more suspicious."

"Why did she run off?" asked Jeremy. "Why didn't she call the police?"

Detective Shaw tried to explain. "We all do crazy things when we are terrified, Jeremy. I suspect she did not trust us to protect her. Plus, Mrs. Smothers knew what the gang members were capable of."

Then it was Heather and Jeremy's turn to review their involvement (much of which they had already shared with Johnny). Periodically, they were asked questions about their experience—and even their motives.

Officer Kraus, upon hearing of the plan to break into the museum, reacted. "You crazy kids...always trying to play detective. Look where it got you." His voice began rising. "When you knew Johnny had been pushed through the window, why didn't you just report things to Mr. Tompkins?"

Heather sighed and replied, "We just wanted to get the lay of the land before talking to any adults...particularly him. You have to admit that we have been helpful before."

Officer Kraus just rolled his eyes. "Do I understand you couldn't be sure who captured you? You didn't catch a glimpse of him before being thrown in the truck?"

"He had our heads in his grasp, and it was dark," explained Heather. "Plus, he kept pulling on my hair."

"And what about going to the hideout? Surely you could see something." Herb was getting exasperated.

"Calm down, Herb," advised Detective Shaw. Turning to Heather and Jeremy, he asked, "Were they tall or short? Could you tell?"

"Definitely short," Jeremy replied.

"Look," Officer Kraus interjected. "He had to be one of the Smothers brothers. Johnny told me there were only four men in the hideout besides himself and Mr. Tompkins, and he didn't recognize any of them. Plus, he only heard the names Tommy and Skippy tossed around."

"I do remember one thing as we were escaping," added Heather. "Whoever it was that brought us to the hideout made the others pretty angry. They were yelling at him."

Officer Sheridan then stepped in. "Well, that would explain things, wouldn't it? Boris Smothers was identified at the site. My bet is that it was Boris who abducted the kids. I'm thinking he got into it with the gang leader, and they left him behind to die. Besides, his brother, Iggy, is the one they found dead not far from Fort Wayne."

Detective Shaw turned toward Chief Olsen. "Right, and if Boris was trying to retrieve the key, he may have been lurking around the museum on Friday night."

Sam then walked over to Officer Kraus and said, "Perhaps this would be a good time for you to speak to Johnny Turnbow's memory of things."

Officer Kraus sauntered up to the podium and stretched his arms off to each side. Chief Olsen tolerated his flair for the dramatic. "Now, folks, there has been a lot of discussion about a silver key. Obviously, the gang wanted the key. Perhaps Mr. Tompkins discovered the importance of the key. But it was Johnny Turnbow who eventually found it and learned what it opened."

Officer Kraus then explained how Johnny discovered the key, along with the business card of Dr. McDougal. When he and Chief Olsen had arrived at the museum on Saturday morning, Johnny was in the basement. Officer Kraus explained how Johnny discovered the door that led to the tunnel. The silver key provided him access. He related how Johnny had spent the greater part of the morning exploring the tunnel, and then his unfortunate discovery of the hideout.

At that point, Detective Shaw interrupted. "You say Johnny found four of the gang members at the hideout. Two of them went back into the tunnel and returned with Mr. Tompkins. That would explain Thaddeus' disappearance."

Detective Shaw paced up and down, stroking his chin. He then continued, "This is beginning to make some sense. I thought all along that Dr. McDougal was involved. Mr. Tompkins visited the professor. He must have learned that there was a greater importance to the wooden leg. Let us presume for a minute that Mr. Tompkins found the key that Mrs. Smothers lost. Then it was snatched out and under from him by Johnny. On Saturday afternoon, he begins a search for it, thinking it will lead him to the leg. He runs into Harvey Scrima and Skippy Forrester just as unexpectedly as Johnny did. They both end up as 'guests' at the hideout."

Officer Plank then stood up and motioned for attention. "Officer Sheridan and I are a bit late to the game here, but up to this point, no one has been able to say why this danged wooden leg is so sought after."

At this point, Emily Quig slowly stood up and raised her hand.

"Yes, Miss Quig…you have something to add?" asked Chief Olsen.

"Perhaps this would be a good time to read my statement," Emily offered.

Detective Shaw motioned for Officer Kraus to step down.

"But I have more I wanted to say about my conversation with Johnny," protested Officer Kraus.

"Later, Herb," said Sam. "I think Miss Quig is right. Reading the statement will answer Officer Sheridan's question."

Officer Kraus stepped out from behind the podium. "Can anyone follow protocol, just once?" he was heard to mutter.

There was a hush that settled over the conference room. Even Daryl and Doris were anxious to hear Emily's story. Though they had an inkling of what she had been through, their understanding was short on details. The truth was, with Detective Shaw and Chief Olsen caught up with Mrs. Smothers, none present had looked at Emily's statement. That was not to downplay the importance of what she had to say, but no one had had any contact with Emily. She had not been part of their adventures. Until Officers Plank and Sheridan had found her ambling down Highway 12, the only people Emily had been with were Dr. McDougal, his assistants Marvin and Mr. St. George, and only some of the gangsters.

Therefore, expectations were great. To Emily's credit, she had patiently listened to all of the museum intrigue, hoping her nightmare would end and she could return to campus. Detective Shaw stood ready to read, but Emily stopped him.

"Detective, sir, would you mind if I read my own statement?"

"Don't see why that should be a problem. Are you sure you are up to it?" Detective Shaw asked.

Emily smiled weakly. "You betcha," she acknowledged. "Besides, there may be some things I want to add."

STATEMENT OF EMILY QUIG

My name is Emily Quig, and I am a freshman at Bradford State University. In my first semester, I received permission to take the Principles of Archeology class. I was truly looking forward to it, but at the last minute, the professor who was to teach the class had to take a leave of absence. Dr. Winston McDougal took his place. The past three weeks, I struggled with the class and sought help from Dr. McDougal so I could pass. Little did I know this would lead me into a sinister plot that would threaten my life and introduce me to several unsavory characters.

Dr. McDougal offered to help me get a passing grade if I would assist him with a project involving the museum in Benson County. It seemed a harmless offer, and I accepted. Little did I know the professor planned on stealing a museum artifact. My role was to get into a museum case and pull out a wooden leg. When I had second thoughts, he threatened to harm my parents. There was a Mr. Tompkins, the museum's curator, who visited him on Friday afternoon. It made me sick to my stomach when I was forced to put sugar in the curator's gasoline tank.

Mr. Tompkins must have caused him some real grief because he had to change his plans regarding the theft. Initially, I did not see why the professor was so obsessed with the wooden leg. But obsessed he was. He summoned me to his office on Saturday afternoon. That is where I first met Detective Shaw. I alerted my roommate, Doris, that if I did not return by a certain time to call the campus police. I was very scared for my life. He caught on that I may have alerted her to the affair, so I had to call her and reassure Doris nothing was wrong. What the professor did not know was Doris and I had worked out code words if either of us got into any trouble.

Dr. McDougal dressed as a woman and we left his office. I was hoping Doris had come to witness what I was going through. But I did not see her in the hall. We were picked up by a pizza van and transported out of town. Though I did not know it at the time, Doris and her friend Daryl followed the van, but I think the professor caught on, and we took a dirt side road. We stopped for a while, and the driver painted over the lettering on the van. Dr. McDougal and I sat under a tree, and he reviewed my responsibilities.

Soon we were on our way again and drove to a farmhouse off of U.S. Highway 12. I never went in, as the driver (whose name was Marvin) drove the van to the back of the farmhouse next to a black limousine. We stayed there until summoned. I was able to pick up that the limo driver's name was Mr. St. George. He and Marvin seemed to know each other.

I lost track of time, but the sun had set on Saturday evening when I was transferred to another vehicle—a sporty model. That is where I first met two men; one was called Harvey but had the nickname "Mad Dog." The other was called Skippy. There was a man in the back with me, but I never caught his name. Harvey was very hairy and short—resembled an animal. Skippy was tall and skinny and wore a fisherman's hat over his bald head. The man next to me looked not to be messed with. Not huge, but muscular.

As we headed toward the museum (at least I thought that was where we were going), there was a tremendous explosion toward the south. This seemed to please everyone, so I figured it had to be part of their plan. It must have been a half hour or so before we pulled up to the museum. All of us got out. The men surveyed the grounds, and we went in the back entrance. I believe it was Skippy who went around to the front porch and discovered someone there. I think he knocked the person out.

Once inside, my job was to get in the back of the case housing the wooden leg. The professor had gone to great lengths to use some kind of technology so that it appeared the wooden leg was missing. But it really wasn't. There was a very small opening in the back of the case, which I got into with the help of a tiny key. I pulled the leg out and the three of us trundled off to the basement. The biker lookalike did not accompany us upstairs, by the way.

My understanding is that we were leaving the car and going back to the farmhouse by other means. We walked to the far end of the basement and came to a tunnel. Two men met us at the entrance. One was new, but he looked to be related to the first. After some words, we headed down the tunnel. The new guy was pretty dirty; he must have had something to do with the explosion, I figured.

What happened next was bizarre. We came to an overhead opening where it looked like we were to exit. Skippy and the other dude went up first. Then it was to be my turn. But the first muscle boy pulled out a needle of some kind and moved toward me. Before I knew what was happening, Harvey/Mad Dog confronted him and stuck him with the needle instead. We left his body in the tunnel. When we got outside, his lookalike wanted to go back in and retrieve the body. That caused a stir, and before I knew it, there was a knife in the guy's back. Now two men were dead. I don't know why I was spared.

We found some horses and took off through fields, crossing a creek at one point. I had lost all feeling. The entire evening was one bad dream. We eventually reached the farmhouse. Skippy took me inside the barn in back, so I don't know what exactly happened for about the next hour.

Eventually, Mad Dog came back for Skippy. I think they were supposed to kill me, but they didn't. Mad Dog just told me to keep quiet and hide behind the haystacks. Soon I heard planes take off.

To my horror, when I ran outside, I saw a lit fuse moving toward the farmhouse. So, I ran back in the barn and buried myself in a huge pile of hay. When nothing happened, I went back outside to find the fuse was extinguished. I guess they were trying to blow up the farmhouse for some reason. Upon waking up, I began to walk up the highway in a daze (I know I slept somewhere, but I can't remember). That is where the officers found me.

Emily had left out a few details and added some. Throughout her entire statement, she kept her composure. It was a masterful performance.

A Gem of a Dilemma

Cooksville, Tennessee, was not quite the best place for getting a valuable gem cut. The Timur Ruby could not be sold as it was. For one thing, it would be immediately identified, and that would likely expose Scrima and Forrester as thieves. At the least, it could alert Dr. McDougal to their whereabouts. For another, few in the valuable gem business could afford to purchase it, making it very difficult to fence. The customers Mad Dog had in mind were more low-key and would only recognize the stones he was selling as rubies.

Mad Dog had hoped they might be transported to Mexico or somewhere close to the United States border. He had a contact on the other side of El Paso who would have been a great help. Now, our two crooks were in a bit of a bind. In Tennessee, they were fish out of water. Fortunately, Mad Dog had only given Miss Quig a portion of the payment he had received, so they could easily secure a motel room. This they did on Saturday night.

Cooksville had grown some from the sleepy town it once was. It now housed a state university and offered two major shopping malls. Its population was approaching 20,000 people. Most of the urban development was south toward the interstate, however, and along with it, the majority of the community's hotels. That was just fine with Mad Dog, though. Coming from the north, the first place they came in contact with was Al's Manor Lodge...sixteen ground-floor units that attracted a less affluent crowd.

Mad Dog and Skippy had decided to bring the pilot with them, as any alternative would eventually tip off Dr. McDougal to their location. It was late at night when they awoke the desk clerk. The kid behind the counter was probably making some bucks while attending college. His blond hair was tied up in a ponytail, and his lack of enthusiasm was evident.

"One room or two," he drawled after noticing they were a party of three.

"Just one room with two beds works," replied Mad Dog.

The clerk shoved the key to room 118 toward them. "That will be $22.95." He paused. Giving Mad Dog the once over, he added, "In advance."

That business being concluded, they shuffled over to their room. To say the room was bare bones was an understatement. Two twin beds with horrible orange blankets, a rickety table lamp, and a dresser with one drawer missing greeted the trio. The bathroom had a shower, but, as Skippy soon learned, it only offered lukewarm water.

"What are you going to do with me?" blurted out the pilot.

Mad Dog shoved him down on a bed. "I haven't quite decided. We may still have need of your services. For the moment, you best be on your best behavior. Of course, you realize we have to lock you in the bathroom tonight. Can't risk you trying to escape."

The pilot was not huge, but he did not relish sleeping in the bathtub...particularly a wet one. Still, he was not about to mess with his hosts. He still had a vivid memory of Skippy's pulled knife from earlier in the evening. Walking from the airfield to the outskirts of Cooksville, he kept an eye on Skippy, not knowing what he might do next.

Having survived the night and then enjoying a hearty breakfast at J.J.'s Diner the next morning, they returned to the motel. Skippy could tell something was rattling around in Mad Dog's brain.

"So, Mr. Pilot, you got a name?" asked Mad Dog.

"Ted. My name is Ted," the pilot uttered.

"Well, Ted, tell me what your orders were after you dropped us off in St. Louis," pursued Mad Dog.

"My job was done," Ted responded. "I was free to return home."

Mad Dog gazed at him intently, trying to discern if he was lying. "And where would home be?"

"I run a little courier service out of an airport in northeast Indianapolis," Ted answered.

"You got any jobs pending?" countered Mad Dog.

"Tuesday I am supposed to take some corporate dudes to Chicago," Ted replied. Ted was not a young man; he'd flown for major airlines for over ten years before deciding to go into business for himself. There were bags under his eyes from too many sleep-deprived nights. His jaw appeared too large for his face, and his brown hair could be seen to be receding.

"You got family?" continued Mad Dog.

"Been divorced for two years. Just got a German Shepard that keeps me company." There was a bit of sadness in Ted's voice.

"Well, then," said Mad Dog. "How about we make it worth your while to take a little detour. I'll double what the boys are paying you. I need to get south of here...say New Orleans or Miami. How far can your plane go without refueling?"

Ted thought a while before replying. "We would have to make just one pit stop. But what guarantee do I have that I will be able to leave once you are done with my services?"

Mad Dog burst out laughing, and Skippy smiled. Mad Dog slapped the pilot on the back. "Good point, sir, good point."

When Mad Dog laughed, and it wasn't often, you could see he was missing some molars. He actually could have made a good Halloween pumpkin, though a hairy one.

"Been asking myself that very question," replied Mad Dog thoughtfully. "We can't have you going to the police. And heaven knows what our former boss will be up to."

Mad Dog walked over and put his hand on Ted's shoulder, which made the pilot cringe. "I think the answer is we need some time. You're going to have to stay at our destination for a week. To be fair, we'll pay for your lodging. Can you do that, fly boy?" Mad Dog thrust his face into Ted's.

"Just need to let my neighbor know to feed and take out the dog," Ted responded softly.

"Then I think we have ourselves a deal, Ted," declared Mad Dog. "Let's go get you some petrol."

*   *   *   *   *   *   *

In a surlier mood was Dr. McDougal. While he was able to get the flight plan for his chartered plane to St. Louis from the airport authorities there, no one could tell him where it was headed after the pilot broke off his approach. The professor sat in the hotel lobby of the Drake Hotel, strumming his fingers on the small table next to him. His bushy eyebrows suddenly rose as he got an idea. Dr. McDougal jumped up and strode toward the business office.

With his long arms stretched outward and resting on the counter, he patiently waited for an employee—any employee—to show themselves. Eventually, a rather thin, gaunt young man whose hotel uniform barely fit entered the room. He seemed surprised to see the towering person before him.

"Is there something I can help you with?" the young man asked innocently.

"I wonder," said Dr. McDougal in his best academic voice, "would you possibly have a drawing compass anywhere on the premises?"

"Don't get many requests for those, sir," the employee replied quizzically. "But this is your lucky day. The hotel does not have one to my knowledge, but I do."

He leaned over across the counter. "Don't say anything, but I was doing a little homework during my break. I'll get it from my satchel." Then he winked.

Dr. McDougal responded with, "Excellent!"

Soon the professor was back in his room, scrutinizing a map of the United States. Placing one end of the compass near Webster, Indiana, and extending the pencil end to St. Louis, he drew a circle. It had occurred to him that the plane he had chartered for the gang had enough fuel to get to St. Louis and back. Therefore, the farthest the plane could fly and still get back to Indiana was the distance to St. Louis. Assuming the plane had not gone far before changing direction, that distance of 243 miles was the maximum the plane flew before returning home. Then Dr. McDougal drew a wider circle of 486 miles in case the plane flew as far as it could go before having to refuel.

Somehow, Dr. McDougal could not see Mr. Scrima wanting to land in Oklahoma. In fact, if he were in Mr. Scrima's shoes, he would want to fly in the opposite direction of the original flight path. Something inside told him they were south of Kentucky. He was going to need the assistance of Mr. St. George and Mr. Fish. They would be arriving Sunday evening. In the meantime, he knew the name of the pilot in question. While he may not be able to communicate with the pilot directly, with a little research, he could try his home. Dr. McDougal had a feeling Lady Luck was with him.

*   *   *   *   *   *   *

"Are you kidding me!" screeched Officer Kraus. "The wooden leg was in the museum the entire time?"

The whole Webster police force was dumbfounded. The entire time they were at the museum since Thursday, the leg had been right under their noses. Detective Shaw's suspicions about Dr. McDougal were confirmed. Even his sharp mind, however, could never have perceived the extent to which the professor would go to steal the leg.

"I want to repeat my question," interjected Officer Plank. "What was so dang important about a wooden leg that this professor would spend enormous effort and money to steal it? Why wouldn't he hire these goons to just go in when the museum was closed and lift it?"

"Exactly," added Officer Sheridan, removing his sunglasses to make his point. "You're telling me that several good and bad men have died for some kooky elaborate operation to take a museum piece."

Both were staring directly at Detective Shaw as they spoke. The detective paced up and down. He turned to Emily and asked, "When you took the leg, did you notice anything unusual about it?"

"There were some markings on the bottom, but I really did not have time to examine the leg," Emily answered, rubbing her forehead. "Mad Dog had it in his possession all the way to the farmhouse."

"Wait a minute, wait a minute!" interrupted Officer Kraus. "It's coming to me. Hold on."

Officer Kraus was moving around the room like a man being attacked by hornets. "When I went to the museum on Friday, Mr. Tompkins was looking over some papers."

Now the officer was hitting the side of his narrow head. Then he stopped upright and exclaimed, "It was a shipping label. That's it! A shipping label. He had me read it. There was a number that caught Mr. Tompkins' eye." He paused. "It was three thousand something."

That caused Chief Olsen to start thinking. "You're right, Herb. When we confronted Thaddeus on Saturday morning, I asked him about the bill of lading and any value attributed to the wooden leg. He also had a bunch of charts and drawings borrowed from Dr. McDougal…or so he said."

Chief Olsen continued, "Herb, when you spoke with Johnny, did he say anything about what he found in Tompkins' office?"

"We didn't get that far, Chief," responded Officer Kraus.

"Jeremy and Heather, you had some time with Johnny," said Chief Olsen, turning toward the two. "Any discussion of his time alone in the museum?"

"We spent the time we had mainly sharing our experiences of escape, I am afraid," noted Heather.

The one person in the room who could have cleared the air on the wooden leg's value was Emily Quig, who chose not to speak. Her statement left out her support of Mad Dog's plan to double-cross Dr. McDougal. She knew of the existence of the ruby. Emily also did not divulge her relationship with Mad Dog Scrima, nor the fact she had been compensated.

Officer Sheridan then stepped forward. "Listening to what all of you have just said and taking into consideration the immense trouble this Dr.

McDougal took to steal the wooden leg, I suggest there was something inside the leg. Plus, I don't think your museum curator was forthright with you, Chief. He'd visited the professor. He was well acquainted with the artifact's history. He must have known what the gang was after. I think that is why he ended up in the hideout."

Heather then jumped in. "Detective Shaw, do you think Mr. Tompkins is still alive?"

Officer Sheridan did not answer her question but asked one of Emily before Detective Shaw could answer. "Miss Quig, you said to Officer Plank and me when we found you walking down the highway that we should check out a farmhouse. And then you also mention going to a farmhouse in your statement. What happened there? Do you know?"

Emily gave a weak smile. "I never went inside, but Dr. McDougal and Mad Dog did. The gang was standing around the porch when I first arrived. Like I said before, they intended to blow it up."

Detective Shaw stepped forward. "Heather, if Mr. Tompkins is still alive, I suspect he is in that farmhouse. Perhaps it is time we go check it out."

"We still need to put some effort into pursuing the criminals, Sam," suggested Chief Olsen. "I think Officer Kraus and I should stay here and work with our Shiloh County officers in getting the word out. Perhaps you should take Officers Plank and Sheridan with you and locate the farmhouse. If Miss Quig is up to it, she should accompany you to help you locate it."

Detective Shaw nodded in agreement.

"Could I offer a suggestion, Chief Olsen?" asked Doris Guice. "Emily has been through a lot. How about Daryl and I tag along to give her some moral support?"

"I'll go along with that, but first do me a favor and give Mr. Kostov a call at headquarters and fill him in on our whereabouts," replied the chief.

Officers Plank and Sheridan rolled their eyes and mumbled, "Who needs sleep anyway? Highly overrated."

Heather and Jeremy suddenly felt very left out. "What about us, Chief?" they asked in unison.

"Yes, of course, of course," Chief Olsen muttered. Summoning Officer Kraus, he said, "On second thought, Herb, why don't you take Heather and Jeremy back to the museum and give the office there a thorough searching. Report back to me with what you find."

Better informed, but not necessarily in high spirits, the group broke up to embark on their respective missions. In Webster, church had let out long ago, and more folks were checking out the explosion site. Mr. Kostov was repeating, "No comment," to the press and eventually hid in the restroom. Melody Stippich was getting ready to take her husband home from the hospital. Ben and Jenny Turnbow were continuing to hold vigil at Johnny's bedside. Gang members were gone or dead.

Amidst it all, the Benson County Museum stood empty and lonely. Scarred by the activities of the past three days, it was almost as if the museum was grieving. It knew the wooden leg would never return.

The Farmhouse
Reveals Its Secret

The team of six moved south on Highway 12 in two vehicles. Officers Plank and Sheridan occupied one squad car with Emily, and Detective Shaw followed in his car containing Doris and Daryl. Since Emily was the only one of the bunch who knew the location of the farmhouse, she had to be the one to point out to the Shiloh County officers where to turn off the road.

As her party approached the dirt road leading up to the farmhouse, Emily leaned forward with her hands on the front seat and counseled, "You need to slow down, Officer Sheridan. We're getting close. The road you want will be on your right, partially hidden by two rather large bushes."

It was only a matter of minutes before Emily pointed to the entryway. "There it is, Officers," she announced.

The afternoon sun peaked from behind some altocumulus clouds above the farmhouse roof. It was easy to see why the structure was not visible from the road. The dirt road swung around to the right to face several mature beech trees. In addition, two large oak trees stood on either side of the front porch. The exterior of the farmhouse had seen better days, its wood now a dull gray.

Officer Sheridan eased his Chevrolet sedan toward the house. It was obvious other vehicles had been there. As Detective Shaw pulled up, they all exited and headed toward the porch. Eventually, everyone stood on the porch and surveyed the farmyard.

"Certainly looks peaceful enough," offered Doris.

Daryl slowly swung his head side to side. "So, Emily, this is where the gang gathered before you headed to the museum?"

Emily stared into space, reconstructing the recent events in her mind. Her green eyes welled up as she remembered the range of emotions she had experienced over the past twenty-four hours. Mostly, she had come to the conclusion that Professor McDougal was a nasty, nasty man. Emily had made a conscious decision to do whatever it took to bring him down, as much of a long shot as that seemed.

Detective Shaw brought her out of her reverie. "Can you walk us through, Miss Quig, what you experienced here?"

With that, she said nothing but led the group around the side of the farmhouse. "See that barn?" Emily asked. "That is where we hung out while the professor and Mad Dog were occupied inside. The limo driver, Mr. St. George, parked his fancy car inside the barn. Marvin—I don't know his last name—parked the van alongside the barn. You can see its tracks. I could not get out of the van until it was time to leave for the museum."

Emily showed no emotion, and her friends knew coming back to the farmhouse was painful for her. Doris, a head taller than Emily, put her thin arm around Emily's shoulder.

"Emily, I can't imagine what it was like with these thugs," she said in a consoling voice. "You were very brave to get through things in one piece. I think I would have freaked out."

Officer Sheridan then stepped forward. "When we picked you up this morning, Miss Quig, you made a point of saying bad things happened here. What did you mean by that?"

The question caught Emily unawares, and she had to stop a moment to think. "Ah, I'm not sure...not sure I was thinking clearly."

Doris interjected, "Officer, go easy. She's been through a lot. Emily was probably just reacting to everything she had been through."

"Perhaps Miss Quig could just relate what happened when Mr. Scrima and Mr. Forrester brought her back here from the tunnel," suggested Detective Shaw.

Emily nodded her head quickly and gave Doris a look that indicated she was okay with responding.

"Like I said in my statement, Detective, they brought me back to the barn and told me to stay put. Then I heard planes, and everyone had left," she replied.

"Yes, of course," noted Detective Shaw. He began pacing again. "But from your statement, Jarvis Bolton tried to kill you in the tunnel. He certainly did not get the idea on his own. Obviously, if Scrima and Forrester had wanted you dead, Mad Dog would not have intervened. Let us assume it was Dr. McDougal who did not want any witnesses to the evening. I am wondering why you are still alive."

Everyone was now staring at Emily, wondering what she would say. Emily gulped. She did not want to divulge her relationship with Mad Dog.

"Maybe he thought I was dead," Emily speculated. "I mean, I never saw the professor when we returned."

"So, you are saying Mr. Forrester basically saved your life by hiding you in the barn?" continued Detective Shaw.

"I don't know. I don't know!" insisted Emily, who burst into tears and began sobbing.

"Oh, come on," objected Doris and Daryl in unison. "Are you kidding me?! After what this girl's been through, you're trying to have her determine what was in the demented minds of her captors? You've got to be kidding!"

Detective Shaw just held up his hand as if to say, "Enough." He then motioned for Officers Sheridan and Plank to come over.

"Are you thinking what I'm thinking?" Sam asked.

Officers Sheridan and Plank looked at each other. It was Officer Plank who spoke first. "Sounds to me that all things were not right in Denmark."

"Assuming Dr. McDougal wanted Miss Quig eliminated, it seems Mad Dog Scrima and the professor were not on the same sheet of music," added Officer Sheridan.

"I'll go a bit further," stated Detective Shaw. "I think Harvey Scrima has pulled some kind of double-cross on the good doctor. Gus, I think you hit the nail on the head. There was something valuable inside the wooden leg."

After Detective Shaw finished, he stood rubbing his chin, and gazed toward the farmhouse. "Well, let's go look inside the farmhouse and see if we get any more revelations."

The group marched up the porch stairs and pushed open the front door. While there was evidence of recent activity—a beer can here, a bag of potato chips there—for the most part, the farmhouse was a neglected edifice. The drawing room on the left housed an old piano, a ragged circular rug, some bookshelves with a few worn volumes, a saggy, moth-eaten sofa, and a lamp that leaned halfway to the floor. On the right was once a dining room; the only piece of furniture was a long table with no chairs. On a small table lay three china dishes, each broken in different places.

Directly in front of them stood a staircase leading to the upstairs. Detective Shaw divided the team in two with Emily, Doris, and Daryl surveying the downstairs and he and the officers investigating the second level. There still was sufficient light inside the house, as few windows had any curtains. For the most part, though, there were no working lights with the exception of the kitchen fixture. Emily and friends found dirty dishes in the sink and a pot of what appeared to be leftover spaghetti sauce.

Upon reaching the landing, Detective Shaw and the officers observed two bedrooms on the left and two on the right with a connecting hallway exhibiting two large paintings of rural landscapes.

"You guys take the left. I'll take the right. Give a holler if you need help," instructed Detective Shaw. He was not sure what his last statement meant. The farmhouse appeared vacant.

The bedrooms were similar in that each had a bed, a dresser, and empty closets with a few hangers. Detective Shaw saw nothing in the first bedroom. He would find Thaddeus Tompkins in the second. Sam Shaw was a seasoned veteran of the Webster police force. He was a consummate law enforcement professional. But what he witnessed in the front upstairs bedroom made even him cringe. In the overstuffed chair to his left sat what appeared to be a dead young man. Slouched, wearing a red Indiana University T-shirt and rumpled jeans, the assumed deceased was probably in his early twenties. His blond hair was matted with blood. Directly in front of Detective Shaw was Mr. Tompkins. He wore his usual black slacks, white shirt, and ratty suit jacket. Lying on the small bed, he appeared petrified, his mouth open and eyes half shut.

First, Detective Shaw checked the condition of the young man. He seemed to have a faint pulse, but considering how long he likely had been in the chair, Detective Shaw concluded he was in a coma. Next, he moved slowly over to Mr. Tompkins, half expecting him to come back to life. It was obvious, however, that rigor mortis had sent in. Since Thaddeus was stiff as a board, he had been dead for at least twelve hours.

Detective Shaw closed the rest of his pale eyes. The room stank, and Sam tried not to gag. He abruptly turned and exited the room.

"Gus, Roger, you'll want to see this…or maybe not," beckoned the detective.

Together, the three more closely examined the victims and agreed the young man had been hit with a blunt object. As for Mr. Tompkins, they discovered small puncture marks on his forehead. More business for the morgue.

Detective Shaw almost did not see the wooden leg at the foot of the bed. "What do we have here, gentlemen?" he posed.

From what Emily Quig had shared, it seemed odd that the leg would have been left behind.

"One of you summon Miss Quig up here," directed Detective Shaw. "Maybe she can shed some light on the subject. But examine the leg in another room. We're declaring this bedroom off limits."

Once congregated, Emily related that she had last seen the leg with Mad Dog. Why it was left behind, she did not know.

"But you did say, and the evidence supports it, that the gang was going to set the farmhouse on fire?" asked Officer Sheridan.

Emily affirmed her statement. After some animated discussion, the group decided that perhaps this was just another stunt to throw the authorities off track. Even if the wooden leg was the real one, they agreed the valuable item inside of it was likely gone. Detective Shaw would have it sent up to the state crime lab for examination. In the meantime, an ambulance would need to be summoned to take Mr. Tompkins back to the morgue. The innocent victim would need to go to the hospital for further examination.

Next, they surveyed the grounds at back of the farmhouse and could see tire tracks heading west. As they walked back to the police car, Detective Shaw tried to make sense of what they had discovered.

"I am going to believe, until proven otherwise, that Dr. McDougal did not intend for Miss Quig to live to testify as to his guilt in this whole matter. I am also going to accept the fact that he likely does not know the farmhouse did not go up in flames. In other words, in his opinion, wherever he is, he does not believe we have been able to pinpoint him as the mastermind behind the theft. At the very least, we have him as accessory to murder and attempted murder, not to mention arson, kidnapping, and civil endangerment. I think it is time to call in the FBI and locate where Dr. McDougal has flown."

* * * * * * *

Chief Olsen was doing his part in that regard. With the help of Officer Campbell, together they were trying get a handle on all air traffic out of Shiloh County Saturday night. Both agreed that the county airport was probably the point of departure. Thanks to Miss Quig, they knew the getaway was by plane. This was yet another fact Dr. McDougal was unaware of. In actuality, he did not realize he now was a targeted man. Therefore, as he planned to track down his traitor henchmen, the professor did so with less caution than he should have.

After contacting air control towers in Springfield and Peoria, Illinois; South Bend, Terre Haute, and South Bend, Indiana; Louisville, Kentucky; Columbus, Ohio; plus the Illinois and Indiana Air National Guards, Chief Olsen thought he had come up with something. The Fort Wayne air traffic controllers reported a medium-sized aircraft on the southern fringe of their airspace around 9:30 p.m. heading east-northeast. The pilot, when contacted by the tower, indicated a flight plan to Cleveland, Ohio. Controllers advised the pilot to adjust his flight path by twelve miles to avoid any possible collisions.‡

The air traffic controllers in Cleveland reported only two private aircraft landings on Saturday night, both coming from Detroit, Michigan. They suggested that the plane, if hauling contraband, may have flown "dark," meaning off radar. The controllers also suggested that Chief Olsen may want to contact Canadian authorities, as it was not uncommon for private aircraft to try and leave American airspace undetected.

---

‡ *Dr. McDougal had retained the services of a Gulfstream GIIB aircraft, which would have fit the description of a medium-sized private jet.*

The Citabria B plane that flew Mad Dog and Skippy to Cooksville, Tennessee, would have had no such issue, as it could fly low enough to avoid any commercial aircraft. The pilot only had to check in when he got close to the Cooksville Municipal Airport.

As noted before, Dr. McDougal did not suspect the authorities would be closing in. So, when he got to Toronto, he had no sense of urgency. Result: advantage to Chief Olsen.

*   *   *   *   *   *   *

Officer Kraus once again felt he was being relegated to low-end action. Upon reaching the museum, he mumbled, "Well, let's get this over with."

The office was much as Mr. Tompkins had left it. But, up to this point, no one had examined the map Thaddeus had brought back from Dr. McDougal's office. It lay slightly curled on his sturdy walnut desk. Heather was the first to notice it.

"This looks interesting," she shared. Heather spread her arms over the map to get a full view.

Officer Kraus and Jeremy joined her, each on one side.

"It's a map of the Caribbean," Heather added. "Look here. An island has been circled. I believe it is St. Lucia."

Jeremy reached over and moved Heather's right arm so he could turn over the map to examine some writing he saw.

"There seems to be some kind of list on the reverse side," he said excitedly.

With Officer Kraus' assistance, they turned the map over.

"That bill of lading Mr. Tompkins brought to my attention put some value on the wooden leg," Officer Kraus reminded Heather and Jeremy. "Perhaps we have found some kind of inventory."

They almost missed the last entry. Then, Heather let out a shout.

"Here we go! Timur Ruby!" Turning to Officer Kraus, she asked, "Didn't you say that Mr. Tompkins actually mentioned a figure of three thousand pounds?"

"Where are you going with this?" questioned Officer Kraus.

Heather pushed her amber hair out of her face and tried not to sound exasperated. "So, within the inventory on the back of a map of the Caribbean, we find listed a Timur Ruby. The bill of lading for the wooden leg seems to give a value of three thousand pounds. That makes no sense. A ruby worth three thousand pounds does."

Then Jeremy chimed in. "Yeah, and according to Johnny, the story behind the wooden leg is that it was taken to England via ship from the Caribbean."

"Well," surmised Officer Kraus, "this just confirms our conclusions at the Shiloh County police station. If you are correct, the item of value we all have been wondering about is this Timur Ruby."

Further investigation of the office did not yield anything interesting. The folder that Mr. Tompkins had scrutinized so carefully was not on the desk. He'd likely buried it in his file cabinet or squirreled it away somewhere. In any case, while it would have provided the trio with more background information, it would not have tied the ruby directly to the wooden leg.

Before they left the museum, Officer Kraus called Chief Olsen and shared their epiphany with him. Chief Olsen, in turn, shared that Dr. McDougal's plane had probably headed to Canada. It only remained for Detective Shaw to share his team's discoveries.

The Plane Truth

Dr. McDougal intentionally did not attempt to land at Toronto International Airport. To draw less attention to his aircraft and to facilitate an unscheduled landing, he opted for Billy Bishop City Airport instead. Situated on the shores of Lake Ontario, Billy Bishop was a favorite of corporate fleets. Since passengers could not go through customs there, however, arrivals had to have a Canadian passport. This Dr. McDougal had acquired (on the black market), and so he entered Toronto virtually unnoticed.

His associates, though, landed at Toronto International from Chicago. They did have to go through customs, and, therefore, their presence could be tracked. As a result, Dr. McDougal's plan was for Mr. St. George and Marvin Fish not to stay at the Drake, but on a boat owned by a professor from the University of Toronto.

Dr. McDougal was no fool. He knew none of them could stay in Toronto. Once he had the ruby broken down so it could be fenced, they would leave town. The professor calculated that would take no more than a week.

Now his plans had been foiled. They would need to leave town empty handed. Not only would Dr. McDougal have to expend extra time and energy to retrieve the Timur Ruby, but he would also have to accomplish the task with diminishing funds. In other words, he would have to get creative.

The taxi carrying Mr. St. George and Marvin pulled up in front of the Drake Hotel in the early evening. The Drake was an old, dignified hotel with a multitude of ornamental woodwork. The lobby hearkened back to another era. Beautiful oriental rugs lined the floors. Two large mirrors with gilded frames faced each other from opposing walls. A huge glass chandelier hung from the ceiling. Dr. McDougal sat on a purple velvet sofa facing the entrance.

The professor stood up as his two supporters entered the lobby. He turned toward the elevators, and they followed him. Soon they all sat in Room 813 with a view of the Toronto skyline.

"Gentlemen," began Dr. McDougal. "We have been stabbed in the back. Mr. Scrima appears to have swapped the ruby out from under our noses. In all likelihood, the pilot of their plane has been forced to change his flight plan. Our payday has been postponed."

After he gave Marvin and Mr. St. George time for his statement to sink in, the professor continued. "My calculations, based on the amount of fuel they had to work with, put them somewhere south of Kentucky. Unfortunately, I cannot afford to retain the services of our chartered plane. I need for you to reflect on our best way forward."

Mr. Fish spoke first. "We figured something had gone south. I was hit from behind with a rake, and when I came to, Mad Dog and his sidekick had taken the satchel and boarded their plane. If they thought they were absconding with the rest of the loot, they were rudely awakened."

"I have been thinking, Boss," chimed in Mr. St. George. "I'm not sure Bolton successfully fulfilled his mission."

Dr. McDougal gave him a cold stare. "Go on," he said.

"I think Mr. Scrima and Mr. Forrester eliminated the Bolton brothers and took on a new partner," offered Mr. St. George.

Dr. McDougal stood up, and his face grew pale.

"Not only that," added Marvin, "I reached out to my boys in Bradford City, and they report there has been nothing on the news channels about a farmhouse fire. The only thing getting coverage is the explosion. One good thing—the Bolton gang has been prominently featured on the local newscasts."

"What I am hearing from you, then, is that Miss Quig is quite possibly alive," Dr. McDougal said in summary. Both accomplishes nodded.

The professor went on. "That means our cover could be blown. So now we probably do not have the advantage of surprise. Getting back the ruby will very difficult."

"Perhaps we should just hightail it and lay low for a while," suggested Marvin.

Gritting his teeth, Dr. McDougal's face grew red. "We have come too far to turn back. In fact, there is nothing to turn back *to*. I have burned all of my academic bridges." Calming down, he continued. "Of course, if you both want to start waiting tables, Toronto has a variety of restaurants."

Mr. St. George, always the voice of reason, then spoke. "We will now have to travel by land. We will also have to alter our appearances. There are no alternatives. I suggest we get a good night's sleep and get out of town first thing tomorrow."

Before they could make further plans, there was a knock at the door. Dr. McDougal motioned for Mr. Fish to answer the door. Standing in front of him was a bellhop.

"I have a message for Dr. McDougal," he said, peering into the room.

"You can leave it with me; I am his assistant," replied Mr. Fish.

The young man hesitated but then delivered the message. "A woman called not too long ago. We rang your room, but there was no answer. She asked for your room number, as she said she wanted to send up some wine. The woman did not leave a return number."

Marvin tipped him a buck and then shut the door.

"Did you hear that, Boss?" asked Marvin.

Dr. McDougal nodded his head, "yes". "My friends," he announced, "I think I will be sharing the boat with you this evening."

* * * * * * *

The Cooksville Municipal Airport was not a hotbed of activity on Sundays. There were a couple of owners working on their aircraft, but the man who usually occupied the tower was putzing around in Hangar 1. There was a solitary refueling tank to the left of the south runway. After a bit of searching, Mad Dog, Skippy, and Ted tracked down the airport employee.

"Excuse me, friend," greeted Mad Dog. "Can we get our plane refueled? I've got cash."

The man looked up from the tire he was patching. He was definitely a good ol' boy. He wore a sleeveless undershirt, and a cigarette hung loosely out of his mouth. "Would love to help ya, really would, but no fuel available until tomorrow morning. We're plumb out."

"What kind of operation do you run here?" protested Skippy, taking a stride toward the man.

Mad Dog threw his arm across Skippy's chest, stopping his progress. "Look, friend, we really need to get out of town today. Even a few gallons would help."

The man stood up and scratched his head. He was on the thin side, and his jeans hung off his waist. "You see those two fellers there?" he replied, pointing. "May be that one of them would let you siphon a little from their planes. They only fly Wednesday afternoons. So, for the right price…"

Mad Dog knew what that meant. He would be taken advantage of. At that instant, Ted stepped in.

"Even if they shared some fuel, it would not get us far," the pilot explained. "Why don't you let me contact the guy who hired me. I could throw him off our trail. Could buy you some time until the fuel comes in."

"The man who hired you is a university professor who would make a great mob boss," responded Mad Dog. "You better have your story down pat if you think you are going to trick him."

Actually, Mad Dog kind of liked the idea. By now, the professor would have figured out he had been double-crossed and could be hot on their trail. Still, why would Dr. McDougal believe the pilot if he assumed there was a gun at his head? Suddenly, an idea came to him.

"By any chance, did your employer give you an idea where he would be headed?" Mad Dog asked.

"Not exactly," replied Ted. "But he did give me a phone number. I was supposed to check in after I dumped you guys."

Not a lot of help, thought Mad Dog. *But maybe there is a way out of this after all.*

"Write it down for me, Ted," instructed Mad Dog. Then he turned to Skippy. "Go to a pay phone and get me the number for the Webster Police Station. Perhaps if we put a little heat on the professor, he will have less time to think about pursuing us."

Mad Dog thanked the airport employee and indicated they all would be back late on Monday morning. It did not sit well with him that he and Skippy would have to lay low, but patience would have to rule the day. Now to put his little plan of diversion in motion.

*   *   *   *   *   *   *

George Kostov finally left the men's restroom and was relieved to see no vehicles parked outside the station. He sat down in Chief Olsen's chair and swung his feet up on the desk. With his head sagging into his chest, his double chin became more prominent. It seemed a good time to finish reading the Sunday paper. George liked being given mundane assignments and being out of the limelight.

Unfortunately for him, he was not five minutes into his reading when the phone rang. He nearly fell out of his chair. Fumbling the receiver, George sat up and said rather briskly, "Webster Police Department, how can I help you?"

The voice on the other end belonged to a man. "I understand you may be looking for a Dr. Winston McDougal."

Poor Mr. Kostov struggled to recall the names of the gang members everyone had been talking about. "That could be," he stammered. "Chief Olsen would be the one to confirm that."

"I'll make it easy for you, you country bumpkin," was the response. "This is a number you can reach him at. Got a pen or pencil?"

George scrambled to find a pen and got ready to write. "I'm ready," he replied.

"767-886-0322," was what George heard. Then there was a click, and the voice on the other end was gone. What Mr. Kostov did not know was that the man calling was Ted, the airplane pilot.

Over the past two days, there had been a number of strange crank calls coming into the Webster Police Station. In fact, earlier on Sunday, one excited caller claimed that he had seen an alien aircraft hover down over Granger's Woods and emit a beam resulting in the blast in the ground that was announced in the morning paper. Therefore, part of George's reaction to the call was to not take it too seriously. Still, he did not want to incur the wrath of Chief Olsen, so after pouring himself a cup of coffee, he dialed up the Shiloh County police headquarters. After a few minutes of waiting, Chief Olsen came to the phone.

"You had better have something important, Kostov," he growled. "We are in the middle of tracking down Dr. McDougal, the university professor."

"Interesting you should say that, Chief," responded George. "Got a call from a fella just a few minutes ago claiming he had a good contact number for the professor."

Chief Olsen's reaction was a puzzled one. Who would call with a contact number to aid in the investigation, particularly when he had tried to keep a close hold on any information related to the theft of the wooden leg? All the public really knew was that some kids went missing and there had been an explosion. Of course, there was some curiosity about the museum being closed on normally the biggest weekend of attendance during the entire year.

The bottom line was no one should have even connected Dr. McDougal with the case. However, if George had a number, what harm could there be in checking it out?

"Share it with me, George. Couldn't hurt. By the way, is everything else fairly normal at the office?" asked Chief Olsen.

"Steady as she goes, Chief. Ready to copy?" came back George.

Chief Olsen took down the number and set it aside for the time being. He and the other police on hand had been busy connecting with air tower controllers on the Canadian side of Lake Ontario. It took a while to gather information, but in the end, they had procured a solid lead. Among all of the private aircraft arriving Saturday evening, only three had come from across the lake. Two had taken a normal flight path and landed at Toronto International Airport. They both carried several passengers and had departed from Cleveland. The third was a bit of an enigma. Controllers at Billy Bishop City Airport had received a request for an unscheduled landing. The pilot had reported a mechanical malfunction. They could only report the plane had seemed to come from the south and was parked at gate 6B.

Chief Olsen and the Shiloh County police were just about to alert Toronto authorities of their most wanted list when the call from Mr. Kostov came in. Chief Olsen was sitting in a command post of sorts, and other phones were manned by Officers Dean and Campbell. Trooper John Bigelow of the Indiana state police had stopped in to share some paperwork and was immediately put to work, too.

Chief Olsen raised his arm, and in his booming voice, he asked for everyone's attention. "Hold up on the phone calls, gentlemen. We may have a lead on Dr. McDougal's whereabouts."

He then handed the phone number in question to Officer Dean. "I would like you to make this call, Officer Dean. The professor does not know you. If he does answer, perhaps you can keep him on the line for a while."

Officer Dean could hear the phone ringing for what seemed an eternity. Finally, someone picked up.

"Drake Hotel, can I help you?" said the voice on the other end.

"Yes—could you connect me with a Dr. Winston McDougal?" Officer Dean asked.

"Let me ring his room," replied the desk clerk. Officer Dean waited patiently, strumming her fingers on the table.

"There seems to be no answer. Would you like to leave a message?"

"Not right now, but can you tell me which room he is in? I would like to send up a bottle of wine," Officer Dean said coyly.

"That would be room 813," was the reply.

Officer Dean thanked the clerk and then hung up. Turning in Chief Olsen's direction, she announced, "He is staying at the Drake Hotel in Toronto. Room 813."

Chief Olsen stroked his chin and thought for a moment before saying, "Somebody get me the FBI field office."

*   *   *   *   *   *   *

Detective Shaw and Chief Olsen were in agreement. It was time to bring the FBI into the equation. Thanks to Heather and her discovery, they knew Dr. McDougal had been after the Timur Ruby. Assuming the wooden leg found in the farmhouse did not contain the ruby, Dr. McDougal probably had it. If they acted quickly, the professor could be arrested before morning.

Detective Shaw had the *look* on his face. Chief Olsen sighed and rolled his eyes.

"What now, Sam?" he asked, a little exasperated.

"For one, I don't think Miss Quig is telling us everything. For another, I am not sure Dr. McDougal has the ruby," Detective Shaw shared.

Chief Olsen sat down in a chair facing Detective Shaw. Resting his hands on his large knees, he paused before he spoke.

"Sam," he said quietly. "It is time to let go of this case. Let's just let the FBI pinch Dr. McDougal and get some answers. This case has now gone interstate and actually outside the United States. We've gone as far as we can."

Detective Shaw sat with his hands supporting his chin and said nothing. Chief Olsen reached out and touched his arm.

"We need to get everyone home. We know how to get ahold of Miss Quig if we need to."

"Guess you're right, Chief," replied a resigned Sam Shaw. "I understand Herb already is delivering Heather and Jeremy to their homes?"

Chief Olsen nodded in the affirmative.

"Okay, I'll send Miss Quig and her friends back to campus after I make sure I have their contact info," agreed Detective Shaw. "Are you going to hold a press conference tomorrow morning?"

"Going to have to, Sam," answered the chief. "We need to squelch the rumors about the explosion and account for all of the bodies. I'll likely schedule it for noon so none of the media feel left out."

With that, Chief Olsen went back into the command post and set things in motion to turn the case over to the FBI. Detective Shaw gave Daryl, Doris, and Emily the good news that they could go back to their dorms. They weren't the only ones leaving the Shiloh County police headquarters. Officers Sheridan and Plank were having a last cup of coffee in the break room before finally calling it a day.

"Frankie, this has been the most bizarre case I have ever been associated with," commented Gus Sheridan. "There are a couple of disconnects I have been mulling over, and now I believe I have some satisfactory explanations. Hear me out and tell me if I make any sense."

Gus stood up and began to brief his partner. "I can buy the fact Dr. McDougal would go to great lengths to steal a ruby and hide its identity. But I think initially he viewed it as a fairly easy heist, though the preparation cost him a chunk of change. A couple of flies in the ointment, however, caused him to make some additional expensive adjustments."

"First, he must have lost flexibility on his choice of dates. Having to steal the wooden leg on the busiest weekend of museum visitation definitely complicated things. The leg would be moved downstairs and have added visibility, maybe even twenty-four-hour protection. The professor had to find a way to make it easy for his hired hands to carry out their assignments. In my opinion, the insertion of the hologram was a late addition to his scheme."

"I also don't think he originally intended to blow up the hideout. But I think he decided a diversion was needed for insurance. Timing was essential, because Dr. McDougal had to make sure there was enough time for the gang to steal the leg and make their getaway. He also had a plane to catch. Any delays would be devastating."

"The second surprise was the museum's security system. Mr. Tompkins was certainly an eccentric. He never lost faith in the value of the leg and was, in the end, correct. I remember my grandfather had this crazy security apparatus installed in his home office. All of his important papers, bonds, and even some cash were hidden in his safe. The wiring was so weird that only he could disarm the alarm. I think he had a button under his desk. It seems to me the museum had a similar setup. When Dr. McDougal discovered he could not disarm the alarm, merely breaking the glass would not work. He did discover the backdoor to the case, though, which I think Mr. Tompkins had totally forgotten. If entered carefully, the case's alarm would not be set off. Enter Miss Quig. The trick was to have someone tiny access the door. Getting a wax impression to duplicate the key was not a challenge for someone who built a tunnel to the museum's basement!"

Officer Plank wanted to interrupt and make a comment, but Gus held up his finger to his mouth to quiet him.

"I'm almost done, Frankie. Have patience," Gus continued. "Including Miss Quig, however, meant for her eventual demise. Dr. McDougal knew, if left alive or around, she was the one person who could identify him. Gang members would all fly off in one plane, he in another. I suppose he could have kidnapped her. Perhaps he did not want that burden. Once Mr. Tompkins showed up, he even added the piece of staging the farmhouse killings to make it look like Tompkins and an accomplice stole the leg, but that went bad. He even was willing to torch the farmhouse for added effect."

"From Miss Quig's statement, Dr. McDougal gave the assignment to Jarvis Bolton, a real thug if there ever was one. I am not sure I understand that, and I certainly do not understand why Harvey Scrima chose to leave the team. We need to understand, though, it was to Mr. Scrima's benefit to leave Miss Quig alive and well so she could testify against the professor. That she has done."

When it was clear Officer Sheridan was done speaking, his counterpart clapped loudly. "Bravo," exclaimed Officer Plank. "Are you going to share your analysis with the others?"

Officer Sheridan put his arm around Frankie's shoulders and replied, "Not tonight, Frankie...not tonight. I'll file something with the office tomorrow. To be honest, all I think anyone cares about at this point is nabbing the professor."

The two then walked out of the Shiloh County police headquarters, arm in arm. They were ambivalent to the chatter behind them and had every right to be so.

The Best Laid Plans of Mice and Men (Oft Go Astray)

Jeremy was lacking his usual degree of enthusiasm for the start of school. Normally, he and Johnny would be headed to Mark Twain Elementary School together. Since they were entering sixth grade, they had reached the top of the elementary school social ladder, so to speak. He and Johnny had looked forward to this day all summer. Now, Jeremy had been assigned to accompany Hans to school.

It was hard to put aside the trauma the three friends had been through over the past weekend. Perhaps a good dose of normalcy would be just what the doctor ordered. Buddy was beginning high school, so Jeremy's mother was more focused on his brother's preparation. Since elementary students started school at 7:50 a.m., Jeremy and Hans were able to exit the house without a lot of doting attention.

"Mom, I'll make sure Hans gets home from school. See you around three!" yelled Jeremy. Both he and Hans waved as they bolted out the door. One thing he did have to look forward to: Johnny was coming home later in the afternoon, and his family was going over to the Turnbow's for a welcome home celebration. His mom would make a cherry pie—he was sure of it.

* * * * * * *

Things were a little less hectic over at the Stippich household. Mr. Stippich was not reporting for work due to his injury. Mrs. Stippich promised Heather she could go in to school a couple of hours late. With everything her daughter had been through, a full night's sleep was more important than reporting on time for the first day of school. Heather, super achiever though she was, did not protest.

At 8:00 a.m., Heather came stumbling downstairs in her pink cotton pajamas and plopped down at the kitchen table. Her mom was busy making scrambled eggs and bacon for Dad. The smell was delicious. Too bad Heather was not particularly hungry.

"What would you like, dear?" asked her Mom.

"Just some toast and jam," said Heather. She was rubbing her eyes while strands of hair kept falling into them.

Mr. Stippich was settled into his recliner in the family room. He had the TV on, ready to watch the morning news. Soon he was beckoning to his wife and daughter to join him.

"Melody, Heather, you have to come watch this. Channel 13 is broadcasting from the museum!"

Mrs. Stippich took the food off the stove for a minute and hustled Heather off to their brown leather sofa. A reporter was reporting from the museum's front porch (the same porch Bill Stippich was stuffed under the past Saturday evening).

"This is Julia Hornbeck reporting from the Benson County Museum. We have just learned the museum was the site of some sinister doings this past weekend. The main focus seems to have been a wooden leg exhibited on the second floor, which was reported missing last Thursday. Mr. Thaddeus Tompkins, museum curator, also went missing on Saturday. Three Webster youths thought to have been lurking around the museum on Friday also disappeared but have since resurfaced."

At this point in the broadcast, pictures of Mr. Tompkins, Heather, Jeremy, and Johnny appeared on the TV screen.

"Lurking!" exclaimed Heather jumping up as she spoke. "Are they implying we were a part of the theft?"

"Relax, Heather," advised her dad. "It's just news. No one is accusing you of anything."

The reporter continued. "One of the youths, Johnny Turnbow, is in serious condition at Benson County Regional Hospital. The other two,

Heather Stippich and Jeremy Murkowski, have been released to their parents. Earlier this morning, the FBI alerted law enforcement agencies in ten states to be on the lookout for members of the Bolton gang who were released recently from prison. Harvey Scrima and Skippy Forrester are wanted for murder, burglary, kidnapping, and several other charges. A Bradford State University anthropology professor, Dr. Winston McDougal, is suspected to be behind the museum theft and responsible for the enormous explosion near Granger's Woods this past Saturday night."

It seems anyone wanted by the law is always pictured in the worst possible light, and the three accused were no exception. Mad Dog looked like he had just escaped from a zoo and Skippy from an insane asylum. Dr. McDougal resembled a mob boss.

"That's the guy who kidnapped Emily Quig," shouted Heather pointing at the professor's picture.

Miss Hornbeck continued, "The museum behind me is closed until further notice. Chief Bartholomew Olsen from the Webster Police Department just announced that there will be a press conference at noon to provide us with further details. Channel 13, of course, will be covering that live. This is Julia Hornbeck reporting from the Benson County Museum."

With that, the screen reverted back to the news station, and the Stippich family ceased to pay attention.

"It looks like you have become a celebrity, Heather," chuckled Mr. Stippich.

Heather was scowling with arms folded.

"Oh, Bill," scolded Mrs. Stippich. "Don't tease." She then turned to Heather. "Do you want to just stay home from school today, dear?"

"What I want to do is hear that press conference," pronounced Heather.

Bill and Melody Stippich looked at each other.

Bill then announced, "And that is what we will all do. Your mother will make grilled cheese sandwiches, and we will eat lunch here in the family room."

A slow grin spread across Heather's face. She knelt down by her father, picked up his hand, and held it to her face. "That's why I love you, Dad," she shared.

*   *   *   *   *   *   *

Agents Nichols and Robertson had good working relationships with Toronto authorities. Based out of Buffalo, they periodically had to track down undesirables who were trying to escape the United States' arm of the law. When they contacted Inspector Murrow on Monday morning, he was eager to help. As a result, by midmorning, they were entering the Drake Hotel. After speaking with the desk clerk to make sure Dr. McDougal had not yet checked out, the FBI agents made their way up to the eighth floor. Inspector Murrow kept an eye on the hotel lobby while he assigned two sergeants to stake out the rear of the hotel.

Agent Nichols knocked sharply on the door to Room 813. When there was no answer, the bellhop used the house key to gain entry. The two agents pulled their guns, and with arms outstretched, they yelled out, "FBI! Freeze!"

The room was incredibly silent. There were no occupants. Except for towels on the bathroom floor and a turned down bed, there was no evidence of anyone having occupied the room. Agents Nichols and Robertson looked at each other, a bit disappointed.

"Do you think they knew we were coming?" asked Agent Robertson.

"Hard to say," replied Agent Nichols.

"I did leave them a message last night that a lady had called looking for a Dr. McDougal," offered the bellhop.

"Do you recall who answered the door?" inquired Agent Nichols.

The bellhop, a good foot shorter than the agents, removed his hat and scratched his head. "The man who answered the door was mostly bald with a touch of whitish hair. I'd say he was in his early fifties. He had a ruddy complexion."

Agent Robertson followed up with, "Did you see anyone else in the room?"

"There was a rather large man wearing a vest and a white shirt sitting in the stuffed chair." The bellhop pointed to it as he spoke.

Agent Robertson continued. "What was the message you delivered?"

"Just that some lady called and wanted to send up some wine. We deliver phone messages in person when one of our guests prefers not to answer the room phone," clarified the bellhop. "We have a lot of people stay here who put a premium on their privacy."

Agent Nichols turned to Agent Robertson, who was playing with his neatly trimmed moustache. "That must be how the local police tracked down his location," he surmised.

After checking for any clues, the agents and the bellhop returned to the hotel lobby. They found Inspector Murrow smoking his pipe and resting against the main desk.

"Let me guess," chuckled Inspector Murrow. "This so-called Dr. McDougal gave you the slip."

Agent Nichols did not answer but instead confronted the desk clerk. "You sure no one checked out of Room 813 this morning?"

The answer was no. Agent Nichols scowled. "Thanks to our friends in Indiana, I am afraid Dr. McDougal and company suspected something." He then addressed the inspector, a portly and distinguished man. "This might be a good time, Inspector, to set up checkpoints at the usual locations. Though I am skeptical they will use normal transportation alternatives."

Based on what Emily Quig had provided, the agents had drawings in hand showing what Mr. Fish and Mr. St. George possibly looked like. The bellhop's description of the man he encountered resembled the image of Mr. Fish.

"You might also want to share these mockups, Inspector, of two men that we think are with Dr. McDougal. The three of them can't have gotten too far overnight."

*   *   *   *   *   *   *

Accompanied by a tiny dose of anxiety, Ted, Mad Dog, and Skippy Forrester headed up the road to the airport. They had waited until midmorning to leave, as Mad Dog figured the aviation fuel would not arrive much before then. There was little conversation along the way. Soon they had reached the entrance road to the airport with its accompanying sign reading, "Cooksville Municipal Airport: Gates close at 10 p.m." To be honest, the sign needed a new paint job. Even from the half-mile distance to the hangars, the trio could see a fuel truck parked adjacent to Hangar 1. Mad Dog smiled, and they picked up their pace.

The same individual Mad Dog and Skippy had spoken with on Sunday was yapping away at the fuel truck driver. This time, he wore an old leather jacket. Mad Dog hailed him as they approached.

"Hey, mister, how much a gallon for the fuel?"

The man squinted at them and then replied, "Ain't you the fellers from yesterday?" He paused as Mad Dog and Skippy got closer. "Yeah, you are. Well, sure, we can help you. Cost will be $3.29 a gallon, but you will have to wait until Mr. Hathaway fuels his bird." Then he pointed toward the hangar nearest the truck. "There's a snack room of sorts right inside that door. You can get a soda and chips while you wait."

"Thanks," said Mad Dog. Then the three trudged off toward the hangar.

Once inside, Skippy plopped down in one of the four folding chairs surrounding a circular table. Behind him were two vending machines; one dispensed Coca Cola products, and the other held snacks. As they had eaten breakfast before leaving for the airport, no one was interested in their offerings. Ted took another chair, and Mad Dog just stood there with his arms folded.

Ted (whose last name was Williams) seemed resigned to his fate. Ted sported jowly cheeks to accompany brown thinning hair. Now approaching sixty years old, the last few years had not been kind to him. After his divorce, he rarely saw his kids. His charter plane business paid him enough to cover the rent and his bar tabs. Ted sat with his cheeks in his hands, just wanting to get on with things. He had that in common with Mad Dog and Skippy.

Skippy placed his hands behind his head and began to wax poetically. "You know, Harvey, maybe we should cut Ted in on the action." He winked at Ted as he said it. Skippy then turned to Ted and said, "How do you feel about Mexico, partner?"

Mad Dog just shook his head. "Skippy, why would Mr. Ted here want to spend a relaxing existence in Mexico when he has everything he could possible want in Indiana?"

If they were expecting a reaction from Ted, they did not get one. Though Mad Dog and Skippy were not his usual clientele, he long ago had lost any energy for anything out of the ordinary. His main goal was to come out of this job alive.

About the time the refueling was finished and Mr. Hathaway's plane was preparing to pull up to the tank, a police car pulled up in front of Hangar 2 and an officer got out. As the fuel truck pulled on past him, the officer walked around to the rear of the hangars.

"Hey, Billy, I got the most daggone story to tell you. You won't believe it. Some professor up in Indiana broke into a museum and made a real mess of things. Bodies all over, and one hell of an explosion. Came across the wire this morning," said the officer.

Billy walked up to his friend. "Ya don't say, Big Bob. Did they catch the guy?"

Officer Big Bob Titus, who had a particularly jovial demeanor, replied, "Not yet. It seems he had this gang to help him. Some escaped— in planes to be exact. That's why I drove out here. You may want to keep your eye out for anything unusual. Not that anything exciting ever happens in Cooksville, though."

Mad Dog had heard a vehicle pull up and peered through the small window to see the squad car. He motioned to Skippy, and they both cracked open the door toward the airfield to try to catch the conversation. They could only make out a small part of it but did see Billy point toward the hangar they occupied.

The two then walked over to Ted. Mad Dog pointed his finger at Ted's chest and said, "This is your lucky day, Ted. You get to prove how great an actor you are. In a couple of minutes, a cop is going to walk in here, and you are going to tell him you are taking us to Knoxville so we can meet up with our party to do some late summer mountain fishing. For the time being, our names are Matt and Sid. Got the picture?"

Ted's body language indicated he had—and just in time, as Officer Big Bob entered the room.

"Good morning," he greeted. "My friend, Billy, said you made an unexpected landing here yesterday."

Mad Dog gave a sign to Ted to reply. "That's right, sir," replied Ted. "The boys in Bloomington shorted me on fuel, and I had to make an unexpected stop."

"Where you headed?" inquired Big Bob, hands on his waist.

"Trying to get to Knoxville. My passengers have signed on to a fishing junket up in the Appalachians," answered Ted, looking toward Mad Dog and Skippy.

"Kind of late for fishing, isn't it?" asked a skeptical Big Bob.

Mad Dog stood up and walked over to the officer. "I suspect there will be more drinking than fishing, Officer," he explained. "Bunch of us get together in this old cabin every other year to renew friendships and talk about the ones who got away."

Big Bob seemingly liked the answer and let out a big chortle. He slapped Mad Dog on the shoulder. "You don't say. But why didn't you just fly commercial?" he asked.

Mad Dog moved a little closer. "Our wives swore that if we ever took another 'fishing' trip, our belongings would be in the front yard. Ted here was kind enough to give us a lift."

Ted then joined in. "It was not a problem, as I was headed to Pittsburgh eventually, anyway."

Officer Big Bob thought a moment and then said, "Well, gentlemen, go get refueled and have a good trip." He then shook all of their hands and returned to his police car.

"You're next up, friends," announced Billy. "Time to get your plane ready." The group then headed out the backdoor of the hangar.

Officer Big Bob sat in his car and radioed the Cooksville police department. "Harold, you know the wanted poster that came in by wire this morning? I think two of those varmints are now at the airport. Meet me at the coffee shop with Ernie, and we will join forces. Make sure you bring extra guns and ammo."

A Watery Exit
For the Professor

"Hurry, Dad, you're going to miss it," shouted Heather. "Chief Olsen just stepped up to the podium."

Bill Stippich placed the last of the grilled cheese sandwiches on a plate and hustled on into the family room. Chief Olsen looked very official as he cleared his throat. The Stippich's 24-inch color TV made the chief look wider than he really was. Heather lay prone and close to the screen while her parents sat farther back on the sofa.

Chief Olsen and Detective Shaw had gone over what was to be shared with the press. At 11:30 a.m., Chief Olsen was on his third draft when Officer Kraus informed him it was time to go. The crew from Channel 13 wanted to test the mics. Chief Olsen slowly stood up as if there were anchors on his feet. *How do you sum up the events of the past few days?* he thought. The faces of the victims kept showing up in his mind. He repeatedly whispered to himself, "Just the facts, Barty, just the facts."

Chief Olsen took some solace as he faced the various reporters with Mayor Balducci, Detective Shaw, and Officer Kraus sitting behind him. The mayor had been particularly supportive and blamed the whole affair on Mr. Tompkins' obsession with the wooden leg. "We should have transferred that infernal leg to the Smithsonian long ago," he was heard to mutter.

Soon it was time to start. All of the Indianapolis stations were in attendance, along with Channel 57 from Fort Wayne. *The Associated Press* had decided to assign a stringer to the press conference.

"Ladies and gentlemen, members of the press, and honored guests: it is with a heavy heart I address you this day," began Chief Olsen. With the press conference being conducted on the steps of the courthouse, it was a good thing the wind had died down. The chief was having a hard time projecting his normally robust voice.

"Last Thursday, Thaddeus Tompkins, curator of our county museum, reported a theft of an artifact from the museum collection...specifically the wooden leg normally housed on the second-floor landing. As we investigated further, it became obvious this was no normal burglary. Developments in the case led us to the Bolton gang, a group of men formally associated with the First Bank of Indiana bank robbery."

"Unfortunately, upon learning something was amiss at the museum, three of our local kids decided to get involved in solving the mystery. We have previously identified them as Heather Stippich, Johnny Turnbow, and Jeremy Murkowski. On Friday evening, Heather and Jeremy were abducted while attempting to break into the museum. Their friend, Johnny, was pushed into the basement earlier and stayed inside after Mr. Tompkins locked up."

"Fortunately, they managed to escape later that evening while being taken to what we learned was the gang's hideout. On Saturday morning, Heather and Jeremy found the farm of Tom Barlow, and he eventually returned them to Webster and they were reunited with their parents. Johnny was not so lucky, as he found an underground tunnel leading to the hideout and was captured."

"You are familiar with the explosion west of Granger's Woods on Saturday evening. This explosion obliterated the hideout. Had it not been for the bravery of Tom Barlow and his sons, Johnny would have died in the explosion. Tragically, Tom died saving Johnny."

At this point, Chief Olsen paused to blow his nose and gather himself. Many hands were raised, and questions were shouted at him. He waved the questions off and pleaded, "Please, wait until the end of my statement, if you would. Rest assured, we will attempt to answer all of your questions."

"To continue, the bottom line is all three children survived. Johnny Turnbow is to return home from the Benson County hospital this evening. I cannot say the same for our beloved curator. In hindsight, we believe Mr. Tompkins assumed correctly that the wooden leg contained a most valuable object, the Timur Ruby, known internationally for its size and worth. He did not share his findings with us and suffered because of it. He, too, was eventually captured by the gang. Detective Shaw and Shiloh County officers found his body in a farmhouse halfway to Bensonville on Sunday."

"Due to the outstanding work by Detective Shaw and Officer Kraus, we have learned that the brains behind the operation was Dr. Winston McDougal, professor at Bradford State University. Dr. McDougal pressed a freshman at the university, Emily Quig, to assist in the theft. She was found Sunday wandering along Highway 12 by Shiloh County officers. Miss Quig was able to tie Dr. McDougal to the theft and substantiate Detective Shaw's suspicions."

"Dr. McDougal and two of the gang members, Harvey Scrima and Skippy Forrester, have escaped and are being sought after by the FBI as I speak. Others have died during the operation or when trying to escape. Tommy and Jarvis Bolton and Ignatius and Boris Smothers are dead. We believe there may have been some disagreements between gang members that resulted in their demises. Ignatius Smothers died in a truck accident south of Fort Wayne. Yvetlana Smothers, a custodian at the museum, is the mother of Ignatius and Boris. She is currently in mourning with a sister in Bensonville."

"The explosion of the gang's hideout on Saturday night was likely a diversion to allow them access to the museum. Bill Stippich of Webster, who had been deputized, was stationed at the museum. He was attacked and stabbed in the leg before being overcome. Detective Shaw found him late Saturday night. Mr. Stippich is now home and recovering from his injuries."

"Ironically, the wooden leg was never really missing from the museum. Dr. McDougal used holographic technology to hide the leg from view within its case—thus the reason for the break-in on Saturday evening. On the surface, the intricate planning and preparations for the theft do not make sense. However, when you consider that the value of the Timur Ruby, once broken down and fenced, approaches one million dollars, it is more understandable."

"I want to thank all of the Shiloh County police and hospital personnel who have been so devoted and supportive in our getting a handle on this case. I also want to thank the fathers of Heather, Johnny, and Jeremy for being willing to be deputized and putting their own lives at risk. Now I am going to turn some time over to Detective Sam Shaw who will try and answer your questions."

With that, Chief Olsen sat down and wiped his brow. Officer Kraus patted the chief's knee as a token of support. Detective Shaw approached the podium to a flurry of hands and voices.

"The reporter from Channel 13," acknowledged the detective.

It was Ms. Hornbeck again. "Detective, if I understand correctly, you uncovered evidence of an underground hideout with a tunnel leading to the museum basement. In addition, the gang used a farmhouse off of Highway 12 between Webster and Bensonville. As Dr. McDougal must have been preparing for this theft for a long time, why was no one aware of any of it?"

"We are waiting for a report from the register of deeds office, but probably Dr. McDougal purchased land under an assumed name. We will be interviewing area farmers to see if they noticed any excavation the past couple of years. However, being in such a rural area on the west side of Granger's Woods, it is not surprising no one paid much attention. As for the tunnel, if done intermittently, it could have been completed in secret."

Next up was a reporter from the *Indianapolis Star*. "Our sources tell us the wooden leg was housed at the museum for years. How did Dr. McDougal discover it housed the ruby? Certainly Mr. Tompkins did not know of its existence, and he was the museum's curator!"

Detective Shaw smiled as he recognized the irony of the situation. "Mr. Tompkins likely tipped Dr. McDougal off on the leg's hidden value, as he kept pestering the professor about its provenance. Eventually, Dr. McDougal, being an educated anthropology professor, put two and two together and did some research of his own."

A tall bald man at the rear of the crowd clamored for attention. "Detective, Detective, what about the silver key?"

Detective Shaw strained to see the man. Officer Kraus came up to the podium and whispered in Sam's ear. "That's the owner of that quirky radio station near Muncie. He is always looking for conspiracy theories wherever he can find them."

"And you are?" asked Detective Shaw.

"Harvey C. Goldberg, WXYT. According to Mrs. Smothers' sister, there was a silver key Yvetlana was asked to steal. We understand one of her sons threatened to kill her over it. What gives?"

"Yes," Detective Shaw replied. "There was a key that went to a door in the museum's basement. The gang went to some length to retrieve it in order to gain entry. It was critical to their plans of using the tunnel."

Detective Shaw wanted to go on to the next question, but Mr. Goldberg persisted. "But Chief Olsen mentioned that Johnny Turnbow discovered the tunnel. He had to have had the key to unlock the door leading down into it. There seems to be a lot you guys aren't sharing with us. Like, how and why was Mr. Tompkins abducted?"

"I am afraid we cannot make further comments on Mr. Tompkins' role in the whole affair until we have completed our investigations," said Detective Shaw, remaining calm.

There were several other questions, and some reporters wanted to know when Emily, Heather, Johnny, and Jeremy would be made available for questioning. Detective Shaw did a good job deflecting all the inquiries, and after ninety minutes, the press conference was declared over.

Heather Stippich rose off the family room floor and confronted her parents. "Am I going to have to answer a bunch of questions, too?" she asked with some trepidation.

Her mother gave her a reassuring hug. "Don't worry, sweetheart. Daddy will give our lawyer a call in the morning. I am sure we can get by with a written statement, if needed."

Melody gazed at her husband, who responded with an assenting nod.

Heather went to pour herself a glass of milk and wondered if her friends' parents had lawyers, too.

*   *   *   *   *   *   *

Dr. John Ricardo, a long-time academic associate of Dr. McDougal, scrimped and saved for years to purchase a new Catalina Cruiser. Part of the reason for taking a position at the University of Toronto was so that he could berth a boat at Ontario Place Marina. It was a beautiful boat and had two bunks below the main deck.

Dr. McDougal and his associates stood against the railing facing the Toronto skyline. The clear night made the lights from the city twinkle. While Dr. Ricardo had given them keys to get into the cabin, they did not have keys to start the engine. After several minutes of silence and soliloquy, Dr. McDougal spoke.

"Mr. Fish, among your numerous talents, have you ever hot-wired a boat?"

"Can't say that I have," answered Mr. Fish.

"But you have had experience with other vehicles, correct?" pushed Dr. McDougal.

"That is true, sir, but this a different animal. Willing to give it go, though," offered Mr. Fish.

Even though it was going on midnight, Marvin set out to see what he could discover. He had been working for some time when the professor and Mr. St. George heard a, "Whoop!" Marvin sprung up to the main deck with a big grin on his face.

"Professor, did you want to go somewhere?" Mr. Fish said mischievously.

Dr. McDougal turned to Mr. St. George and asked, "What does the weather look like for tomorrow, my dependable friend?"

"Way ahead of you," replied Mr. St. George. "Should be clear, but wind will pick up in the morning. Water could get kind of choppy."

Dr. McDougal then explained that borrowing his friend's cruiser might be their best avenue for escape. As Dr. Ricardo would have no need to visit his boat until they met up again at the end of the week, he would not be aware of its disappearance until the following Saturday. That would give them a week's head start before anyone discovered the boat missing. Of course, it meant crossing Lake Ontario to New York State—a distance of about fifty miles.

All agreed they would awake before dawn and head across the lake. On weekdays, the marina did not open until 9:00 a.m. unless arrangements were made with the resident captain. So, before Inspector Murrow and agents Nichols and Robertson made their appearance at the hotel, the trio was up and about, ready to embark.

Mr. Fish had checked out the weather reports and reported to Dr. McDougal. Mr. St. George's previous perceptions were confirmed. "NOAA reports there will be choppy water developing this morning. You can feel the wind is already beginning to pick up."

Dr. McDougal took the news stoically. Mr. Fish continued, "If the winds start to come at us directly from the south, Boss, I am not sure this boat is up to the task. Are you sure you want to shove off this morning?"

The sun was just beginning to peak above the horizon, and Dr. McDougal's massive figure was silhouetted by the early light as he stood at the stern of the boat. In some respects, this was the moment of truth for the professor. Waiting another day was really not an option, as the feds were hot on his trail. Dr. McDougal was still determined to track down Mr. Scrima, but he had to live another day first.

"Marvin, my man," responded Dr. McDougal, "we are going to have to brave the elements with courage. By the end of the day, I suspect we will all have learned of what we are made."

Mr. St. George and Mr. Fish exchanged glances that seemed to say, "Here we go." Soon, the engine was purring, and Marvin was easing the cruiser out of the dock. The decision had been made to purposely keep their speed down until they were well clear of the harbor. Mr. St. George and Dr. McDougal stood silently gazing toward the Toronto skyline. Even though clouds were beginning to gather, the view was spectacular. Dr. McDougal's original strategy had been to stay in Canada. Had he not been betrayed, by now he could have been fencing the stone and preparing to move into a rural mansion on the shores of Lake Huron… if he had just been able to stay undetected for a week.

Mr. St. George had a kind face. He was the kind of man you would pick to be your grandfather. Dr. McDougal appreciated his counsel and wit. "Winston, we have been down many roads together. I had hoped this would be your crowning glory," noted the chauffer. A couple of minutes went by.

"I fear this entire operation may not end well, my friend," Mr. St. George continued. "Whatever occurs, I just want you to know that it has been a pleasure to be of service to you."

Normally Dr. McDougal showed no outward emotion under any circumstances. But after Mr. St. George's remarks, tears welled up in his eyes. He was unable to speak and could only place his right hand on Mr. St. George's shoulder. In less than an hour, both men began to feel the boat's speed increase.

"Time to adjourn to the cabin, Mr. St. George," counseled Dr. McDougal.

Mr. Fish kept his eyes alert to any other boats while being mindful of the streaming clouds that escorted them forward. The last time he'd played the role of captain was on a houseboat on the Ohio River. It was obvious to Marvin that navigating Lake Ontario would not be the same pleasant experience.

Endings Can Be Elusive

The dormitories at Bradford State University were on the east side of campus, tucked behind a grove of silver maple trees. There were eight in all. Emily Quig resided in the freshman dorm, Liberty Hall, the oldest of all the red brick dormitories. She shared her room on the third floor with Doris, who was technically a sophomore.

Missing were some of the modern amenities found in the dorms of the upperclassmen. There was no air conditioning. Because Emily and Doris had a south-facing window, however, they were sometimes blessed with a soft breeze. Still, those assigned to Liberty Hall were advised to bring a fan. On Monday morning, Emily did not need her fan, because the temperatures had dropped into the forties the evening before. She did crack the window open a little, however.

Sitting on the bottom bunk, Emily was attempting to wake up. She had slept until 10:00 a.m. Doris had risen early to catch her Art History class. Though there was much Emily resented about her mother, she did appreciate the soft, fluffy pink bathrobe Mrs. Quig had bought for her. When Emily had checked her messages earlier on the room phone, she was not surprised to hear her mother's voice.

"It's Sunday evening, and I can't imagine why you are not in your room studying." It was the same nasal-toned chastisement Emily had put up with all throughout high school. "Call me back, but not after nine. Your father and I are turning in early."

It was apparent to Emily that her mother had no clue what she had been through. That was not surprising, as her parents' only TV functioned with rabbit ears. They basically got one channel and the reception was poor. Robert and Martha Quig could certainly have afforded better. They had a five-bedroom home in the Richmond Hills district. But, as Mrs. Quig was prone to say, "Television is the Devil's workshop." In the Quig household, one listened to classical music and National Public

Radio only. Emily figured that by the time the Fort Wayne papers caught up with the events in Webster, it would be Wednesday.

That was actually good news. Emily had no desire to be yanked back home, and she needed a couple of days to collect her thoughts and perfect her story. Emily had undergone a major transformation. Now, she was determined to chart her own course. Thanks to Mad Dog's generosity, she now had the opportunity. Emily had already decided she would give it a month before returning to the shack off of Highway 12. A nice warm, sunny fall Saturday would be a great time for a bike ride.

Emily's dream had always been to attend a private school, preferably somewhere off the beaten path. She had the grades to apply to better schools, but her mother would hear none of it. "Bradford State is far enough away. And remember, Emily, you have two brothers at Notre Dame," her mother reminded. "You are lucky we can afford any tuition for you at all."

Well, Bradford State University was better than nothing. It also meant she did not have to come home on the weekends—only for holidays. Now, though, many good schools were in play. Emily had already decided she was going to try to get into Beloit College. She understood they had an excellent anthropology department, and no one was going to stop her!

*   *   *   *   *   *   *

Mad Dog and Skippy walked several paces behind Ted and were having a quiet conversation.

"Skippy, I don't trust that hayseed officer any more than I can spit horseshoes," whispered Mad Dog. "While our pilot is refueling, let's you and I have a few words with Mr. Hathaway."

Sandy Hathaway was a local boy with a Piper J-3 Cub. His father owned three restaurants in the area, and Sandy managed one (Othello's). Sandy had every Monday off, and that is the day he always went flying. He was just backing his plane up in preparation to approach the runway when Mad Dog came up to his side window, arms waving. Sandy cut the engine and opened his door.

"What's up, mister?" questioned Mr. Hathaway.

"Our pilot has to get to Pittsburgh sooner than he thought. Any chance you could run us to Knoxville?" petitioned Mad Dog.

Mr. Hathaway scratched his chin. "Don't suppose that would be a big deal. Not so important where I fly as long as I fly," he chuckled. "You guys will owe me a tank of gas when we get there, though. Extra weight and all. Get my drift?"

"No problem, Mr. Hathaway. In fact, we'll treat you to a beer if you'd like," replied Mad Dog.

Sandy Hathaway seemed to like that idea, so he said, "Okay, then. Step on in but use the other door."

It was to Mad Dog's and Skippy's benefit they only had small satchels to bring aboard. Even then, the luggage had to sit in their laps. Skippy looked nervously out the window, but Ted was paying close attention to the refueling of his plane. The Piper Cub leapt quickly into the air heading west and then did a loop to head the opposite direction. That gave Mad Dog a clear view of the airport below. They had taken off not a moment too soon. Three police cars were slamming to a halt in front of Hangar 1. Billy came out to greet them, and soon they were having an animated conversation.

"How long to Knoxville, Mr. Hathway?" asked Mad Dog.

"We've got good winds behind us, so I figure less than an hour," he replied.

"You got any good music we can listen to along the way?" inquired Mad Dog.

"Well, I have to cut off the radio, but don't see that as a big issue. FAA doesn't pay attention to small fries like me. I've done it before when I've gotten bored. How do you feel about country western?" asked the pilot.

Mad Dog smiled. "That suits us just fine," replied Skippy.

Mad Dog now knew they could get to Knoxville unimpeded. If they could get Mr. Hathaway to a bar for an hour or two, they could take the heat off. Even better, it would serve as another diversion that would make it difficult for Dr. McDougal to track them down.

Mad Dog and Skippy had no idea of the greater challenge the professor and his crew were facing on Lake Ontario. They also had no idea that as they landed at the Knoxville airport, Chief Olsen was beginning his press conference. However, they were both savvy enough to know the word was out in the law enforcement community. To himself, Mad Dog made a note it was time for a haircut and some new threads.

*　　*　　*　　*　　*　　*　　*

Chief Olsen and Detective Shaw were having a late lunch at Christine's, a downtown family restaurant at the corner of Birch and Main Streets. It was a favorite haunt of the chief's, as he loved the beef chili deluxe that came with extra onions. They sat in the rear of the restaurant in one of the red leather booths.

"Sam, you saved my lunch at the press conference. I have never been good at those things, and this PC was worse than most," said a very grateful Chief Olsen.

"You did fine, Chief," said Detective Shaw consolingly. "We've all been through the wringer with this one. I think we struck a happy medium with the amount of information shared. At least it bought us some time. I don't think you will need to hold another one until Friday." Detective Shaw smiled as he said it. Chief Olsen just groaned.

Just as the chief was finishing his apple pie, his pager went off. He jumped up and moved over to the passing waitress. "Hey, Margie, okay if I use your phone for a minute?"

"Sure, Chief…you know where it is," said the waitress who continued busing a table.

Chief Olsen headed to the kitchen where a green wall phone sat hanging next to a large calendar covered in scribbling and grease stains.

He dialed the station. Officer Kraus answered.

"You won't guess who just called five minutes ago," challenged the deputy.

"Oh, I don't know, President Reagan?" answered Chief Olsen sarcastically.

Officer Kraus laughed. "That was a good one, Chief. No, it was the FBI. Seems a private cruiser was found floundering in the middle of Lake Ontario this morning. They traced it to a professor at the University of Toronto, who when contacted, said he had given permission for an academic friend to bunk in it for the week. Guess who the friend was?"

"Enough of the questions, Herb. Just get to the facts," replied an irritated Chief Olsen.

"It was none other than our very own Dr. McDougal," offered up Officer Kraus. "Interestingly, he evidently did not have permission to take it out of the harbor. In fact, the professor said he did not know how they managed to start the boat, since Dr. McDougal was not given any keys to do so."

"Well, do they have Dr. McDougal in custody?" asked Chief Olsen impatiently.

"No bodies were on board, Chief," responded Officer Kraus. "The coast guard is sweeping the area as we speak. The FBI thinks any passengers drowned. Waves got quite high this morning on the lake, and it must have been too much for the cruiser."

Chief Olsen had no further comment and advised Officer Kraus he would be at the office in a couple minutes.

When informed of the news, Detective Shaw concluded that either Dr. McDougal and his assistants were dead—with the ruby down with them—or the professor had staged the incident to throw everyone off their trail. Chief Olsen said he thought it hard to discern their escape plan if the lake was as wild as reported. Detective Shaw admitted he did not have an answer.

Once back at the police station, Chief Olsen returned the FBI's call and learned there was an ongoing massive manhunt for Dr. McDougal and associates. In another development, the FBI shared with the chief that the Cooksville, Tennessee police chief had called in a sighting of Harvey Scrima and Skippy Forrester at the municipal airport. Both men had given officers the slip, however, by escaping in a private plane.

Officer Kraus sat in his chair, mulling over everything he was hearing. Stroking his chin, he seemed to be pondering what all the new information meant. Suddenly, he interrupted the conversation between Chief Olsen and Detective Shaw.

"Who's to say Dr. McDougal still had the ruby when he left Canada? Why would he risk returning to the States when he obviously planned to dispose of it in Toronto? He could have just laid low and fenced it once things died down. Certainly he must have had a safe place to go to at some point."

"Not sure where you are going with this, Herb," stated Chief Olsen.

It was time for Officer Kraus to get dramatical again. He stood up, and while pacing, he started to launch his logic at the chief and Detective Shaw.

"The way I see it, gentlemen, is the gang had a big falling out. Otherwise, why was Miss Quig kept alive and returned to the farm? What were Scrima and Forrester up to? Maybe they played the big double-cross and kept the ruby for themselves. Therefore, when the professor found out he did not have the ruby, he began to plan to come back into the country to retrieve it. I'm telling you, if we find Mad Dog, we find the ruby!" exclaimed Officer Kraus.

"I do agree it is rather interesting that Dr. McDougal would choose to use his friend's boat to leave Canada," commented Detective Shaw. "But that may just have been the easiest way he figured he could avoid the law. We certainly know by now we are not dealing with a man who thinks normally about anything; his twisted mind is not founded on rational thought. No, I think Mad Dog figured he preferred not to split his share of the action with four others. I do admit, though, I am stumped by Miss Quig's survival."

"All of this theorizing is really pointless," interjected Chief Olsen. "I think the professor, Mr. St. George, and Marvin, whoever he is, are at the bottom of the lake. In a couple of days, the FBI will put this case in their file cabinet and eventually close it entirely once there is evidence of drowning. Who knows? Clothing may already have made its way to the lake's surface. The Timur Ruby has once more gone into hiding, never to be found again. Right now, I am turning my attention to Mr. Scrima and

Mr. Forrester. Once the feds have their hands on them, I want a crack at questioning them."

With that, Chief Olsen stood up and stretched. "Herb, I'm calling it a day. I have to admit that I am plumb worn out. Did not sleep a wink last night from worrying about the stupid press conference." Turning to Sam, he asked, "Do you think you two could hold down the fort for the rest of the afternoon?"

Officer Kraus was a little miffed that no one would buy into his theory and did not say anything. Detective Shaw assured the chief they would be happy to oblige. He and Herb watched Webster's chief of police get into his car and drive off. Then, it was back to the office to complete a lot of paperwork. The case of the wooden leg seemed to be coming to an end.

*   *   *   *   *   *   *

All the children stood on the front porch at the Turnbow household in anticipation of Johnny's arrival. Buddy and Jeremy stood on the left. Buddy was a good foot taller than Jeremy, and his wavy blond hair was not short. He wore a Chicago Bears hat, white T-shirt, and jeans. Jeremy wore a plain gray sweatshirt and khaki pants. Mrs. Murkowski instructed them to wash up, and Buddy's hair was combed. The boys felt a bit like they were prepared to go to church.

Hans sat with his legs dangling over the edge of the porch. He was not anxious to see summer go and created his own fashion statement by wearing shorts. Hans was old enough that he understood Jeremy had been through a lot. His dad's explanation of the weekend's events was a little short on details, but Jeremy sat down with both Buddy and Hans and went over his night in the forest with Heather. The three boys seemed to have grown closer as a result of Jeremy's ordeal.

Melinda, only a year older than Katie Turnbow, had her arm around her as they sat on the swinging bench. Katie did not have her brother's red hair (hers was black), but it was thick and cropped in back. Katie wore her *Snow White* pajamas and was humming to herself. Melinda's long blonde hair laid over her corduroy jacket. She had put on her best denim skirt and told her mother, "I want to look nice for Johnny."

Jenny Turnbow had returned from the hospital to make desserts for the homecoming. Mary Murkowski, of course, was there to help. Her stout arms and hands did a number on the pie crusts. Now, though, the cookies and pies were set out on the table, and the two mothers leaned against the front door. Each reflected on how close they had come to losing their sons. They could be forgiven if they became a little misty.

It seemed like an eternity to the children, but finally, Mr. Turnbow pulled up in front of the house. Frank opened the door for Johnny and helped him out onto the sidewalk. There were a few seconds of silence, then all the kids started clapping and shouting; Melinda and Katie jumped up and down. They all rushed toward Johnny, and Ben and Frank had to hold them back before they crushed the poor lad. As it was, there was nonstop hugging as Johnny was dragged, more than walked, to his house.

Finally, Johnny raised his arms and pleaded, "Okay, okay, I get it. You're happy to see me. I'm glad to see you, too!"

Katie held Johnny's hand tightly and said, "Johnny, I want to hear all about your adventure; no one will tell me anything."

Brushing away her tears, Jenny Turnbow pushed all aside and escorted Johnny into the dining room. "I made your favorite pie, Johnny, and Dad even got the really good vanilla ice cream to go with it."

Soon, all were yammering away between bites. It was a celebration of both family and Johnny's survival. Johnny felt warm inside, and periodically, he and Jeremy just smiled at each other. It would be so good to get back to school and their old routine. Another adventure was the furthest thing from their minds.

The Ruby Calls the Shots

When it became obvious to Ted, Billy, Officer Titus, and the other officers that Mad Dog and Skippy had flown off with Mr. Harrington, it was just a matter of determining where his plane would be heading.

"That's easy," said Billy. "Mr. Hathaway mostly flies to Murfreesboro. He has a brother that way."

"A good piece of information," replied Officer Titus. "Billy, you contact the Murfreesboro tower, and I'll alert the police in Rutherford County."

Big Bob then turned to Harold Small and Fred Caruthers, his two deputies. "Let's wrap up this shindig. Harold, let the FBI know we have our eyes on those varmints. Fred, you and I are going to make tracks and be part of the greeting party."

With the Cooksville police headed in the wrong direction, and Mr. Harrington's radio out of commission all the way to Knoxville, it was smooth sailing for Mad Dog and Skippy. Mr. Harrington informed the two that they would not be landing at the city airport but would be using the McGhee Tyson Air National Guard Base landing field.

"I don't do well navigating around all of the big planes," explained Mr. Harrington. "They have some small landing strips they make available to guys like me." He noted a look of concern on his passengers' faces. "Oh, don't worry, gents. They have a club where we can get a couple of brewskis."

Mr. Harrington did not lead them wrong, and a couple of hours passed rather quickly. It was the Monday after drill, so they had the club pretty much to themselves. The man behind the bar was actually glad to have some business.

Eventually, Mr. Harrington stood up and announced it was time for him to head back. After some robust handshakes and promises to link up again in the future, he was off. Mad Dog did buy him some petrol for the trip home. Once Mr. Harrington was airborne, Mad Dog and Skippy let out a bunch of belly laughs. Skippy almost fell over.

"Thank God that's over," confessed Skippy. "We may just get out of this mess in one piece."

Mad Dog scratched his armpits and ruffled his hair. "Hey, Skip, isn't that a barbershop over by the base exchange?" They both squinted against the sun.

"Let's check it out and see if we can't recast our images."

The tall African American man sitting in the chair smiled and stood up quickly when he saw potential patrons.

"Gents, you look like you are in need of a good trim," greeted the barber.

"That obvious, huh?" replied Mad Dog.

"Actually, sir, we're joining up with the unit here and need to get shorn," explained Skippy. That was a rather humorous statement, as Skippy maybe had ten hairs under his hat.

Mad Dog stepped in. "What my friend means is that I will be the one getting my ears lowered, and he will take a shave."

What followed was the biggest accumulation of hair on the floor the barber had ever seen. When he had Mad Dog "Air Force ready," Skippy hardly recognized him. Mad Dog really had a small head with pointy ears. His nose looked a lot straighter and narrower than before. You could say he had goblin genes.

Mad Dog kept rubbing his head. "Hey, sir, anywhere one can get a lid around here?" he addressed the barber.

"If you hurry," the barber answered, "you might find something in the exchange. They are open for another thirty minutes. They won't be checking IDs this time of day."

Mad Dog and Skippy were able to outfit themselves with new camouflage T-shirts and pants. They bought some leather jackets for good measure—the nice, soft brown ones that emulated those worn by military pilots. Mad Dog chose a baseball hat that read "Air Force Strong" on the front.

As they finished their purchases, Mad Dog asked the clerk where they might find a lift into town.

The short Hispanic lady answered by saying, "If you can wait a few minutes until I lock up, I'm running into Knoxville to do some shopping at the mall. Slip me a five, and I'll get you downtown."

That is how Mad Dog and Skippy managed to locate the sports bar and grill on Cumberland Avenue. It was late afternoon, and the two friends began to realize how hungry they were. They ordered two double cheeseburger specials. They really didn't need another beer, but they ordered a pitcher of Budweiser to appease the bartender. Mad Dog and Skippy saddled into a booth in a corner of the establishment, out of the way of the after-work traffic beginning to build.

"Don't look at me as if I'm some mutant," Mad Dog growled at Skippy.

"Sorry, Harvey…it's just…you will take some getting used to," said Skippy, trying hard not to laugh.

"Guess I have changed my image," Mad Dog replied. "Sorry for being so short." Then they both laughed at the pun.

"Did you notice the bus station as we drove into town?" asked Mad Dog. "When we're done here, let's mosey on over and see what departures they have going out tonight. I'm not too particular, as long as they have a bus going south."

The partners in crime then plotted further strategy, unaware of the thin Jamaican man staring at them from the bar.

*   *   *   *   *   *   *

Dauntay Vidal could trace his lineage back to the mid-eighteenth century in Jamaica. He was proud of his French heritage but even more connected to the preservation of Caribbean culture. Dauntay had graduated from the University of the Virgin Islands and majored in Caribbean Studies. It was there he met several like-minded individuals who also were members of the Society for the Defense of Caribbean Heritage (SDCH). The Society took it upon themselves to investigate and right wrongs placed upon Caribbean citizens and communities, particularly from the colonial period of European history.

The Society would have disappeared long ago had it not been for the beneficence of one Sir Geoffrey Hubbard, a wealthy landowner residing in the Jersey Islands. Sir Geoffrey had taken an interest in treasure and plunder left by British and Spanish privateers. He was of the mind that what was found in the Caribbean islands should stay there. Fueling his passion was the fact that his great-great-grandmother had been taken off of St. Lucia and hauled to England to be a servant until her death in 1797. You might say Sir Geoffrey took her mistreatment personally.

While the SDCH started off innocently enough, as regular donations came in from Sir Geoffrey, their agenda became more proactive. The

Society also became more secretive and recruited members from all over the Caribbean. Vigilante justice, as applied to the Society, might have been a bit overstated, but certainly vengeance was part of their agenda. With a bottomless budget and friends in high places, their reach was long.

Mr. Vidal and his friends had known of the Timur Ruby for some time. They were familiar with its story and history. In fact, the more zealous among them considered it a sacred stone, a stone that was to be protected and watched over. That is what brought Dauntay Vidal to the sports bar and grill on Monday.

Mad Dog and Skippy were so engaged in conversation they did not notice when Mr. Vidal walked over toward their booth. He towered above them before they looked up. Skippy just about messed his pants and lurched backwards. Mad Dog went into a defensive posture and instinctively put his hand over his hidden gun.

"Dear sirs, do not be alarmed," said Mr. Vidal calmly. "I only need a few minutes of your time."

It was hard to remain calm when a seven-foot-tall man in a white silk shirt was hovering over you with a long scabbard hanging from his waist. In fact, it was all the more astounding that no one in the bar and grill seemed to pay Mr. Vidal any mind.

"Who the hell are you?!" challenged Mad Dog.

Mr. Vidal broke into a broad smile. "Just an interested party. What I have to discuss will be hard to do here," he noted, gazing over the crowd.

"Who says we have any interest in talking with you?" reacted Skippy.

Mr. Vidal raised his thin eyebrows. "A good question, but not relevant, I am afraid. I have a cab waiting outside and suggest you follow me."

He then patted his scabbard, giving a distinct message it would be in the best interests of Mad Dog and Skippy to comply. Mad Dog hesitated for a minute but then decided that if they were going to take the intruder out, it might be better to do it in another location. Both men stood up, and Mad Dog plunked some bills down on the table. They then made their way out of the bar and grill amidst only a few momentary stares.

Standing near the cab on the street and holding the back door open was a shorter man in similar garb. He had a neatly trimmed jet-black beard.

"Where are we headed, if I may ask?" questioned Mad Dog.

Mr. Vidal leaned over the seat. "It is not too far. There is a tiny Cajun eatery across the river a couple of miles. We can talk there uninterrupted."

Initially, Mad Dog wondered if this was someone in Dr. McDougal's employ. But that made no sense. No one should have known of their presence in Knoxville. The next thought he had was they were being abducted. Perhaps this was a unique way the locals welcomed strangers to town. That also seemed unlikely, as why would anyone be interested in shaking them down? He and Skippy gave no evidence of having anything worthwhile to steal.

The cab made a turn down a side street with just a few shops, all rather run down. It stopped in front of one that bore a sign above the entrance: "Mama's Cajun." The establishment did not have windows. There was a screen door that hung crookedly. Skippy was not sure he wanted to go in.

Mr. Vidal strode up to the door and knocked firmly three times. Shortly, a teenage boy answered, and after giving Mad Dog and Skippy the once over, he beckoned them to enter. Inside were several round tables that had seen better days. The restaurant was neat enough, however, and Skippy found himself reviewing the menu above the far counter. Mr. Vidal did not stop, though, and led them to the back, past the restrooms and through a beaded curtain. The bearded man followed at the very rear.

The back room may have been for larger parties, as there was a long table that could seat eight. Mr. Vidal took a chair at one end and his companion the other. He motioned for Mad Dog and Skippy to sit down. A rotund, jolly Caribbean woman then came in, set a bottle of wine down on the table, and gave each of the four a glass. She left, softly singing to herself.

"Look," said Mad Dog. "I don't know what your game is, but you best start talking. We are not as patient as we look."

Mr. Vidal poured some wine in the glasses and then sat back. "Mr. Scrima and Mr. Forrester..." he began.

"How do you know our names?" protested Skippy, beginning to stand.

"Hear me out," responded Mr. Vidal. "Everything will soon be clear." After a pause he continued. "You almost gave us the slip when you left Cooksville. Not that it was easy tracking you to begin with. You are a most creative criminal, Mr. Scrima."

"Who hired you to track us down?" asked Mad Dog.

"The group I represent is beholden to no one, Mr. Scrima," explained Mr. Vidal. "Our interest has been less with the Bolton gang than the object of your theft. We have an abiding deep loyalty to the Timur Ruby."

Skippy gave Mad Dog a furtive glance. He did not like the direction this conversation was going.

"You see," continued Mr. Vidal, "as long as the ruby was safe, we saw no need to recover it. Thanks to a benefactor and some intriguing research, we knew of its existence at the county museum. Mr. Tompkins was indeed a good custodian. I must admit we should have caught onto the plotting of the professor long ago, but he moved methodically and worked hard to stay out of the limelight. When the article appeared in the local paper announcing the theft of the wooden leg, we, of course, took great interest."

Mad Dog and Skippy now knew the reason for the meeting. Fortunately, there were only two individuals between them and the ruby. It would not be easy, but they each began to assess their options.

Mr. Vidal slid forward in his chair. He rested his head in his hands. "We have been observing since last Friday. There have been eyes on the museum at all times. We, therefore, knew of the children's capture. We witnessed the comings and goings of the police and Mr. Tompkins. To be honest, we were a bit perplexed, just like Chief Olsen and Detective Shaw. However, the professor did not let us down. Thanks to Mr.

Tompkins, we decided to keep tabs on the anthropology department. That allowed us to follow him all the way to the farmhouse. Dressing as a woman was an interesting twist. My heart goes out to the coed who got dragged into the entire mess."

Mr. Vidal took a break from his explanation and sipped some wine.

"So why aren't you on his trail?" asked Mad Dog. "He's the one with the ruby. We were just his henchmen. He went his way, and we went ours. We diverted to Cooksville since we figured he would try to do us in. Not to mention we got shorted on our promised payment."

"An honest question, Mr. Scrima," noted Mr. Vidal. "He definitely was our main focus. But then he had you return to the museum. Very strange. Four of you went into the museum, and none came out. The only explanation was the professor did not have the ruby. Fortunately, Mrs. Smothers had a good next-door neighbor. So, when she was in dire straits due to the silver key, Mrs. Smothers confided in her. Lucky for us, Maria was one of our plants. A key has to fit somewhere. Right, Mr. Scrima?"

Mad Dog only glared at him.

"Therefore, when your party did not come out after a reasonable amount of time, we went in. There was commotion coming from the basement, and it was not a great surprise that there was a tunnel. You had the missing leg, and later we learned why it was hidden on the second floor. Then it became a matter of tracking it back to the farmhouse. We didn't need to follow you. We just waited."

"You still haven't answered my question," reminded Mad Dog.

"Ah, quite right, Mr. Scrima," said Mr. Vidal calmly. "It all was going down as expected. You and the professor linked up, and you delivered to him the wooden leg. Then we observed something strange. Only three of you returned to the farmhouse, and Miss Quig lagged behind. Then, while you and Mr. Forrester were negotiating with Mr. Fish, she came from behind and clobbered him with the rake. Why would she need to do that, Mr. Scrima?"

Mr. Vidal waited for an answer.

Mad Dog gulped. "We figured the fix was in and we would not get our share. So, we grabbed the entire bag and made our way to the plane."

"Still," pondered Mr. Vidal, "what was in it for Miss Quig? Did you threaten her? Or did she go along with your plan to double-cross the professor with a motive of revenge?"

When Mad Dog did not answer, Mr. Vidal provided his own.

"Somewhere between the tunnel and the farmhouse, it is our belief that you found a way to retrieve the ruby. You eliminated the other gang members one way or another and convinced Miss Quig to assist you. To be honest, we really do not much care how you compensated her. The bottom line is you possessed the ruby. Sure, we kept tabs on the professor. But when our man at the Drake Hotel informed us the professor discovered he had been double-crossed, we moved all of our attention to you boys."

Mr. Vidal now stood up and looked directly at Mad Dog. Then he said in a loud voice, "It is now time for you to turn over the Timur Ruby!"

The bearded man also stood up and drew his sword. Skippy was suddenly aware that all his dreams were about to be dashed. His hopes for a comfortable retirement and a life of ease were going up in smoke. Rage boiled up in his bosom and he launched toward Mr. Vidal. Just as he reached for the tall man's neck, a sword flashed out of nowhere and Skippy was minus one hand. The bearded man rushed to put Mad Dog in a chokehold before he could draw his gun.

Skippy was moaning in pain, slumped on the floor. Mad Dog was squirming to no avail. Mr. Vidal walked over and picked up Mad Dog's bag. It was only a matter of moments before he found the ruby wrapped in a sock.

"For a minute I thought you may have stashed the ruby somewhere," shared Mr. Vidal. "Thank you for not disappointing us. We have no desire to see you returned to the authorities. We also have no desire to relieve you of any renumeration you have already been given. This is what we have to offer."

At this point, three more men entered the room. Two assisted Skippy up and wrapped his severed hand in ice. They also did the same for his arm. The bearded man released his hold on Mad Dog.

Mr. Vidal continued. "In some respects, you did us a favor. If reports are true, the professor and his associates are on the bottom of Lake Ontario as we speak. It seems they were trying to make their way back to the States with hopes of tracking you down. Unfortunately, their boat was not up to the task. Basically, the threat is over. Therefore, why don't you let us drop you off on a very pleasant island? You should have enough cash to get yourselves situated."

Mad Dog walked over to Skippy. "What about his hand? We can't just show up at a hospital."

"If it's quickly frozen, and if we can get him into an operating room within twenty-four hours, I think we can save it," answered Mr. Vidal. "We have a private plane and can leave immediately for Grenada. There is a good hospital there."

It quickly became apparent to Mad Dog he was being offered an attractive alternative to continuing their quest for the Timur Ruby. If they gave up any further aspiration to possession of the ruby, Mr. Vidal would provide them a safe house and medical care for Skippy. True, they would not be beyond rich, but they could retire to a most comfortable existence.

Skippy looked up into Mad Dog's eyes. "All I ever wanted was to live on an island, Harvey." He then turned to Mr. Vidal. "Any chance I could have a maid and someone to cook for me?"

"You will live like a king, Mr. Forrester," reassured Mr. Vidal.

Mad Dog turned to their benefactor and stated, "I never did get your name."

"You may address me as Mr. Vidal, Mr. Scrima," he replied.

"Well, Mr. Vidal, what is it they say? Discretion is the better part of valor? We accept your offer."

Skippy beamed and began to doze off from the shock of losing his hand. He pictured himself on a beach with a wine cooler in hand. In many respects, Skippy was finally going home.

Epilogue

Halloween would be descending upon Webster in a week. It was always a festive time. Jenny Turnbow and Mary Murkowski went to great lengths to sew their kids' costumes. Normally, Johnny and Jeremy relegated themselves to accompanying their younger siblings around the neighborhood. And it would be no different this year. However, in a magnanimous gesture, Heather asked if she could join their little band. Secretly, the three friends sought closure to a very wild Labor Day weekend. To emphasize their solidarity, they decided to go as the action heroes Wonder Woman, Superman, and Batman.

School had been what the doctor ordered. Even Jeremy seemed to take an added interest in his academic studies. Johnny tried out for a part in his school's play, *Ten Little Soldiers* (and was successful). Heather enthusiastically participated on the middle school swim team on weekdays and began tutoring young children in reading on Saturday afternoons.

The Webster citizenry were astounded at the vivid fall colors emanating from the maple, oak, and tulip trees. It was almost as if Mother Nature was healing the landscape via an intensity of hue. The cavernous hole in the ground that had become a major regional tourist attraction for Benson County had finally been filled in. Boy Scout Troop 401 had accepted the challenge of planting two hundred fifty seedlings that eventually would erase all memory of the scarred land. The farmhouse that became the tomb for Thaddeus Tompkins was condemned by the board of health and was slated for demolition before Thanksgiving. The entire forty acres was to go up for auction at a sheriff's sale.

* * * * * * *

There were several burials in September. Yvetlana Smothers was provided with what remains of her son, Boris, could be found. Iggy's body was transported from the Allen County morgue. They were buried side by side in the St. Thomas Catholic Church cemetery. Yvetlana's sister, Marna, sprung for the plots. Yvetlana moved in permanently with the Kopps after giving notice to her landlord. James had managed to get her a custodial job in the department store. It was to be her place of healing. Unfortunately, what was still painfully obvious by October was that the healing process was still ongoing.

Jarvis and Tommy Bolton had no next of kin that anyone could identify, and no one stepped forward. The coroner decided in the interest of economy and the Webster taxpayers to cremate their remains and disperse the ashes over the pauper's field east of town.

The poor, innocent victim of Jarvis Bolton's creativity turned out to be one Martin Crenshaw, aged twenty-two, of Champaign, Illinois. A senior at the University of Illinois, Martin had been heading south that fateful Saturday afternoon to visit an aunt who lived in Bradford City. Upon learning of his admission to Benson County Regional Hospital, Martin's family and relatives gathered there to await his awakening from his coma. By the Friday after his admission, it became painfully obvious to all concerned that he would be not be coming back to life anytime soon. The doctors advised his parents that even if he eventually came out of the coma, Martin would be basically braindead. At that point, permission was given to end Martin's life. The Crenshaws returned to Peoria, Illinois, and buried Martin in the family plot. Of all the tragedy associated with the case of the wooden leg, Martin's death was the most senseless.

Indeed, if Martin Crenshaw's death was the most senseless, then Tom Barlow's was the most heroic. After taking Heather and Jeremy under his wing, Mr. Barlow could have called it a day. That was not who he was, however. Tom Barlow was a beloved farmer from Benson County. The Barlows could trace their Hoosier heritage all the way back to 1845, when Lucretious Barlow moved his family west from Pennsylvania, having procured 140 acres of fertile land from a War of 1812 veteran.

The Church of the Blessed Savior, five miles southwest from the Barlow farm, overflowed on September 12th. Mr. and Mrs. Barlow had two other sons, Henry and Lawrence, who lived in Cleveland, Ohio. They and Ben Turnbow served as pallbearers. Johnny Turnbow held his mother's hand tightly and brushed away tears with his other hand. Johnny was alive because of Tom Barlow, and he would never forget it.

The quest for the Timur Ruby claimed ten victims. A case could be made that of all those individuals, the one person who controlled his destiny more than the rest was Thaddeus Tompkins. Had he been honest with Chief Olsen from the very beginning, had he not given into his greedy desires, and had he not become a thorn in the side of Dr. McDougal, Mr. Tompkins would not only still be alive, but he would have continued his stewardship over the Benson County Museum.

The irony of all ironies was that Thaddeus Tompkins became the beneficiary of a groundswell of sympathy and reverence unlike any could have predicted. Because the details of his involvement were never made public, Webster residents began to populate the museum porch and grounds with flowers and testimonials. The popular view was that Mr. Tompkins died trying to protect a valuable artifact—as if he'd died in the line of duty. The museum board met and unanimously agreed that the museum should be renamed the Thaddeus Tompkins Memorial Museum. Mayor Balducci felt the entire public response was a bit overdone. Still, he could not avoid taking advantage of all the goodwill surrounding the former curator.

So, there it was. On the first Saturday of October, Mayor Balducci presided over a ribbon cutting ceremony and the unveiling of the new museum sign. Frank Murkowski and Ben Turnbow each got up on a ladder and helped install the sign above the museum's entrance. Admission was free for the day, and a constant stream of visitors flowed through. A newly formed Museum Ladies' Guild served ice cream sundaes and accepted donations for their cause. Their first goal was to raise enough money to have a portrait commissioned of Mr. Tompkins, which would join the others in the semicircular hallway.

A recently graduated student of museum studies out of the University of Indiana was assigned to be the interim curator. By October, an active search was in motion to find Mr. Tompkins' successor. On the day of the ribbon cutting, Officer Kraus did not hide his disgust with the entire affair, while Chief Olsen kept busy accepting congratulations on his handling of the wooden leg's theft. Sam Shaw stood nearby with a smile on his face. Thaddeus Tompkins accomplished in death what he couldn't accomplish in life.

*　　*　　*　　*　　*　　*　　*

The law enforcement community as a whole tended to defer to the next level of authority. Therefore, it was easy for Chief Olsen to accept state police jurisdiction over the museum theft investigation, even though the theft occurred in his own backyard. In turn, the state police had no problem looking to the FBI for guidance once the perpetrators of the crime left the state of Indiana. As a result, when the bureau determined the case was closed, there was no protest…Except from Officer Kraus, of course, who felt he had it all figured out and that Harvey Scrima and Skippy Forrester needed to be tracked down. Unfortunately for Herb, Mr. Scrima and Mr. Forrester were considered small potatoes. Officer Kraus did get sympathetic ears from Officers Plank and Sheridan, though. One night, over a few beers, the three officers thought a private investigation into uncovering the Timur Ruby was worth the effort. Needless to say, they eventually agreed nothing much good would come from stirring the pot. Officer Kraus, to his grave disappointment, realized deep down the entire affair was now beyond his pay grade.

The week before Halloween, the Webster Police Department was preparing for their annual crusade against vandalism. It didn't matter how many yards would be strewn with toilet paper, but *whose* houses were covered that was important. Normally, there would be some kind of tomfoolery taking place on the museum grounds. This year, even the high school students would stay away.

Over time, the existence of the wooden leg and the ruby would take on a life of its own. Theories abounded and interest never really diminished. This was the reason the fake wooden leg was provided a position of honor in the glass case on the second floor of the museum. A good mystery never really has a satisfactory solution. The Widow Ruenzel summed it up in a most tidy manner. When asked about the wooden leg, she replied with raised eyebrows, "Dead men tell no tales."

*   *   *   *   *   *   *

The Sunday before Halloween was a gorgeous day. Beside the color of the terrain previously noted, the sky was robin's egg blue, and there was not a cloud to behold. By three in the afternoon, the thermometers were registering near seventy degrees. A number of folks were out and about in Shiloh, Dodge, and Benson counties. One of them was Emily Quig. The tiny coed wore denim jeans and a matching jacket. During the first two months of the semester, she had undergone somewhat of a makeover. Her formerly long brown hair had been transformed into a pageboy, and Emily began to wear more makeup. Doris accused her of trying to become a trendsetter.

Emily's external appearance was a reflection of her internal metamorphosis. Confident, reserved, and radiating a quiet optimism, Emily buried herself in her studies. She had been doing some group dating on weekends, however. Emily discovered she had a real interest in spooky movies.

This particular Sunday, Emily Quig had managed to convince a fellow archaeology student, Bennie, to take a ride north on Highway 12 to revisit the farm that was the bearer of painful memories. For a week or so, Emily had acquired a certain notoriety after all of the details of Dr. McDougal's plotting came to light. Doris and Daryl were happy to comment on Emily's ordeal to those who would listen. Eventually, things died down. Even Emily's parents acquiesced to letting their daughter stay in school after the administration guaranteed she would be well looked after. Emily postponed the trip to her aunt in Chicago.

Bennie was a nice enough young man, though definitely an introvert. He and Emily were more or less drawn together due to personality and an intense interest in all things ancient. They were an odd-looking pair, however, as Bennie, six feet tall and thin, hopped on his moped to head out of town. One of Bennie's attributes was he did not ask a lot of questions. He accepted at face value that Emily was likely just seeking closure on a very traumatic experience.

First, they wandered around the farmhouse, not going inside as the board of health had roped off all entrances due to safety concerns and the impending demolition. Emily spoke little but pointed out where she and the gang members had been. As they returned to their starting point, Emily put her hand on Bennie's shoulder and asked, "Could you give me a couple minutes, Bennie? I need a little alone time. I won't be long."

Emily then headed through the field, now filled with brown grass, and reached the old shack that had been her "hotel" that Saturday night. The rusty shovel was still where she left it. It was not long before Emily had retrieved the envelope of bills; it was a little dirty, but no worse for wear. Stuffing the money in her purse, she returned to Bennie, and they were soon headed back to the university.

✳   ✳   ✳   ✳   ✳   ✳   ✳

A case could be made that if there were any winners in the whole sordid affair, they would be Mad Dog and Skippy, living a comfortable existence on a Caribbean island. True, Skippy had limited mobility and not much feeling in his right hand, but they wanted for little. There was no danger of the authorities ever finding them. Mr. Vidal was true to his word and provided them with islanders to wait on them hand and foot.

Still, the two surviving gang members had given up their freedom. In some respects, it was similar to the upscale accommodations afforded to political prisoners who were spared contact with the riffraff. Therefore, truth be told, it was Miss Emily Quig who survived and benefited most from her involvement with the wooden leg's theft. She had evolved significantly in just two months.

It is common to most sidebars of history that the most poignant, important events are basically lost to cultural amnesia. Would anyone remember the role of Miss Emily Quig in years to come? Certainly, no one would have claim to the total truth of her experience, unless she eventually wanted to share all of the facts. No, indeed, "The Mystery of the Wooden Leg" could easily have been called, "The Transformation of Miss Emily Quig."

✱   ✱   ✱   ✱   ✱   ✱   ✱

Halloween night finally arrived. The streets of Webster were bustling with trick or treaters. Officer Kraus cruised slowly down neighborhood streets with his bubble light flashing. There would be no monkey business on his watch. Mr. Kostov handed out candy at the station.

The Turnbow, Murkowski, and Stippich families used the occasion as a reunion of sorts. There was hot chocolate, sugar cookies, and cherry pie for the taking on the Turnbow porch. Johnny, Jeremy, Heather, Buddy, Hans, Melinda, and Katie bobbed along as they took a grand circuit from Elm Street to Main Street and over to Pickett Street via Johnson Drive. They then traveled down Heather's street (Plum Drive) and back to Johnny's house. Melinda and Katie had both dressed as fairy princesses. Buddy went the pirate route, and Hans was his mate.

By the way all the children carried on, it was as if there had never been any kind of adventure two months past. That is a delightful attribute of children. Wounds are allowed to heal, and bad memories can be tucked away into a mental closet. There was no discussion that Halloween night of what the next adventure would involve.

After everyone was safely home, bags of candy emptied, and children tucked into their beds, anyone who may have bothered to wander by the museum would have seen a flickering light on the second floor. Looking more closely, they may have seen a shadowy figure pacing back and forth past the window. To the more senior of Webster's citizens, any report of those observations would have elucidated a smile. They knew Mr. Tompkins never intended to leave the museum.

The End.

Published by Nico 11 Publishing & Design
www.nico11publishing.com

Be well read.

ISBN 9781945907753

51800 >

9 781945 907753